Margaret B. Wright

Hired Furnished

Margaret B. Wright

Hired Furnished

ISBN/EAN: 9783337122409

Printed in Europe, USA, Canada, Australia, Japan

Cover: Foto ©Andreas Hilbeck / pixelio.de

More available books at **www.hansebooks.com**

HIRED FURNISHED.

BEING CERTAIN

ECONOMICAL HOUSEKEEPING
ADVENTURES IN ENGLAND.

BY

MARGARET B WRIGHT.

BOSTON:
ROBERTS BROTHERS.
1897.

STARS INDICATE LOCATIONS OF THE "HIRINGS."

TO THE

BELOVED COMPANION OF THESE HIRINGS,

My Son.

PREFACE.

WHEN the author of this little book returned to her own country, she was greatly surprised to discover how vast the multitude to whom Europe is still an unrealized dream. "On the other side," every summer is so full of Americans that one absent long years from home naturally supposes that we all get there, rich and not rich, somehow and some time. Even if fewer of our country people went "Across" every year on their own responsibility, it almost seems (at least over there), that very few escape the scores, even hundreds, of Personally Conducted Parties whose advertisements occupy so much space in our newspapers, and themselves so much in European steamers, hotels, and railway-trains.

Nevertheless, the fact is, that as many (or more) remain at home as ever go abroad, remain to hope for, and to dream of the happy day, ever and ever so long delayed, when they too may set forth to wander in the world of art and story. Even are there still others who scarcely hope at all, but merely dream of what might be, if dreams and dollars were the companions they almost never are. For it is as sure as fate that dreams and dollars can scarcely exist together, dollars so soon put an end to dreams by turning them into realities.

With thoughts chiefly of these two classes of stay-at-homes, the story of these happy, these more than happy, "Hirings" was written. It is so little a matter after all, even for moderate purses, to go abroad, and that too without the breathless and cursory glimpses, really only squints, at storied Europe, of the "personally-conducted," that one who knows longs to tell every tired teacher, every over-worked college professor, every toiling author, indeed everybody with dreams and time, how it may be done. "Time?" Time is money, we are often enough reminded; yet thousands of us have more time than money, time that perhaps cannot better be used than in the place of many dollars otherwise necessary for seeing Europe. Why should not a college professor's sabbatical, for instance, be spent in exploring beautiful England, hiring cottage and villa homes for six weeks or three months at a time, thus with always a delightfully inexpensive *pied-à-terre* to return to from far and near wanderings, on foot, on bicycle, by cheap railway trips? The author, with that famous work on hand that is to set the universe aflame by-and-by, what reason that he or she should not write in a "Hired-furnished" among English downs, among English meadows, in rustic villages, upon the English coast, rather than in a dull American village or expensive city lodgings? The gain to health, and thus to the *magnum opus*, would be incalculable, for all out-of-doors exercise in England would naturally resolve itself into walking miles away to historic castles, manors, picturesque hamlets, places and things immortal in song and story. In the space of a year, even of six months, very much of England could thus be familiarly known, and England lends herself most exquisitely to passionate pilgrimages, even in winter, with her gardens duskily abloom in November, her waysides and fields yellow with primroses in February, her meadows green all the year, even under light snows. Except during the one wild storm that comes usually in January, it is possible for the ardent pedestrian in England to walk as many miles as he pleases every day of the year. In many parts bicycling also is practicable, but not always in the soft southern counties, where the frost darts into the ground and out again at its own wayward will.

As is told in these pages, furnished cottages are abundant all over England, hundreds to be obtained at the prices named. In answer to our own advertisement came offers from Ramsgate, Margate, Worthing, Deal, Folkestone, Dover, Littlehampton, Broadstairs, Colchester, Canterbury, Cookham, Herne Bay, Great Marlow, Aylesbury, Winchelsea, "Near Fareham," "Near Salisbury," Farnham, Basingstoke, Reading, with half-a-dozen others so near London that the fog spoiled them for our purpose. We advertised but once; our whole supply (in England) came from that one source.

Established in one of these cottages or villas, living expenses are as much under one's own control as in one's native village or city. The stranger need have no apprehension that his nationality costs him dear in the purchase of potatoes, bread and butter, as it does cost dearly in any continental market-place. The English provision-dealer, whatever his wares, is exactly as honest as those in our own country; the farmer who brings butter, eggs, and vegetables to the cottage door gives not an ounce less to the pound that his customer is of Boston or Chicago, and not of London. Even did the carnal man prompt him to give only eleven eggs for a shilling, instead of twelve, the business man of him would know that the customer could not read the local papers without learning the market prices of everything.

One important consideration of an English winter

is the cost of fuel. That cost seems absurd to us, with our ever-devouring furnaces, our consuming coal-stoves, even our hearty grates. English winters are damper than ours, but indescribably less biting. Outside of London, where the sun shines, summer grates are usually quite sufficient for winter tenants, with the best coal at twenty to twenty-five shillings a ton, usually about twenty-two. On the southern coast, as at Worthing, the bedrooms, even of invalids, need very little or no artificial heat, and drawing-room fires burn dimly until evening. It is the same on the west coast. Englishmen themselves might criticise this statement, having so little idea of what Americans mean by " a good fire."

" Hiring-furnished " has not often been tried by Americans in rural England. Two at least of the small number of those that have tried it enthusiastically recommend the plan to those dreamers who are forever " haunted by the horizon," and for whom imagination gilds and refines into fairer than palaces, temporary homes in a foreign land that only ten or twenty dollars a month may " hire furnished."

CONTENTS.

		PAGE
HIRED FURNISHED		I
THE DOVE-COTE		48
FORT CHEER		79
MARTIN AND LA VIEILLE		107
"UNCLE PETER"		126
GARRISON SERVICE		138
IN THE JERSEY "STATES"		145
SARK		155
A LITTLE DASH INTO FRANCE		189
GUERNSEY		224
HAUTEVILLE HOUSE		239
NELLIE PALMER		255
THE ISLAND OF ALDERNEY, ITS PEOPLE, AND ITS COWS		270
THE LADDER		298
CLOVER VILLA		325
"S. S."		351
AN ACQUAINTANCE OF MRS. CLOVER		364
PHŒBUS		369
WINDY HOW		375
WORDSWORTH'S "PARSON SYMPSON"		407
MONA		428
SUNDRIES		449

Hired Furnished.

" LET us take a country house,"sneezed she.

" Why not a dozen?" croaked he.

She declined to be suppressed.

" Yes, why not a dozen, one at a time?"

The afternoon was not gray, although a winter afternoon in London. It was not the dirty gray of afternoons suggesting old kitchen nuns whose devotion is elbow service rather than knee. Even a dirty gray would have been auroral compared with it. It was a filthy brown, almost a greasy black, the hue of mendicant monks, and its odor was — well, it was if possible even worse than a begging friar's. The drawing-room seemed full of smoke, sewer gas weighted the air, the lighted chandelier struggled ineffectually to lessen the gloom, and both he and she kept each other company in uncouth noises, all because this was November in London. Fifteen minutes before, she had come home in a piteous state, having gone out to buy a lamp because of that fog-choked chandelier. She had managed to find her way to the nearest shops in Oxford Street, although with extreme difficulty. The lamp could not be sent home, no goods were being delivered in this dangerous darkness, so she took it in her good right hand, the left carrying the porcelain globe. "Though I meet all the dukes and duchesses of the English peerage," she magnificently thought, "neither right hand nor left will I hide." She knew very well that the sharpest eyes in the peerage could see neither hand.

Returning, the lamp-bearer came to grief. She utterly lost her way, the way familiar to her for years. Impossible to see the names on the street corners ; impossible to define any landmark ; impossible to recognize any shop or house passed every day. Whether she had missed the right turnings she could not tell ; that their own familiar door was but a hand's-breadth away she tried to hope. Twice she stopped to ask where she was. One answer was, "Somewhere between Kentish Town and Victoria ; " the other, "I wish I knew myself, Madam." Grotesque forms drifted past her with vague outlines and shrouded faces ; but for constant gasping, choking, coughing, she might have fancied them ghostly fleers from Pluto's realm. She knew them to be of flesh and blood by the sympathy of her own suffering. Imprisoned odors of sulphurous chimney smoke ; of dead and living flesh, the rank out-put of butcher shops and public houses, — stung her throat, scalded her eyes, scorched her nostrils. Tears ran down her cheeks ; she heard them drop upon her ribbons, and she knew that channels of lesser grime were thus marked upon her countenance. Yet she dare not wipe a single tear away or reduce her blackamoor aspect, for to put down lamp or globe even for a little instant was to lose sight of them forever.

Then a gleam of something like hope, for somebody brushed closely by whose hobbling gait and crooked figure she often saw in their own Square. "I have only to follow this lunatic," she thought, "and he will conduct me home."

Then he vanished utterly, and left no wrack behind.

In the course of time, black bitter time, some one of the distorted spirits of the fog proved to be a Giant Greatheart. His face she never saw, but he took her by the shoulders and turned her nose from north to east. "This is Store Street," he said. "You know your way from here, I suppose."

So did she "suppose," that inkily weeping wanderer, but in less than three minutes she wished she had clung to Giant Greatheart no matter what his face might be, and refused to be parted from him.

Then, O Joy! Then she heard a blessed voice crying at brief intervals, "This is Gower Street," and she hoped everybody gave the invisible angel twopence as she did. A little farther on another heavenly voice sang, "This is Torrington Square," and she was at home; that is, after counting the doorsteps till she came to No. 999.

"I was just going out to look for you," he said anxiously. Then he added, "But I never should have known you from a chimney-sweep."

A laugh, a hollow, mocking, horrible laugh, issued from her sooty lips at the bare idea of looking for anybody on such a day.

"Let us take a country house," said she. "Let us answer some of the many advertisements of seaside and country villas to let at a nominal price for the winter. Let us go into the sunshine bathing Albion's white cliffs and kissing English meadows outside of black London. Let us hear what the wild waves are saying, and keep the rust from somebody's summer grates; the moth from our own daily toil."

Whether the earth-rending concatenation of sound that answered her was of admiration or derision she never really knew.

They decided to advertise in the " Church Times." " It goes into all the rectories and vicarages of rural England," she said, "and all the spinsters read it."

For their seventy-five cent advertisement they received threescore answers. There were villas, cottages, and if not mansions, at least houses that were neither villas nor cottages, but brick and substantial, gas-lighted and in seaside cities. Three of these letters were amusing inasmuch as they offered three villas at Ramsgate in the same street and with consecutive numbers.

Two of the letters the lady read aloud as fair specimens of them all.

" This one is from a place 'near Colchester,' but it seems too far away for our little time now.

" DEAR MADAM, — In answer to your advertisement I wish to say that I have a most comfortably furnished detached cottage to let. Would take ten shillings per week from quiet small family.

" The house is situated three or four minutes from sea, with good views of same. Ten minutes' walk from Frinton Station on G. E. R. Two hours from Liverpool Street Station. Five minutes from Church and dissenting mission room. Bracing air, splendid sands. Immediate possession may be had.

" Yours truly,

" ———— "

"He does not state number and character of rooms," they observed. "We have not time for a correspondence on the subject."

The next was more definite and was from Faversham.

"MADAM, — Seeing your advertisement of this day for country cottage, I beg to offer one to your notice containing Draw'g and Din'g and Kitch., three good bedrooms, and other offices comfortably furnished. Would let it for six weeks at ten shillings per week. The house is detached and situate near Dover and Deal, and church near, about twenty-five minutes from station and about ten minutes' walk from the Bay. Can be seen by arrangement.

"Yours truly,
"_____"

The Americans carefully put these letters away for future use and chose Pevensey Villa. Now Pevensey Villa was only an experiment. It was hired by the week and only for six weeks, so the Americans were less exacting of requirement than had their hiring been for a longer period. Indeed, their paramount desire was to flee away the very soonest possible from darkness and gnashing of teeth, so they engaged without seeing it the villa to which was the shortest flight. Afterwards, when they found that this was not only the most economical but the most delightful way of seeing and knowing beautiful England, they became very high and mighty in their requirements, and picked and chose among their *Mems* as though they were spending fortunes in hiring furnished.

Darkness was falling when they left their train less than two hours from London. Only two other people descended where they did, and the aspect of the little station was not smiling. Neither was that of the crouching village outside, which seemed a moist, unpleasant body, with a bad cold in the head. They found that they were still two miles from their villa, two dank, damp, dumb miles, to be done in a hired coach from an adjacent stable, a huge coach that loomed high above wayside cottages as though it were carrying Brobdingnagian princes.

Darkness had entirely fallen when at the end of a perfectly flat ride between draining ditches they came out through wide gates and saw the sea before them. The coach seemed driving straight into the water, but before the final plunge it was arrested by two running figures, — a man in a fisherman's jacket, and a woman in the most extraordinary head gear they ever saw. These proved to be their proprietors, who had been on the watch for them.

"You see, sir, if you'd driv up to henny hother villa to let," said Mrs. Pumpkin-Hood, "you'd never got haway."

Mrs. Pumpkin-Hood, they learned later, must always be addressed in a robust voice, not that her ears were dull, but because she never quitted that thickly wadded pumpkin-shaped hood day in (or night, it is believed) or day out, while they knew her; this was a matter of rejoicing to them so long as they believed they had thus come upon a Dickensesque landlady, a tribe distinguished for immovable bonnets.

Pevensey Villa proved to be a double one, peaked and puckered with beatings of the seaside weather, flat on the flat ground, a little white picket fence about it, and directly facing the sea.

The Americans had the favorite side, their proprietors told them, and as the Americans saw, it being the one most open to the wide view of universal flatness. A bright fire welcomed them ; the sitting-room was the very picture of a home nest, with its large glowing lamp, its snugly drawn window-shades, and lace curtains.

" Are we in clover ? "

She must have spoken with vigor, for Mrs. Pumpkin-Hood quickly replied, " No, mum, no such villa in Pemsy Bay."

" Pemsy — " thus Dr. Andrew Boorde named Pevensey when he willed away his house in 1547; thus the inhabitants name it still.

While Mrs. Pumpkin-Hood ran over to her own house for sheets, one other table-cloth and four towels, the entire " linen " of the villa, the new-comers took observations. But first the lady wrote in a book — " *Mem*. Lucky I brought towels ; never hire furnished without bringing extra towels and table-cloths."

The sitting-room was undeniably small, but then two persons so closely related as these do not need a large one ; if they insisted upon largeness, why, there were the French windows opening upon a little balcony ; *they* were like cathedral doors. There was a neat carpet, fresh wall paper, " ornaments," including a thermometer on the mantel, and window-shades that came down on the run but went only crawlingly up again. The little wall closets beside the fireplace had empty shelves, but the space beneath was a chaos of bottles, left by previous tenants. Neither of the Americans remarked that the key must be turned to keep the sitting-room door closed, or that the outside door would shut only by argument of a stalwart kick, then open again only by means of another from the outside. Not yet did they know that to every one who rang at that front door during their hibernation the salutation through the frail barrier should be, " Would you mind to kick?"

But both noticed that the sitting-room was beautifully warm, and that the little round table was brightly laid in readiness for the chops and bread they had brought with them, and the keen hunger given them already by the change of air.

"And so near the Infinite, the Eternal Sea," she reverently chanted as she set the steaming teapot down.

" What's the matter with its nose?" he asked.

.   .   .   .

" Beds aired? Yes, mum ; slept in 'em ourselves last night."

Considering the chronic dampness of beds in England, particularly seaside beds, this was extraordinary thoughtfulness. The lady asked vaguely but sympathetically concerning possible rheumatic twinges in the weather-beaten substance of their proprietors.

" Never 'ave henny," answered the pair.

Days later, when the conversation touched in its flight upon that perpetual hood, " Nooralgie," the wearer explained, and the strangers were much disappointed. For do not Dickensesque landladies wear eternal black bonnets only to show which way the wind is listing?

Fires were soon lighted in four rooms (the two comfortable attics left unexplored), and after a cosey evening by the sitting-room fire with the wild waves hinting unutterable things through the chinks of the French window, they went to bed before the lights of Hastings burned low or those of nearer Eastbourne.

She awoke from her first sleep to find herself in a coffin. Above that lidless coffin rose the damp walls of a tomb, a mildewed tomb, a shattered antique tomb smelling of things long dead, of seasons gone to decay. Upon the coffin's edge horrible shapes grinned and capered, clutching, snatching, clawing shapes, named Rheumatism, Fever, Neuralgia, Everydisease and Death. Outside the tomb, far away from that *danse macabre*, she heard the wild waves saying, "Well aired? Slept in last night? Go to, thou dunce's duncely daughter! Those beds have not been slept in save by the mists (which are not misters) since the bathing season ended."

"And here it is almost Christmas!" she cried. "Come, arouse thee, arouse thee, my perilously sleeping one, and help me pile these bedclothes before the fire!"

"'Bed is bed, however bedly!'" he quoted in yawning. "What do you expect, — all the luxuries of the season, even to a truth-telling landlady, for our paltry two dollars and a half a week, 'linning and plate' included? I doubt if some of them are not missing even at fifteen dollars a week in the height of the summer." (By "plate" the sleepy one meant five lead forks and eight spoons of pure pewter. "I will *mem* them," she had said, and wrote down "*Mem*. Never hire furnished without bringing our own silver."

Glorious sunshine beat broadly into the sitting-room the next morning as they tilted fragrant and exhilarating even if nicked cups before a blazing fire. Two long toasting forks were in the villa's furnishing, and they gleefully made the toast as they needed it, bronze and piping hot.

"We are like young Wordsworth and Dorothy toasting their breakfasts before the fire in Dove Cottage," she said.

"I cannot imagine Wordsworth doing anything for himself, even making toast," said he. "Dorothy toasted for both. That *was* a sister!"

The hint, if one was intended, fell upon deaf ears.

"Ceylon tea," she smacked, "delicious at only fifty-five cents a pound! No wonder England makes the worst coffee in the world."

Only a stone's throw from the breakfast table the sea sparkled with scarcely a murmur. Almost as near, one of Pitt's martello towers, meant to frighten the French, gleamed like marble, albeit really a most ramshackle and mouldy affair, stuffed with somebody's hay. This was their nearest neighbor of the line of seventy-five towers encircling the coast from Eastbourne to Hastings.

"We do not need to be more cosey," he magnanimously confessed.

"I hope London fog is thick enough to dip with a spoon," she purred, albeit not particularly vicious, as women go.

Pevensey Bay is not picturesque. It has no trees, no white cliffs, no beetling rocks, no verdure even in summer, and its "terraces," "places," and "villas" are all dolefully new, though faded. It is a hamlet of cheap summer cottages and one shop, squatted upon the edge of a marsh euphemised as Pevensey "Levels" and upon rough shingle, blazing, glaring in summer, in winter hideously bare though never bleak. The marsh (pardon, the "Level") extends from the ancient seaport of Pevensey where William the Norman, that famous warman, landed with his motley crew of artisans and land-pirates. Deposits from a tiny river and the receding of the sea have formed the present site of Pevensey Bay; over the very spot where the villa stands, the adventurer's fleet sailed twice at least, for from Pevensey he sailed six months after the Conquest for his first visit to Normandy.

William, the burly, half-savage landgrabber, to the Americans was still very much alive in that Saxon region. They grew upon such familiar terms with him that they occasionally referred to him as "Willie," even "Bill," after the fashion of their favorite New York weekly, by way of variety in such continual mention.

Within walking distance (a "tidy walk," the natives would call it) is the spot where Harold fell, taking with him all the sympathies of these late-arriving Americans — the battle-field where the greedy Norman became forevermore "the Conqueror." At night the glow of Hastings edged the disk of their darkness; whenever they returned by train from their many excursions, their way from the station ran through the grounds of a Roman castle already a ruin when the Norman landed beside it; in the same spot, many say, where Cæsar landed a thousand years before the Norman was born. This Pevensey Castle stands upon a slight eminence, and its ivy-grown walls are a landmark for miles. Its fifteen massive towers buttressing the walls were added probably soon after the Conquest, by one of William's half brothers, the Earl of Morton, to whom much of Sussex was given.

In this castle in 1399, Lady Pelham, who had valiantly defended it against King Richard (although women must not vote because they cannot fight), wrote to her " trewe lorde," the earliest letter extant in the English language. Here, in 1405, young James the First of Scotland spent some time of his captivity in England ; and here in 1419, Queen Joan of Navarre, widow of Henry Fourth, was imprisoned by her stepson. But perhaps none of those distinguished people ever occupied so high a position in the castle as these undistinguished Americans did. Since those prison-days, time has been busy filling in the roofless ten acres, till now the village path through the walls is within a few feet of the top of the towers. Probably when Lady Pelham chewed her goose-quill and gazed out of window-slits meditating how to spell her letter to her " Lordes hie worschippe," she sat a hundred feet or more below the sodden path where, from a continent she never heard of, certain Americans passed and fancied they could teach her.

" The insolence of thinking to teach a valiant dame who taught a king bitter knowledge, that ' yhowr awnn pore I Pelham ' is not the latest style in the adjustment of letters," retorted one of them to the other. " Don't tell me that correct spelling is not vulgar, the trick of schoolmarms and proof-readers ! Chaucer's spelling was entirely Chaucerian ; Goethe blundered as he pleased ; Swift allowed Stella twenty misspellings in one letter. Neither Romney, George Morland, nor Turner could spell ; Monk and Marlborough spelled fortuitously ;

Washington put as many *n*'s as he pleased in his ginn; Queens Mary and Anne spelled in true Stuart fashion; Victoria is by no means always vulgarly correct; no king of England and no hero has ever spelled as correctly as a board school-mistress. Then think of Jane Austen with her 'arraroot,' her 'neice,' and 'tomatas.' Don't tell me — "

" I won't," said he.

Pevensey has had distinguished visitors that have not been prisoners. The house is here in which tradition says the original of all Merrie Andrews was born. Tradition insists that not only here he was born, but that in the very next parish was the Gotham of which he wrote merry tales. Dr. Andrew Boorde is usually spoken of as physician to Henry Eighth. His name appears in no household books of the Court, and the only authority for such courtly association is his own word that he " waited on the King." Tradition represents him as a sort of sixteenth century bohemian, seeing many countries and many men, loving flesh and wine, or living upon " a peny worth of whyte bread a hoole weeke," and finding it enough for an honest man " unless he be a raveneur." Boorde began as a Carthusian monk, but he was unable to bear the " rigouosity of the religion," and became a physician and a very roaming one, as is shown by his own writings. " I have travelyd specially about Europe and part of Affrycke throwow and round about Christendome," he wrote. Tradition says that he frequented markets and country fairs, haranguing crowds, disposing of his remedies and enlarging his practice by his drolleries and buffoonery, thus becoming known as " Merrie Andrew " and the

original of whole generations of " Merrie Andrews "
who were the companions and allies of quack
doctors and mountebanks. Sussex tradition insists
that here in Pevensey he wrote the " Merrie Tales
of the Wise Men of Gotham " that have been
printed with his name ever since his own century.
It says that he was not on good terms with the
village authorities, and that he wrote ostensibly
about those " foles of Gottam," while really ridicul-
ing certain known actions of their own. That he
owned a house here is not tradition, for he gave
away " my house in Pemsy " by his will. Neither
is it traditional that he roved in many countries,
" in divers countries by the practyce of physyck
for his sustentaysion," a profession which certainly
requires stability of position for success, unless it be
a bohemian success of a " Merrie Andrew." An
editor of Early English text, Mr. Furnivall, one
of the most amiable natural dispositions and the
very most cantankerous literary temper, denies with
asperity everything that tradition says. Not the
Gotham of Sussex was meant, says Mr. Furnivall,
but probably the Gotham of Nottinghamshire,
renowned for the foolishness of its inhabitants, and
Dr. Boorde never wrote the tales. He repudiates
the idea that Boorde ever frequented country fairs
and made himself a " Merrie Andrew." But as
the Early English Text Society can substitute
nothing definite for tradition ; as it can draw its
inferences only from other of Boorde's writings
(very vague inferences they are) ; as it is compelled
to acknowledge that he died in the Fleet (as rovers
so often have died), and cannot tell why ; as it cannot even tell when or where he was born (except
that he was born in Sussex) ; in fact, as it does *not*

disprove the Merrie Andrew tradition to any other satisfaction than its own, — all who love tradition have every right still to believe that Andrew Boorde was a roving and a Merrie Andrew, "a lewd and ungratious pre'st" (priest), as he was written down thirty years after his death, and given to wine and wantoning, alternating with hair shirt and cold-water penance, just as the bohemian poet, Paul Verlaine, was wont to alternate, and many another besides King David.

Mr. Furnivall would argue that a man who wrote piously must be pious, and a man who was pious could not be a Merrie Andrew or write the Merrie Tales of the Wise Men of Gotham. King David was the author of the Psalms, yet King David's private life was not set to the tune of Old Hundred. As for the Sussex Gotham, the name still adheres to a land and the site of a manor near Pevensey; and Sussex, Boorde's own country, is notoriously "Silly Sussex" in parts to this day. The marshy soil, horrible roads or rather no roads, so deep with "myre and dyrt" that so late as the last century people have gone to church drawn by oxen, made travelling almost impossible. Villages lived entirely by themselves, without acquaintance with other villages but a few miles away, which were considered "furrin parts." A Sussex man once returned to his native hamlet saying that he was "tired of furrin parts." He had been six months in a village sixteen miles distant from his own. Under such conditions there was constant inter-marrying within a limited circle, and this going on for generations with the natural result, the "foles of Gottam," as well as the Silliness of Sussex generally.

The Americans, after examination of both sides

of the question, decided to accept Tradition's say of Andrew Boorde, finding that say so much the more interesting and picturesque, although not even Tradition would tell them why so clever a man, and one with other houses to will away besides this one in Pemsy, died in the Fleet.

"A very wise man," remarked the lady. "'Beate her nat,' Boorde advised husbands concerning their wives."

"Did he not say 'God made her subject to man?'" observed the other Villain. "What did that mean but a right to beat her at discretion?"

"He wrote, 'Let every man please his wife and displease her not,'" recited Mistress Villain much as if reading from notes, "'but let her have her owne wyl for that she wyl have, who-so-ever say nay.' Bless his merry old soul! How modern he was for an age we consider barbaric! '*Homo* is the Latin word,' he says, ' and in Englyshe it is as wel for a woman as for a man, but woman is a man in wo, and set wo before man and then it is woman, and wel she may be named a *wo*-man, for as muche as she doth bear chyldren with wo and peyn.' Imagine him," she continued, "standing on a cart surrounded by gaping yokels, a close-shaven man like a monk, wearing a little cap and one straight stiff feather, with woollen hosen to his waist, and under his ordinary short cotes a petycote of scarlet to keep his stomach from 'croaking,' and over all a doctor's long cloak or robe. Imagine him selling his cures, and telling those Tudoresque Englishmen that 'the woman is subject to the man *except when* the white mare is the better horse.'"

That same evening, with feet on the fender, as they spun their usual fancies both blithe and pensive, they managed between them to enrich English literature with rhymes in remembrance of Merrie Andrew Boorde.

THE LOST BROTHER.

Seven Wise Men of Gotham were they,
Yet none too wise to unbend to play,
When the sun was hot and fields scorched brown,
And nothing whatever was doing in town,
And the river ran near and wimpled cool,
And rested in many a placid pool,
To tempt those men from sordid toil,
From the stewing streets and the August broil,
To bathe fevered frames in limpid shade
And find failing forces thus remade.

So the Wise Men started by dawn's first light,
Having for fear of not rising sat up all night,
And soon the whole seven were cucumbery cool,
Immersed to their necks in a slumbery pool.

" Ah ha ! " cried a Wise Man, pulling on his hose,
" How lucky we are no one of us to lose
In those fathomless depths whence we all emerge
And whose raging billows might have wailed our dirge ! "
(The fathomless depths were two feet deep,
And their rippleless surface smiled in its sleep.)
" Are you sure ? " asked another in mild surprise.
" We were Seven at starting, if I trust my own eyes
Now I see only Six, and does not that show
That one of us lies in those fell depths below ? "
(The Wise Man in counting saw each of the others,
But forgot to count himself among all his brothers.)

" You 're right ! " cried the others, after horrified pause
And each counting himself in oblivious clause,
" We 're but Six, as is plain ; at dawn we were more,
So surely our brother has ne 'er come to shore.
Ah ! How can we bear that dear brother to lose,
Or how carry home the dolorous news

2

To weeping aunts, sisters, cousins, and mothers,
Widows, orphans, relations-by-marriage, and brothers ?
How can we endure that dear brother to lose,
Not the best of us worthy to tie up his shoes ?
He surely was wisest and best of us Seven,
For of such is always the Kingdom of Heaven ! ''

So they wept and wailed with clam'rous refrain,
Then by fits and by starts they counted again ;
But always forgetting that each counter was one,
Came always to same number when the counting was done.

Their grief grew tremendous, and its clamour rose high,
Thus attracting attention from a man riding by,
Who stopped his old horse to demand all the whys
That the day should be rent by such hideous cries.
" Our brother ! Our brother ! " was all they could say ;
" We were Seven at dawn, we 're but Six at mid-day.
We 've counted ourselves a dozen times round,
And always the Six reiterated found.
The Seventh is missing, hence the truth is quite plain
We shall never see our dear brother again."
" Gad ! If a Seventh you want," cried the man in amaze,
" I 'll make you remember where he is, all your days ! "

Then he gave one a lash with might and with main,
And the Wise Man yelped like a bulldog in pain.
" You 're *One !* " said the lasher, to which lashed agreed.
" You 're *Two !* " and the second was lashed twice with speed.
" *You're Three,* and *you 're* Four, *you 're* Five, and *you 're* Six :
You 'll remember your numbers by the number of licks."
Then — with lash more cutting than ever — " *You 're* SEVEN ;
Thus you see you 're not yet of the Kingdom of Heaven ! "

The Seven howled together with agonized glee,
Thus suddenly restored their dead brother to see.
" God bless you ! " they chorussed, all prancing with pain,
" But for you we should never have been Seven again ! "

" Quite equal to Wordsworth's ' We are Seven,' "
said one of them. And the other agreed.

Pevensey Bay is not picturesque, but what care
they for picturesqueness, the twinkling, twittering,

fleeting hordes for whose pleasure its exists? It is a cheap bathing place, made cheap by its total lack of natural beauty; where children dig all day in the summer sands, and bathing costumes dash from bedrooms straight into the water and drippingly back again. A constant succession of short holiday folk, shopkeepers, and office clerks and their families, dashes through the hamlet during "the season," few remaining more than a week or two at a time, and all leaving more or less, generally more, of havoc and smash behind them. The Americans needed not to ask who nipped the teapot's nose and lost the stove lid-lifter, and corkscrewed the poker, and robbed the oven of all its grates, and lost every key to cupboards and chests of drawers, and broke the thermometer's back and the spirit of all the upholstery in the villa except of the beds, which were perfect, even luxurious, as English beds always are. They needed not to ask concerning the brief summer tenant.

Evidently the villa gave outward signs of the warm life within, for they all came, butcher, baker, milkman, grocer, from Pevensey beyond the marsh (pardon, beyond the Level). Even the sewing-machine man came, two of him for every week they stayed, and ten machines the lady waved away, — the first with mildness, the last without. Every day came the rosy maid whom they named "Ivy Leaf," so perennially fresh, so full of sturdy life she seemed, however the wind blew, the snow flew, whatever the wild waves were saying. Every morning she came from a market garden in "Pemsy" with her brilliant complexion not even suggestive of blousiness, not even of a "cabbage" rose, but of wild pink roses blowing over a distant hedge, with the most cooing, winning voice in the world, a pretty accent, every *h* in its place, and an enormous basket from which one might select the order to come later. She went to every house in the hamlet every day of the year. " She's been offered any price to go to London with summer visitors for child's nurse," said Mrs. Pumpkin-Hood, " but she likes this business better."

The Americans found that even nicked cups and saucers, scarred platters, and a wounded tea-pot need to be washed after use, the mattresses to be turned every day, and then the dreadful ashes !

Likewise the more dreadful shoes.

An old adage names " Sowsexe full of dyrt and myre," and a writer so late as 1771 facetiously asks, " Why is it the oxen, the swine, the women, and all other animals are so long-legged in Sussex ? May it be from the difficulty of pulling the feet out of so much mud by the strength of the ankle that the muscles get stretched, as it were, and the bones lengthened ? "

" What a swinish advantage," she remarked. " Women are the only animals obliged to keep their feet clean. Don't tell *me* that women are not shamefully put upon — don't tell *me* — "

" I won't," said he.

" To be sure," said Mrs. Pumpkin-Hood, " there's the Widow Rogers who will take your washing home. She will be thankful to do everything in the forenoon except cooking, for four shillings a week."

Which the Widow Rogers did do, and perfectly, so that the Pemsy Villains were as independent of coals, ashes, and mud as Sussex swine or oxen.

When the laundry basket came home the first time, — "Are you taking a nap?" he called from the sitting-room.

"I'm not snoring!" came the indignant answer from the kitchen. "I'm only smiling over the disappearance of London fog from the clothes!"

The dinners of these Villains came at night. Digestion waits better upon appetite after the brain's work is done for the day. The Mistress Villain prepared joints and vegetables herself; the sweets and deserts came from Pemsy shops or were brought home from Eastbourne or Hastings, where English plum pudding may be bought by the yard, or mile, and steamed, resteamed, re-re-steamed, so long as an inch of it is left. Mince pies too, the size of an American jam tart and entirely of fruit without admixture of meat, were perennially fresh by means of a tiny tin oven fitted to an oil lamp (*Mem.* The lady had written "Never hire furnished without my oil lamp and oven").

"We are in the very heart of the *H* topsey-turveyism, I mean the very 'art of it," said one of them, "yet Sussex speaks English, antique English, and it says pie for pie just as we do in America, and not tart for pie as London does."

"Just so," said the other of them. "Sometimes these Sussex expressions make me wonder for a moment how this ' strong Saxon English,' as they call it, ever became so ' Americanized.' We both thought at first that yesterday's landlady was speaking American when she said the table was 'out of kilter,' yet an old Sussex benefaction left money to keep the parson's breeches from getting 'out of kilter.' Londoners sometimes smiled at our use of the word 'crock,' yet the Sussex proverb tells that at the rainbow's end is a *crock* of gold, not a pot."

"When I was a child in my native Maine, we were very funny when we dialogued 'Wat's your name?' 'Pudden tame;' yet here in Sussex the dialogue is ancient, and the answer 'Pudden ta'em' means either 'pudding at home," or as wiser ones say, 'pudding and a broach,' or a draught of beer. We sometimes added, 'Wat's your nater?' and answered 'Pudden-tater;' but that addition was undoubtedly of our new world."

But apropos of these dinners. These Americans knew the bloom and the beauty of California fruit even when imprisoned in tin. One morning the lady of the villa added to her order for the day, "and a tin of peaches." The grocer's grin was wider than Mercutio's wound, for it was as wide as a church door.

"You 've 'ad 'em hall! 'Ave sent for more," he remarked.

With books and work and healthful play the days flew by on wings. They were calm, still days, with that delicate sunshine Americans never see in their own startling land, the golden light softened by transparent mists, as a girl's blushes by her bridal veil. Sussex "dyrt and myre" was sticky but not deep, although too much so for bicycling, so they trotted many miles instead of rolling them, and almost buried Mrs. Rogers in her native soil.

One day it might be Battle Abbey where the Conqueror willed that prayers should forever be offered up for the souls of those who had fallen in the memorable conflict, prayers forever before the high altar erected on the very spot where Harold's standard had waved. " Perpetual prayer ! " what a mockery ! What a mockery is "perpetual" anything in a world that never for an instant rests from perpetual change ! Now the original abbey is level with the ground, and only the site exists of the high altar, where no prayers are said unless the sightseer includes one with his sixpence to the guide.

The present Battle Abbey is a ducal dwelling shown to *hoy polloy* on certain days of the week. It is said to be haunted, not as one would suppose by mailed knights, but by a nameless old woman of weird and terrible aspect.

" Do you ever see a weird old woman in the grounds ? " a lady asked the guide.

" Her Grace the Duchess," he answered. Evidently "weird" was too much for him.

Sometimes it was a walk to Beachy Head, where in 1690 "the English got one of the very few lickings they ever got not administered by us," remarked a Pevensey Villain, with filial pride in a parent hard to lick. Other times quaint bits of Sussex architecture embedded in " restorations " lured them for miles, or a storied castle, an historic manor, a quaint churchyard, even once a search for the grave in which a queer corpse was buried. At the funeral of a renowned smuggler a mysterious tall stranger in a cloak stood by the grave. When the coffin was lowered he exclaimed, " I am not there ! " with which quite unnecessary remark he disappeared. A century afterwards the coffin was found to hold only stones. " The man didn't gain much," they agreed. "His own coffin by that time held less."

Delightful beyond description to walk in rustic England even in winter, for one may scarce walk a mile anywhere without coming upon some relic of ages past, some shrine of poetic history, some ruined temple of forgotten fame, some broken altar of faith, or some ghost of romantic art. Besides, there are always exquisite pictures of true English farmhouses and cottages, old when our Declaration of Independence was new, some older than the history of Plymouth Rock; houses wrapped in living green, with low hanging eaves and massive skeletons showing through solid walls. No one was like another, and every one they saw between Pevensey and Herstmonceaux Castle they vowed was more antique, more picturesque, more utterly, unspeakably enchanting than all the rest.

"Ah! *this* is poetry! This is what it is to *live!*" quoth she, wiping the mud from her English boots on the wayside grass.

They were English boots and no mistake. Nowhere on this rolling globe could they ever be mistaken for anything else. They were as solid as iron, and as impervious to water or dampness as a man-of-war. They were laced in front high up the leg, they had Jacobean gables for toes; they endured for years, and they cost three dollars. Ugly? Yea, verily, they were of unmitigated, absolute hideousness, in which a number three foot made tracks whereby scientists might imagine to follow some extinct mammoth. They however did perfectly all they were bought to do, — kept the feet warm and dry whatever the road, for ever so "tidy" a walk. In New England's ice and snow they would be worse than useless, would keep the wearer oftener on her shoulderblades than her heels, because of their stiff-soled slipperiness. In all her years in England this American never wore out a pair of galoshes, and on their winter tramps and summer mountain climbs "Stumpity-Thump" her companion named the occupant of those iron-bound, Jacobean gables.

Poetry? Pages, volumes of it; volumes which included lunches of bread and cheese in wayside inns, and afternoon tea in another inn miles nearer their hired-furnished. And *such* tea! "Shall we ever be able to drink the concoction we call tea at home?" they wondered, as in the humblest of parlors they drank at sixpence apiece elixir that ought to make any mandarin purr and prattle; elixir that slid divinely over the tongue to mount to the brain, to descend to the heart, to rummage through all the veins and make the drinkers rise to Olympian heights of bliss and power. "Now I understand Hazlitt's intemperance," one said, and the other agreed. "I never could understand it before I came to England."

Hazlitt was really a tea-drunkard, and weaned himself from brandy by its means. He would sit for hours over his strong, black tea, silent and motionless as a Turk over his opium, for tea served him precisely in that capacity. He was very particular about the quality of his tea, using the most expensive he could get, and when alone consumed nearly a pound a week. He always made it himself, half filling the pot with tea, pouring boiling water upon it, and almost immediately pouring it out. So fascinating to him was his beloved tipple, so deep the blissful peace into which it threw him for the time, that not even the intrusion of a dun, to which he was at other times so abnormally sensitive, could wrest him from his repose. When he died he said, " I have had a happy life," and must thus have remembered only his tea-happy hours. For otherwise he was very miserable. Unhappy with his two wives, he tormented himself with a foolish passion for a lodging-house keeper's daughter ; was in money difficulties at times, and in the bitterest of literary and political quarrels. Evidently tea washed all those hateful memories away. De Quincey also was excessively fond of tea ; Shelley was an inveterate tea-drinker. What miles of poetry and prose Englishmen have written about tea, beginning with Waller, who pleased the tea-drinking spouse of Charles Second with a sonnet declaring that —

> " Venus her Myrtle, Phœbus has his bays,
> Tea both excels,"

and continuing —

> " The Muses' friend, Tea doth our fancy aid,
> Repress those vapours which the head invade,
> And keep the palace of the soul serene."

Very early in the history of tea Englishmen recognized it as a brain-elixir, softly thrilling the nerves to lyre-like trembling, bringing out whatever of music was in the instrument, an æolian quiver quite different from the vibrant effect of coffee.

Poor forgotten Nahum Tate wrote a poem, " Panacea," about 1700 to represent all the divinities contending for the honor of standing as god-parent to tea, which honor finally fell to Phœbus. An Anglicized Frenchman, Pierre Motteux, wrote

another recommending tea to all who exercise
their brain, to all who would

> " On soaring wings of contemplation rise
> And fetch discov'ries from the skies;
> Ethereal *Tea* your natures will refine
> Till you yourselves become almost divine."

They all unite in singing it the Phœbean drink,
even though we know that Ben Jonson never put
a teacup to his sack-swilling lips ; that Shakespeare never heard of the Phœbean elixir, or any
other of the stalwart Elizabethans.

> " ' And I remember,' said the sober Mouse,
> ' I 've heard much talk of the Wits' Coffee House.'
> ' Thither,' said Bundle, ' you shall go and see
> Priests sipping Coffee, and *Poets Tea*.' "

Writers rapidly multiplied in England after tea
became a popular drink, doubtless because so
many more brains were clear than when sack was
man's beverage morning, noon, and night. They
were not of the Elizabethan breed of writers, but
they wrote, and in time a *tea-ful* printer set the
world agog with fiction that could never have
been nourished on pipe and bottle, yet that made
many a pipe and bottle man weep.

"Exactly," said one of them; "we have just
been reading the diary of tippling Thomas Turner,
a Sussex tradesman of one hundred and forty
years ago, who sobbed between his cups (not
of tea). ' My wife read to me that moving scene
of the funeral of Miss Clarissa Harlowe. Oh may
the Supreme Being give me grace to lead my life
in such a manner as my exit may in some measure
be like that divine creature's ! ' "

Hartley Coleridge asked somebody to " Inspire my genius and my tea infuse," as if the two easily went together, and wrote, —

> " And I who always keep the golden mean,
> Have just declined my seventh cup of green."

Shelley wrote of it, —

> " The liquor doctors rail at, and that I
> Will quaff in spite of them, and when I die
> We 'll toss up which died first of drinking tea."

" Shall we have another sixpen'orth ? " asked the lady.

" It is to be noticed that no American, distinguished or otherwise, has ever been an excessive tea-drinker, such as Dr. Johnson, for instance, who declared himself a hardened tea-drinker whose kettle never has time to get cold ; as for women — "

" And gossip ? " interrupted the other. " The moment one speaks of women and tea in the same sentence I know that ' gossip ' will follow. Some people never can say ' Margaret ' without ' rare pale,' or mention an underdone joint without bringing in poor old Ben Jonson, or a day in June. Don't tell me that men are not the greatest gossips in the world ! Was not Plutarch a lively old gossip as well as Herodotus ? The author of the ' Memoirs of de Grammont ' said ' The Duke of Buckingham was the father and mother of Scandal.'

" Anatomy-of-Melancholy Burton, before he knew tea (if ever he knew it), wrote, ' Our gentry — their sole discourse is hawks, horses, dogs, and *what news.*' Pepys, Swift (to Stella), Boswell, were kings of gossip. Was ever a better description than Leigh Hunt's of tea-scorning Walpole's gossip, 'the perpetual squeak of its censoriousness?' Lady Blessington wrote that Lord Byron was very fond of gossiping; any little bit of scandal amused him very much. When she remarked this to him one day he laughed and said, 'Don't you know the elephant's trunk can take up the most ponderous things and the most minute? I do like a little scandal, I think all English people do.' Then there was Keats, a very apothecary except for his genius, who when speaking of 'personal talk' said, 'I must confess to rather of an itch for it myself.' None of these gossips drank tea. Byron, Keats, and Walpole airily sneered at it; Swift wrote superciliously against it; the others did not know it.

"Neither Tea nor Woman is really responsible for Scandal. 'Slanderynge commythe of a dronkon hede,' the Goode Wyfe taught her daughter about 1460."

"Yes, let us have two six-pennorth," said he.

Thus the two Villains chatted over their cups in dusky inn parlors, where floors were often tiled, sunken, and bare, walls heavy and low, and those "cups" more like the "dish" of ye olden time than those with which they were familiar, yet would they not change with tealess occupants of thrones.

Why did our ancestors even down to our own century so often say, "Drink a dish," where we more daintily "take a cup"? Was it that the "new China Drink" of which Pepys wrote coldly in 1660, found "cup" already wedded to "sack," and a vessel not delicate enough to receive the

costly beverage ?   When the Oriental leaf was sold
in London at sixty shillings, or fifteen dollars, the
pound, and the liquid made from it taxed at eight-
pence the gallon in coffee-houses, scarce wonder
the coarse cup, boon companion with roaring
sack, was considered unfit for the elixir dealt out
of teapots holding half a pint, into measures
scarcely more than a tablespoonful.   Even so late
as 1703, Counsellor Burrill in Sussex recorded in
his Journal as a valuable gift the three-quarters of
an ounce of *Te* he gave away.   The year after
Pepys' "Cup of *Tee*, a new China Drink of which
I never drank before," that is, the second year of
the Restoration, the landlady in Dryden's "Wild
Gallants" loudly complained, —

"And your Worship came home ill (*drunk*)
last night, and your head was bad, and I did send
for three dishes of tea for your Worship, and that
was sixpence."   Sixpences in those days were as
large as "dishes" were small, and the cost of the
new drink excuses the character in one of those
old plays who "will get the tea ready and *boyl* it
a long time."   Sir Kenelm Digby's "recetes" of
only a few years later teach a better course than
to "boyl a long time," although his "recete" is still
of huge economy, less than one "dram" of the
leaves to a pint of water.   "In these parts," he
wrote, "we let the hot water remain too long
soaking upon the Tea.   The water is to remain
upon it no longer than the whiles you can say the
Miserere Psalm very leisurely."

"Cup" was not in fashionable use much before
the beginning of the Eighteenth Century, "that
hoop-and-teacup-time."   Then Pope and Cowper,
the teacup poets par excellence, never use any-

thing else, "dish" by that time having fallen low in the world.

The new " China Drink," which was first named in English literature as a medicine for tipsiness (Pepys had no thought of literature), long held that poor reputation. Quite naturally, too, it was very early recognized as fit drink of the Muses in place of wine, "which hath heat without light."

Dr. Ovington, a court chaplain to Queen Mary of Orange, named it "*Anti-Circe* inasmuch as it counter-charms the enchanted Cup and changes the Beast into a Man."

"When the tea is brought in," says Sir John Brute, in the " Provoked Wife," " I drink twelve regular dishes." Sir John was a man of headachy mornings, being " drunk ten times in a fortnight; " therefore even so late as his day (1694), those twelve tiny dishes must have been a *dose*. It was so considered evidently by that rough cavalier, General Blunt, in Shadwell's " Stockjobbers." Major-General Blount said of the tea-table, " 'T is ready for the Women and Men who live like Women; adod, your fine-bred Men of England as they call 'em are all turned Women, but by my Troth, I 'll not turn my Back to the Pipe and Bottle after Dinner."

Shadwell's " Stockjobbers " is interesting as containing the first mention of *tea-tables*, and also as evidence that the modern lady's " day " is no new thing. Eugenia, who is described as " a very fine young lady," the reverse of her sister Teresia, who is " a foolish, conceited, affected young Lady," exclaims, " Who that has the Sense of Vertue could endure the piteous Dullness of new Plays, the most provoking Impertinences of how-do-you 's and Visiting Days with Tea Tables!" Evidently Eugenia was "fine" in the sense of being sensible, and regarding visiting days and tea-tables from the masculine or "dosed" point of view. Yet its history shows that tea has been almost the best friend the Englishwoman has ever had.

"If you please," says Touchwood, in the "Double-Dealer," exactly two hundred years ago, — "if you please, we will retire to the ladies, and drink a dish of tea to settle our heads."

Tea was a "settler." It "settled" the "Rake-hells" till not one is now to be found in decent English society. It "settled" the Sir John Brutes till not one such dare show his head among visiting days and tea-tables. It "settled" the tea-table, too, on foundations deep in our civilization, binding families, communities, nations together in pleasantness and peace. Before tea came, England had only its heavy dinner-table, laden with strong meats and stronger drinks. There was no breakfast-table, no pleasant centre for afternoon tea. All through the seventeenth-century dramatists are mentions of breakfast, but never of a breakfast-*table*. The morning meal was then not much more than the ten-o'clock drink, a sop or a bite with it. The family did not gather decently together to the silvery tinkle of teaspoons, the chime of dainty china cups, the hum of lucid conversation.

Sir William Davenant's description of a lady's tealess and tableless breakfast is enough to make all the world of womankind feel closely akin to Lady Gentle in Colley Cibber's "Wife's Resentment."

Sings Davenant : —

"Arise, arise! Your breakfast stays, —
Good water, gruel warm,
Or sugar sops, which Galen says
With mace will do no harm.
Arise, arise! when you are up
You'll find your draught in caudle cup,
Good nut-brown ale and toast."

From caudle cups and morning draught of ale, tea has delivered England, even if it has developed the traditional old ladies who make their living by taking tea at each other's houses.

"Tea," exclaims Colley Cibber's Lady Gentle, — "Tea, thou soft, thou sober, sage and venerable liquor, thou innocent pretext for bringing the wicked of both sexes together on a morning, thou female tongue-running, smile-smoothing, heart-opening, wink-tipping cordial, to whose glorious insipidity I owe the happiest moments of my life, let me fall prostrate and adore Thee."

Then she falls upon her knees, and from her "dish" sips loudly, as nineteenth century Lady Gentles do not from modern "cups."

When originated the popular superstition which links Tea and Gossip together? Who first put into print that the musical jingle of silver, the dainty tumult of china, the fragrant steam of teapots, was a necromantic spell to set tongues awag? Who in English literature not only recognized the potency of the spell, but slandered the character of the wagging? Who was first to make a common-place of "Tea and Gossip?" Naturally it was some man. The words still retain their ancient echo of a gruff voice. It was some man of a century in which only despised Woman loved tea, and arrogant Man did not. Quite as naturally it was some poet or dramatist, for in poems and

3

plays are imbedded the pearls and pebbles of other times, so often to become the traditions and superstitions of our own. " Every woman is at heart a rake," has jaundiced many a man's vision who never read a word of Pope. Without so much as a dream of the manner of our century, Shakespeare has fitted it with sayings for its every day's doings.

Pipe and bottle were not conducive to the wagging of tongues. One closed the mouth, the other clogged the wits, and oftener under the dinner-table than at the tea-table the Blunts were found. Now we see that tea was a silly woman-drink, beloved of chatterers with fancy aided by it, and souls made serene rather than muddled. What wonder that women wagged their tongues over dainty cups and tinkling silver, while their trencher-men lords piped, swilled, and snored !

At the end of the seventeenth century, or nearly half a century after elegant Waller's apostrophe to Tea, Congreve's " Way of the World " took an even more modern view of " that best of herbs " of which Waller wrote. Tea was now rapidly permeating England. The tea-table was a recognized feature of society. In " The Way of the World " Millament insists to Mirabell that she " be sole Empress of my Tea Table, which you must never presume to approach without asking leave." With characteristic insolence those silly women had taken the tea-table as their very own, that same tea-table to which pipe and bottle had exiled them. In Congreve's play Mirabell answers : " To the dominion of the Tea Table I submit — but with proviso that you exceed not in your province but restrain yourself to genuine and authorized Tea Table talk — such as mending of fashions, spoiling reputations, railing at absent friends, and so forth."

We have him ! Congreve is the slanderer, — Congreve, whose plays are full of wine-bibbing male tattlers, backbiters, scandal-mongers, who even names some of his men " Scandal " and " Tattle " and never gives them a cup of tea ! Again in the " Double Dealer," Congreve makes Mille-fond answer Careless's question, " Where are the women ? I 'm weary of guzzling and begin to think them better company," with " Then thy reason staggers, and thou 'rt drunk ;" adding after-wards, " Why, they are retired to Tea and Scandal according to their ancient custom."

After this the deluge ! The poets, than whom in the nineteenth century none are more given to the five o'clock cup, scarce mention tea without the companionship of scandal, or its meeker sister gossip. They are all men-poets, Mrs. Browning with her,

" Then helps to sugar her bohea at night
With your reputation,"

being almost the only woman who does so, and she only in one specified instance, not generally and sweepingly, after the manner of men. Indeed, by the eighteenth century it became a literary and social convention to unite the two, and quite inde-pendent of one's own observation and belief, as we speak of the rising and setting sun, knowing perfectly that there is no such thing in creation.

Pope, however, in the eighteenth century recog-nized the much-maligned elixir as of balmy and amiable effect. He makes Lovet say, " Now stop complaining and come to Tea." Cowper, too, was the poet of the tea-table in its more humane and natural aspect, and without the hateful accomplice Slander seen by so many other poets, — "the cup that cheers," etc.

Tea has had to suffer for keeping bad company. For women are bad, as most poets and playwrights know, — have been bad ever since Eve ate the apple. It was for woman exclusively that the ninth commandment was given, it was for women that Christ spoke the Golden Rule ; Judas must have been a woman in disguise. Woman is the sinner, Tea the innocent sufferer. For long before tea entered Europe, poets and playwrights knew women to live not by bread, but by gossip and scandal. When women were not bright enough to do much in the gossiping-Pepys and scandal-mongering Horace Walpole way, they were such women as Sir William Davenant described (*tea*less women), —

> " — dull country Madames
> That spend their time in studying receipts to make
> Marchpane and preserve plums ; that talk
> Of painful child-birth, servant's wages,
> Their husband's good complexion, and his leg."

" Don't tell *me !* " said she. " Don't tell *me* that tea has not done Christian Service in civilizing humanity. It has turned drunken man's scandal into woman's dainty gossip. Don't tell *me !* "

" I won't," said he.

Often the Villains enticed the landlady into a chat even while regretting that Sussex landladies are not " buxom," as story-landladies usually are, and from her beguiled many a quaint form of Sussex speech or scraps of neighborhood or family history, — " gossip " perhaps.

It might be the gossip of the old rector's approaching marriage with the Lady Faire, whose heart was buried in a slim curate's grave years ago. And the story of her beauty as she rode to hounds when Bretomhurst had another mistress than now, and the country-side was brilliant with scarlet coats. One of their gossips was twin maidens of seventy years, so much alike that the Villains can never tell if one they saw or two. They wore gray ringlets hanging both sides of their ruddy faces, with much beribboned caps, and massive gold chains round their neck and across black alpaca breasts. For the first few. times they did not show themselves to the strangers, but sent their niece, a village maid with townish ideas of dress, who always referred to them as one indivisible person named " harnts." " Harnts was sure the lady's feet were damp, and would she take hoff her shoes to be dried in harnts' happartment ? "

" Harnts could send them some butter-toast if they preferred it with their tea." When the tea and toast were consumed " Harnts oped they were pleased with their tea," which they decidedly were. Other times harnts themselves brought in the tea, a special honor, — one bearing the tray, the other the loaf, from which in England the luncher always serves himself. Harnts were chatty ; they wondered anybody should wish to find stocks and a whipping-post, but directed how to discover them a tidy walk away — they never had seen Lady Pelham, although they had lived under that roof all their lives, and never could marry because when Lizbeth was harsked she could n't leave Liza, and when Liza was harsked she could n't leave Lizbeth. " We don't mind," they remarked, " but it would be pleasant to 'ave the children come 'ome."

" Yes," explained Mrs. Pumpkin-Hood, " we call one Bright, the other Spite. It was Spite who kept Bright from marrying."

Then a few miles farther on, the Jacobean gables were sent into a corner, and in easy slippers and gowns they made merry over re-heated soup, broiled steak, salad, and steamed pudding. The Mistress Villain named a supreme convenience for these scrambled dinners " Saint Trivet," and *memmed*, " Never hire furnished without a blessed trivet." Later came a day that she *memmed*, " Never hire furnished without *two* trivets." To distinguish the two trivets hitched to the same grate she re-named the first one " Saint Makehot," and named the younger, " Saint Keephot."

When excursions were not in order, there were long quiet hours in the sunny sitting-room, with books new and old, books of Sussex history, tradition, archæology, and fascinating domestic diaries of ye olden time that strewed quaint old-world flowers all along the paths they trod. There were other old books that haunt one's memory like a perfume, books one always means to re-read and that one almost never does re-read, as well as old books known by name and reputation for a lifetime but never yet fitting in to the idle hour, which is all they merit. When some time the Master Villain requested Mistress Villain to tighten a button or set a stitch for him, and she cried despairingly,

" Leave me, oh, leave me, kill me, oh, kill me, but do not ask me to do that !" he grinned and answered, " I see ; it 's one of the late eighteenth and early nineteenth female novelists! Whose ' throbbing heart,' ' suspended breath,' ' burning brow ' are you indulging in now ? "

Behold, it was Miss Farrer's " Inheritance."

One day each week came the American papers, enough of them to fill the entire day.

" Bah ! " said a Villain, holding out an extra paper, a Sunday one, not one of their own subscription. "' Mrs. Jim has been wearing her white satin again ; Mrs. Tom looked very lovely in pink ; Mrs. Jack, as usual, wore a white veil and was surrounded by gentlemen ; Mrs. Disc-Spadden was the most stylish woman present !' Bah ! think of reading such rubbish where the eight hundred chaloupes of the Norman sailed."

" You have read it in Pompeian tombs."

" Never ! I skipped it even in Boston, that dear provincial city which so much over-esteems itself as one of *the* cities of the world. Why, Boston young men who have never lived elsewhere in their lives pose there as ' men of the world.' Imagine it ; Boston, which is only the size of Birmingham ! Would not a Londoner grin to hear a Birminghamite name himself a man of the world ? A man arrived in London from Birmingham, — dear me, one is inclined to warn him not to betray over-anxiety about his pocket, and not to trust any man who knew his great uncle in the provinces."

For days and days there was sunshine, and the wild waves sang only of peace to earth and good will to winter people in summer villas.

Which was a very good thing, Pemsy Bay being full of winter people in summer tents. A somewhat curious feature of English life, the life whose heart is the Home, and whose boast that only the English know Home in its deepest sense, is the homelessness of so many English people. In but one other civilized country in the world do so many people live without a vine and fig-tree they can call their own. Hosts of these English people live, or stay, in furnished houses by the month, usually not longer than five or six months in each. They carry all their possessions in trunks, and are " a-tome " wherever they unpack. Every autumn they select their winter quarters, either from past experiences or from advertisements of summer houses " to let for the winter at a nominal rent." Such a plan of existence is much more feasible in mild England than in severer climes, the west coast particularly, because of the Gulf Stream, enjoying a pleasant but somewhat debilitating softness such as New England never knows at any time of year. Where this curious shadowy, flitting, fleeting world homes itself in the summer when country and seaside rents are *not* nominal, who knows? The mystery seems never to have been solved. In the other half of Pemsy Villa was a lively family with a double perambulator. That family had spent three winters in the same furnished house at a rent (from November to June) of $2 a week. When the Mistress Villain asked where they lived between times, " We travel," she was told, and not even the twins were excepted from the *we*. The head of the family was of gentlemanly appearance, and spoke like a person of cultivated intelligence, but he seemed to have no occupation, unless he were an author, in which case his nervous system must have been of most unliterary vigor in a clatter that disturbed even the American side of the villa.

Almost the entire winter population of the Bay was of this intangible, impalpable, mysterious character, without mutual acquaintance, without neighborhood or church society, without any common, even any general interests, — the post-man served them all alike, and the tradespeople from Pemsy; the sewing-machine men, and Ivy Leaf's wooings and cooings over carrots and cab-bages; but more than that there was nothing in common save the sunshine and the wild and mild sayings of the waves. The former drew one or two rather listless gentlemen out upon the shingle occasionally; a governess (apparently) with her charges, and bevies of comfortably, not elegantly, dressed children, some of them children of lodg-ing-house keepers, living here all the year. The Americans were sure some of the gentlemen were distressed authors unable to work in noisy towns, where rents are guineas instead of these few shill-ings, and where tradesmen's bills are more punctu-ally presented. As they noted the springless steps and heavy heads, the Americans wondered if in those heads divine imaginations lurked before springing forth to dazzle a dull world and make yon seedy author immortal.

"The Vicar of Wakefield and Tony Lumpkin were born in a garret decorated with unpaid milk scores and accustomed to duns. Otway choked on a roll; a starving author, Sam Boyse, invented paper collars and carried manuscript to the printer without breeches. Ben Jonson complained of the king, ' He sends me so miserable a donation because I am poor and live in an alley.' "

" They are not to be pitied," continued another of them. " In such sunshine as this, beside such a laughing sea, and with a daily paper from London, one might live all one's life in hired-furnished and not feel homeless."

The daily paper deserved its mention. Every day by a mid-day train from Eastbourne the morning papers were brought by a reckless lad with a gold-banded cap inscribed " W. H. Smith," the name of a vast newspaper monopoly. Usually this lad loitered (when he did not levant into by-roads and fields or stop to bet on dogs and horses) on his way out from Pevensey Station. At the hour he was strictly due the summer hamlet of winter people became visibly astir. Heavy gentlemen with walking-sticks, spare gentlemen in knickerbockers, strolled sparsely up the one flat, wet road toward Pevensey. Now and then a shabby velvet jacket leaned expectantly from out an opened window ; here and there were picket guards of children ready to signal that the wayward urchin was in sight.

" Why do they not subscribe to their daily ? " asked he. " By the postman it would come just as soon."

" But then it must be paid in advance," quoth she.

The wild waves continued their garrulous murmur for at least two beautiful weeks. Not a day of these weeks that the cathedral windows up and down stairs were not thrown open for the entrance of any of the shining gods that chanced that way. The sitting-room encompassed an atmosphere in which June roses might grow and blow, to say nothing of bananas and pomegranates, and in the calm nights through mists of lace the still moon looked upon stirless slumbers.

Then, ah, *then!* Then America sent over the Atlantic, Boreas at his very howlingest. "We have many more and much worse storms," somebody once said to these Americans, "since your country took to managing the weather."

The Villains awoke one morning with cold noses. Getting out of bed was like an icy bath; the villa was dark, the air bedlamic.

"Pumpkin-Hood knew what was coming when she advised an oil lamp left near the kitchen pump," thought the Mistress Villain.

They breakfasted in shawl and overcoat, which kept them from freezing, but did not keep the table-cloth from bulging in spots and waving in places, like a ship's sail loosely set. Twice during breakfast the cathedral doors blew open, and a thousand millions of snowy imps dashed in with biting fury. They rushed in, under and about the door, they lay in a writhing heap in the front entry, and all the while the fire tore up the howling chimney like a kitten with a dog at its tail. He looked crestfallen, she seemed more so.

"What are the wild waves saying?" he asked with ill-timed levity.

"This carpet must stop its bounding billows or I *shall* die!" and her tone was precisely that well known to the stewardesses of ocean steamers. "I *shall* die! Oh, I *shall* die!"

It was a mighty storm; one with bugles, drums, and banners, marching over a shuddering world. The Villains discovered why their side of the house was the favourite, being the coolest. Mr. Pump-kin-Hood assured them "'tain't blew like this in a good five year," and congratulated them that the piling snow prevented the wind from getting under the villa. The lady thought not much was for congratulation when she saw her petticoats expand into Elizabethan farthingales, or the "cheeses" she made at school. The Americans made a great pailful of flour paste. They stuffed every crack and cranny with rags, and pasted all over with thick wrapping-paper. The cathedral window was nailed fast, and peace reigned.

Alas, it was a pallid and shivering peace, for the grate held scarcely more than a spoonful of fire, being but a summer grate.

What to do? Impossible to generate warmth by exercise in a tempest like this kicking at the front door. "Lucky I brought two oil stoves," she said; "never will I hire furnished without them."

She placed a stove in two corners of the sitting-room, the great heat-giving evening lamp in another; the door and side window were curtained with travelling rugs; a couple of bricks placed in the chimney somewhat stayed the dog and kitten; the grate was piled as high as it could hold with red-hot coals. Little thought they to contribute to the cyclonic devastation familiar to their villa, yet beneath its hitherto unheard-of fervors that grate melted almost entirely away. When they returned to London, but an abject, tottering skele-ton of a grate remained to bear witness against them.

" Look at that thermometer ! " a little later one exclaimed. " It looks half frightened to death."

"I wish I had a lemon soda," she gasped.

"A vanilla ice would about fit me," he panted.

There was no question of going out into the wailing kitchen, where even the grates would have danced in the oven had not amiable pre-Villains destroyed or lost them. So at noon, with Saint Makehot's help, the tin of Boston baked beans came gloriously into play, like a star-spangled banner in a Fourth of July breeze. Many hours afterwards, when the long absence of daylight, the drawn shades, and blazing lamp made the hour seem midnight when watches told but half-past seven (their usual dinner hour), the potatoes and canned corn were prepared by the grate fire, and the kitten and dog carried all the scent and steam of the crisp chops up the more mildly raging chimney; the saints between them toasted the mince pies.

Thus for three days, and of those seventy-two hours they voted without a dissenting voice that the cheeriest, the cosiest, the brightest, and pleasantest was the hour of four o'clock tea. They had every requisite for supreme enjoyment of the hour that so great a tea epicure as De Quincey demanded, even to the wind strong enough against which to lean one's back.

"Cosey," said one of them, "what is it to be cosey? We know and feel that we are cosey, but how define it, how put the delight in words? All one can do is to give the causes, the surrounding local color; but can we, or cleverer than we, describe the sensations, mental and physical, that make us purr like kittens, and purr the more cosily the fiercer the storm outside? Leigh Hunt knew what it was to be cosey in bed when a wind was moaning outside ; he did not care how melancholy a wind to the sound of which he could drop asleep in a transport of comfort. To me one of the most delightful bits of Robinson Crusoe was where he made himself snug (or cosey) for the winter. That sense of snugness or cosiness to me is the secret of the charm of stories of shipwrecked crews in caves or islands. How much softer our own beds seem when the blasts dash against our windows, how much lighter, more fleecy, our blankets when the rain beats upon the roof ! Did Spenser not understand this when he wrote of the bed of the God of Sleep, —

> " And more to lulle him in his chamber soft
> A trickling streame from high rock tumbling downe,
> And ever drizzling rain upon the loft
> Mixed with a murmuring winde."

How did our ancestors manage to live without the word 'cosey,' for it is a comparatively new word, you know, and never in use before our century. Some say it is Scotch, and some say it came from the French *causeuse ;* but whatever its origin, Thackeray was guilty of an anachronism in putting it into the mouth of a Countess Castlewood when the second George was king."

" Unconscious cerebration," explained the other. " All through our exquisite comfort, our luxury of warmth, and exhilaration of tea, penetrates an un-conscious-consciousness of what we are escaping from the roughness outside. We are warmer for knowing how cold we might be, we purr because we are not sighing. I wonder if it could not be proved that in most persons who like stormy and rainy weather (as Tennyson, for instance) the domestic instincts are strong ? "

"They must have been strong in De Quincey, at least once a day. Hear what he says of tea-time : " Let it be winter in its sternest shape. The divine pleasure of a winter fireside, candles at four o'clock, warm hearth rugs, a fair tea-maker, shutters closed, curtains flowing in ample draperies to the floor, whilst the wind and rain are raging audibly without . . . you may compute the period when happiness is in season, which in my opinion enters the room with the tea-tray " (" Hear ! Hear ! " shouted both Villains). " For tea, though ridiculed by those who are naturally coarse in their nervous sensibilities, or are become so from wine-drinking, and are not susceptible of influence from so refined a stimulant, will always be the beverage of the intellectual. But there, to save myself the trouble of too much verbal description, I will introduce a painter and give him directions for the rest of the picture. Paint me then a room seventeen feet by twelve, put as many books as you can into this room, make it populous with books, and furthermore paint me a good fire and furniture, plain and modest, befitting the cottage of a scholar." ("Hear ! Hear ! ") " And near the fire paint me a tea-table, and as it is clear no creature can come to see one on such a stormy night, place only two cups and saucers on the tea-tray."

"Sydney Smith thanked God that he was not born before the habit of tea," said Mistress Villain with an air of benediction for all the Smiths. "Will you have another dish ? "

THE DOVE-COTE.

WHEN the Spring God peeped into the windows of the Square, came the usual uneasiness, the uneasiness of migratory birds whose wings tremble for flight, the birds ask not whither. With the primroses came the first quivers, by the time Oxford Street was yellow with daffies those wings were spread.

But to what purpose? What wit or wisdom in spreading ones wings in Cavendish Square?

"Let us again hire furnished," said he, "and find something in the Channel Islands."

"*Tirili! Tirili! Tirili!*" remarked his mate, putting down her *Reisebilder*.

When Bright Eyes answered their letter from Jersey she was sure nothing could be found within their terms. This was discouraging, for Bright Eyes is Jersiaise born and bred for ages, and ought to know.

"*Ought* and *do* are not synonymous. Bright Eyes is born and bred under ceilings twenty feet high," said one of them.

Then they wrote to Le Gallais, the well-known house agent, plainly defining that they did not require to drive a coach and four up to' their dinner plates.

His reply assured them of thanks for their esteemed favor, but he knew of no furnished cottage on the island at their terms, for spring was Jersey's season, when everything was let from engagements made months before ; and he remained theirs.

"Give it up," said he.

"Won't," said she, being a very won't-give-upable person at all times.

They sent an advertisement to the "Jersey Times," and offered exactly half they were willing (if obliged) to pay. Out of the six answers they received (four of them from lodging-house keepers) they fell by mutual consent upon Dove Cottage.

"The description is so quaint," said one.

"The name is so appropriate," said the other.

"Ten and six a week is so very charming," said one. And the other.

"Besides, there 's no choice," said both.

Dove Cottage was in St. Helier's, the capital. This was an advantage in more ways than one, although in one it was highly disadvantageous. The villa offered them at St. Aubin's (everything is so saintly on Jersey that Mrs. St. Smith wrote them from St. Martin's Villa, St. Saviour's Road, St. Helier's) at a pound a week would have given them one great advantage, but it would have been less convenient in just the respects in which Dove Cottage excelled. It seemed preposterous in a way to make a *villeggiatura* on an island and never get a glimpse of the sea without going in search of it. The villa was directly facing the sea, but in Dove Cottage the owner wrote with what they fancied a spirit of boasting, "You would n't know the sea was within fifty miles." This disadvantage was compensated by superior advantages of getting about. The headquarters of all the excur-

4

sion coaches and of the railways are naturally in the capital. It would be pleasant to go home at night to cradle songs of the crooning sea, but that home-getting would not be possible after an early evening hour, except on foot, when excursion cars and railway carriages had gone decently to their night's repose in St. Helier's.

There were other doubts.

" It is a very queer cottage," wrote Bright Eyes. " We are afraid it will not please you ; but then, I know you like queer things."

" What does that mean ?" asked l'Américain.

" Means that there are no statues in the en-trance hall," explained l'Américaine.

" No, it means that your taste is hodd," said he.

He quoted from a London landlady disgusted at seeing her drawing-room " shoot " covered with their fantastic draperies, and her mantel ornaments bundled out of the apartment. " Bright Eyes knows that you are rather hodd, so is not so sure you will object to a queer style of cottage."

" If I am hodd and the cottage is queer? " thought the lady, somewhat dubiously. " Perhaps this is my doom as a 'Discontented Woman,' doomed to be hodd because I always hated cook-ing and the care of carpets and curtains. I'd rather live in a clean wigwam on parched corn than give my days to the elaborate feeding of a family under ceilings twenty feet high. I am daughter of many women with a 'faculty,' yet have I no faculty at all except for happiness where so many women would be abjectly miserable. There was my early girlhood friend Kitty, with a tremendous 'faculty,' and whom I had not seen for many years ; what did she do, almost the moment of our meeting, but show me her cut glass and diamonds; to *me*, who care not two straws for all the cut glass and diamonds in the world! Had Kitty understood this, would she have told me with so much good housekeeperly pride, ' I earned them myself, keeping boarders'? It takes a 'faculty' to do that! I could not but remember what poor facultyless I was doing while Kitty filled her handsome house with folding beds and strange faces. My rooms in a Florentine palace were close under the Italian sky, fanned by ilexes, and perfumed from the flower market below, littered with books and unfinished sketches, and holding few other good gowns besides the one I wore. Those days were quite as hard-worked and busy as Kitty's; they never brought me the least bit of cut glass or the tiniest diamond. What they did give me was happiness, more than which no 'faculty' could ever have brought me. They gave me hourly communion with the mighty ages and the mighty dead, the glory and illumination of their thoughts, their imagination, their art. They gave me a wider outlook upon humanity; a more vivid interest in the concerns of its spirit, its aspirations, endeavors, achievements, failures, triumphs; a clearer knowledge of its knowledges. Those days in which, had I a 'faculty,' I might have been studying the human palate and the management of dirt, I was living on much less money than other women require, on a hundredth part of that necessary to make Kitty smile. Up there in an *ultimo piano*, with my head almost striking the sublime stars, Giotto's campanile was my neighbor, the refuge of Boccaccio and the fair story-tellers my perspective, Vallombrosa's leafy heights my horizon. Many toil-earned hours of liberty were spent in dreamy wanderings through the Medicean city; hours in old churches and convent gardens, hours in the Uffizi and Pitti galleries, where, never, never, never should I have wandered with so clear a head and eye had I been doomed to a 'faculty.' I am born of a long line of New England housewives ever since my fore-mother Elizabeth at thirty-two left her English home, but not her English household ways, and went over with her English children to our Plantation of Massachusetts Bay; yet as a New England housewife I am a failure, a 'Discontented Woman,' when it comes to statues in the entrance-hall. Why was I born thus to loathe the luxury of fine and famous housekeeping? Why can I never look but despitefully upon rare viands, upon carpets that cost hugely, and silver shining vaingloriously, not one of which add to comfort, but only to pride? Why would I rather bang rusty tin cups in leaky tents than tinkle cut glass and silver? Why do I gloat over hardtack in the byways of travel and flout the spongecake of five-o'clocks? Why do I prefer the open sky to frescoed walls? Why could I never cook even fairly, toil and moil as I may in a fine kitchen, yet so triumphantly excel other women over a camp-fire or the rickety range and oil-stoves of a hired-furnished? Why could I never pound a nail, except my own? Why am I shod with iron indoors; why am I shod with air when once outside? Why am I so often a 'Discontented Woman'?

"Am I a 'Discontented Woman'?"

"A regular Mark Tapley," said he.

She was just beginning to purr when he added:

"Providing you have neither shopping nor fine housekeeping to look after. You see, Madam, you are not of the New England housewifely stuff at all. You've had Indian fighters in your line, bold hearts that tracked lurking foes in mysterious ambush through dense forests and beyond unknown rivers, and knew by the stars the way through deadly morasses. You have had many a brave adventurer sailing strange seas to bring home to Old England and to New the fruits and spices of other climes, and strange stories to thrill even veins that seldom grew hotter than over preserving kettles. You understand, Madam, do you not, what writers on the duties of women who hate highly-civilized housekeeping never do under-stand, that you have fore-fathers in your blood as well as fore-mothers?"

"Many more of them," she proclaimed. "I remember this much of my ancestral fighting days that I never see Pot and Pan Philistina, full of pious reproach for other women that I do not yearn for her scalp. And I never hear nice old gentlemen, whose ancestors must have been all fore-mothers, laying down the law of 'true womanliness,' that I do not long to tell them that they should have begun earlier, and taught our fathers not to sail and fight, but to knit and spin."

"Going to the Channel Islands?" remarked their English friends. "Beastly passage!"

"No word for it," she moaned, the gray and windy morning that they rolled between Guernsey and Jersey in company with a score or so of other dull-eyed, huddled mutes. "No wonder so many English people declare they would rather be tossed twelve hours in a blanket."

"These appear to have breakfasted on olives and bananas," said he.

There never was an Englishman who did not loathe olives, however much he may pretend otherwise. When an Englishman can eat a banana without nausea he plumes himself upon being an absolute cosmopolite, completely purged of every John Bullish prejudice.

The lady shuddered.

"Never mind," consolingly; "we are nearly there. Just think of Sir Walter Raleigh two days and two nights getting to his lieutenant-governorship of Jersey in 1600."

The English Channel has a bad reputation at best. Between England and the Islands it is much worse than between England and France, but when it comes to the currents and eddies, the swirling channels and sunken reefs between Guernsey and Jersey, the English language is an insufficient vehicle for the wrath, hatred, and loathing (particularly the latter) inspired by it. The steamer leaving Weymouth at two A. M., upon the arrival of the London express, stopped two hours at Guernsey from about six in the morning. In the chill dawn Guernsey seemed very high, very cold, very remote, — a lonely scramble of vague roofs and spires upon a cloudy hill, whither was no temptation to climb, and which was less interesting than the motionless cabin of the Lynx.

Jersey came in sight, a dull mass of greenish gray, now rising, now sinking, between long yeasty billows, not long after the Lynx bounded away from Guernsey. Came in sight, that was all. It stuck stubbornly against the horizon, and refused to budge, strain and pant as the Lynx might.

Sometimes when it disappeared, at least one of the olive-tinted mutes fancied it had gone to the bottom of the sea. Oh, joy! Oh, bliss, to follow it there!

Notwithstanding the island's shocking behavior, it was only ten o'clock when their carriage drove up to the steep hill of St. Helier's from the steamer landing. Nothing reminded them that they were not in some provincial English town. The streets are narrow, the shop displays modest; always so, it is said, because the island's climate rusts everything meant to shine. Only conspicuous announcements of the largest stock of something or other "in the Channel Islands" would have reminded them, had they forgotten it, that they had reached a part of the world which once seemed as remote and improbable to them as the interior of Tartary or mountains where Mahatmas hide.

"Remark," said she, "St. Helier's street dust is laid with salt water."

"Remark," said he, "every other shop window announces an infallible preventive or cure for sea-sickness. The fact is apparent that Jersey is surrounded by — "

"Bitter regrets," she whimpered.

"Remember," said he, "New Jersey, 'an island in Virginia,' was given to Charles Second's brother, the Duke of York. Remember, in May, 1650, many passengers, much merchandise, and goods of all sorts, set sail from just about where we now stand, bound for 'New Jersey in Virginia,' only to be captured by Parliamentarians just outside."

Their carriage drove up to Dove Cottage; almost drove over it.

"Perfidious woman, you meant to scalp me!" one of them exclaimed.

"Perhaps it is larger inside than it is out," she humbly answered.

The cottage, blunt upon the street, was snowy white with a very green door. It was of white-washed stone and seemed cold. It was in a narrow street, or alley, running between the high walls of gardens on one side and even lowlier cots on the Dove Cottage side. It was as ugly a street as could possibly be, without grime or squalor. A tidy middle-aged woman, who early informed them that she was "Devonshire not Jersey," met them at the door, and introduced herself as "Martin," Martin who cared for them so long as they remained Doves as were they babes of her own gotten from the Lord with many prayers. Kind Martin, silent, respectful, honest, pleasant, faithful, dear Martin! To be welcomed upon an unknown threshold by one like you was worth all that ground and lofty tumbling from England, worth even the nauseous struggle from Guernsey, worth more than words can tell; for to two Americans it idealizes forever the whole race of reduced English widows who serve in dove-cotes for four shillings a week.

"I told you so," said the lady with curling lip. For behold, even as she had said, the cot was larger inside than out. On the street side it was a mean little cot, with narrow, dungeon-like door between two windows, the roof remarkably near the doorstep. A tall man would almost hesitate to enter, without holding to his forelock with both hands. Whoever did enter, found that the front entry was midway of the stairs, one half the stairs rising to a tiny sitting-room and bedroom, the other descending to another bedroom and a kitchen-dining-room. Thus on the front side the dove-cote seemed half a story high, on the back it was two good stories. As if to impress upon these Americans the folly of too speedy judgments the two-story side was in a garden fragrant with Jersey bloom, musical with the hum of honey-seeking bees. The dining-room windows looked out upon this garden "all a-growing and a-blowing," as did also every room in the cottage. When the back door was open a full tide of golden fragrance filled the cot.

The narrow stairs were covered with oilcloth or linoleum, as was the kitchen-dining-room. The two bedrooms and sitting-room were carpeted with half-worn but perfectly neat ingrain ; the lace curtains were undoubtedly the relics of ampler draperies descended from more magnificent windows. The woollen table-covers were neat ; indeed, everything in and about was spotless, except the sitting-room mantelpiece, hung with a lambrequin of cretonne and spottily decorated with bouquets of hideous artificial flowers under glass.

"These are what made the cottage 'queer' to Bright Eyes !" exclaimed the Mistress Dove as she denuded the shelf.

"Our picture gallery," said one of them, "isn't it also rather queer? "

" Baronial hall," said the other.

They were standing in the front entry between the two sections of the stairs. The entry and stair space was lined with dark polished wood : here and there upon the sheeny surface hung the cheapest of colored prints of the early Victorian time. Coquettish Isabelle arched her neck and puckered her mouth at much neck-clothed George the Fourth ; the Princess Victoria showed her teeth under a too short upper lip at a fur-trimmed Napoleon crossing something or other, as one might choose to imagine. The whole noble company was bought, perhaps, for half-a-crown and was dear at that.

In every respect, apart from its artistic aspect and except no water or waste pipes, the cottage was entirely satisfactory. As for water, what matter so long as Martin brought and carried, they never knew whence or whither?

" Another time we must advertise for a ' queer ' Cottage," they agreed.

In the dining-room-kitchen (with the dining-room aspect marked, the kitchen invisible except at cooking times) a white robed table was set, as if for the breakfast of a pair of dolls — dolls with very human appetites, however, or rather *in*human — after a Channel passage. Never was bread whiter, butter yellower, milk richer, tea more delicate yet of healthy body, never was a breakfast-table set in a more radiant sphere of summer-time bloom in March, if only one did not turn backward to note the tiny range (given occasionally to smoking, it must be confessed), hidden by curtains, when it was cold. That range *was* cold much of the time they were Doves, for Mrs. Dove had not failed to bring her oil stoves and oven which reheated the delicious evening rolls for the morning, boiled the eggs and made the coffee or tea. As for the ubiquitous breakfast fruits from California, they needed no cooking.

" I thought you might like to taste the Jersey

wonders," said Martin, bringing in a plateful of golden brown objects. The instant those American teeth touched the discs of golden brown thence came a gush of melody as were the discs coiled pipes of merry Pan.

" Dough — " she piped.

" Nuts," piped he.

" *We* call them ' wonders ' " said Martin, smiling but halfly. " I don't mind in the least what you call them, for I am sure you like them."

Honest Martin ! " Dough " seemed to her a slight aspersion upon the exquisite doneness of her " wonders."

" We have never seen them before in Europe," they told her. " They are not made in England or on the Continent ; perhaps America owes them to Channel Islanders who went early to the colonies, although, to be sure, the Dutch vrouws of New York made famous ones."

For that day only Martin did the marketing, her contract including only the forenoon's work. Afterwards the Doves did their own provisioning, and always in the old Market, where Jersey farm women sit and ply their knitting-needles, jabbering in their antique gibberish ; never in the new market under the great glass dome where the market-women wear bonnets, speak English among themselves, sometimes read penny dreadfuls, sell not from gardens of their own, and where a bustling flower-woman in the very centre cheated them nearly the first time they tried. She was evidently an Englishwoman ; had she been pure Jersiaise, the name on her stall would have been Boulanger.

Mrs. Dove wished she had done the marketing

that very first day when she saw the extravagant excess of salad brought in by Martin.

" Enough for three dinners," she expostulated ; " we like it fresh."

" A penn'orth," explained Martin. " I did not think to get less."

Poor Martin seemed rather disturbed when bid to examine the shops for various of the tinned fruits and vegetables with which these Americans were wont to tide over the nongrowing season.

"I think the grocers have them," she said mildly; "but nobody uses them here except very seldom ; they are so dangerous."

" How, dangerous?"

" Poisonous. Three people were poisoned by them last week, and several the week before. Our doctor was once poisoned himself, the only time he ever tasted any."

" Is he the doctor who attended all these other poisoning cases?"

"Yes, 'm."

Mrs. Dove laughed.

" I 've heard of this same doctor in France, Italy, and England," she said. " When he cannot give a better cause for a violent bilious attack he always asks if you 've eaten anything tinned within six months. A doctor who fancies himself poisoned is always sure to be keen about poison forever afterwards. *We* have eaten hundreds of tins in our lives and never were ill a moment from it."

Martin did not look in the least convinced. Neither did she seem an atom more so the day they left Dove Cottage and she surveyed a cairn of tins under the garden wall.

" I suppose they ain't really like hus," they heard

their landlady say to Martin over the pile. "They ain't like hus or they would be dead copses this very minute."

Then Mrs. Dove remembered the aged sea-woman, once heard rebuking a younger one.

"In my seafaring days," she said, "we lived upon potatoes and salt beef on long voyages until the potatoes grew bad, then on salt junk and bread. You, nowadays, have all the fruits of the earth, and the abundance thereof every day in cans, with only one of which we should have made a never-to-be-forgotten festival. You ought to thank God for your ' tinned stuff ! ' "

Would any matron-since-many-a-year become a bride again and begin honeymoon housekeeping upon a new and fairy scale? Would she feel young pulses throb and thrill with the triumphs of acquisition, — one thing at a time and countless throbs, two or three things at a time and thrills almost infinite? Would she know the young wife's joyousness of prowling among bargains, even penny and tuppenny ones, turning over slightly imperfect or imperceptibly damaged arti-cles, picturing how much this would add to the æsthetic grace of the breakfast-table, how *that* would make the tea-tray shine, thus building up a dainty nest, bit by bit? Would she know again bridely glee over the unwrapping of parcels at home with triumphant assertion, " *There!* all that for eighteenpence? " Would she be a house-furnishing bride again with a perfectly clear con-science, that thus she is spending less than her city tram-fares and is laying up for Martin in the end? Then let her, after months of London lodgings, dumb mantel clocks and muslin flowers under glass, of monotonous white and gold china and carpets and couches free to any body's guineas, — let her then hire furnished some lilliputian cot in a sunny garden, a dove-cote with a few, very few, slight deficiencies of table furnishing, perchance a mild scantness of fruit saucers, a cream jug too large or too ugly, no distinctive butter-dish perhaps. Then if her wedding ring does not brighten up and fancy itself young again, young, foolish, and preposterously happy, alas, she might as well have remained a maid and lectured upon anti-vivisection and the rights of cats. Never, in their home across the sea, had these Doves cooed over anything as they did now whenever Mrs. Dove came back from town. One day a glass cream-jug for sixpence filled their souls with young rapture. Another day six deep saucers at a penny each increased their sum of dual joy and portions of peaches and cream; a fancy glass for threepence, the nick thrown in, set them up in a spoon-vase and happiness; fivepence well spent gave them as good as a crystal sugar basin; a wild, wild shilling thrilled them with ecstasy and a dashing preserve stand. Their daily table to them was really pretty, for the Jersey air makes linen whiter than driven snow, and with not more than three dollars spent in honeymoon purchases their contentment was increased by many a dollar's gain. The bride one day even regretted that their present hired-furnished included such faultless bed linen. " I saw such beautiful sheets and pillow-cases," she told, " I ached to buy them. What a pity we paid that extra sixpence over our ten shillings a week for linen."

The bride did forget herself so far as to accept

with blushes a pot or two of blooming plants, and to set them upon the wide window-sill among books from the extensive Beresford circulating library, with as youthful grace — Ah, well ! why not carry May into October when one can?

One day, as she displayed her purchases, " I ordered four histories of Jersey at the library, and three novels in which the scene is Jersey ; they will arrive when the boy makes his afternoon round," she remarked. " The man at the delivery desk asked me if I had ever seen any of the American magazines ! "

" Heavens ! If you spoke in your present voice he need never have asked."

" It 's my best American accent," she continued nasally. " When the man spoke of the magazines by name I told him I knew them all, as I am an American. He exclaimed, ' Impossible ! you have no accent.' ' Yes, I have,' I answered. ' You do not use it then,' said the man, still unconvinced. So you see now, I am using it ! He said the American magazines were popular here only for the pictures ; readers do not care much for the letter-press, he thought. English patrons of the library did not think much of anything American, they were mostly military families, and had n't yet forgiven the American revolution."

" What a long tail that revolution has ! How generous of these half-pay military families to be amused by our picture books ! Yet we never find the ' Atlantic Monthly ' in when we ask for it. I suppose these inheritors of revolutionary dislikes are looking at its pictures ! "

" I guess so," she answered, in a voice that made him clap both hands to his ears. " You see they do not recognize Americans, except those who do all their talking as tea-kettles sing. Only yesterday Bright Eyes remarked, ' How strange that one never hears of Americans that are not nasty and never knows one that is not nice ! ' "

Jersey is the largest of the Channel Islands and the sunniest, having its chief exposure from north to south instead of *vice versa* as Guernsey has, only eighteen miles away from point to point, although thirty by steamer. Guernsey, nearer the broad Atlantic, is more subject to fogs. Whenever the postman was late and no letters by eleven o'clock, the Doves were sure the Lynx, the Antelope, or the Gazelle, was caught in a Guernsey fog, however brightly the sun was shining upon Jersey. At such times they almost broke their necks craning for sight of the signal pole that tells St. Helier's just where in the Channel its letters are. Jersey, in fact, is universally known as "the sunniest spot in the British Isles." The climate is balmy, at times relaxing, while Guernsey and Sark brace like quinine or champagne. Thus Jersey is more favorable for delicate lungs than for lazy livers. In its scenery it is as good as a continent for variety. Within its coast line is every character of miniature picturesqueness from the pastoral to the heroic. On the north it rises precipitously with echoing caverns, cliffs and sea-sucking gorges. There the billows surge and beat against impregnable rocks with every fury of infinite nature, while but a small turn of the coast calms those furies to sunny and rippling laughter. There cannot be more dulcet shores and inland vistas than at Anne Port for instance, where the Jersey Lion sleeplessly watches France. The island is twelves miles at its longest, eight at its broadest. With these little dimensions are its wonderful miles of green lanes. Lanes? Nobody knows what lanes may be till he has wandered and lost himself for hours, he fancies forever, in those emerald labyrinths, winding, turning, circling, bow-knotting themselves into the very blindest of mazes. It is said that there are five hundred miles of these Gothic lanes into which the sunshine never penetrates and where the leaves lie from many and many a dead summer; but the estimate should be altered to say there *were* five hundred miles. The exceeding dampness of these romantic lanes has been found a cause of disease, hence many of them have been thrown open to the day by cutting down trees. The prosperous potato culture (early potatoes for Covent Garden) of the island has also caused much havoc among trees, a havoc bitterly resented by Jersiaises of twenty-foot ceilings who had their early potatoes just the same when the island was yet tangled with lanes. Jersey bids fair to turn into a great potato patch in London's service, a cruel promise indeed to these gorse-golden commons, these flowery meads and meadows, these waving orchards and spangled thickets of wayside rose and berry, these rugged hills and dreamy vales set in a girdle of gray sand dunes, and grayer precipices.

Always the Doves were amazed, then angered, to see how this market greed has vanquished every consideration of beauty and fitness. Imagine garden plots by the hundreds in front of cottages of considerable pretensions and thrifty farmhouse doors, laid out in the designs favorite in small front yards; crescents, hearts, ovals, diamonds, all encircled with wide borders, and all of potato plants. Where lilies should grow are potatoes, where roses might perfume the air, potatoes add a few pennies to the pocket.

"Those people all eat inferior potatoes," said indignant Myra. "Jersey potatoes go to London and poorer ones come to us from French farms."

Sir Walter Raleigh and his potato zeal in Jersey, are not gratefully esteemed by our dignified Myra.

"That explains why Bright Eyes the other day was so much interested that I was writing upon 'The Potato,' when I am ashamed to say the subject was only Plato," laughed a Dove.

Potatoes bring money to Jersey, but also danger. They bring hordes of French peasants every year from the coast only thirteen miles away, for the annual work of planting and harvest. They are a class of easy morals or none at all, and Jersey thus receives an enemy to its own sobriety and thrift. In ancient days Jersey feared the Frenchmen of battles, now it has reason to fear the Frenchmen of peace. In the old days it built towers and forts to keep them away, now little steamers dart to and fro, and Jersey has only its laws for its protection. Its government uses its law of banishment freely, so evildoers have only to be brought before the court to be banished for years, or for life, as the case may be. This is cheaper than keeping them in jail, but what happens if the banished defy the law, and return, nobody seems to be able to tell. Another law, devised chiefly for protection against the French, forbids the sale of land to any foreigner. This law so vexed the Doves that they yearned to buy their cot and live in it forever till they were assured that *they* were not foreigners, only those detested French. The menace to Jersey is what is called the "seeding" of the island by French farm people. Many come over from Normandy every year for the potato season, and learn for the first time in their lives the ease of life free from taxation. They are eager to remain, and for that purpose hire themselves by the year upon low terms. If they are of a decent sort they make themselves extremely useful to their employers, live on almost nothing, and save money. The French make the very best of servants, workmen, and laborers, and are in much higher esteem as such than the shiftless and insolent English. In time the Jersey farmer and his wife grow old or wish to move into town. They cannot sell their farm to their faithful French servants, but they can sell to any children of those servants born on the island. The French couple are given easy terms and buy in the names of their children; thus the "seeding" takes place by which the farming part of the island has become very largely French. Fortunately that "seeding" is as yet counterbalanced by the continual increase of English population in the towns, Jersey being extremely popular with retired army men whose systems have been rendered sensitive to the harsh English weather by long service in hot climates. The French farmers themselves become Jerseymen as much as they can, in their delight at freedom from the taxes that bowed them down *là-bas*. The Channel Islands are free from all taxes save their own, that is, they are entirely free from English taxes. They pay nothing to the Crown; why should they, when they as a part of Normandy conquered England and gave it kings? Even to this day, loyal Channel Islanders often drink a health to "Victoria, Duchess of Normandy *and* Queen of England." Very curious is the fact that these islands are so supremely proud of their Norman origin, yet no term of contempt is greater in Jersey than " Norman." Even to call a man *"espèce de Normand"* is scarcely better than naming him a dog. Centuries ago, as Matthew Prior wrote, it was the same to call a man " Englishman." The Channel Islanders, the real ones, not English arrivals of only a few generations ago, see an infinite distance between the eleventh century Normans that they are, and the nineteenth that they are not. They are a proud people, to whom even the English are parvenus, proud of their little archipelagoan nation, its sturdy independence, and its ancient laws. The islands have Home Rule in its broadest, fullest sense; have each its own parliament, its own judiciary, entirely independent of England and also of the others. In Jersey a man may marry his deceased wife's sister, in Guernsey, Alderney, and Sark he cannot, and each island has its own immigration laws and laws of banishment. They have no representation at Westminster, and want none, for such would reduce them from their position as an insular nation to that of mere English shires. The Crown, as representative of ducal Normandy, furnishes a lieutenant-governor to Jersey and one to Guernsey, but in all the island legislation, he is of inferior rank to the Bailiff, the chief island officer, whose dignity dates from ancient Normandie. In the States (*États*), the island's legislature, are two thrones, the highest of these for the Bailiff, the other for the Queen's officer, the lieutenant-governor. The Bailiff must always be present, the governor may do as he chooses, and is rarely present.

Very many curious laws and quaint practices still exist from ancient Norman days, such as Normandy itself forgot ages ago. Seigneurs still hold certain rights or fiefs, and every man who buys or sells land must look well that seigneurial rights are properly hunted up. The seigneur may be as poor as Job's turkey, he may be a Tasmanian tramp, may be working in a Californian mine, or selling calico in a London shop, but his "rights" still exist, be they so many bushels of wheat or so many ducks and capons, inherited from his ancestors. He may have not one single inch of land of his own, but pounds and shillings belong to him by rights of his forefathers. It is amusing to read of the measures of wheat, the eggs, fowls, etc., due to the Queen every year, not only as Duchess of Normandy, but for other seigneurial rights that have come to her by lapses in direct lines, by forfeitures, etc. These, of course, nowadays are all paid in coin of the realm. " *On* the paper," as the islanders say, the Doves read that the chief rents of her Majesty for the year were "wheat, 10s. per quarter; capons, 5s. 6d. per couple; fowls, 3s. 9d. per pair; two score eggs, 2s. 6d." When Victor Hugo lived in Hauteville House, in Guernsey, Charles Hugo wrote that his father paid the Queen (Duchess of Normandy) "two pullets a year."

Only the other day of A. D. 1897; we heard of a quaint survival of feudal tenure in these islands. The manor of Sainte Hélène, in Guernsey, was purchased some years ago by Miss von Gersdorff, a German canoness. With the manor were sold the *droits du seigneur*, and the canoness became henceforth châtelaine, or *dame du manoir*. Recently Miss von Gersdorff presented herself before the Royal Court, and then and there, before that august assembly of island notables, renounced all the rights of "chief rents, field rents, champage, and poulage," due to her from her tenants. While releasing them in perpetuity from these dues, she still retained her rights as lady of the manor.

For the benefit of those unversed in Norman law, "champage" is the twelfth stack of any kind of grain grown on the rented fields, and "poulage" are the fowls due each quarter from the tenant to his liege lords. These dues were probably originally devised for the maintenance of the seigneur's table. That even at the present day these dues fall heavily on the tenant may be inferred from the gratitude of those released.

Headed by the seneschal, or bailiff of the manor, they presented Miss von Gersdorff with what the local paper calls a "testimonial of their thankfulness for such generosity." This testimonial took the solid and practical form of a silver tea and coffee service, and silver tea-kettle, on an oak and silver tray. On the tray was engraved in French, "Presented by the tenants of the manor of Sainte Hélène to Miss Margaret M. A. R. von Gersdorff, canoness, lady of the manor, in recognition of her having voluntarily surrendered to them in perpetuity all rights to the chief rents, champage, and poulage."

When the islands were finally separated from

Normandy, being all that was left to miserable John Lackland of the Crown's continental possessions, many seigneurs were obliged to choose between English John and French Philippe, and to surrender either their Norman or their island estates. The surrendered island estates reverted to the Crown. It is somewhat curious, although perfectly comprehensible, that the two most worthless kings of England, John Lackland and Charles the Second, are the ones always most respectfully named in the Channel Islands. Indeed these seagirt rocks are the only places in the world where they are mentioned without contempt.

The old law of heritage still holds in these islands. At the doors of the court-house, or of the legislative building, may be seen posted lists of dead proprietors whose estate in default of direct heirs of his body (brothers and sisters not counted) reverts for a year and a day to his seigneur. When William IV. of England died in 1837, without direct heirs, a certain fief of the Crown owed rights to an island seigneur, who claimed them, and received a royal indemnity to release his *vassal*, the King, whose subject he himself was !

It was as a vassal of France that John Lackland was summoned to appear before Philippe-Auguste. His refusal to appear under charge of the murder of his nephew before his seigneur suzerain resulted in loss of his Norman fiefs, and decided the fate of these islands.

Another curious survival is the *clameur de Haro*. This *clameur de Haro* is a right of appeal by which any person considering himself wronged may call upon the law in the most peremptory and efficacious manner possible. The origin of the custom is unknown ; some say it is descended from appeals to the justice of Rollo, first Duke of Normandy, and is an abbreviation of Ha! Rollo! Others contend that the cry is even more ancient than Rolf or Rollo, and that Haro was a Frisian chief. Whatever its origin, its power is magical. Let a man find, or believe he finds, a neighbour over-building upon his land, any trespasser upon his estate or rights of any kind, and he has only to take with him two witnesses before the offender, then to fall upon his knees, and, lifting up his hands, cry " *Haro ! à l'aide, mon prince ! on me fait tort !* " (Help me, my prince, I am wronged). At these words everything stops instantly. Workmen upon a wall, diggers in a field, cutters of trees, all drop their tools as if by a command from heaven. For his life no man dare make another move, except to leave the place. Nothing more can be done until the court can decide between the two, and the aggrieved party has this much assurance that not another stroke can be struck at his rights. The court must attend to the matter at once, for it holds the place of that invisible prince, dead and dust a thousand years but mighty yet by the magic of his name.

Some years ago before the " Wild Jerseyman " and " Flying Islander " ambled so decorously across the island a certain judge was bitterly opposed to their introduction. He was a man of the olden time and as much opposed to innovations as was the Jersey farmer who ordered in his will that his coffin should not go to its grave by any of the newly opened lanes, but be carried through the old emerald labyrinths, though thus the distance was twenty times as much and his coffin in island-fashion carried on men's shoulders. For some Jerseymen, as well as some other men, do not in the least care how much it costs to have their own way when somebody else foots the bills, or carries the coffin. This judge had talked against the projected railways, voted against them, done all he could save call on the invisible prince. It is to be said that *mon prince* cannot be invoked without enormous expense to the invoker if he be found to have unjustly invoked. All other business must be set aside at once and the whole machinery of the island law directed to that appeal. Hence the *clameur* is rarely used where the case does not seem to demand instant action. The angry judge thought this case did, for the ground was being turned and labourers had begun work to introduce into peaceful Jersey the hateful screaming things which Jerseymen had comfortably done without since the world began. He went out before the workmen, this doughty and determined old Jerseyman, and knelt in the dirt before them. With hands raised in supplication, he cried *" Haro ! Haro ! à l'aide, mon prince ! on me fait tort !"*

In an instant, the twinkling of an eye, the work ceased. Horses were stopped in their tracks, spades were arrested in the ground, men were reduced to absolute inaction. Nothing more could be done till the officers of the court came to decide if *mon prince* had been justly or unjustly invoked. In this case the decision was against the judge ; he was forced to pay enormously for his mistake, and died soon after, a ruined man. Even *mon prince*, the invisible hero of unknown ages, was on the side of progress and railways; the poor old Jerseyman had not given him credit for so much modernity.

Wherever there is a suspicion that the *clameur* may be raised against repairs to a house or garden-wall, or against the foundation of a new one, the business is usually done in the night. A man who is angered to find a foot (or an inch) of his lot built upon, may decently go to law as other men do, but he cannot appeal to *mon prince* after the work is done. Thus it is said that very much Jersey building *is* done in the night. Once upon a time, Jean and Jean, father and son, cutting down trees on some disputed territory suspected the intention of a neighbor to appeal to *mon prince* against them. That same day Jean *le jeune* stood beside one of the tree-cutters, a stranger to him, and made a remark or two. The other Jerseyman, the labourer, paid not the slightest heed, and Jean concluded that he was pretty deaf. He shouted, " My father wishes this one left," whereupon the other looked up with a grin.

" You are the son of Maître Jean? I thought you had come for the other party, with the *clameur de Haro*."

The Doves found all this romantic, fascinating, enchanting. Seigneurs, fiefs, tribute, homage, the language of heroic days, somehow seemed to turn their dove-cote into an eagle's nest upon a hoary ocean rock, or the loftiest branch of eternal forests swayed by the eternal sea, a coign of vantage overlooking all the centuries. They dreamed, and awoke not when they recognized the noblest seigneurial names upon butchers' carts and fish-barrows; names once to make vassals proud of their vassalage, now of forgotten fame, save to inquisitive foreigners like these Doves.

"After much searching, I found canned corn to-day," she meditatively said. "The dealer, not knowing me for an American, kindly explained to me that it was a new vegetable just coming into use and much liked by many. I could scarcely find tongue to answer him, for I saw that he was a de Paisnel, a de Carteret, or something equally glorious."

"Shall we have some for dinner?"

She bowed her head low upon her book.

"*Haro! Haro! à l'aide, mon prince!* If here is n't a horrid American wanting his green corn among these descendants of seigneurs, these ghosts of heroic ages called 'dark.' *Haro! Haro! à l'aide, mon prince!*"

One interesting ceremony of the island is the annual June procession of parish officials through highways and byways with long staves. If any branch or drooping vine is touched by the staves the owner is fined. Naturally a day or two before the staves there is much activity in the way of tree trimming all over the island. In spite of this activity, there is usually a considerable levy of fines, a great delight among the staff-bearers being to fine each other. As the fines go to providing the officials with a banquet, the fining among themselves is taken in good part, even when it is suspected that something of an arm's-length has been added to the regulation staff. The origin of this custom is found, as so many Channel Island customs are, in ancient Normandy. In the olden days, men with long staves preceded the Holy Sacrament carried to dying beds, in order that nothing might interfere with its passage through the lush lanes. In those days the staff-bearers went on foot. Now they ride in a char-à-bancs, yet their staves are still of the antique length.

Over the wall of the dove-cote peeped a wonderful wallflower. All the island flowers are wonderful, so rich and brilliant, beside their English sisters like fairy princesses beside beggar maids. Especially are the wallflowers radiant and robust, climbing like housebreakers, peeping over a hundred walls, stealing to the sills of a hundred windows, making the day glorious with gold stolen from the sun.

This particular wallflower winked and blinked at the staff-bearers, nodding her brilliant head as much as to say, in most impudent fashion, "Don't you wish you were I, with banquets furnished every day from earth and heaven, at root and outermost petal? Don't you wish you were I with a white table spread always before me, the winds bringing me nectar, the dews ambrosia, while you silly staff-bearers must lunge and thrust from a hired wagon to fine enough for one big dinner a year!"

When the Doves reached home that night, their almost absurdly tall and thin landlady waved phenomenally long arms at them from her door.

"I will have to pay a pe*nal*ity for your wallflower," she shouted. "There's been a perfic e*pid*ermic of fines to-day. They shall get arf-a-crown from me. I went out before they came and tried to reach that sarsy wallflower on a chair with my humbril. I couldn't reach it by a foot. 'Ow them raskils must' a stretched!"

"They never fine your lilies," comforted Mrs.

Dove — " your Jersey lilies, that tower like columns of ivory with central spark of living fire."

"Bad for them if they did!" Madame De Longue confessed.

The Jersey Lily. The name is familiar to us, even though its associations are less than fair to those who have never seen the real flower blooming in island gardens a miracle of stainless beauty.

Nevertheless, the Jersey lily is really the Guernsey lily and transplanted thence. On Guernsey it blooms more brilliantly and earlier; grows to more regal height. It is a native of Japan (the *Amaryllis sarniensis*) and came by accident to Guernsey, in the reign of the virtuous Charles Stuart. It was a dreadful thing, of course, when that English vessel all the way from Japan had struggled so nearly home, only to be wrecked in the cruel Channel. That any good could come of that tragedy of destruction, no man would have dared prophesy. That a blessing of beauty for balmy Guernsey was in those cruel waves, who would have believed, even had such prophets been ten thousand,—that Guernsey taking bits of the wreck to her breast would enrich herself, even in hard money, the value of the lost ship and its cargo countless times over, would have seemed but a bit from auld wives' tales.

When the great ship went to pieces the water was strewn with wreckage. Nobody ever thought of securing little brown objects very like onions that danced hither and yon on the waves; how long those onions floated who knows? Nobody knows how many ebbing and flowing tides took them nearer and nearer to land or whether one breaker or many finally swept them beyond the sea's reach in beds of soft warm sand.

Years afterwards a governor of the island in the reign of Charles II. was struck by the beauty of certain flowers blooming in the sand near the shore. The island people assured him that they had always been there, that they were indigenous, even though never found save in that one place. Being something of a florist he knew the value of the prize, and had them transplanted and cultivated, sending some roots to England, where they were greatly admired. It became a favorite in England and on the Continent, but nowhere flourishes so well as under the trees of Guernsey. One might fancy the flower held yet in its heart golden gratitude for the soft warm sands that received and cherished its sea-drenched ancestors. Very little care is bestowed upon the Guernsey lily ; its soil is never fertilized but slightly covered with sea sand. They grow in beds, hundreds of them together. It is a very capricious flower. It must have been by pure caprice that after so long floating on buffeting waves it chose to make itself at home in the Guernsey sea sand to wave its radiant heads in defiance of its chill for years without the slightest effort to become naturalized elsewhere on the island. In England it can be made to blossom a second time only with the greatest care, and even in Jersey it is not at its best.

FORT CHEER.

CAME Bright Eyes to the dove-cote one morning, as Bright Eyes often came, yet not often enough.

"To-morrow shall be a good day for the Fort, so be ready by ten," she said.

The Doves fluttered with joy. For they had long ago in London heard beautiful stories of that Fort in sunny Jersey, where, one afternoon in every week during fine weather, Bright Eyes and her lovely sisters are "at home" to their friends. They had heard of the dainty teas and merry luncheons served upon velvet sward within the parapets, of those dainty teas even upon the sunny parapets themselves, looking across shining water to cathedral spires of *la belle France*, the spires of Coutances to which diocese Jersey belonged in ancient days. They had heard of tea-parties taking refuge without loss of gayety in the cosey guard-house when the winds from France became too boisterously enamored of the company, or the rain kissed fair faces wantonly. On that side of the island is a string of Martello towers like those between Eastbourne and Hastings in Sussex, together with three small forts, all long ago dismantled before the pipes of peace. Several of these towers are hired by the year from the island government by families and parties of friends, who tidy, dry and furnish them for picnicking purposes, rendezvous for shrimping parties, and for afternoon teas, with cards and parlor games. "Fort Cheer" is much the most important of these. It has a moat, now dry, across which one walks a shuddering bridge. Inside mighty portals, although decayed, are two houses of one room each, and a space of satiny turf sheltered by high walls. Fort Cheer was erected the year of the Stamp Act that so infuriated the American colonists. Pitt did not intend to scare these far-away growlers (he little dreamed what thunderbolts were forging in the West) with the four guns and dozen red-coats of Fort Cheer. He meant only that the frog-eaters yonder should feel sleepless eyes upon them. The French call them *boule-dogues*.

One goes to Fort Cheer from St. Helier's by carriage, or takes to the "Wild Jerseyman." Jersey has two narrow-gauge railways, the "Wild Jerseyman" and the "Flying Islander," neither of which has ever been arrested for fast driving. A little journey on the "Wild Jerseyman" gives an American a very complete consciousness of remoteness from home, a consciousness made somewhat fantastic by imagination of a foreign remoteness greater than it is. The prim little carriages trundle primly between stations where almost every word uttered, and they are many, is in a language never heard before, however wide one's wanderings. Now and then a few words seem familiar, but the whole swing and sway of utterance, the lights and shades of intonation, are new and strange to the Americans. It is curious that this patois is interchangeable with the most perfect French, and the patois-speakers have no difficulty in understanding a Frenchman, however often he may be checked by words from them. The names of the stations too are distinctly French, Hâvre des Pas, Grève d'Azette, Samarès (*sur-les-Marais*), Le Hocq, La Rocque, Grouville, Gorey (or Gouray). At various of these stations stout countrywomen get in and get out, with full or empty baskets from St. Helier's market, and begin the tale of their adventures in the vast metropolis before they are fairly squeezed out upon the platform. In one carriage a party of deputies to the States (or *États*) as the island parliament is named, discusses some *projet de loi* in the same incomprehensible tongue. Bright Eyes, born to this variously-corrupted mediæval-ism, translates to the Doves, but, asked to write a word or two of it down, becomes, like our troops at Bull Run, "shockingly demoralized." Modern Parisian French is much more easily written by Miss Bright Eyes.

Within Fort Cheer only one of the old guard-houses is in what somebody styles " polite condition." The tumbling one shelters wood and coal ; the other, spick and span, is newly lined with lustrous wood, floor, walls, ceiling. A roomy closet holds the table service and tea-kettle, permanent dwellers in Fort Cheer. A long table and many chairs are ready for hospitable service indoors or out as the heavens declare ; the grate is of grandmotherly proportions compared with the puny imp of which the Americans made an *auto da fé* in Pevensey Villa.

But what to say of the view from the ramparts ! A poet's, not a common scribbler's, pen should describe that stretch of blue and golden water, with horizon visibly haunted by the poetic mystery that is *la belle France*, France so well known to everybody, but ever an enchanting ideal seen from this filmy distance, — the billowy inland roll of rich verdure, the wooded heights, the gorse-gilded common, the wayward roofs and spires of Grouville and Gorey, all completed by as picturesque a ruined castle as ever haunted romantic dreams.

Gorey Castle, "Mont Orgueil," has a very definite and positive history of attacks, defences, and surrenders, of political prisoners and heroic deeds, as well as dark ones, but, for all that, its architecture seen from the Fort is of fairyland only, or the dream world. From Fort Cheer it is also at times stern and massive yet, hurling contempt upon the modern world and its cowardly warfare mowing down hosts by machinery and not man to man with spear, dart, and javelin, or even awkward blunderbuss and God with the bravest arm. At other times it is a dusky giant wounded and crouching beneath a cloak of thick ivy upon its rock. Then, in a fleeting instant, it becomes an aerial vision, vaporous, floating, bodiless, the poetic memory and no more of brave deeds and heroic thoughts, of dashing chivalric ages that died so long before the nineteenth century was born.

"It was built in the reign of Henry II. on the site of one of Cæsar's castles," said Mentor Karl; "there are dolmens behind it, as you shall see, and bits of Roman masonry in their keep." Jersey was for the King during the parliamentary wars, while Guernsey declared for the parliament. Charles II., then Prince of Wales, was twice secretly on the island during his exile from England. Jersey was very proud to have acknowledged his sovereignty when he had none elsewhere ; so, for a time he was king of Jersey and of nothing else. It is said he was proclaimed King by a Carteret or two and in presence of a score or so of people, and that he never ceased to laugh all his life long at the pompous insignificance of that first proclamation of his sovereignty. He was nineteen, but already with vicious habits and friends. He did not come to the island in any heroic guise or manner, you may be sure. He wore deep purple, the royal color of mourning, for his father, while the Duke of York, then fifteen, wore the deepest black. Their retinue of 300 was mostly cooks, valets, hair-dressers, although there was one ferocious looking creature with a moustache who was the chief tailor's wife. They nearly ate Jersey out of house and home. Charles lived at Elizabeth Castle, near St. Helier's, but often rode out to Gorey Castle. During the Civil War, Puritan Prynne was imprisoned here and amused himself by writing bad poetry.

> " Mont Orgueil castle is a lofty pile
> Within the eastern port of Jersey-isle,
> Seated upon a rocke full large and high,
> Close by the shore next to Normandie,
> Near to a sandy bay where boats do hide
> Within a peere safe from wind and tide.
> Three parts thereof the flowing seas surround,
> The fourth north westwards is firm rocky ground.
> A proud high mount, it hath a rampier long,
> Foure gates, foure posternes, bulwarks, sconces strong,
> All built with stone on which there mounted lie
> Fifteen cast pieces of artillery,
> With sundry murdering chambers planted so
> As best may fence itself and hurt a foe.
> A guard of soldiers (strong enough till warre

Begins to thunder) in it lodged are,
To watch and ward it duly night and day,
For which the king allows them monthly pay.
The Governor, if present, here doth lye;
If absent, his lieutenant deputy.
A man of war doth keep and lock
The gates each night of this high tow'ring rocke.
The castle's ample healthy and
The prospect, pleasant both by sea and land,
Two boist'rous foes sometimes assault with losse
The fortresse which their progresse seems to crosse,
The raging waves below which ever dash
Themselves in pieces whiles with it they clash."

To tell the truth the Channel Islands have never distinguished themselves by additions to the world's literature, even although they were early in the field. Wace, who wrote the "Roman de Rou" before Dante dreamed the "Inferno," was a Jerseyman, and said so in twelfth-century French.

"Je di et dirai ke je suis
Vaice de lisle de Gersui,
Ki est en mer ver l'occident;
Al fieu de Normandie assent."

The poet Abraham Cowley, who was some time upon the island, wrote from his quarters in Elizabeth Castle, where also Lord Clarendon wrote a portion of his history —

"For you must know, kind Sir, that verse does not in this
island grow,
No more than sack."

The usual insular conditions of isolation and constant intermarriages for generations probably explain the fact that the imagination of the Jersiais never rose to much height of poetical and artistic creation. All the same, it sees its name occasionally in the history of English art and literature, Millais, the President of the Royal Academy was of a Jersey family, our own Henry Thoreau was of Jersey descent. Mrs. Manley, whom Swift scorned as a New Woman of her time, was born here in 1667. Her father, Sir Roger Manley, was Lieutenant-Governor of Jersey. She early lost her mother ; her father, of literary tastes, paid little attention to his children, so that they ran wild. She was early deluded into a false marriage (at least, so she herself told), and began that adventurous career of love-making, novel-writing, and quarrelling with the " Tatler's " Steele and Swift, quarrels that have made her quite as notorious as has her " New Atlantis." Swift once rebuked Stella that she spelled no better than " the Mrs. Manleys," by which he must have meant the New Woman of the time. One of his "Tatler" papers represents her under one of the vague personifications common to those essay-ists as poisoning by smells and restoring to life by the same. He wrote of her more plainly when he told Addison " she writes as if she had about two thousand epithets and fine words packed up in a bag, pulled them out by the handful, and strewed them over her paper, where about once in about five hundred times they happen to be right." Swift might have improved his own man-ner while so severe upon the New Woman who was learning to write, and said " *one quarter* of her epithets," etc. Mrs. Manley is reported to have been of as scandalous private life as she was of public writing, but we may remember in our idea of her that she was " New " and that all her censors and judges were men who scorned a wo-man writing in direct imitation of the men of her day, having no other model. But all this was long after the little girl ran wild within the precincts of Elizabeth Castle, in Jersey, till she was eight years old, when the family returned to England. Her story and fame really have no relation to these islands, for she was English, a race then foreign here. "I am heartily sorry for her," Swift wrote to Stella; "she has generous principles for one of her sort, and a great deal of good sense and invention; she is about forty, homely, and very fat."

Abraham Cowley was here not on business of the Muses, but on business of the King and Queen. He at that time resided in France with the Jermyn family and was trusted with a cipher correspondence between Charles I. and Henrietta Maria.

"In that gray house between the Spanish chestnuts on Gorey Heights, George Eliot wrote 'Janet's Repentance,'" said Mrs. Dove. On May 12, 1857, she wrote in her journal of the blooming orchards hereabout and of the castle. She hated the wind; it is curious how often she mentions winds with annoyance in her journals, continually complaining of them. So she meant to express gentle contentment when she wrote "Jersey trees have no distressed look about them as if they were ever driven back harshly by the winds. It is like an inland slope suddenly carried to the coast," she wrote of this part of the island.

"To hate the wind, unless indeed one be utterly devoted to one's frizzes, which George Eliot was not,— does it seem possible?" said Amy.

Hate the wind! not one of those fair and brave islanders could understand how such a hate could be, they in their wind-singing home where rarely come raging tempests. To them the wind means music and soft caressing. To George Eliot the wind meant only a bother. She was born in a flat, windless country and was not cradled with its lullaby. Moreover, she never liked wild elements of nature or character. She had no sympathy for what we may call the Gothic in humanity. The wild north wind to her was only a lawless blusterer; for the Arctic fields, the beetling precipices, the gloomy mountains and valleys of which he sings, she cared nothing at all. No romance was in her spirit, the mystery of our outlying universe had no fascination for her; personal comfort was her greatest good. To her there was no mystery in life, all is to be understood by a careful and conscientious study of human nature and the interplay of character. When she wrote her least realistic and therefore most romantic novel, she must even leave a land where the loud winds are keen, and place a story without hero or heroine but only with characters, in a sunny city where, even if the winds do blow down from the Apennines at seasons, George Eliot never stayed to hear what they say.

How different from Victor Hugo, who asked concerning the wind the questions we ask concerning our souls: "Whence? Whither? Why?" and who heard them sing all the legends of the ages, all the music and the poetry of our divinely created earth.

"George Eliot could never be a poet, with all her conscientious trying," said a Dove. "She might have heard 'choirs invisible' while she lived had she been a poet and loved the wind."

"As you do," smiled the other Dove.

Which was a family joke. Once in the height of the palm-reading fashion a hand had been read as that of an artist, "probably a musician, one subtly sensitive to sweet sounds and gifted in interpreting nature's most noble and most subtle emotions through music."

"Stay!" said the owner of the hand. "I do not play a single musical instrument, I understand not a note of music. I care for no music except of the wind and the sea, and such as reminds me of them."

"Precisely what I mean," answered the unabashed palmist.

Ah, Bright Eyes, laughing, serious, sweet Bright Eyes, with native grace enhanced by utter artlessness and unpretension, you did not know, that sunny spring day when that Jersey party of ancient island and more ancient Norman lineage, proud to have been Norman freemen before the Bastard made earls and dukes of his vulgar adventurers, admitted to its circle a pair of Doves in whose Anglo-Saxon veins the Norman drop was small and pale, what an unfading memory you added to the choicest memories of two lives. You never thought that, in years to come, with roaring tides between those birds of the far West and your island shores, those bright faces and pleasant voices of Tom, Karl, and Annie, Florrie, Amy, George, Philip, Ada, Belle, would live in fadeless springtime together with a vision of smiling island and radiant sea, so long as those Doves know summer from winter, day from night!

How much those Jersiais and the Americans found in common besides doughnuts, Sunday morning baked beans and *pie* as England knows them not ! How freely they criticised the English, to whom all were faithful friends and true, loving them as brothers and sisters, even as husband and wife ! How much they found in common in their forms of English speech kept apart on both sides of the ocean, on island and on continent, from the exotic adoptions and corruptions of England itself since America inherited and the Channel Islands accepted, the dominant and domineering English tongue ! Jersey habitually speaks three languages. Its native mediæval French, as their Duke William spoke it, has developed into something new and strange in the course of centuries ; they nearly all speak English ; and the educated speak continental French. As they say themselves, not one of these languages do they speak perfectly, which few do, even those to a language born. In the English the Jersiais seem never able to deal successfully with *shall* and *will*, as neither do the Scotch or Irish, however highly educated. It has been known of Scotchmen at Oxford to refuse help on this point, preferring to prove their nationality by their ignorance. Jersey has not spoken English so long as America. When the Mayflower took the Stuart English over the sea the Channel Islands still universally spoke their antique Norman-French. At the beginning of this century that same French was the language *par excellence*, and only the educated portion spoke English. They spoke it with a sort of hidalgo contempt for it as for all things not of ancient Normandy, and always as a foreign tongue. Even yet the Norman-French is the domestic language of many who never utter a word of it away from home. All legal business is carried on in French, all legislative and judicial action. " We deliberate in French," said a deputy, "but we speak English." In all the twelve parishes of Jersey and in every church one of every two Sunday services is in French, although the service is Church of England. Bright Eyes tells us that the opening and closing prayer of her Dorcas society is always in French. It is the same, perhaps to a slightly less degree, in Guernsey. In Sark the insular French is entirely the language of the island ; religious service in English is held only during the summer, when some visiting clergyman officiates, for the benefit of other visitors. In all the islands the changes in their original language have been differently produced by circumstances peculiar to themselves. The Jersey-French is a medley of old French intermingled with modern expressions and Gallicized English words curiously pronounced. Fifty years ago there was a marked difference of language, even among the different parishes. A Jerseyman, writing then of his native isle, declares that there were more dialects in Jersey than in ancient Greece. Of late years an English garrison on the island has helped greatly to spread English among the lower classes. In such case the mixture of north-country English, cockney English, and the island accent is fearfully and wonderfully made. The landlady of the Doves, widow of an Englishman, served this mixture to her English-speaking tenants and assured them that they need never be bilious if they " het enough hile to carry off the boil." The same lingual witchbroth sometimes gives the parish of Saint Ouen three names, — *Saint Euens, Santowan, Saint Owen.*

An interesting specimen of this insular Jersey-French is here extracted from a little book purporting to be a series of letters written by a *centenier* (constable) of St. Ouen, from Paris, during the exhibition of 1889. He is represented as —

Bram Bilo (Chant'nyi d'St.-Ou), San viage à l'exposicion ov sa chiethe femme Nancy, et chin tchi vites dans la ville de Paris.

PARIS, septembre 1889.

MOUSSIEU, — Nos y v'chin dans chu Paris, éd pis hier ô sé.

J'nos embertchimes avan'hier dans le baté dé Granville, man couesin Liés et ma belle-mèthe étais v'nus nos condithe dans la van, avec not boëte.

J'eumes une fiethe peux justement comme le baté tchitai la cauchie, car, ma belle-mèthe tchétai v'nue dans le steam pour vais la machine, s'étreuli hor-bor les fiers en l'air en montan sus la plianche pour s'en r'allé. Lé captaine n'arrêti pon pour la r'pètchi, mais y criyi "Go ahead," sans pus s'jèné; heutheuseman qu'un matlo dans un baté la r'pètchi par san cotillon. J'cré pas qu'oul' en mouoro oquo chute fais.

J'avaimes empauté des sauchisses et un mio d'muothue dans un pagas, et j'acati eunne bouteille de bière.

Enfin j'arrivimes à Paris ! Tchi train ! Tchi comba a chute station ! Nancy mé ténai tight par lé bras de crainte dé s'èdgethai, et, ma fé, ou'l avé raison. Yen avé du monde et du bri ! ! J'én savais pon dans tchi hôtel allé, et tandi que j' regardais atouore de mé, un homme s'en vint m'dithe : " Mylor cherche quelque chose ? " Vethe-d'ja, j'lis dis, puoriez-vous m'inditchi un hôtel respectable et pas trop chi? Y répouni qu'oui, et la-d'sus j'nos n'allons — y voulai portai ma casse, mais " not for Joe," 'n'lis laisse pas s'fit Nancy, chès p'têtre un pickpocket !

Y nos condisi à un grand hôtel, mais l'proprié-

taîthe nos dis tchi n'prenai pas des gens de not'
espèce. "Queman," j'lis dis, "savous bein qué j'sis
Chant'nyi à St.-Ou!!" V'la tchi l'radouochi, et nos
v'chin dans s'n'ôtel, au siexième estage.

Le preumi jour, j'nos proumnimes dans la ville.
Y'en avé ti d'chu monde, et des carosses et des
tremway, et des boutiques, et des églyises! My
eye, tchi grande ville!

J'montimes dans un tremway tchi nos condysi lien
comme de St.-Aubin à Gouérey sans sorti d'la ville.
J'vinmes des gardins, des pars, des pythamides, des
églyises et des estatues.

Nancy fut tout-à-fé chotchie par ches estatues là,
et dé vié, y'a d'tchi faithe ruogi escrivain — y sont
presques toutes nues coumme un ver, ches estatues
là, pas tan seuleman eunne pathe de cauches.

J'dis au coachman du tremway que j'tai honteux,
et i'm réponni que probablyemon si l'presidan avé seu
que j'nos en vinmes, il éthai fai mettre des kéminses à
ses estatues. J'cré casi q'chu coachman là s'motchai
mé.

Oprès nos être proumnés tchique temps, vin
l'euthe du diné.

J'entrimes dans un restauran et je d'mandi au
ouaiteur tchéque y'avé à mangi. Y nos aporti un
papi sus tchique étai écri chein qu' y'avé, mais j'ny
comprins rein, ni Nancy entou. L'ouaiteur nos dis
qu' nou zavé ammor de qu'manchi par le potage.
Ch'là m'étonni, j'lis dis qu'à St.-Ou, nou qu'manchi
par la soupe. Là-d'sus y nos apporte eunne bollée
de bouillon tchi'l applé du consumé.

Enfin, oprès qu' j'eumes diné, j'nos proumnimes
oquo eunne demieuthe, et pis coumme Nancy étai
un mio faillie, j'rentrimes à not' hôtel et j'nos
quochimes ben lassés.

J'vos écrithai oquo prechainement si ch'la vos
fait plyiaisi.

A bétos, vot' vièr anmin,

BRAM BILO.

"Please sign the paper which is *pleated*," the boy who brought the cider told Mrs. Dove, and she knew he meant the *folded* paper, even though he did not say so, nor yet *plié*.

But when another asked in perfectly pronounced English, "Are these tins of Homer for you?" she could never in the world have guessed what he meant to say but for her knowledge of French. "Homer" would never suggest aught to eat, unless one remembers that *homard* in French means lobster. Yet again, when one serving man complained, in perfectly unforeign English, "John takes too much foot," it was necessary to know the meaning of the French saying, *Il prend trop de pied*, to understand his good English.

Once upon a time Karl told them a bread riot was stirred against one of the Lemprières who had bought up and stored great quantities of grain. It was chiefly a woman's riot, and women went shouting up and down : —

"Allons, mourons sur la plièche pustot que par une disette languissante, le bouan Gui nos a donnet du grain et jelle garderons en dépit d'schez bougres de Lemprière et d'lus cour."

Mrs. Dove was much less interested in the story of old Prynne imprisoned in this Castle and writing poor verses, or in the tragedy of the Bandenellis, father and son, trying to escape by ropes of sheets only to be dashed in pieces on the rocks, than she was in the brave protracted defence by a woman.

"Just as sure as one comes across the history of a castle anywhere," she declared, somewhat recklessly, "just so sure history tells of an obstinate defence by a woman who may not have a voice in governing because she cannot fight (by the same reason she has no right to the teeth in her head). There was the brave defence of Pevensey Castle by Lady Pelham, 'yhowr awnn pore I. Pelham'; the Castle at Pontorson by Du Guesclin's sister Julienne, after her traitorous maids had betrayed her to the English; Peel Castle, by the dauntless Countess of Essex; Gorey Castle, by Lady de Carteret; then, if you want strategy, there was clever Mrs. Hungerford during the Parliamentary struggles, who telegraphed from St. Aubin's to her husband, seneschal of Elizabeth Castle. She established an entire code of signals by means of her clothes line, and by his glass, her imprisoned husband could distinguish a shirt between two petticoats or *vice versa*, shirts between sheets, or sheets between shirts, and read the whole domestic history of his family, and the condition of affairs on the island, punctuated by stockings and handkerchiefs."

" To be sure, women have always been cruelly down-trodden," replied the other Dove. " Have you not read of that Jersey woman, wife of Pierre Fallu, who, one Sunday in March, 1552, took a pair of paternosters to church and refused to give them up to the Connétable on demand. Perhaps you remember her punishment? "

The laugh was against the lady. For, as everybody knew, Madame Fallu was condemned by the court for her popish contumacy — that her husband be sent to prison !

" Every night at midnight," Legend-gatherer George was saying, " the ghostly sight was visible to whoever peeped from windows. Everybody was within doors, for everybody would have as soon have met grim death as that spectral procession moving slowly across Gorey common just over there. Every night as the clock struck twelve it moved, an ancient procession the like of which had never been seen by living eyes upon the island. A procession of silent figures, in cowls and long monkly garments, followed a coffin which seemed to float in the air. The long pall trailed upon the ground, the grim train followed silently and slow with bowed heads. Whither the ever restless dead was bound, going every midnight to a grave it never reached, or if found, never to rest therein, nobody knew. Nobody, indeed, dared to ask."

" Does it pass yet ? "

" No," said the narrator, solemnly. " One night as the silent train wended its way across the common a posse of live men barred the way. They tumbled the coffin from off the shoulders concealed under the pall. They stripped the monkly garments from the ghosts and found, — what do you think ? — a coffin full of " run " French brandy and some of the most respected inhabitants of the island. Jersey was a nest of smugglers in those days. I have heard old men tell of cutters darting between here and France, drawing scarcely two inches and running with sails flat upon the water. Steam has spoiled all that," and the dignified and law-abiding Jerseyman almost sighed.

" You have heard of Pinel First, King of the Ecrehous? " asked somebody. Everybody had heard of him, of his abdication since the Queen's death, and his recent death in the snug harbor of the hospital. For years he and his wife lived alone upon a tiny islet of the Ecrehous, a heap of rough rocks between Jersey and France, forming an island of nine square miles at low tide, at high tide only two, and, like all the other Channel Islands, once a part of the Continent. Even these two miles are cut up by intricate channels. Upon one of the bits are the remains of ruins of a thirteenth century abbey built there when the Ecrehous rocks were the top of a hill belonging to France, and where neighboring villages went to hear mass now that the sea had made an impassable marsh between them and the church at Port Bail in France. The Channel Islands themselves were separated from the Continent during the eighth century.

Upon these rocks King Pinel and his Queen had their kingdom, — monarchs of all they surveyed, and their royal palace one squalid room. King Pinel I. was a wild, aboriginal Jerseyman, rough of speech and manner, living chiefly by vraic gathering. At low tide his special kingdom was some rods in circumference, at high it was scarcely more than the ground covered by his hut. The Queen, his wife, managed to cultivate one or two spots of sand where the tides came but a few times a year, and thus they lived in royal state. He accepted the title given him in jest as his legal and legitimate title, and felt his royalty such a fact that once he communicated with a sister sovereign, doubtless the only sovereign of whom he ever heard. He or his queen wove a couple of fancy work-baskets, which he sent to the Queen of England and the Princess Beatrice. In return, the Queen sent him a comfortable coat in which he at once had his photograph taken. One day King Pinel came over with word that certain strangers had left some casks upon the verge of his kingdom and he suspected that they contained French brandy waiting to be " run " after dark. Immediately, custom-house officers sailed away to the lonely Ecrehous and brought back the casks. In the presence of higher officers they were opened and found to contain sea-water. King Pinel was hand-in-glove with all the runners. How he probably smote his shanks with glee, when he pictured the discomfiture of the excise men !

The long table was spread out-of-doors. Doubtless it was a groaning board under so many good things, but nobody kept still enough to hear its complaining. Exquisite Jersey cider made from orchards such as George Eliot approved, peaceful untormented orchards upon serene slopes, yielding cider without a thought of sourness or tang of bitterness, pure juice of golden apples, not too sweet yet not *brut* and with stinging sparkle caught from the ever-present sea ; sandwiches of ham, beef, chicken, cheese, with mustard or without, French *saucisson* or English sausages, as one *should* or *would*, a vast pile of " wonders " in compliment to the Doves.

" Shall you have some apricot pie ? "

" I *shall*," answered the Dove addressed, " although I need it not, but because you name it ' pie,' as it is, and not ' tart,' as it is not, being covered."

" Of course we always call it pie," declared the Jersiais. " We never are done disputing with English people concerning the proper difference between a covered pie and an open tart."

" Hast thou a strawberry mark upon thy left arm ? " fondly asked one of the Americans.

"We recognize the same distinction, a distinction that was English until London fell under the influence of French cooks. Because French cooks call their meat pies *pâté*, London cooks thought it fine cookly manners to translate *pâté* into pastry and confine pie strictly to meat-pastries. London claims to hold the sceptre of the world's English, yet is not above corrupting the good old English of its forefathers at the bidding of cooks. In almost all the provinces, the rural parts of England, pie is pie to this day. Those provincial old maids were tarnished by seasons in London who disliked to mention rhubarb because it suggested medicine, so offered their guests portions of 'spring-fruit-tart.' Which was the true Englishman of the two who met at a picnic, the Londoner who asked for 'a bit of that fruit tart,' or the country squire who answered 'there's only this *borry poie*' (berry pie)?"

In 1676, Lady Fanshawe wrote during her foreign travels, "They have a fruit called a massard, like a cherry but different, and makes the best pie I ever eat." In 1705, Dr. King wrote in his "Art of Cookery,"

" Choose your materials right, your seasoning fix
And with your *fruit* resplendent sugar mix,
And thence of course the figure will arise
And elegance adorn the surface of your pyes."

When, in 1739, West wrote to Walpole, it was certain he had no intention of writing other than pure English. Yet we read in the letters promise of "a gooseberry pie big as anything." Twenty years later a plain Sussex tradesman, Thomas Turner, to whom the English of Walpole's correspondents and King Charles' courtiers was good enough for use, wrote in his diary a resolve "to eat nothing *for breakfast* but water-gruel, varied occasionally by a fruit Pye." In 1813 the future Cardinal Newman wrote to his mother from Oxford, " We live well here, we have gooseberry, damson, and apricot pies." Had he been told they were not pies, but tarts, he might have wondered how many tarts the Knave of Hearts could have stolen that summer's day when we all spoke English, or why busybodies had a finger in every pie that was fish, flesh, or fowl, and therefore without plums. We, too, if inquisitive, might ask why it is that we never see, even in London, a tart-dish, but only the pie-dish, in which the "tart" comes to the table. Does even London ever hear of a mince-*tart*, albeit absolutely void of aught but fruit. Tom Moore wrote of —

> " The cold apple-pie his lordship would stuff in
> For breakfast to save the expense of hot muffin."

Surely England's laureates write in English. What was Southey's language when in 1789 he wrote his Pindaric " Ode to Gooseberry Pie "? Charles Lamb was an undeniable Londoner. " George Dyer has introduced me to the table of an agreeable old gentleman who gives hot legs of mutton and grape pies," he wrote in 1800.

Ruskin surely wrote English superior to ordinary Londoners. In his autobiography he tells of his childish enjoyment of gathering the fruit for " cherry pies." Yet we do not speak English if, being Jersiais or American, we do not ask for tart when we wish for pie !

" Yes, Bright Eyes, I shall have some of the apricot ' pie.' "

"Under the sheeny blue and gold," said Captain Philippe, who has Jersey history at his finger-tips, "Under this motionless surface Jersey chimes and crosses lie. At the Reformation, to which Jersey took most readily, having always been under the influence of a high class of Huguenot ministers, fled from France, all church images, chimes, and crosses were sold to France to help pay for fortifying Elizabeth Castle, and much against the wishes of Jersey people. The vessel bearing them away to St. Malo struck upon a rock and sank, to the joy, mingled with sorrow, of many a Protestant Jerseyman. They are down among the mermen now, but what use can that pagan people make of them in their green-vaulted aisles?"

"Mermen! Do you imagine the touchy mer-folk did not move their habitations from the English Channel with the first steamboat that churned up their roofs? What sort of a degenerate must the merman be who would cling to green aisles into which a mass of cinders came ploughing now and then, to say nothing of champagne bottles and bones of fish, flesh, and fowl?"

"The mer-folk may be gone, but disembodied human spirits, as defiant of water as of air, may wander there among submerged churches and the ruins of their mortal homes. They would know the uses of holy chimes and crosses. I wonder we never hear those chimes when the Channel is as calm as now. During a phenomenally low tide in 1735, when Jersey was left in the midst of a wilderness of weedy pinnacles and domes of rock, the remains of a submerged village were distinctly seen. How many others there may be nobody knows, left from the days when one could walk dryshod from here to the centre of the diocese at Coutances, to which all of the now 'Channel Islands' belonged.

"In 1203, the Ecrehous became an island, having for a long time previously been high and dry land in the midst of a marsh. It was given to the monks of Val Richer to build a church to God and the Virgin as the inhabitants (it was *très peuplée*) could no longer walk over to Port Bail to hear the mass. Ancient MSS. speak of various parishes of Coutances now under this blue and gold. There our chimes and crosses lie."

"Listen," said one of the company, "I hear them now."

Everybody listened, all heard.

On the soft wings of the wind, floating dreamily over the parapets of Fort Cheer came gushes of mysterious music. It came from No-Man's-Land, bound by neither space nor time, the infinite vagueness where hides forever the poetry that never enters into words, never reveals itself save by subtle thrills that touch the spirit and flee whither even thought cannot follow them. It was faint and far enough away, yet near enough to echo of clashing wine cups, and ringing pitchers of silver and gold at the bridal feast of pagan Rollo with the Christian princess Gilla. Shivering amid the deeper tones of wassail, one might almost hear the plaint of a girl's grief at her forced bridal with the barbarian enemy of her weak royal father and of France; the sixty-years-old husband who would behead all her French attendants in his own Norman capital, Rouen; the girlish weeping and shrill lamentation of an age when women wept as loudly as the children they rarely ceased to be. Yet nobody fancied it the echo of a bridal an hundred and fifty years before William the Conqueror was born, the bridal by means of which Normandy became a recognized duchy and fief of France, for now the sound of silvery chimes floated slumberously over the grassy parapets, chimes soft and low, chimes wrapped in space, in clouds, in foam, chimes swinging upon sway-ing tides in cool green twilight. Their melody seemed even to come nearer as the slumberous wind wavered to and fro.

"French excursionists from Port Bail," ex-plained Captain Philippe. "Coming over to do Jersey in eight hours. They are singing to keep their courage up upon the raging deep and before facing the perils of a foreign tour. We have many such every summer. Excursions come all the way from Paris and 'do' us in sixteen hours from start to finish at the Paris railway station. We often go down to the pier in town, to see these excursions arrive. Heavens what a chatter! It's exactly as if flocks of wild geese were suddenly released from captivity. They are usually small shop people, clubs of them who almost never leave home save on a day's excur-sion, and this is a momentous event in their lives. They begin to criticise *ces Anglaises* the instant they land, and with a spice of venom added to every criticism, we think, by their vague impres-sion that our islands rightfully belong to them and that perfidious Albion somehow did them out of u   They fully believe us bowed down with woe (and England's yoke), because we are no longer French. The whole company gets into excursion cars and rides round the island, stopping only for dinner or luncheon at some of the tourist hotels, then back again to their steamer, and in their own beds by midnight, under firm conviction for the rest of their mortal lives that they have made the tour of modern England, and know *au fond la bêtise anglaise,* '*puisque j'y étais.*' Should we tell them we have been united to England longer than Scotland has, than Wales or Ireland, they would only shrug their shoulders and say '*Tant pis pour vous.*'"

"We hear them as far off as this sometimes," dainty Flo was saying, "moaning with sea-sickness — nobody is ever so sick as a Frenchman — and sobbing, '*O ma mère, si tu savais comme je souffre.*'"

Everybody laughed. Everybody always does laugh at a Frenchman's almost invariable devotion to his mother, whether on earth or in heaven, — not that the devotion is ridiculous, but his manner of exploiting it.

After luncheon, a walk round the coast, passing the Jersey Lion on the way. Its head is up, its aspect watchful, one eye is upon Coutances spires, the other upon a mite of a steamer bustling over to France. It never turns its head even when apostrophized in five languages, Parisian-French, Yankee-French, Jersey-French, Jersey-English and New England-English, for it is only a rock after all. Legend-gatherer George bids them notice wherever they see them, the farmhouses and cots, where the widow has fastened herself like a solitary barnacle upon the original homestead. Mrs. Dove looked upon them with sadness. "To this it comes," she thought, "to this it all comes; the happy bride who came in her youthful hope and strength to a husband's home, who worked with him, planted, tended, watered, weeded, harvested, sinks in time away before ever-encroaching youth. The world is youth's ; the power, the strength, the joy thereof. When youth comes, youth goes, march we must in the awful procession, the bride becomes in time only a barnacle on her son's rear wall."

"You see," said Legendary George cheerily, "we house our widows well. When a man dies, and the son and his wife own the homestead, that little addition is built to the main house that she may still live on the premises."

"How very kind," agreed Mrs. Dove. "And when it is the wife who dies? Does the husband then retire into one of these widow-pens?"

"He usually takes another wife," explained Legendary George, — "a young one to help him on the farm."

Some of these widow-pens seemed as ancient as the house itself, some almost new. Occasionally one seemed even older than the house, more weak and faded. "The son who built that cheated his mother with cheap workmanship and material," said suspicious Mrs. Dove.

She said no more, but deep in her heart she bitterly felt the injustice of social and political laws, that doom a woman to become so absolutely a part of her home that she has no horizon, no atmosphere, outside of it, that enjoins upon her to be only a home-maker, to live in her pans and kettles, to become a part of her carpets, to take every stain in the floors, every crack in the walls, every darn in the curtains, to the very centre of her consciousness, only to be ejected from everything when her master dies.

"No," one of the Jerseymen was saying, "we have no definite law of primogeniture, but the spirit of our laws is decidedly in favor of keeping property and estates always in the same family."

On the lintels of many of the Jersey houses is the date of erection carved in stone. Often this date is accompanied by the united initials of the husband and wife who first owned the house and lived in it. When this first couple were a bridal pair, building their nest, the fact is sometimes indicated perpetually by two sculptured hearts transfixed by an arrow surmounted by the initials and with the date beneath. The Doves knew this was a practice not peculiar to the Channel Islands, for they had seen the same in Sussex, and they wondered if it were not some relic of habit from ancient Northman days. In Sussex sometimes what the Doves called an "epitaph" accompanied the initials and date. They never saw, but Sussex Archæological Journals told them of one antique inscription carved in fine relief —

> "When we are dead
> And lay'd in grave,
> And all our bones are rotten,
> By this shall we
> Remembered be
> Or else we were forgotten.
> "R. & D. T."

Who were R. and D. T.? Who remembers them? How long have they "lay'd in grave," and where?

Fools, fools, fools! Our poor shifting dust, thinking to keep its memory on earth by pyramids, by colossal tombs, by massive lintels with deep inscriptions!

"A classical dictionary is better than any inscription," said the Dove lightly, who thought not admiringly of such short cuts to learning. He referred to the fact that not far from St. Helier's is the ancient farmhouse in which our old friend Lemprière was born in 1766. He was an Oxford man of Dr. Johnson's college (Pembroke), took holy orders, and was always a schoolmaster in England, where he died in 1822. The famous dictionary was finished when he was but 22. He was three times married and left many children. The farmhouse in which he was born is quaint and gray. On the lintel of the door one may read, " C. L. P. 83. S. C. L. 1766." As his father's name was Charles, these were probably the initials and the marriage year of his parents. What was meant by 83 nobody could tell.

Over the great chimney-piece in the kitchen on a lozenge-shaped stone is the inscription —

" 1647
M. D.
E."

Who were they, M. D. and E., in the year that Charles the First still wore his head, and his vicious son not yet King of Jersey?

MARTIN AND LA VIEILLE.

"I KNOW of nothing more utterly discouraging than to be disappointed in one you have trusted."

Mrs. Dove said this as if it had never been said before. One would suppose from her face and voice that hers was the first soul since the morning stars sang together into which the iron of disappointment had entered. Her whole appearance suggested spiritual bedragglement and forlornness ; the condition of a glowing soul that had chased a rainbow and returned from afar laden only with mud.

"Chestnut," remarked her mate.

"Only four times," and the mud grew heavier. "Pity, if four times finding her in this state and remarking upon it must needs be chestnutty. Go and look at her yourself and see if you don't say as much, and more."

He went. He saw. He returned.

"Only a trifle redder in the face than usual, and I believe she is rattling the dishes more than I ever heard her, but even that might — "

"You know perfectly that when we came home yesterday and the day before it was precisely the same. Martin's face was red, her eyes very queer, her hair fairly stood on end ; she was all trembling and tottering, so that she leaned against the wall and stuttered and rambled as she talked.

Yesterday it was even some time before she opened the door to us and then it was with something in her hand that she tried to hide."

"It looked to me like an innocent dust brush," said he.

Sadly, solemnly she whispered —

"I fear it was a bottle."

The house of their proprietor as well as their own opened upon that blooming garden; so did the cottage in half of which Martin had lived for years. Thus it happened that, although Martin owed them service only during the forenoons she was always ready to skirt the garden and enter the ever-open back door whenever she could serve them by some little short-timed attention. As their front door key was evidently from some "misfit parlors," and turned with difficulty, she frequently let them in when they rang their bell upon their return from their rambles. At first nothing peculiar had been in her manner or appearance. For the first week or two she had opened the green door, cool, silent, respectful, as they had always known her. Then came the anxious unhappy day that she opened the green door to them with whirlwind motion and fury-ridden countenance.

"What if anybody should have delirium tremens in a dove-cote," said Mrs. Dove, with a scared look. "Why, there is n't room."

The speaker's idea of this horrible malady was not very well defined. It was a sort of decadently artistic incoherency of snakes racing through the sitting-room hissing, up and down the stairs and dining-room walls. She was indignant when the other Dove laughed aloud.

"Excuse me," he said. "But the idea of Martin taking up more room than she can help does tickle one!"

As it happened, Martin was not their only annoyance just then. One or two persons had called and gone away without leaving cards. When the Doves were deeply buried in their reading and writing, as they usually were when at home, it was no simple matter to answer the door-bell. They were little accustomed to the sound of door-bells. and had not yet realized the responsibility of hiring a furnished one. In London, all they knew of bells was that a handle must be pulled when they desired to enter a house, and that somebody must have pulled their own London door-bell before the servant brought them a card or message. Now at the disquieting sound so very near, one or the other of them would look up in mild surprise to ask, "Was that a bell?" as if it were as likely to be flute or bassoon. Whereupon the other in as sweet a daze would murmur, "Is it a door-bell?" as if trams or trolleys might be clanging down their alley. Then the other would murmur, "Is it *ours*?"

Finally, these momentous questions settled, the necessity was recognized that somebody must go to the door. Should they telegraph out of the back windows to Martin that visitors were at the front, or go to the door themselves? That question was generally settled by finding that Martin was not at home, or at least not about the back of her cottage. Then only remained the question *which* of the Doves should answer the door-bell. This depended upon which was nearest to the surface of the surging tide of books and papers, and was a matter not to be decided off-hand. The result was that when the green slit between the white walls of the Dove-cote was opened, behold nobody was there.

"Who would imagine the Jersiais so impatient?" they remarked the third time this happened. "Whoever it is quickly turns the corner and is out of sight. I wish we were not so near the corner or that they would leave their cards."

"Probably they are glad of any excuse, like our undergrads at Oxford."

This always cleared their brows. It brought up such a pretty picture of one trembling freshman ringing at their door, and a shivering group on the opposite side of the street rushing wildly away when the door was opened.

"How they must have hated us for knowing their parents and for inviting them," the Doves laughed. "No men on the face of the earth are so bashful as young Englishmen."

"That reminds me," said Mrs. Dove; "here is the account I have just finished of one of those Oxford lunches where we were guests, and our hosts *not* freshmen. Let me read it to you : —

"The wide windows frame an exquisite view of a dreamy garden. Over that space of softest green bordered with brilliant flowers, the summer mist broods like an iridescent dove. Through the pebbled quad immediately beneath those wide windows, how many young feet have fared to and fro, feet that have since left immortal prints upon the sands of time. How many noble visions and high resolves that bare quad has known, does know, will know, when we are dust.

" The room is large and handsome, with oaken panels and ceiling; even though the stairs and landing outside seem beggarly to one who sees nothing to reverence in steps worn deep, and walls blackened by countless scholarly generations. Up and down this staircase, in and out this very room, fifty years and more ago, daily passed a knot of students and thinkers whose names have since been connected with the most important religious movements of the century.

" The walls and mantels are covered with photographs and ·engravings, with brackets, and homelike ornaments. Books are in profusion upon swinging cases; the rugs are artistic upon the varnished floor. It is like the spacious and pleasant drawing-room of a refined home, without a trace of bachelor untidiness, or of the rowdiness not always hidden in a Harvard student's room. The lunch table is another picture. Our young host is healthy, handsome, and (we hope) wise.

" Five students and two strangers sit at table. Behind us a solemn 'scout' passed noiselessly backward and forward, so noiselessly that when the lobster salad should give place to cold duck, behold ! no scout was there.

" ' A don in the room below is giving a lunch,' grumbled our host; ' he has gobbled the scout.'

" Thereupon five Oxford men turned waiters, and, more or less dexterously, deposited salad plates upon the deep window-couches and elsewhere, resetting the table from the sideboard.

" ' Ekker! jolly for the digegger,' they say with laughter.

" What language is this, of ancient peoples and

forgotten times? See what it is to be unlearned in learned Oxford !

" ' " Ekker " is exercise, don't you know?' they explain; ' " digegger " is digestion. When a man walks in the park he takes a " pagger ; " when his people come to see him they are "straggers," or strangers.'

" ' Easy enough when you once get the swing,' said the youth known as ' Father William,' because of his thinning hair. ' Breakfast is " brekker " in the Oxford tongue ; when a man makes lunch his first meal of the day it becomes " brunch ; " and a tea-dinner at the Union Club is a " smug " at the " Ugger." '

" ('Who was Agabus?' 'Who was Candace?' 'Who was Mother Lois?')

" In at the flower-clad windows at mystic intervals these strange questions swept. No answer came, so far as we could hear ; but answers there were (or failures at answers), we knew. For in response to a guest's astonished question, 'Jubilee' and ' Le Petty' (Le Petit) explained together, ' Cramming for Gossers.'

" So very clear ! Yet the 'stragger' soon understood that ' Gospels ' is a severe examination at Oxford, and, from window to window of the quad, friends ' cram ' each other with leading ' Gosser' questions.

" ' A sort of amateur pupship,' ventures one of the straggers, whereupon the five explode. They explode again and again, as they dart about the spacious room seeking a hole or corner not already occupied with discarded dishes, till the guest fears somehow to have put her foot in it, yea, both feet.

"Yet she was right, after all; for a man who 'coaches' for 'exams' calls his pupils his 'pups' dropping the last syllable of 'pupils;' and many an Oxford man looks forward to no more brilliant career than a lifelong 'pupship.'

"But what does it mean when Jubilee calmly asks Father William across the sweets : —

"'Keeper-Creeper to-day?'

"'Don't you know?' he explains to the stragglers. 'One of the dons is always known as "Creeper" and to "keep a creeper" is to attend one of his lectures.'

"Hark! What bold thumping is this upon the antique stair? Are 'young barbarians' again 'at play,' that shouts go with it, not all of laughter?

"Our host goes out and returns. '"Lily" and "Lulu" are helping "Samson" to the train,' he explains; but nobody believes him. Later the stragglers know that two Merry Men, mad for mischief, had undertaken to 'rag' a room. Under pretence of helping the occupant to the train, they cast coal-scuttle, books, boots, etc., into an open trunk, and were trying to dump it down the stairs. When our host saw the comedy Lily and Lulu were tugging desperately trainward at one end of the trunk, Samson contrarywise at the other. All were hot and very red, and victory was undecided where to perch till a sudden thought struck Samson. Instantly he ceased to pull homeward, gave a sudden push trainward, and Lily and Lulu sprawled at the bottom of the stair, while Samson strode triumphant with his luggage to his room.

"Then to the stragglers the five tell stories. They tell of another unpopular student whose

8

room was 'ragged' in similar manner, but gave different results. The rag*gee* defended his lecture-notes, pyjamas, boots, and best hat, which the raggers were mixing indiscriminately, with tongs, poker, and zeal, so strenuously that his 'stove-pipe' was not smashed, his lecture-notes not inextricably mixed; but two Merry Men went about with black eyes for a few days thereafter bleating piteously, 'so deucedly ungentlemanly, doncherknow.'

"Our company agreed with them!

"One evening some of the five saw a Youth in the quad who seemed like one of the Arabian Nights, half flesh, half monumental marble. But in this case the magic was reversed; for the upper half was black, being full evening dress, while the lower was a pair of silken tights.

"A group of Merry Men were vigorously pushing, or trying to push, something into the letter-box.

"'He was going out to dine with a rip in his trousers; we will send them home to be mended,' they chorussed. The Monumental Youth was one of the most prankish of Merry Men himself, and took this revenge for many a joke of his own in perfectly good part. But the letter-box did not. It resisted bravely till it broke. Upon the bills ('battels') of every man in college a shilling was charged for the letter-box wreckage, as it is the practice to charge such wrecks. The letter-box cost, perhaps, thirty shillings; the assessment resulted in several pounds. The colleges never lose money by student antics; the cost comes upon the students themselves, Merry Men and unmerry alike.

"Our host shows a huge bunch of cheap canes, perhaps two score of them.

"'We buy them at wholesale, a penny each, and keep them on hand for presentations.'

"Every Oxford man must carry a 'stick,' as it is called. Without that distinctive mark a student is 'disgragger,' to the University. Sometimes a new man, never having been bothered with a cane, and caring all for study and naught for undergraduate tradition, neglects this tradition. Then men of his own college present him with penny canes, leave them in his room, at his door, his place in chapel, his seat at table, till the man in sheer self-defence is obliged to cane himself, though he lose one every hour. The 'straggers,' saw one day in the 'pagger,' a recluse 'grind,' who carried his stick tied to one of his buttons.

"'We presented him with twenty canes and sixteen umbrella handles before he gave in,' the straggers were told.

"The lunch comes up from the 'Common Room,' and though the viands are dainty and rich, the menu is not extensive for many calls. Thus the first lunch of lobster salad (or salmon and cucumber), cold duck (or joint), lettuce salad and cherry pie, with fruit and bonbons, is quite epicurean. So is the second, in another man's room ; likewise the third, with the only change in host and guests. Then one begins to suspect a sameness. The suspicion grows, till after the fifth, one suspects no more.

"One of our hosts has his room draped with Star-spangled banners, not as clean as they are in their own country.

"'He sends his national standard to the wash with his shirts,' chuckled our English friends.

"' *English* dirt !' answered our host.

"' You would call washing your flag a "core," in America, would you not?' one asks, in all seriousness.

"' Core?'

"'Yes, "core." We often find the word in American stories, *c-h-o-r-e.*'

"' No,' said the American, 'it is not a "core," and Washington pie is not "jam sandwich," though you English call it so.'

" All laugh, for these discussions are frequent and always good-natured. One day in a meeting of a college club of which an American was a member the reader of the essay, forgetting the Yankee element, spoke of 'the sordid commercialism of the United States.' What was his astonishment to hear the company burst vigorously into a bar of Hail Columbia."

"I remember," said Mr. Dove, "asking my scout one day if he thought we had enough for my luncheon-party, the supply seemed rather small."

"' Are there ladies of the party?' Savage asked.

"' Yes.'

"' Then quite enough, sir, quite enough. Gentlemen never eat so much when ladies are present.'"

As if in echo to Hail Columbia, had come a postman's rap at the green door.

" Only an island letter ; our steamer letters came hours ago," said the Doves, and they did not hasten to see. "It is probably only an invitation."

A little later Martin came with the evening milk. Said Mrs. Dove, " Please bring me the letter on the entry floor."

" Why does she not bring it? Why is she so

interminably long about it?" after a long time asked Mrs. Dove.

"Ask me another," said he.

"Martin!"

"Madam!"

"The note!"

"Only an advertisement, Madam; I took it down to the fire."

"Queer thing for her to do! Why not bring even an advertisement upstairs instead of down? Do you see, she has that strange, wild look again; and just hear how she handles the kitchen poker and tongs!"

When, a day or two later, Martin had carried two other advertisements downstairs instead of up, she was formally requested to deliver everything found under the letter slit the moment it came.

The very next time they succeeded in letting themselves in with their own key they found the little stair-landing, or entry, littered with bits of torn paper.

"Dear, dear!" mourned Mrs. Dove, "I am sure Martin is queer again to-day, or she would never do this, and so openly too. She has not even taken the trouble to burn the circular or circulars."

"It seems to me we are objects of considerable interest to the dwellers in this little corner of St. Luke's parish," said Mrs. Dove one day. "Just see the heads in those cottage windows as we pass."

"Probably it has got about that we are Americans, and these heads are watching for our appearance in feathers and paint. Americans are rare in this quarter; even if these people ever saw any before us, they did not know them from English. But now they know what we are, they look to see something new and strange, like the Great American Sachem who drove four horses tandem through the streets of St. Helier's a year or two ago, and drew teeth without pain in Royal Square, and took the crutches of cripples away."

They turned the corner as he spoke. As he spoke they saw a flying figure disappear up the hill. Within the instant they rang at their own door; before he withdrew his hand from the bell a fury stood on the threshold. The woman's hair stood up; her eyes blazed; her face was crimson. She struck out blindly with a rolling-pin.

" Take that, you sneak ! "

The rolling-pin came down with a thump. It hit nobody but Martin herself, whose knees must have been black and blue for a week. Her face was not black and blue, but every color of the rainbow, when she recognized a pair of timid Doves in place of him for whom she had lain in wait.

" It 's the butcher's son, sir, up by the Rouge Rue and his gang," she gasped, and the Doves could not but notice how soft and sweet her voice was through it all. " He 's been ringing the bell and hiding every day and stuffing paper through the letter slit. I shall go to the school-master of St. Luke's or to the rector about him. I pulled his hair for him yesterday, but he is too quick for me."

" Devotion, not drink," said one of the Doves, remorsefully. " Think how she tried to keep from us that these young hoodlums were trying to surprise us in our American *costume d'intérieur*."

"What a pity we did not bring our lariats," said he.

Probably Martin lives in memory none the less radiantly because of La Vieille. The contrast was stupendous. La Vieille might have lived for no other purpose than to make Martin regretted, and go to her grave the most successful woman who ever lived.

The Doves could not have Martin the second year that they hired the dove-cote. Behold, some highly offensive officer — the Doves were sure he was red-faced, blustering, and read only picture-books — had incorporated Martin into his kitchen as head cook, entirely regardless of the rights of the American flag over the chimney-piece in Dove cottage. So Martin was lost to them, but they could have La Vieille, their landlady wrote, who would do everything for them, including the cooking, for the same terms. Mrs. Dove had seen La Vieille and was doubtful, but knew not what else to do.

Behold La Vieille, who met them where Martin met the year before, but with what a difference! She did not smile a welcome ; the Americans never saw her smile upon any occasion. She was of English parentage, about fifty, and could not speak the island French or any other, as she spoke English only by jerks and sputters as if afraid it might choke her. She had but one eye and but one tooth ; she was nearly stone deaf and would not be persuaded of the fact, which made confusion worse confounded by her pretence of understanding. She invariably understood crossways and up-side-down, "because everybody nowadays mumbles ;" and she was given to weeping over the dinners because Mrs. Dove had insisted upon seeing the pan washed before the roast went into the oven. Dirt lay thick under the sofa and chairs till Mrs. Dove took upon herself to sweep it all into the middle of the rooms over night. That La Vieille did not pass the heaps unobserved, as Mrs. Dove almost thought she would, was proved by the sound of loud weeping that filled Dove cottage early the next morning before the Doves were up. La Vieille could not read or write, and for a time she had an innocent little manner of bringing their letters to the Doves. She took them through the garden in at their landlady's back door to have the superscriptions read to her that she might know the master's letters from those of the missis, and *vice versa.* Complaint, reproach, was useless ; she could scarcely hear a word, but at the spectacle of an offended face burst into violent weeping, and ever and forever the words, —

" But I never have any followers."

Followers ! That hideous, one-eyed, toothless spinster ! She was enough to frighten a whole garrison into decorous behavior, even though " followers " in a garrison town are the pest of almost every household, as they are the lifelong misfortune of many a serving-maid. One evening, the Doves heard an earnest confab in the street before their cottage. Two women talked together in the shadow of a wall ; one was crying bitterly. What was said the Americans did not hear until the woman who was not weeping burst furiously to the other : —

" Them sojers oughter be drownded."

" Followers," remarked the Doves. " See what La Vieille is spared."

" Followers ! " exclaimed their landlady. " They

are the pena*l*ity we pay for conquering Hinglund. The hisland is overrun with red-coats, I couldn't turn my back that my 'ouse wasn't full of 'em, heating my provisions and a-dancin' down my floors. I had to take La Vieille in self-defence, as the least of hevils."

"Wherever we go," remarked Mrs. Dove, "we find bitter complaints of servants. Nowhere do we find them better than in our own country, where complaint is loudest. It seems to me every country has its own form of complaint. In our own free and equal country the insolence and independence of the servants is almost their universal fault. We think it an insupportable fault; we do not stop to consider that French housekeepers suffer just as much from the immorality of their serving-maids in youth, from drink and snuff in age; that English housekeepers are continually at their wits' end for service because of dishonesty, drunkenness, and followers. To tell the truth, our American housekeepers ought to be thankful they are no worse served; that drunkenness is almost unknown, thieving rare, immorality not one of our domestic crosses. Don't you remember the night we were to dine at Oakhurst, and two cooks were in the kitchen, the extra one in case the regular proved drunk and incapable? The dinner, such as it was, was tossed together by the butler's wife, brought in by telegram because both cooks were snoring under the kitchen table together. Then at our lodgings in Cavendish Square, when our landlady turned out three cooks in succession, and brought up our Sunday supper herself, having left the fourth cook weeping on the cellar stairs because she was a ' poor orphanless child.' "

Because of La Vieille Mrs. Dove that second year saw much more of their landlady than the year before. Madame de Longue told many an interesting story of the island folk, one of which was not altogether new to the Americans, for it had made some stir in their own country.

Several years ago, one Sunday evening two young shop-girls returning from church met two young men of their acquaintance. The young men proposed a moonlight row upon the water. They took two boats and rowed merrily away from the island. The boats became separated and one returned without the other. After some time the young man of the other boat came to land in an exhausted condition. He tried to explain that his boat was adrift with the young woman and without oars, but nobody believed him because he was French and a stranger. To be a stranger and French in the Channel Islands makes a man at once distrusted, even though almost any Jerseyman pressed to the point will acknowledge that the reason is not so much the French character as Jerseymen's inveterate dislike of Frenchmen. The young man said that he lost an oar overboard ; in trying to recover it he accidentally went over himself ; he knew nothing better to do, he said, than to swim ashore for assistance. Boats went out in search of the young woman, but after long search came back without tidings. The young man was arrested charged with the murder of the girl, and lay in prison for two months awaiting trial. The girl's family went into mourning, which, as they were in poor circumstances, was handsomely furnished by a town torn with sorrow and wrath for the murder of a Jersey girl by a pestiferous Frenchman. Then came a Bank holiday when all the island was free to go where it pleased. A great part of them chose to go to a certain hotel on a certain bay some miles from St. Helier's to view the body of the unfortunate girl washed ashore by the tides. Everything in the shape of a carriage, car, or wagon was pressed into service, hundreds went on foot; the concourse at the hotel was amazing, the proprietor reaped a tremendous harvest, and not till everybody had gone home without seeing any murdered body washed ashore did it dawn upon public comprehension that the proprietor of the hotel had played a very clever advertising trick by means of the sensation rocking the island. A week or two afterwards the community was electrified by a message from under the sea. It was a telegram from a clergyman in Newfoundland stating that the young woman was safe in his family. The island went almost wild with joy that an obscure shop-girl, of whom almost nobody had ever heard before that fateful Sunday night, was not murdered, but safe in a foreign land three thousand miles from home. Telegrams flew thick and fast under the Atlantic at government expense. The island thus learned that the girl in the boat, after the Frenchman's cowardly desertion of her to save himself, had drifted out to sea for twenty-four hours. Even while Jersey boats searched for her she despairingly watched the London packets steam from Jersey. She waved her hat and screamed with as much effect as a gnat in a cyclone. Still she drifted away, away, till, sick at heart and in body, she lapsed into a swoon or stupor. When she awoke a sailing-vessel was not far away, and she succeeded in attracting attention. She was taken on board, treated with every kindness and respect by the captain, a Frenchman from St. Malo bound to Newfoundland. Although only fifteen miles from Jersey he could not alter his course, which would mean thirty miles for his slow craft. He gave up his cabin to her, clothed her in dry clothes that were not womanly, and at St. John's delivered her to the clergyman's family. The affair became a public one, for the Jersey legislature, always paternal of government, assumed every expense of the Jersey girl's home-bringing. She was clothed handsomely and sent first class to England, where her family was sent to meet her. The day she returned to Jersey, three months after drifting away in the dark, was a public holiday. Shops were decorated, flags flying, the streets were filled with an eager populace loaded with flowers. As she stepped ashore from the great steamer, handsomely dressed, having gone so shabby away, she stepped into banks of flowers and loud hurrahs. " Hef she 'd been the duchess of Normandie herself she could n't 'a' had a sweller home-comin'," said Mrs. Dove's landlady. The honest captain of the schooner, even though a Frenchman, received his share of the island's enthusiastic gratitude. A handsome purse was presented to him, and a memorial piece of silver; he was publicly invited to visit the island as its guest, but modestly declined so heavy an honor.

"Then what became of the heroine?" asked Mrs. Dove.

" She went to France to visit the captain's wife and family, then came home and went into the shop again. A while afterwards she was married. I don't know if she is living on the island now or where."

Said Mrs. Dove that night at dinner, "After dinner I want you to set me adrift in a boat." Then, after a pause, "But nò; islands, like republics, are ungrateful; they allow their hobjecs of hinterest to sink so far out of interest that nobody knows whether they are on the island or off."

Nevertheless, this same paternal care of the island government for the islanders that made an island-affair of the island girl is shown everywhere. The debates of the *États* do not scorn to discuss all the pros and cons of a woman's domestic circumstances when considering whether to give her a hotel license or not. The Doves heard one such deliberation, where it was decided to give such a license to a girl who, although very young for such a position, had an elderly aunt living with her !

" UNCLE PETER."

THE Americans had always cherished a quiet fondness for an unknown relative of a distinguished American man of letters. That unknown grand-uncle was the last link that connected the American family, now entirely extinct, with the curiously remote island of its paternal origin. Curiously remote, one says, for the reason that the Americanized branch of the family became, not only more thoroughly New Englanders and Yankees than very many descendants of Pilgrims and Puritans, but because they were always absolutely without longings for the Old Home, the country of our nativity, the beautiful England and its dependencies that is New England's mother.

Henry Thoreau was entirely satisfied with his own little corner of life ; he never expressed the slightest desire to go to Europe ; no thread of pre-natal love and memory stretched though ever so imperceptibly between him and Jersey whence his father's Uncle Peter now and then sent greetings. Curiously remote the Island of Jersey must indeed have seemed to the American Thoreaus because remote from their sympathy and interest. It were as though the insular habit of their ancestors lived in them still, even on a continent.

In 1772 a young John Thoreau sailed away from St. Helier's forever. Jersey was his native island; it was very vivid and positive to his consciousness that final day; he knew every street and alley of St. Helier's; probably not a corner of the island, not a bay or promontory of its coast but was as definite as an actual picture in his imagination. Little could he have believed then that he would in time almost cease to think of himself as a Jerseyman at all, that he would forget to speak of his native island even to his sons and daughters of another nationality than his own.

None of the Jerseyman's descendants ever knew why or how he thus sailed away. In Jersey it is supposed that he made one of a crew of some Jersey privateer, of which there were many at that time, and that he got to the colonies without intending to get there and in some way unexpected to himself. His family knew nothing save that he was shipwrecked and suffered great hardships.

This boy of nineteen evidently spoke English. It is probable that he and his brother Peter were the only ones of the family who wrote it easily; for the latter is the only one who ever wrote to the American Thoreaus, and with his death all communication between the families ceased. These two, Peter the younger brother, left to continue the father's wine trade in St. Helier's, the next older first keeping a store in Boston, then living for years on Concord Green, maintained an intermittent correspondence till John died in 1801. Even then faithful Uncle Peter did not lose sight of his American nephews and nieces, but from time to time sent them an epitome of the family history upon his side of the Atlantic, telling them, in 1801, of their grandmother's death, only a few weeks after the death of her American son. In every affectionate letter he wrote also of their cousins, his own children Peter and Betsey. It had taken so long by slow-sailing ship for tidings of the death on Concord Green to reach Jersey that Marie Thoreau, aged seventy-nine, had passed away, having been but a year a widow, without knowing that her son John, unseen for thirty years, had passed on before her.

In writing his simple, affectionate letters to his distant kindred Uncle Peter little dreamed that he wrote for unborn generations, little dreamed that his artless chronicles would be printed as a portion of the history of a New England Worthy. He little dreamed that many a year after he was dust two pilgrims from New England would search long for his forgotten grave that they might leave there a garland of remembrance, and pansies for gentle thoughts. He little dreamed that pilgrims from his brother's far country would seek for his descendants with far and wide questionings, by graveyard hauntings and the searchings of church registers, finding at last Uncle Peter's granddaughter in none of these, but young, smiling, happy in her own Jersey home, and immensely surprised to be an object of pilgrim quest.

It was Mrs. Dove who came home almost breathless one day, saying, "I have found them!"

Her mate did not need to ask who, and merely said, "Where?"

"Not ten minutes walk from here; she's been there all this time that we've been ransacking not only Green Street Cemetery and Grouville churchyard, but the memories of everybody we knew, as well as many we don't know. The librarian, who does n't believe in my accent, introduced her husband; he's of an historic island family. Don't you remember we read of a fighting parson, Rev. Du Parq, grandson of a protestant refugee from France, and himself a retired military chaplain, who took command of the artillery at St. Ouen's and sent his bullets into the invading Prince of Nassau in 1779? Her husband is one of those Du Parqs, and he — she — they — we — he — I —"

"Do stop for breath to tell me who *she* may be."

"Uncle Peter's granddaughter, of course, his very onty-donty-own, and she was born Sophia Thoreau, cousin twice removed of Henry Thoreau of Concord; but I care less for the cousinship than I do for the granddaughtership, for she's Uncle Peter's, and his only descendant on the island except her own son, and he says she will come to see me —"

"Who says so? Uncle Peter's granddaughter's son?"

"No, Uncle Peter's granddaughter's husband, descendant of the fighting parson and father of Uncle Peter's great-grandson, who ought to be proud of his ancestry."

In Uncle Peter's letters to his niece Elizabeth Thoreau, published in all biographies of her nephew Henry Thoreau, he speaks of his son Peter, then a lad. The children of this lad are now only two. Of the two, one lives in England; the only one left upon the island is the eldest. The name Thoreau no longer exists in Jersey, where once it was so numerous and so honorable, save upon many gravestones. Uncle Peter's youngest Jersey descendant is thus not a Thoreau, — a clever lad of sixteen, familiar with many American books, curious about America and thoroughly acquainted with his cousin Thoreau's fame and writings.

The Doves found Uncle Peter's granddaughter in such an ugly-visaged house that it were easy to pity her. The street was ugly, dusty, close ; the front door seemed grimly shut without any intention of opening with a welcome. It was not so blunt upon the street as the dove-cote, but might just as well have been for any superiority in the becomingness of amiability.

"In Jersey it is about as silly a thing as one can do to form an opinion of a house from the street side," whispered a Dove as they waited in her sitting-room the coming of Uncle Peter's granddaughter.

For, behold, the marvel was wrought anew that had so amazed the hirers of Dove Cottage, and the house was twice as large as it looked, as toward a smiling sea it turned a smiling face. Between the smiling side of the house and the island's calm edge was a sunny garden, blooming, fragrant, drowsy with the hum of bees, jocund with the songs of birds.

"Jerseymen have become Anglicized at least thus much," said a Dove. "They know how to keep the best for themselves."

Enters Uncle Peter's granddaughter, and grand-niece of the ex-privateersman on Concord Green. But how so young, this daughter of the lad Peter of whom Uncle Peter wrote to America in 1801 as already well-grown? Why so fair, so bright, whose father to-day would have been more than a century old?"

The granddaughter laughs.

"You see," she says, "my father, 'the lad Peter' as you call him, was married three times, the last time at sixty-four with a girl of nineteen. By none of the marriages save the last had he any children. My mother's father and mother were considerably younger than my father. I can remember hearing my grandmother tell of my birth and the white-haired old man flying down the hill to announce the birth of a new Thoreau. I wonder if he was not less delighted later," laughed the low soft voice, "when another was born, and then twins. For we were a lively family and annoyed him with our pranks. The white-haired old man never seemed to us as our young mother seemed, — he wanted quiet and peace; we would not let him have it; being in the majority we had our own way. Although my father was forty-six years older than my mother he out-lived her three or four years, dying in 1867, at seventy-eight years of age. I wish I had asked him all about my grandfather, the Uncle Peter of my American cousins, but I never did. I have heard him speak of a sister, my aunt Betsey, but I never knew that I had American cousins till we learned it by the Henry Thoreau biographies."

The granddaughter has a soft and exquisitely modulated voice. Mrs. Dove ventured to ask if that voice was an island voice, a Thoreau voice, or essentially an individual one. Unsuspecting why the question or the effort to trace a musical genealogy, the wind-sweet voice answered : —

"It must be a Thoreau voice, for my sister's and mine are frequently mistaken one for the other."

"Don't you remember," a Dove was telegraphing to another Dove, with every possible eloquence of wink and blink as the granddaughter busied herself with the teacups, "don't you remember somebody told us that half the charm of Henry Thoreau's poems was the wind-sweet voice in which he read them?"

With calm eyes the other telegraphed back : —

"Of course ! did he not flute to the owls and tree-toads of Walden Pond, seeking unconsciously to find again the long-forgotten music of the wind-swept, sea-cradled island home of his race?"

With the tea came the granddaughter's son, learning now at Victoria college as a foreign language the French that (in its island form) was the mother tongue of his mother's great-grandparents Philippe Thoreau and Marie Le Gallais, just as Henry Thoreau in Harvard College studied as a foreign tongue the language of his great-grandparents Philippe and Marie Le Gallais Thoreau.

"Whenever I see Americans," he says, "I ask them about Henry Thoreau." Then he added, quizzically, "They generally answer, ' Henry Thoreau? who was he?' "

It is a far cry from great-grandparents to great-grandchildren, yet to these Americans Uncle Peter's granddaughter and Henry Thoreau seemed very near akin, just because Philippe and Marie Le Gallais Thoreau, a respectably undistinguished couple who lived, loved, worked, and died so long ago, bore the same ancestral relation to both.

Unlike most youths of sixteen, Uncle Peter's great-grandson has interest in his ancestors on both sides. He regards them, however, synthetically, as those Shades are so often regarded, and distinguishes sinner from saint, dreamer from warrior, firebrand from man of peace, only as "one of them." "One of them" defied the all-powerful De Carterets and gained his suit at law which proved him stuff not to be trodden on. "One of them" cast bullets for Jersey's enemies in the church cellar. "One of them" did *this*, "one of them" did *that*. For to this we all come when our throbbing flesh falls away, our burning hearts are ashes, and in the world of the disembodied we leave the earth of our little raptures and agonies to our children's children's children; we are no more than an ancestral "one of them."

"Don't worry," said the young Dove, whose mission it always seemed to smooth the asperities of the elder's fate. "Don't worry. Do we ever distinguish our great-grandchildren-to-be save as 'one of them'?"

Uncle Peter was born November, 1755, when George the Second was King of England and a sorry representative to Jersey of the proud dukes of Normandy; he died in 1810. It is proof of his faithful family affection that, although he was but seventeen when his brother John sailed away forever into the west, at fifty he was still writing to that brother's children, and sending them a picture of the ancient town in which their father was born. It is evident that the desire to maintain these relations was chiefly on his side, for he complained that his letters remained unanswered. Young people are always more indifferent to such ties than their elders; none of the American Thoreaus realized the value, in more ways than one, of their

Uncle Peter's friendliness. John and Peter Thoreau were of the nine children of Monsieur Philippe Thoreau and Marie Le Gallais, who were married in 1749. Only three of these were sons, but quite sons enough to perpetuate the name, one would think, knowing the perpetuating power of so many original "three brothers" in America. Philippe, the eldest son remained on the island, and his line lingered there till the last son of Maître Thoreau of Grouville emigrated to New Zealand years ago. They were a family speaking always the island language and keeping up the habit of French Christian names, while the John branch and the Peter bore English forms of often the same names. The second son of Philippe and Marie became an American, the third became Uncle Peter, and remained a Jerseyman till he died. He kept up the island habit of naming the first son for the father, the first daughter for the mother. For this reason Jersey genealogies are easy to trace, even if only on tombstones. In America, Jerseyman John Thoreau did the same, and there were three Johns till the last died a bachelor, one of a family of spinsters and bachelors. The eldest daughter of John Thoreau was Jane for her mother, her sister was Marie, or Maria, the name of her Jersey grandmother. Another sister was Sophia Thoreau, as was born Sophia Thoreau, the sweet-voiced lady who smiles over cups of exquisite tea at the Thoreau enthusiasm of these American Doves.

When, in 1801, Uncle Peter wrote to his American relations of his son Peter, their cousin, the lad was about eleven years old, running about St. Helier's in long worsted stockings and knee breeches, and doubtless with ambition for a bobbing queue as long as his father's. He grew up to the family wine trade and during many years had charge of a branch house in London. In 1855 he made his third marriage, with a Jersey girl of nineteen, the very year, perchance even the very day that across the sea Henry Thoreau recorded in his Journal having received for safe keeping from his Aunt Maria the family heirlooms of Uncle Peter's letters. Maria Thoreau and the bridegroom of sixty-four were own cousins, yet we hear of no wedding announcement such as Uncle Peter would have been sure to send; and although these letters were for " safe keeping," they did not prompt to any renewal of Thoreau ties. The American Thoreaus were insular, even with their continental admixture of blood and their continental birth.

The granddaughter showed the Doves portraits of her father the lad Peter, a quaint little old gentleman, swallow-tailed and brass-buttoned and seeming long generations away from his daughter Sophia. " One of them " he seemed and scarcely more ; very much more and merely " one of them," than eighteenth-century Philippe or Marie seemed.

" Moral," telegraphed a Dove, " unless you want to be merely 'one of them' to your own children, don't marry at sixty-four."

" We won't ! " telegraphed chorus.

The Americans sought long for the graves of Philippe and Marie Thoreau and faithful Uncle Peter their son. Beside the latter, one at least of the Americans wished to kneel in the soft grass amid the æolian music of sunny Jersey, and thank his shade for the faithful kindness of his life. They never found those graves, though many a stately stone bears the name of Thoreau, even of Philippes, Maries, and Peters. Uncle Peter was buried near his father and mother in the parish churchyard of St. Helier's. Thirty or forty years ago it was found necessary to widen the road outside the churchyard, and thus to encroach upon a space of graves in which slept many Thoreaus. The ashes of Philippe and Marie with several of their children, including Peter, were carefully removed, but as the inscriptions upon their tombstones had perished, it is now unknown where their bones were laid.

Opposite the churchyard still stands the decrepit house from which Philippe and Marie Thoreau were buried in 1800 and 1801, in which Philippe, John, and Peter, with their sisters, Mary, Ann, Elizabeth, Jeanne, Susan, and Catherine Thoreau were born. From that house John Thoreau departed, having but a few steps to go to reach the water over which he would never come back again, in 1773, when George the Third was King of Jersey and eke of Concord Green. It is a prison-like square house, of some pretensions in its day but now a ghost of its former self. It went with the Philippe branch of Thoreaus, and some years ago was sold out of the family by the last male of the island line, the one last heard of in New Zealand where he is said to have a large family. The old house is in process of restoration for purposes entirely unconnected with the wine trade, and is regardless of ghosts, even Uncle Peter's.

"The Philippe Thoreaus?" said the granddaughter; "yes, I dimly remember being taken out there to tea as a child. I should have known more about them had my father not died while we were still so young."

"Don't you know," almost gasped one of the ancestor-worshipping Doves, "don't you know that Maître Thoreau was great-grandson of your great-great-grandparents? Don't you know that he was always an old-school Jerseyman and never spoke English when he could avoid it? Don't you know that he was a gentleman farmer at Grouville and church-warden, till he shocked everybody by becoming converted and joining the dissenters; that he married two wives and took a fatal cold while collecting the census?"

Uncle Peter's descendant's answer was rippling music.

"Only you Americans find out so much more about us than we know," said the granddaughter.

GARRISON SERVICE.

THE regiment in garrison at Fort Regent is a Yorkshire one, mostly north-of-England men, with the north-of-England *burr*, so different from the London and south-of-England accents. Wordsworth was a north-of-England man, and he made no bones of rhyming " girl " with " squirrel," thus leaving proof to generations after him that he pronounced " girl " *guirrel*, or " squirrel " *squirl*.

This garrison service is open to all who choose to attend it. Many do so choose because of the music ; it comes immediately after a service entirely in French. Those upon the island who do not speak both languages are very few, and every church of the twelve parishes has at least one French service every Sunday.

In some of the back parishes the knowledge of English is almost scanty, and the Doves noticed that some of the rectors used a form of English, considerably corrupted by French. As one of the rectors once said, " We speak both languages badly, but we prefer to abuse the French."

All of these rectors are Jerseymen by birth ; no other can hold a benefice on the island. They are English university men ; some even have had English parishes. Yet so delicate a thing is language, so subtle its tempters, and so hidden its pitfalls, that even these educated men by no means keep theirs pure and undefiled. In the lower classes it is much worse, and some speak a motley French patched with much English, some ragged English patched with French. Jersey-French even of the upper classes, everybody knows not to be French-French. For even though the words are perfect French, the idioms are not, and the construction of sentences continually suggests English.

The Parish Church of St. Helier's was built a century before we were even "discovered." In 1341 it stood here just where a church has stood ever since. In the old times it was a Norman church, and continued under the ecclesiastical jurisdiction of a French Bishop long after the civil authority of the island was English.

Now the Channel Islands are a part of the diocese of Winchester. The late Bishop was suspected of resenting that fact, and the necessity of crossing the dreadful channel occasionally to look after this part of his flock. He appeared to consider his Channel Island lambs something neither fish, flesh, nor fowl, and greeted every child with, " *Parley voo Fransy ?* " — a question to take the child's breath away ; as if a Boston boy were asked, " Can you speak English? " This good Bishop always scolded very much because the churches were not warm enough for him, always ate good dinners, and, at least, once upon a time asked that he might be allowed to sup before meeting the invited guests. Immediately after supping, the good Shepherd of Souls and Vicar of Christ felt quite unable to meet the invited company and retired to bed.

Before the Reformation, 1565, this church and others possessed the right of Sanctuary. Directly from the gate by which we enter the churchyard, a road twenty-four feet wide led straight to the sea and by it the offender must either leave the island or give himself up to the legal authorities. The church did not thus give immunity to crime, but protection against the oppressions of feudal lords. The descendants of both feudal lords and oppressed, still bearing ancestral names, now sit side by side in the church.

The present church has a low Norman tower, and the roof is upheld by Norman pillars ; otherwise it has no air of antiquity.

From the gallery the Doves looked down upon what at first sight seems a solid red carpet. These are red-coats, still the same as when a hundred years ago the term " red-coat," expressed unspeakable hatred to a people across the sea. We notice how unbecoming the red is to those sandy-haired high colored Englishmen, many of them mere boys with still the rustic bloom upon them of Yorkshire farms and hamlets. In blue or gray they would look another race of men, refined simply by a change of dye. Now they have a hot and angry appearance, and one regarding them (who chances not to be English), is reminded more of steaming lobsters than of iron sons of Mars. They seem somewhat restless, and have the usual British soldier air of being exceedingly well groomed and oiled. At the listlessness we do not wonder when the stately rector sits him down.

Beside the altar, the regimental band takes the organ's part. The bandmen are lavishly decorated with white braid, on red coats, and have fringed shoulder caps precisely like women's. To eyes not English, especially eyes remembering the simple dignity of American uniforms, as well as the Italian which is somewhat like it, these red and white popinjays tempt to a shooting out of the lips. Certain Americans that day regarded them from seats of the scornful. Any proposition to change the dress of the English soldier, so associated with England's glory, would rock the British empire to its foundations no doubt. But could there possibly be a martial thrill the less for a few thousand leagues the less of this white-popinjay trimming?

The responses are feeble. The prayer for the Queen receives fewer than that for the Princess of Wales, whose gentleness and heart-break over her poor weakling son have ever since drawn her to the hearts of the islanders. A volume of sound was expected from this churchful of throaty Englishmen, but Tommy Atkins comes to church only because he is led lamblike to the slaughter of his preferences. Much rather would he roam the streets of St. Helier's with a silly round cap over one red ear, the ideal of dashing and heroic beauty to nurses and parlor maids.

The sermon, — was it one? It certainly was delivered in a preachy tone, by the dark, Frenchy-looking young curate with a French name, who, by the way, repeatedly used *as* in the place of *so* and *that* in precisely the manner so reprobated in Americans by James Russell Lowell. The Thing had a text (or at least one was given out), and it had " firstly," " secondly," "thirdly," and " finally." But it had no head, so far as the finite understanding could see, no middle, and no end, though it came to a close in due course. Well may poor Tommy Atkins seem listless. To sit within sound of this and its like fifty times a year is enough to reduce any man to gibbering idiocy who really listens. It is a written Thing, and it treated of pain, toil, humility, patience. It viewed all these, not from the spiritual side, or rather did not view them at all, but boyishly mouthed the views of the aristocratic and conventional Established Church.

Pain, toil, humility, patience, are the duty of Tommy Atkins, and he must not forget that he and his low-born hordes are put here to toil and suffer for the high reward of achieving humility and patience. Christ was a dumb carpenter for thirty years, but he was Christ all the same, and would have been even had his tongue never been loosened.

The natty little curate gave Tommy a thoroughly Class-Thing. A bicyclist speeding through the church could have seen that, and that the carpenter ideal — not the divine, not celestial thought and heaven-aspiring endeavor — was for red-coats, but pain, toil, humility, patience. "God hath himself appointed that many shall work for a living, as Christ himself set an example," saith the Preacher, while in seats of the scornful certain Americans scoffed that it be deemed Christlike, that it even be "working for a living" to take the Queen's shilling, to be garbed like a boiled lobster, and to loll uselessly about the streets of Peace, or else go forth to kill and be killed.

When they came out of church the red-coats were forming into rank in the square, whence they strode fortwards to notes of fife and drum.

Even before those notes died away others were heard. Those notes were not music, but they made a vigorous and stirring noise. Soul and body went to blowing and pounding; zeal and strength of purpose were behind them. Worn-out thoughts, dead conventions never made so much clamor, and the Doves wondered if after all poor lowly Tommy Atkins might not be better reached by loud and lowly Salvationists than by High-Churchism, condescending from Heaven only knows how many classes above him.

Another time, another curate. What could poor Tommy think, if he thought at all, of two such antipodean views of his duty?

This curate's name is thoroughly English. He is not a man to resign his curacy in a miff were young ladies of the parish to sing Gilbert and Sullivan curate songs at him with deep expression. Rather would he sing back at them.

Evidently the Reverend Mr. Stott intends to meet Tommy on Tommy's own level. Hence his Tommyatkinsesque style of language. He intends to be practical and hopes no " blagguds " are among the men and also hopes they tell no " tarradiddles." " The man is a duffer who don't try to get at the top," although only a Sunday or two ago he must stay where God placed him, remembering that his toil and humility are God's will. " Sin is no fluke," the Jerseyman with an English name tells them, and they must " stuff themselves with truth as we stuff our shoes with shapes, — not stuff ourselves as the anaconda does, who stuffs and sleeps."

The whole burden was, Get up, get on; have your nets out for draughts of fishes; if you are a stupid Tommy Atkins, make up your mind that you must work a heap harder than your friend Tommy who is less of a dunce, etc., etc.

Is such a difference in views the difference between a Jerseyman with a French face and name and a Jerseyman with an English name and face? the Doves wondered.

The responses were all led by the band, which band also punctuated the prayers by blowing saliva from out its trumpets. The services ended by Saving the Queen, who is Duchess of Normandy.

IN THE JERSEY "STATES."

DAYLIGHT comes dimly through windows of stained glass ; a single torch burns from the roof. Under an oaken canopy are two sculptured thrones, one of lesser height and evidently of smaller dignity than the other. Before the two thrones stands the royal mace, presented to this august company, or rather to an ancestral company, by Charles II., of England. The floor of the handsome chamber is well filled with about fifty men. None of them are quite young men; gray heads and bald predominate, as they always do among the Solons of nations, little and great. From the gallery one hears an unfamiliar roll-call. Not only strange names, but stranger titles. "Jurat de Quetteville," "Connétable de St. Helier's," has no English sound ; neither has the breathless gabble with which the nervously brisk *greffier* recites the conventional form of excuse for absentees. It is not English, and keenly interested working-men discuss the proceedings in whispers that are not English.

Were yon roof vaulted, instead of cumbrously flat and heavy with renaissance ornament, were that burning torch not palpably gas, we might almost persuade ourselves that this is a Norman council hall, and we looking down upon lieges doing homage to a feudal lord.

Yet no ! For even while we listen and while amid the names of many *connétables*, we half wait for that of the Breton Duguesclin, Connétable of France, we catch a sound of later days and of a later spirit in the roll-call for "*Député de ceci*," "*Député de cela*." What have feudal days and baronial halls to do with deputies, or deputies with them ?

In reality the scene is a *séance* of the Jersey "*États*," or " States ; " and these fifty men are the august legislators of the little island nation in the English Channel, which has " Home Rule " in the largest sense, with no representation at Westminster, and preserves to this day strong traces in laws and lawmaking of its Norman origin.

" Jerseymen first, Englishmen afterward," these Channel Islanders invariably declare themselves. Yet they are English in daily speech and habit, thoroughly English in loyalty, and with even more than the Englishman's inveterate and ineradicable feeling of superiority to all Frenchmen.

The Jersey "*États*," or " States," are represented by twelve jurats (from *jurat, jurez*, comes our " jury "), one for each of the twelve parishes of the island, and chosen for life ; the *connétable*, or mayor, of each parish, a deputy for each and three for the capital, St. Helier's, and the twelve rectors.

Deputies and *connétables* are elected for three years, rectors sit as long as they hold their benefices. Two Crown officers, attorney-general and solicitor-general, are also in their seats, where they may speak but may not vote ; the president, or *bailli*, occupies the higher of the two thrones, the lower empty in the absence of the governor. This latter officer has no vote, yet has the right of veto. Both governor and the bailli, Sir George Bertram, hold office from the Crown.

The governor's is an English office ; the bailli, or bailiff, is the ancient title and office descended from Norman time. He still swears, on taking office : " *Faire droit au peuple, baillant et déli-vrant à chacun bonne et brière justice, au petit comme au grand, au riche comme au pauvre, sans exception de personne,*" etc.

The bailli is also chief judge in the Royal Court. The viscount, or sheriff, has a seat but no vote, neither can he speak without special permission. All matters discussed in the "States" are only "*projets de loi*" till they receive the royal assent, although as provisional enactments they are valid for three years. The "States" have no real con-stitution ; only an antiquated tangle of inherited laws, traditional precedents, and modern amend-ments. Yet so attached to "things as they always have been" are the Jersiais that the brilliant Attorney-General has lately brought no end of hornets about his ears by simply stating the truth, that the island has not, and never has had, what it needs, a constitution. Reforms move slowly, like the solemn stars, on this soft, sunny isle ; and only within three years have the more hasting and less resting of the workers secured the secret ballot.

Upon the left of the throne sit the jurats, as a body the baldest, grayest, most draught-avoiding and becapped of the Assembly. On the right are the rectors, younger, and headed by the Dean of Jersey, who, however, sits here only as the Rector of St. Helier's. The rectors are English in appearance, though all are "Jerseymen first." The Established Church puts its stamp upon its priests quite as much as does Rome. They are all university men; some have had English parishes, many have English wives. They are really the most English section of the "States," although their English speech sometimes is decidedly *jersiais*.

Among jurats, *connétables*, *députés*, are some faces as un-English as if the island had never been riven from France. Yonder sits a seigneur and jurat busy with penknife and finger-tips. He wears a gray business suit and sits quite in American fashion. Even thus he might be a mailed knight of eight centuries ago, jousting and tilting with those who became his ancestors, for his very face and figure we have seen upon scores of Norman tombs.

Among the deputies asleep on the back seats are several that one almost remembers to have bargained with in the markets of Normandy, and a *connétable* or two in conspicuously English clothes (or capital imitations) are brothers of excursionists over from France for the day.

What more interesting to us Americans than the bill presented now by the Rector of Grouville, and which he presents, he says, "*en tremblant*," though we see no sign of it. This rector is known as the "States' Jester," and wears his cap and bells with many a witty and sarcastic fling.

The *séance* is dignified, yet not formal, and order is fully maintained by the five fingers of the bailli tapping upon his desk. Informality is natural in so small a chamber, with men who have known of each other from the cradle ; one cannot but remember the gavel banged to death so often in our own Congress, as well as the spectacle of the President of the French Chambers pumping madly at his bell and failing to pump therefrom silence.

The bill asks the *optional* substitution of English for the French, to-day, as always, *de rigueur* in the "States"; that is, that each speaker may choose in which language to speak. The Rector has read in the paper, he says, that the newly elected Jurat Lemprière, son of the Seigneur of Rozel (and of the Classical Dictionary family), has declared himself in favor of English in the " States " ; so the Rector prepared the bill that (Monday) morning.

At this several voices shout : *" Hier ! hier !"*

In no wise disconcerted by this insinuation of Sunday work, the Rector argues his point, that the legislative language of the island is not the language of the people represented by that Legislature ; that the use of it obliged everybody to learn two languages whether he would or no ; all legal papers, bonds, contracts, deeds, etc., continuing not the nineteenth-century language of the island, not even the eleventh-century language, but a language mixed and compounded of them and others, — neither Norman-French, French-French nor English.

" Why compel a plain farmer of Grouville to learn two languages, each imperfectly ? " asks the Rector, dramatically, then answers : " Because he must build his barn in English but must not sell it so ! "

The Deputy of St. Martin's follows with, *" Je seconde ; "* and we smile. For this was instant proof of one of the Grouville rector's assertions.

Not "*Je seconde,*" but "*J'appuie,*" the deputy would have said, had he spoken "French-French" and not Jersey French. As little Norman, or "French-French" was also the round and robust, "Hear! hear!" bursting forth every now and then.

Another speaker hoped "the States" would make the bill a *projet de loi,* and assured them that if they refused to do so the press of England would take the matter up and give an offensive publicity to the fact that the English language had been rejected by the Jersey "States." Neither was it by rejecting such a bill that the "States" would conciliate those Jersiais who clamored for reforms, etc. Only one or two of the speakers, so far, has spoken what could honestly be considered good French. The accent is not Continental, even when the grammar is and the words are. The greater the facility, where all were facile, the more apparent that the cadences, intonations, the whole "swing" of the sentences are insular when not actually British. But now the stately Dean arises — the stern-faced, dignified Dean, who so rarely smiles, and then as if it hurt him, — and small wonder, since his name is *Baleine.*

The Dean thinks the question serious. He is confident (in full-mouthed accents of Britain) that the "States" are not *en touche* with the islanders, who are so prompt to throw discredit upon the Assembly.

"The people do not consider the 'States' as representative," reiterated the Dean. "Last year the 'States' passed a resolution that Jerseymen were proud that French was their legislative language! Could anything be more ridiculous, or contrary to fact?"

"Hear! hear!" he was answered.

Dean Baleine (or Whale) speaks French with massive deliberation. His subjunctives roll forth as if to organ music. Sometimes, although rarely, he recalls those subjunctives and corrects them. The wildest, maddest, merriest listener could never mistake that French for his mother-tongue, nor yet the tongue of his father; yet Dean Baleine is a native of Jersey, as all Jersey deans and legislators must be. He never would have said "*en touche*," meaning *en rapport*, but for his Oxford education and long ministry in a Yorkshire parish. His French would have been less of a perfect accomplishment than it is, and more a gift of circumstance.

Somebody argues for the bill that it is unjust to "Queen Victoria" to compel her to read all State matters of the island in a foreign tongue. This draws the attention of our gallery to the fact that these islanders are indeed Jerseymen before they are English; for no Englishman ever names "Queen Victoria," but always "The Queen." The rectors only never fail to speak of *Sa Majesté*, and the natty Attorney-General, who looks like a very much refined and younger Sir William Vernon Harcourt, and whose name is William Venables Harcourt Vernon. Yet even the rectors speak of "*la presse anglaise*" as of a foreign one, as they might name *la presse française;* and everybody speaks of the "Government of England" and not the "Home Government."

The Connétable of St. Helier's rises to speak. This connétable, mayor of the capital of the island, is a very important personage, and evidently never forgets that fact. He speaks against the bill, and no wonder; for his French is as rapid and rushing as Niagara, his accent perfect, his "swing" entirely Continental, though his entirely French name has been Jersiais for generations. At what disadvantage *he* would be with a change of languages, one who runs needs not stop to read. This chief connétable of the island is *bon bourgeois*. In port and mien he reminds one of Gambetta. Even his raiment is not English, though ten paces away the Attorney-General sets him a pattern of lavender trousers, buttonhole bouquet, and Bond Street tailoring. Thousands who might be the Connétable's brothers trot the dusky streets of provincial France, knowing no more of the language of Perfidious Albion than "English Spoken Here." He has a French wife, never speaks English when French will do as well, and he gesticulates as Frenchmen do. At this moment he agrees with the Dean that the people are not "*en touche*" with the "States" (he twinkles mischievously at the Briticism); but that want of touch is not the contest of languages, but the wish of the people to expel the clergy from the "States."

Thereupon the Dean, who with all his dignity, culture, and commanding position and presence, is a remarkably diffident man, starts, actually blushes, and exclaims, "Exactly!"

The Connétable hopes the "States" will reject the proposition till the people themselves ask the change.

To the onlookers it seems strange that no allusion is made to the dignity and picturesqueness of antique habit in this matter. Nobody names Duke William, or the later ducal kings, whose fortunes carried the Channel Islands to and fro between two nations without even changing their language. Nobody repeats the common Channel Island boast, " *We* conquered England, not England *us !*" Nobody referred to the fact that the sovereigns of England rule here as Norman dukes. Nobody appeared to think of the Great Past at all save some New-Worlders in the gallery, who, without any great past of their own, are much addicted to that of other peoples. Nobody seemed to look at the question at all otherwise than with prosaic and utilitarian or prejudiced eye.

A hayseed legislature of regions wild and woolly could be no more matter of fact.

The motion was lost by 21 to 12 votes. Of the eight rectors present three voted for the bill, three voted against it in spite of their deliciously British accent and costumes, and two abstained from voting. The Norman knight also refrained from voting, although him alone certain galleryites wished to see voting for English. For this Norman knight is of the famous family to whom Charles II. on his restoration gave a grant of land in North America. That land was named *New* Jersey, and upon it were settled some 300 poor people sent to make their fortunes there from this right little, tight little Jersey of old. Our present Norman knight is a direct descendant of the Jersey De Carterets. The name ended with the direct male line two generations ago, but our Norman knight coming into possession of the original De Carteret seigniory of St. Ouen's, through the female heirs, assumed the family name and transmits it to sons. He lives more in London and on the Continent than upon his Jersey estate, is a London clubman, a famous yachtsman, and withal the living portrait of men who bore shields and the leopards of Normandy into many a fight and foray.

SARK.

"BANK-holiday 'five-pounders!' 'week-enders!'" Mr. Dove expostulated.

"Never mind ! *We* have been 'five-pounders' and 'week-enders' ourselves before now, and harmed nobody. We can come back if at the pier we find the company of the usual London bank-holiday quality," argued Mrs. Dove.

He was afraid, being a man. She was not afraid, being a woman. He was afraid that some of the wild young London clerks, off upon their Easter holiday with from Friday to Monday's cheap excursion tickets and five pounds to spend in three days, might make themselves too manifest on this excursion to Sark. Jersey was to-day over-run with them ; he begged Mrs. Dove to choose some other day.

"Steamers not running on other days," she pointed out to him, " we should be obliged to take one of the large English packets to Guernsey and remain there over two or three nights for the weekly steamer to Sark. We cannot afford the time."

"Bank-holiday 'five-pounders !' 'week-enders !'" he repeated disconsolately, having a thoroughly masculine yearning for the last word.

The small Commerce had very little holiday air, bank or other, when they reached the pier.

Not more than a dozen people were standing about with shawls and overcoats, and they were not (ostentatiously at least) English "week-enders." Some of them were undeniably French, others of the different Channel Islands; only two betrayed themselves as English by guide-books and lively discussion of the "National Budget." In time others came, none of bank-holiday aspect (at least London bank-holiday), and by nine o'clock the Commerce, without levity or unnecessary bustle, took up its joyless way.

Joyless? — and a holiday excursion? Strange but true; for the slow Commerce must cut her way to Sark on the bias, and the English Channel cut on the bias is something to make the whole animal kingdom joyless from molecule to man. Nor is it altogether of algebraic certainty, that passage. Many a harrowing tale doleful tongues had recounted to the Doves, of excursion parties turned to abominations of desolation between these islands, overtaken by fog or met by sudden tempest, and rolling upon sickening billows without food for hours upon hours, even unto twenty-four. One party starved two days so near land that they heard cocks crow and dogs bark, but the steamer must not move in the darkness lest it strike a fatal rock.

Fortunately it was not a bad passage, although not one of the twenty-five passengers could make up their minds to that effect, the ever-cheerful Doves excepted. In considerably less than three hours the lazy Commerce was within the mountain shadow of Sark. Then came the first realization that this was a general holiday, even though "banks" were almost the last thing to think of in the midst of this vividly picturesque commotion. Two other steamers were already landing excursionists from Guernsey in small boats; bright holiday attire flashed across the shadow of boats, steamers, and island rock; the bright water flashed in spaces; people called to each other in French, English, Jersiais, Sarkais. The Doves whispered in American : —

"Did we ever see anything so foreign in all our days?"

Who could dream that Britannia rules these waves? Who dream that these lithe, swart boatmen jabbering beside the Commerce in an unknown tongue with gestures utterly unbritannic sometimes claim to be "Angleeshman." Yet on this feudal rock left behind from the Middle Ages, Queen Victoria is Sovereign Lady as much as she is anywhere outside the three chief islands.

Were her Majesty to visit Sark, the little island of her many-island empire which keeps most to its ancient ways, she would seem much more of a foreigner than President Faure, for instance. In all these islands the close neighborhood of modern France is distinctly evident; one never gets away from it even when the shimmering coast is out of sight. Whole streets in Jersey are French. French servants are in many families; French workmen are at command; even the English of the common people has a French construction of phrase and sentence. It is really France, nineteenth-century France, only a couple of hours distant, that one feels in the other islands. In Sark it is France of ages ago, the ancient Normandy which was still antique Normandy when some of its families were transplanted from Jersey to Sark three centuries ago. The Channel Islands were not mere sea-girt rocks belonging to Normandy. They *were* Normandy, a large portion of maritime Normandy, and their inhabitants ancient Normans with continental possessions as well as insular. No change whatever came upon them, their character, laws, and manners, by their Duke's conquest of England. They had nothing whatever in common with England, and looked upon Britain as a conquering race looks upon the conquered.

Somehow and strangely the scene reminded the Doves of their first landing on Capri. There was quite as vivid an impression of remoteness from their natural habitat, the clamor was quite as dramatic and unintelligible, the boatmen were as picturesque as those Mediterranean Raphaels, Giuseppes, and Paolos. Yet they knew without touching it that the deeply blue water had a tang and a bite unknown to the volcanic, but no bluer Neapolitan Bay. They know that these jabberers can all speak a sort of English if they choose ; there are no girls in the boats ; above their heads, unsoftened by fig, olive, and vines, unsoftened by anything, rises a sheer wall of rock three hundred feet in the air, to cast a cold shadow over and far beyond the Commerce, the shadow of Sark.

Only the rock-dwellers themselves, Frenchmen and perhaps a quarter of the other islanders of the Archipelago speak of the rock nowadays as, "Cerq," as all who knew of it did once. To Englishmen and to Americans, strollers like those Doves into by-ways of travel, it is the Island of Sark.

Sark is one of the wonders of Europe, and its multitudinous caverns teeming with animal life make it one of the wonders of the world. It is a granite rock in the sea, against which the surges beat and bellow forever, tearing it into the strangest, most grotesque forms, rending into caverns and tunnels, gnawing it into gothic pinnacles and spires, tearing it asunder bit by bit. In the sunniest day these inaccessible ocean-caves and monstrous fissures echo the eternal chant of the sea; in storms the surges almost become silent from infinite power of rage. All about the rock are deep bays and caverns between masses of towering granite, and invisible except from the sea. These were long a favorite haunt of pirates and smugglers, whose cavernous treasures the tides hid. Elsewhere the sea has pierced fissures under natural bridges; even the interior of the island is lined with gorges and ravines. Some do not run down to the sea, but terminate in precipitous cliffs. Upon towering Sark, sometimes called "Dizzy Island," the stranger feels that beneath him is a dusky, mysterious world, haunted by strange histories and . romantic tragedies, — a world of mystery hidden from the most daring climber, the most experienced boatman.

Scores of skeletons from ages long gone may even yet be whitening there, hid forever from the disintegrating light of day. Skeletons of fighting monks hurled from their sanctuary, skeletons of knights in armor, of corsair and smuggler and pretty maids stolen from convents and school, seem to the stranger even yet to be smiling the same sneering awful smile that all the living world carries under its masks. The strangers in this connection are very likely to remember what is usually spoken of as the Tragedy of the Mother-in-Law.

A young English couple with the bride's mother, one blowy day sixty years ago when both sea and sky were of ominous aspect and the Sark boatmen of evil prophecy, wished to return to Guernsey in the small open gig in which they came to Cerq the day before. Everybody tried to persuade them not to tempt fate, but if they must go that day at least to take passage in the large island cutter which was about to leave for Guernsey. The young couple might have been persuaded but for the wife's mother, who insisted upon the needless expense of a cutter passage, when their gig return was already paid. She prevailed and the tiny open boat put out. In a very few minutes it entered one of the terrible currents that sweep among the rocks and almost instantly capsized. The two sailors and the husband were carried out to sea and seen no more; the ladies floated for awhile on the current with desperate cries, but sank before boats could reach them. The bodies were never recovered nor any trace of the ill-fated boat.

A part of the story is grewsome. The following year a Sark fisherman discovered in the stomach of a large conger caught in the very current where the gig capsized the ivory handle of a parasol which belonged to one of the ladies.

The Sarkais themselves, numbering about 575, seem only a lively sort of linnet clinging stubbornly, unimaginatively, to their 1274 acres, their islet three miles and a half long by one and a half wide.

"You never shall understand it," a Jersey-man was saying, "try as you may. Among islanders who neither read nor wrote it the mediæval Norman-French has come to be this lingo, unintelligible everywhere on the globe except on Sark and its master isle Guernsey, eight miles distant. Neither Jersey nor Alderney can understand it; although it came from France, by the way of Jersey, a Frenchman can make no more of it than you can. These boatmen give orders for sailing and trimming their boats with the same nautical terms, it is said, used by French sailors in the time of Louis XIV."

The Americans try to imagine the fate of their mother-tongue, unwritten, unread, and exiled for centuries on an island in the Gulf of Mexico. No wonder the Sark patois became *sui generis* when their island is so absolutely inaccessible. Once upon a time the Lords of the English Admiralty were out upon a tour of inspection. They had given no notice of their coming, so there was no preparation on Sark to receive them. They cruised about till they were tired of trying to find a harbor and finally steamed away having found none.

The Doves alighted in the boat of one named Pierre. He had every appearance of a Norman fisherman, or rather Breton of the olden time. He wore almost precisely the costume those continental fishermen have much discarded for hats and caps bought in town. Pierre wore the *tricot* or knit jacket known in America as a "Guernsey" or "Jersey." His young face was bronzed and covered with heavy wrinkles, his head was covered by a scarlet cap with long tasselled end floating upon his shoulder, — exactly the costume of Gilliat in Victor Hugo's "Travailleurs de la Mer." Pierre's vocabulary, in anything comprehensible to the Americans, was evidently limited. He told them he could not give them change for the half-crown they offered him, for he had but "one cheelang." Thereupon they spoke to him in French and he answered, not in patois, but in queer French, although better than his English. But when he finds that they can make the change regardless of his shilling and give him his exact fare, he speaks no more in any language whatever.

The tiny pier is crowded with women and girls watching the arrivals. Alas and alackaday! Here the more sensitive adaptability of women to varying conditions proves itself yet once again. Though Thrones totter, Principalities and Powers reel, the Sarkais never dreams of doffing his tricot or (once adopted) quitting his flaming head-stocking. Let but a single visitor come in a city frock and in a week the younger Sarkaises will have developed something more or less like it. The display as the Doves walked the length of the little pier suggested that last summer's departures had unanimously left their hats behind them, especially when they recognized Oxford College colors on the bands.

Alas, too! and alackaday! for the self-consciousness of feminine adaptability sitting upon walls of masonry at the base of a feudal rock in the sea, and meeting the gaze of arrivals from the modern world, — that smirking self-consciousness, so different from the adorable *abandon* of russet-cheeked Léon, Pierre, Henri, and Jean. "Look at us!" it cried without speaking a word. "And observe your error if you imagine we are only dairy-maids of Sark. Don't we go every week to the Market at Guernsey, and can we not trade our garden vegetables in that metropolis of fashion, Peter Port, for milliners' roses and poppies gone only a bit to seed?"

From the pier and the ragged feet of the rock they passed through a grotto littered with wheel-barrows, nets, and tackle. But for that grotto, which is no grotto at all but an artificial tunnel, they would be obliged to soar aloft and scale the sheer rock like geese in baskets. Even so late as 1866, when a new seigneur built the present harbor to enable arrivals to land less often upon their heads, there was not so much as a cart road upon the island, everything was carried to the top on men's backs or clumsy sledges. The manor was then a dilapidated farmhouse, the lord, very much of a rustic.

One of the two tunnels through the island's outer wall is as old as the Sarkais themselves, having been built by the first lord, Helier de Carteret, to whom after the monks had aban-doned and the pirates been driven away from "Cerq," Queen Elizabeth gave the seigneurial rights in 1563, and who came over from Jersey with forty families and lived with his young wife in a thatched "manor house" of mud and stones. They brought the Jersey Norman-French with them, now the unintelligible patois of Sark.

This first seigneur was of the De Carterets, to one of whom, Sir George de Carteret, Charles the Second afterwards gave territory in North America to be called New Jersey.

"Shall we never reach the top?" panted the

lady, climbing, ever climbing, this almost perpen-
dicular gully between solid earth-walls, said by
guide-books (and guide-books cannot tell a lie)
to be a "charming valley," but which valley
might be one of Upas or Deadly Nightshade for
aught they knew.

Surely there will be an end to the torrid toil in
time. "All things end that begin, do they not?"
they said, "even deep gullies on small islands."
That day they doubted it.

But though there was no End, there was surely
a Beyond, for high above their heads they heard
the island jargon tossed from height to height;
and for those echoing heights, that aerial Beyond,
they strove.

In a glorious, a triumphant instant they emerged
from that Valley not of Shadow. They stood
rejoicing upon a pleasant table-land waving with
green and gold, veined with shadow-vaulted lanes,
and streaked with fair roads, in the very centre
of which towered aloft, a far-away landmark, a
mighty Bishop with white, lawny arms extended
in benediction, Bishop Windmill grinding the corn
of the islanders at the seigneur's expense.

Round all was the divine, the infinite sea.
They were almost lifted from their feet by the
sudden glory of the revelation, and by the thrilling breath of windy uplands catching them in
godlike embrace and lifting them from heaviness
it seemed forever. No wonder limp Jerseymen
come here to be "braced." They were not
cool. Nevertheless nothing is more certain than
that they would have turned the very coldest of
shoulders to whoever had dared hint that that
vergeless Radiance, that dazzling mystery of tragic

depths over which the creature crawls like a
mite, was only the trafficking English Channel,
scratched by dingy tugs, rumpled by peddling
tramps, smutted by colliers, its verge only twenty-
four miles away. In the distance sleeping Jersey
floats, and nearer sleeping Guernsey. "It cannot
be the Jersey where we this very day were reft
from our breakfast by screams of the fussing
Commerce. Nay, it is a poet's dream, a Lotus
Isle of haunting memories and music, a Slumber
Land of divine phantoms; perish the thought
that it is at this moment the Jersey of noontide dish-waters and greasy bones," declaimed
a Dove.

"St. Peter's dome!" said the other irrelevantly.
At least so it would have seemed to any but that
Dove-cote pair. They knew differently. Years
before, all one long winter in Rome their palace
windows took in a dream of distant Tivoli. The
days were often cold in Rome, and through the
piazza a bitter wind sometimes swept, or rain fell
in cold sheets. All that winter Tivoli was a
dream city upon a slumbrous hill, a city of nebulous spires and roofs, shifting, floating, visionary,
a mystery of unearthly loveliness, haunting the
horizon, to fill the soul with a very rapture of
longing. Then the time came that they left
Rome behind them and crossed the campagna
to Tivoli. Through filthy streets, amid beggars
whose like was on a thousand easels, they managed to get to their *appartamento.* It had been
reported to them clean, it was not; and clouds
hung low, and foul smells rose high upon Tivoli.
The lady stepped upon the loggia and for a
moment was silent. Then a peculiar sound drew

the other to her side. And thus together they
saw, deep in the enchantment of distance a golden
star blazing in the heart of a filmy cloud, a dream
city with nebulous spires and roofs, a very Celestial City to fill a soul with rapture of longing.

"I would reach it though upon hot ploughshares," she murmured.

"No! Rather should it remain a dream forever," said the wiser one. "What fools these
mortals be to pluck the heart from every poetic
mystery! 'What is Man? When he's before the
Altona Gate he wants to be in Italy, and when
he's in Italy he wants to be back before the
Altona Gate.'"

Cerq was known to Rabelais in 1540. Panurge
speak of it and its neighbor Herm as *Terres des
voleurs et larrons*, and its inhabitants as worse than
cannibals. Its inaccessibility, its numerous caverns
and deep low-tide harbors hidden entirely at high
tide made it of greatest service to lawless sea-
rangers of every sort. Even now the very sight
of its romantic architecture almost intoxicated one
of these innocent Doves with fierce yearnings to
go and be a pirate too.

"Away with fan and parasol! Avast there,
bottines de Pinet and *gants de Dent!* Avaunt
Bond Street tailoring and complexion of Oxford
cloisters! Away! Away! Away! And Ho,
Minions! Unto us slim rapiers, burly cutlasses
and scimitars of flame! Let us swear dashing
oaths, Love. Let us swagger with magnificent im-
precation and wear thing-um-bobs of velvet and
what's-names of leather to our knees! Let us
be Bold and Bad, Love, Boldest and Baddest of
Buccaneers!"

"The Seigneur would soon clap you into jail!" he answered, and both laughed.

They had heard of that jail. Once upon a time a vagabond Sarkaise was committed to jail for a term of twenty-four hours. Finding herself somewhat ennuied she complained to the constables that it was impossible for her to breathe with the door shut. The constables appreciated her difficulty, allowed the door to remain open and the prisoner's gossips to bring their knitting and to squat on the threshold. Once upon another time the bailiff and jurats (from *jurat* our word "jury"), over officially from Guernsey, were met by the Cerq prévôt with bitter complaint that he had to keep the prisoners at his own cost. The authorities asked how many prisoners he had had that year. "Eh mais," was the answer, "none this year." "How many last year?" "One." "How many the year before?" "Well, I cannot tell; I am only prévôt since two years."

The most dashing history connected with Sark is of the first years of the thirteenth century and Wistace le Moigne, or Eustace the Monk, who, after a wild and romantic career on land and sea was killed in a naval battle 1217. There were two brothers "Eustace" of either Flemish or Boulognese origin, both of whom were educated men, and both of whom threw off their cowls for helmets and visors. The story of their exploits on land bears much analogy to that of Robin Hood. Ravaging any territory they were invariably kind to the poor and tender to the helpless, but filled with ferocious hatred to fief-holding priests and barons. They were poisoned thorns in the flesh of Philip Augustus. The Comte de Boulogne

could not sleep because of them. As bandits and
outlaws they became a centre of a world of myth
and fable. Adam le Roi, who wrote fifty years
after Wace and who was a minstrel at the court of
the Duke of Brabant, is supposed to be the author
of an amusing poem describing Eustace as studying the black art in Spain, and how he gave himself up to piracy and the various elfish tricks he
played upon his enemy the Comte de Boulogne.

In 1202 the brothers disappeared from before
the archers of the Comte de Boulogne, to appear
in 1203 on the side of John Lackland, of England,
in his troubles with the King of France. They
were evidently mercenaries, though such brave and
brilliant fighters, for they were willing to fight upon
either side. In 1205 they were sea-rovers and
full blown pirates in name of the worthless John.
In his name they scoured this part of the Channel,
and they took possession of Sark in the king's
name. They were both excommunicated by the
Pope, which may have stirred superstitious fears but
did not reform their manners ; a price was put
upon the head of *Wistace l'aîné* by his suzerain,
Comte de Boulogne, which the count never was
called upon to pay. John Lackland himself was not
sure of their purchased loyalty, and demanded as
hostages for that fealty the wife and daughter of the
elder Eustace and the uncle of both. With this
daughter came mischief, as mischief came to Eden
with Adam's daughter Eve. Nobody knows what
the young daughter of this wild blood thought of
miserable John Lackland, but it is told that he was
conquered by her charms and gave her a palace in
London, an estate in Norfolk and the seigneurie of
Cerq. It is extraordinary how this paid fighter

fought sometimes upon the side of France, sometimes of England. In 1211 he was in the English service, then in a quarrel with the king about his daughter, he disguised himself in one of the many characters he delighted to assume, penetrated through the territory of his old enemy, Comte de Boulogne, reached Philip Augustus in Paris, and was given the charge to reorganize the French fleet. Again he came into the Channel, this time with French ships. Sark was still in the hands of his brother, the younger Eustace, who was there with his family. With him was the uncle and the lovely daughter of the elder Eustace, both of whom had escaped from John. Where the wife was is not told, or how long the fair maid had remained contented on a savage island after the rough luxury of a king's palace. In 1214 one of John's officers, D'Aubigny and his chevaliers scaled these tremendous walls in a net and with a *coup de filet* took the daughter prisoner together with Eustace the younger, the uncle, and forty-four other prisoners. The daughter was sent to England and put under the charge of the Abbess of Winton, — a way robber-kings had with their stolen beauties and complacent convent superiors. Eustace the elder, with his French archers and sailors then pillaged Folkestone, and a little later descended upon these islands to intercept three galleys sent by John to reinforce D'Aubigny, thus to avenge himself for the captivity of his daughter, brother, and uncle. D'Aubigny was probably driven off from the island, for he was one of the few barons left to John on Runnymede. At any rate, John was obliged to free the brother and uncle, but he still clung to the daughter, who was held till his death a year later, in 1216, when the Abbess of Winton gave her up to her father. Eustace the Monk was beaten in 1217 by John's bastard son Richard, and his head paraded on a lance that all might know that the famous sea-pirate and land-robber could frighten the world no more.

"Minx!" remarked a Dove, poised upon the edge of a sheer promontory, a brutal tusk of Sark thrust outward toward any threatening invader. "Minx! Don't tell me she did n't throw the net herself down to D'Aubigny and her royal lover's men? Don't tell me she did n't run under the *coup de filet* as fast as her mediæval legs could carry her! Don't tell me she was not frightfully ennuied on this island in a thatched hut and only island fare, a week's sail from England, although now only five or six hours' steam! Don't tell me she did n't hate a place where she could not replenish her hair-dye, where she could n't spread the tails of her gowns, and attract attention to her jewelled girdle and head-dress! Don't tell *me* — "

"I won't," said the other.

In the sixth century Sark was in the possession of monks, St. Magloire, said to be a Welshman, their superior. He came to the island in 565, and the spot where he built a cottage for himself, and cells for his sixty-two pupils, is still called the Moinerie. There are still left a few traces of his monastery in the grounds of the seigneurie, notably an old holy water stoup from the monastic church. He died in Jersey, and was buried in Sark. He is storied to have slept there peacefully through all the wild changes of French and English possession, for about three hundred years. But it happened that in the ninth century a king of neighboring Brittany promised to build a monastery for some poor monks, if they, by hook or by crook, could procure some holy relics to put in it. Then these honest monks bethought them that on lonely Sark was the unprotected grave of a saint whose bones ought to fill the King Nomenoë's requirements. They sailed over to the dizzy island with a bag, tradition does not say how large a bag, and they returned with bones in that bag. The King kept his promise and built a magnificent monastery to receive the bones. This was the Monastery of St. Magloire de Léhon, and one of the fine edifices destroyed in the revolution of 1793.

For centuries Sark was first one king's then another's, overrun by cutthroats, soldiers of fortune, renegades, and stragglers from two countries, the Barry Lyndons of their time. Hosts of these swashbucklers were secretly allowed to man and provision galleys at St. Malo for piracy upon Sark, or anywhere else, so long as they only relieved the country of their presence. In 1549 again only a few monks were on the island; the robbers took easy possession and lived upon that impregnable rock, by preying upon Guernsey and Alderney and such unlucky vessels as sailed within their horizon. It was then that Panurge told Pantagruel that Cerq was an island of assassins and worse, for " *ils nous mangeront tous vifs.*"

Upon towering little Sark then came a bit of history like the story of Troy's wooden horse. Some Dutch or Flemish adventurers in 1555 begged permission to bring to land, and to deposit for prayers in the holy chapel, the coffin of their dead commander. Permission was given provided every man came unarmed. Up the terri-·ble rock they were lifted, for there was no entrance tunnel then, and upon the sunny table-land, with bowed heads and signs of grief, they followed the coffin to the church. At midnight they broke the coffin open, armed themselves with its contents, and drove the other robbers into the sea. For years Sark was deserted; then Queen Elizabeth gave it to Helier de Carteret in 1564, and to De Carterets it belonged until 1731.

The farmers of Sark are still forty land-holders, as Elizabeth's De Carteret divided the land. They cannot divide their land or sell an inch of it from the main proportion. They cannot sell to each other without the seigneur's permission; they rarely ask that permission, and for the best of reasons, — nobody wants it. Stout is their rock-clinging. Not for Cerq are dreams of adventure in other climes, not for it thrilling quests on far seas, not for it nature's pageantry of other zones. The Sarkais are almost without the sailor instinct of their sea-neighbors the Bretons; *boats*, not *ships*, are their desire. Upon their bit of rock they find all they need and ask, the bread their fathers ate, and with no more butter or jam than they had.

If ever a farm is sold upon the island, the seigneur is entitled to every thirteenth pound of the purchase-money. He can (and does) compel the Sarkais to keep the roads in order. He is really King of Sark. Though under the control of the Queen's representative, the Lieutenant-

Governor of Guernsey, Sark is in a sense (a small one) independent. The seigneur or feudal lord has the right to appoint the officers of the court; that is, the seneschal or judge, his deputy the prévôt, and the greffier. The seneschal has complete jurisdiction in petty offences, but his right of punishment is limited to three days of imprisonment, or a fine of "three livres tournois," or about four shillings. Where such gentle punishment does not fit the crime the offender is sent to Guernsey. There is a Sark Court of Common Pleas, composed of the forty householders, and at which the lord must be present, either personally or by deputy, and his consent is necessary for the enactment of any ordinance. Absolute veto of anything relating to island affairs is his right. He could forbid any visitors if he chose.

What an atmosphere of picturesque romance envelops the word "seigneur." With what clang of arms, what clarion cries, what music of beating hoofs, comes down through the centuries vision and echo of the seigneur's tribute of armed men to his king. What pageantry of waving standards, shining armor and emblazoned shields, flits with the words "lord of the manor," to show the nineteenth century what it was to be a feudal lord, what it is to hold the lordly rights of many a lordly generation.

The Seigneur of Sark is only a plain "Mister." A seigneur could never be otherwise in these islands. The Norman seigneurs of the Channel Islands were not nobles; they were merely men entitled to bear arms, and without other dignity. In all the islands they were a rustic gentry, with little or no superiority in manner of living, and in close relations with the people and the *bourgeoisie*. Their manors were thatched and their courtyards no cleaner than those of their neighbors, who were their tenants. Within comparatively few years the Seigneur of Sark was " untutored," although not precisely " savage," and his manor-house or *seigneurie* less than a decent English farm-house. The father of the present seigneur was nothing more knightly and bold than a clergyman should be. He bought the manor and its rights when they came into the market at the death of the seigneur before him, Pierre Le Pellew, who was drowned as so many Sarkais are in crossing over to Guernsey.

Pierre Pellew was a headstrong man who thought he knew more about wind and weather than the islanders who bade him beware of the rising tempest. He wanted to go to a dinner in Guernsey to which he had been invited, and probably felt that he and storms were too old friends to do each other harm. The whole island watched his boat as it tossed on the waves, every man, woman, and child with heart in mouth. It was not a long watch. The sea swallowed him within a mile of his island home, swallowed him and the boatmen, who had gone much against their own wills. The island rector, a Swiss (who never learned English), saw the tragedy and was so affected by it that for many a year, some say as long as he lived, he never dared leave the island.

When the Reverend Mr. Collins bought the island it is said that he was very much surprised by the power he bought with it. When the islanders, in conventional speed, addressed him as a superior being he had much ado to keep from laughing in their faces. He made a just and generous seigneur and was always a gentleman. His son, the present seigneur, is given to nocturnal adventure on land and sea, arriving on Guernsey and Jersey at any hour of the night, and consorting more congenially with rough sailors and the odd fish of waterside inns than with men of his own quality. When the Doves saw him, he was driving a horse furiously, at least held the reins in hand, with a very red face and a meaningless smile.

The rights and title belong to the estate. Seigneur Peter may come and Seigneur Paul may go, but the rights go on forever, that is, forever thus far. Those of Sark have never ceased since Queen Bess gave them, and added thereunto a cannon which any one may see in a little tower back of the *seigneurie*, and upon which read " Don de la Reyne au Seigneur de Serck, 1573." Those rights have not ceased, though once only a foolish woman was left to carry them on. In 1779, on October 20, Madame Le Pellew, widow of a seigneur and guardian of his five children, took the lord's seat in the *Chefs Plaids*. The only record at hand of her administration is the decree that " whoever shall sell anything on the island without consent of the seigneur or his representative, shall pay a fine of fifty francs, of which one quarter goes to the King (of England), one quarter to the seigneur, the other half to the poor." This regulation or law is writ in French, as is all official business to this day. Information is not to be unearthed as to whether Seigneuress Pellew took command of the island army or not; for there was one in her time. The army, of about twenty bold warriors, existed until within a few years ; the Rev. Seigneur Collins was its last colonel, and drilled it upon occasions with merely a military cap and sword worn with his clerical suit. Some who remember these brilliant occasions, when Peace and War kissed each other, say the army was disbanded by the Reverend Colonel Seigneur in disgust that he could not make it stand upright. Therefore, were he called upon for service to his sovereign, it would not be with lance and javelin, with arrows tipped with iron, with marching men and waving banners, but with Bank of England notes.

Nothing is necessary to become a feudal lord of the nineteenth century in the Channel Islands, but money enough to buy a marketed manor, and to be of Channel Island birth.

On the serene table-land is no village, though every cluster of two or three farms has a name, always a French one, as Rousel, La Frégondée, Le Fort, etc. Indeed every crag, promontory, cave, everything has its name in that language. The wonderfully picturesque thatched cottages and farm-houses are widely scattered, and as there is but one shop the delicious lane upon which it stands does not call itself High Street. About the ugly modern church, of date 1822, the homely nests gather somewhat more closely, and are known as *La Ville*. This group of half a score of houses is of course the capital, for here is the school and the famous prison. There is the " Rue du Sermon " as the French Huguenots called the way to church ; "going to Sermon" was their habit, as the modern is " to church." Services in the church (although Church of England) are always in French, except on midsummer afternoons when an English service is held for the sake of visitors.

The author of the French translation of the

Book of Common Prayer was a Channel Islander, John Durel. He was born in Jersey in 1625, and entered Merton College, Oxford, at the age of fifteen. On account of the troubles caused by the Civil War he like many other students retired to France and took his M. A. in the college of Caen. He then studied Divinity (as many Channel Island clergymen do still) in France, at the Protestant University of Saumur, and in 1647 returned to Jersey as chaplain to Sir George de Carteret.

The liturgy was read in French for the first time on Sunday, the 14th of July, 1661, in the chapel of the Savoy, London, — Mr. Durel preaching in the forenoon, Mr. Le Couteur, then Dean of Jersey, in the afternoon. In 1662 the French translation was published. In 1669 John Durel was made D. D., in 1677 Dean of Windsor and of Wolverhampton, and Rector of Witney, also Registrar of the Garter. He died on the 8th of June, 1683.

In La Ville of Sark are also the rustic schools where moon-faced, foreign-looking boys and girls are promoted to English after sufficient proficiency in French, and where they speak neither, once out from under the master's eye. There too is the ancient thatched building, now a farmhouse, until 1822 the church of Cerq. A Wesleyan chapel is in La Ville, but the idea of Norman-French Methodists on a rock of the Middle Ages was absurdly incongruous. There are also two graveyards, old and new, the latter round the ugly church. In the old, a weedy enclosure within high hedge-walls, the inscriptions are nearly all in French. More than one Huguenot sleeps there in sunny peace, fled here from the Royal Rascal who revoked. Over the church-yard-graves English is less unfrequent. "De Carteret" occurs upon them many times. The Doves remarked it also upon "Notices to the Public" (always in two languages), signed by the "connétable" or mayor (not constable) of Cerq. The name flourishes, though the "dynasty" be no more. Compared with some of the Sarkais their present lord is a *parvenu*, and "Collins" does not sound like a Norman name.

Entering the ugly church the Doves fell a-wondering. Who could have worked this miracle? Who transformed this Mission of St. Prig into a temple of the shining gods? No man had hand there save as menial, they were sure. Those hands were worthy to wave laurel branches and with bare ivory feet to keep ever aflame white fire on altars of snow. *She* was patrician, they knew as well as if they saw her, for only the taste of generations of culture could have thus transformed mean posts of painted pine into columns of flawless pearl ensphered by mists of the dawn, with font, altar, and canopy of alabaster, upon which the fairest of the Olympians had breathed blue and rosy clouds.

The seigneurie is near this capital of Cerq. It is a comfortable modern mansion, with a tower and the usual insular indifference to views of the sea. Hundreds of better form the residential suburbs of Boston.

The ancient chapel of the manor stands close by, a tiny block of thatched stone. The holy-water stoup is said to remain from a sixth century church upon the same site, and of which also a small pile of stones remains. An ancient metrical life of St. Magloire, written in old Norman-French, describes very minutely how the Monk of Léhon in Brittany made him into a "relic."

In the courtyard of the seigneurie they met a milk-white steed. The lady beside it had no falcon on her wrist, and none could imagine the milk-white steed a palfrey, because of its bray. The lady was not riding to joust or tournament, she was the English governess driving the nursery out in a cart. The gardens, open to the public, for the present seigneur follows his father's generous example, are said to be fine. In them figs ripen and English green-house flowers bloom in the open air.

"*Rien! rien du tout!*" the old gardener assured them; "the vicarage ladies took every camellia for Easter Sunday."

Those vicarage ladies! How the Americans wished to see them, ivory-footed and with laurel boughs wending their way through the "rue du Sermon," to services at St. Prig's. How they wished to see their divine faces as they sang there our own familiar hymns turned into French.

"All the same," remarked one of the Doves, "*we* are only bank-holiday excursionists, and a joke to them."

There are two Sarks, — Sark, and Little Sark. Little Sark is the space of two or three small farms separated from the main island by a terrific chasm. At low tide this chasm is walled and floored with murderously jagged rocks; at high tide the sea roars through it. The incessant action of tides upon a mineral vein in the island rock has made Little Sark, but has left a natural bridge between the two about 290 feet above high-water mark. At this exposed end of Sark the winds are fierce at times, and tragic tales are told of its work. In earlier days, before this bridge was guarded as it is now by a wall of solid masonry, the children of Little Sark going down to La Ville to school often crossed on all fours for safety. "I seldom crossed so," a Sark woman afterwards told the Doves on Alderney, "for when the wind blew father always met us on the Great Sark side and helped us across." Many traditions connect this *coupée* with the master passion of love, as greedy of victims on Sark as elsewhere, even although all are akin. Rival lovers have met there, it is said, and only one has ever been seen again ; for the tide rises twice a day, and even on Sark a man may not be missed in twelve hours, particularly if he be of Great Sark and she of Little. One story of these tells of the lover who came home, ghastly, dishevelled, stung by mysterious torments, yet dumb as the rocks against which the consuming sea beats. He disappeared from home and was known to haunt the foot of the rocks in his boat, like a spectre, ever looking downward as if expecting the sea to give up its dead to accuse him. He was seen no more in La Ville ; when he came home at rare intervals he never spoke. He was supposed to be under the spell of one of those mysterious obsessions which are so often the fate of island people largely intermarried, and none save two or three suspected the hot, panting encounter upon the bridge, from which one man had gone over and one returned thus scourged by silent furies. One day the obsessed skulked about *la coupée* as he always did when not in his boat. He saw a bridal party approach and cross in couples. As the bride and bridegroom came close upon him he gave a terrible cry and fled to the edge of the precipice. He was caught midway and found to be raving mad, having seen the living faces of his rival and his love, and believing he saw them in death's world; a violent fever followed, the man recovered, went decently to his farm again, and never spoke of the mercy which cast his rival, who was his brother, into a safe cleft of the rock instead of upon the jags below.

Until comparatively late years the church tithes were paid in the ancient manner of an actual portion of the produce of a man's land. One lowering day a Jean, Léon, or Paul shouldered a huge load of wheat to take to the rectory barn. The wind was wild from storm caves of the Atlantic, and the neighbors advised him to wait for a stiller day; but Jean or Paul, or Léon had already waited till almost the last day for paying his tithes; besides, he needed new milk-cans and a rake by the next boat that should go over to Guernsey. The wind was not so very high, it was in his favor, and he was sturdy on his legs, as everybody knew. People on Little Sark watched the huge mass as it sped all too swiftly on its way. Nothing could be seen but the moving yellow load, the man being entirely hidden beneath it. It sped like a winged bird till the narrow bridge was so nearly crossed that the watchers began to breathe freely, though the wind over the stubble abated none of its wild jeering. Suddenly the yellow bird rose an instant in the air, was caught there by a monstrous gust and whirled over like a single straw. The next moment the broken fragments of a man strewed the rocks below and never since has Little Sark paid its tithes from its backs, but from its pockets.

The Americans walked all the long day, save during the one hour that they rested on a vine-clad rock. Strange that so much walking may be found within so little space; that the broad roads seem so much like broad roads elsewhere, in breadth, even in length. During many min-utes' walk, the sea often is not seen at all, only pleasant farms, blooming orchards and gardens, with sleek cattle feeding upon sunny slopes. The charm of distance even is not lacking, at least an illusion of distance; and sometimes Bishop Wind-mill loomed grandly vague, spiritualized by a remoteness of perhaps only two miles. From various points, Little Sark, high in air, seemed almost a part of some other far away island. What is called distance is, after all, chiefly a matter of one's own eyes and imagination, and fairyland lies very near to those who most earnestly desire it.

Said a Dove, looking upward and away beyond where they knew an awful chasm, a valley of the Shadow of Death, was spanned by a narrow bit of rock beyond which was dazzling light: " Hark ! Do we not seem to see horses and chariots, and to hear trumpeters and pipers with singers and players on stringed instruments, before beautiful gates of a celestial city? "

" No, dear," said the other, " I do *not!* I do not wish to see. I do not wish to hear. I do not wish to end our pilgrimage. It is heavenly as it is."

Among Mrs. Dove's *mems* was this: " Never take luncheon at a hotel when time is precious."

Time was precious, yet not less so than the other hours that golden one during which they perched high above the singing sea and decided that they were greater than emperors, as they certainly were higher. "Give me health and a day," they quoted from Emerson, "and I will make the pomp· of emperors ridiculous." While they lunched, wrapped in the very heart of august Nature, and dreamily talked of Eustache le Moine and his naughty mediæval daughter, of fights and stratagems, of archers and scaling ladders, of corsairs bold and blood-thirsty pirates, of passion's tragedies, of fate, free-will, and heredity, which is fate, half their fellow-excursionists sat upon the piazzas of hotels and wondered what to do next now lunch was over.

"*Mem*," wrote the lady upon the tablets of her memory : " Always provide sandwiches of potted meats for excursions ; they leave no greasy fingers, and fate, free-will, foreknowledge, need not wait for the picking of a bone or the rending of a slice ; always take a bottle of wine, and camp without regard to water ; always take cheap glasses and Japanese napkins to be left behind ; always be provided with a fish-net or twine bag to be folded away empty after luncheon, as if it did not exist."

" *Tout de même*," she murmured, as they rose from that golden hour, " *Tout de même* if every bank-holiday-maker leaves olive-stones, orange-peel, penny glasses, paper napkins, and a bottle behind."

With care she gathered everything together, stuffed the glasses full, and placed them beside the upright bottle. "Now I have done up the dishes, come, let us be heavenly pilgrims again, only taking good care not to reach any final city."

Refreshed and with health, although with now but half a day, still considering themselves greater than emperors because happier, they again took up their pilgrimage. Coming towards them by a circuitous route comprehending both sides of the road, they recognized a co-excursionist, a five-pounder and week-ender, one of the morning's clear-headed debaters of the Budget, who gravely wished to know if " lay, gem'l tell ware " he was. Next, a ravishing old woman, with broad-brimmed hat tied under the chin, and a little woollen shawl worn fichu-fashion across her breast, who was going to her cows for the mid-day milking. She carried the usual narrow-necked vessel used for milking in all the Channel Islands, and which only expert milkers can use, the art of hitting the small orifice being acquired only with long practice. The Americans always wonder what sort of milking-vessels were used while this amphora was in process of evolution, unless it really descended from the antique civilizations. They never found out, for no milkmaid or milk-matron was ever found to acknowledge that she had ever used any other than the narrow-mouthed, rotund-bodied utensil.

In former days, these were always of earthenware. Now that they are of tin they are much lighter to carry, but it would be asking quite too much of the conservative farm people of these islands to change the form of vessels from the shape used on Duke William's Norman farms. Duke William the Conqueror must somehow seem to the Channel Islanders a patron-saint of cows. At every cattle show, and in every list of prizes are

Duke, Duke William, Duke of Normandie, Duke
Rollo, The Conqueror, Duchess, Duchess Matilda,
La Duchesse Mathilde, La Normandie, La Duchesse Galla, together with Dukes Henry, John,
and Stephen, and their feminine forms galore.

"Voulez-vous me permettre de faire votre portrait, madame?" asked Mrs. Dove, swinging the
kodak into view. The milk-matron evidently
knew the use of the black box, for she instantly
placed herself in one of the usual stark, staring posi-
tions. But when the kodaker sought a more favorable point of view, in the interests of the picturesque
as the picturesque is understood beyond the circumference of Sark, the milk-matron demurred.

"Comme ça vous ne verrez point ma physionomie."

"Physionomie," they laughed in each other's
sleeves; "has n't that a fine insular flavor? Were
she at home in modern French how much more
easy to say ' figure.'"

The milk-matron was gathered into the black
box, a very tit-bit of foreign picturesqueness, and
was pleased to receive the London price of a quart
of milk.

Next, a shifty group of shock-headed, half-naked
urchins were snapshotted, tumbling in and out of a
row of picturesque cottages while gossiping mothers
plied knitting-needles in companies of two and
three. Knitting was formerly the one great in-
dustry of the Channel Islands for both men and
women. The Guernsey and Jersey jackets known
all the world over were once all of domestic knitting. In those days not only women incessantly
plied their needles, but their husbands and sons
were rarely without them. Fishermen knitted be-

tween the setting and drawing of nets, knitted even with a line in hand ; sailors took knitting to sea for their watch off or on. Nowadays all women knit, but no longer for exportation, and the men do not knit at all.

"Wonder if they still eat gooseberry soup," said one of the Doves.

In the seventeenth century somebody wrote to London from Sark of the "generous belly timber to be found here, very pleasant to the gusto, so that an epicure would think his pallat in Paradice if he might but always gormandice on such delitious ambrosia." The three staple articles were fish, fowl, and rabbits ; of the two first many varieties. To Mrs. Dove's disgust this "belly timber of Paradice" included not a fruit or a vegetable save such as were made into a certain "extraordinary and most excellent pottage made of milk, bacon, coleworts, mackerel, and gooseberries, boyled together all to pieces, which our mode is to eat, not with the ceremony of a spoon, but the more courtly way of a great piece of bread furiously flying between your mouth and the kettle."

At five o'clock, tea at the Victoria, whence certain Guernsey excursionists had not budged since the morning arrival. Then down to the Commerce amid the same foreign picturesqueness of the morning, the darting boats carrying passengers to two steamers, the confusion of languages, with shouts as one and another of the bank-holidayists lost his feeble balance and almost fell into the gloomy water. The Budget-debaters of the morning were separated, probably forever, one taking passage on the larger boat to Guernsey and thence to England or France, the other, he who had earlier asked the

Doves where he was, apparently left behind. On board the Commerce was much bargaining, as Jersey people bought lobsters and crabs in which Sark abounds, to take home to their own island which has none, and where even the fish-market is largely supplied from Billingsgate. One week the Jersey papers advertised that twenty thousand oysters would be sold for a song in Jersey's Saturday market. They sold for four cents a dozen because England would have none of them at any price, hearing that they were fattened where rivers emptied sewage into the sea and thus they were breeders of typhoid. One week thirty thousand were to come, for not yet had Jersey caught the alarm. They never came, but went to a watery grave, being caught and held in a fog till even typhoid were pleasant compared with them.

As the Commerce lazily got up steam and lazily jogged away from Sark, wild signals were seen from a pursuing boat. The chasing and signalling was not for the Jersey-bound steamer, but the larger one puffing away to Guernsey.

"Imbeciles," said a Jerseyman, "I never went on an excursion to Sark in my life that somebody was not left behind. That couple have been spooning on a hotel piazza all day. They shall have to hire a boat or wait for the regular steamer on Saturday."

The Commerce crawled; the sea was gray, the air bitterly cold. Everybody was silent. Even the steward, fidgeting about with a brown teapot, smiled no more.

"How pleasant to be with our friend the Budget debater, under a warm hedge on Sark," chattered one of them to the other. "Virtue may be its own reward, but so also is unvirtue."

It was not yet dark when they reached Jersey, for twilight is long in these latitudes, even though figs, oranges, and lemons ripen in sheltered spots in the open air. Just before them, as they disembarked, marched their friend the Budget debater, as sober as a judge, having comfortably slept off his bank-holiday in the warm cabin while sobriety chattered its teeth and curved its spines above.

Cold, tired, hungry, one half that dovely pair strode sternly up St. Helier's slope, the other half feebly wabbled behind. The Dove-cote turned upon them but a chill white face with two blank eyes, and a shut mouth of bilious green. No sign of welcome, no hint even of life was about the sulky-visaged thing. They put the misfit key into the misfit lock, with gloomy realization that even as the most jocund youth must go out in shadows of age, so a glorious bank-holiday may have the most cheerless of evenings.

Behold! Martin smiled welcome with her cups of tea to cheer, and also to inebriate very much more than the noontide claret. The tiny dining-room was balmy with comfort; a dinner for such gods as like steak, mashed potatoes, salad, with cider, cake, pears, and doughnuts, exhaled an intoxicating aroma.

Then they rejoiced that they were born to go bank-holidaying upon Cerq, for seventy-five cents apiece the round trip, and sixpence apiece for their Victorian tea.

And behold, wise Mrs. Dove did not even say, "I told you so!"

She waited for some future occasion.

A LITTLE DASH INTO FRANCE.

" Only ninety minutes."

" Yet no," said Mrs. Dove, meditatively, " let us leave it, a land in which no man dwells; a phantom country echoing mystic music of the spheres; a cloud vision stirring the passion of our desire. Let us leave it, the haunting of the horizon in whose inmost mystery our fiery chariot swings."

Mrs. Dove seemed to take for granted that their translation would require but one sweet chariot swinging low.

" Bless my soul! " exclaimed the other Dove. " Have n't you lived years in France and rowed no end of cheating trades-people and lazy servants? Have n't I heard you say scores of times that you 'd rather be whipped than go into a Norman market and jabber ten minutes over every potato you bought, rather than pay the ' *hors nous* ' price those market people demand of you? Where, for instance, was collected your famous gallery of Roman Pontiffs? "

Those Pontiffs! Well that malicious Dove knew what a sore point that subject was.

One day Mrs. Dove had gone into the Bon Marché with only gold in her purse, one piece of which was changed at her first visit to a *caisse.* At her second visit to a *caisse* a silver piece of fifty centimes was cast back at her as a Roman coin.

Now l'Américaine was entirely aware that these papal coins were no longer of any value in France. She had intercepted and circumvented very many attempts to " do " her with them as a foreigner. She was equally well aware now that that portrait Pius IX. had been given her in part exchange for her gold, since she came into the Bon Marché. Naturally she was indignant. She made her explanation, which was curtly dismissed. Then she shut her teeth, and vowed to rid herself of that papal portrait before she left the place. She proceeded to make various small purchases to be paid in small coin, always including among them Pius IX. At every *caisse* that fat, smirking pope was cast back at her. More and more angry she grew, till ready to cry aloud, " He may be worthless, but he's the Head of your Church ! " only that then she knew her despised Ninth Pius would never leave her heretic porte-monnaie.

Half a score of times at least she bought some unconsidered trifle, for the sake, and only that, of hiding her puffy-cheeked Head of the Church with more valid silver, and offering it at a *caisse*.

Alas ! The Bon Marché was too sharp for Yankee sharpness. Finally she gave up the struggle in despair and went home, offering her pope to the omnibus conductor on the way, only once more to have it contemptuously flung back at her. Arrived at home she told her story of wrong, opening her porte-monnaie as she told.

Behold, she had *three* Heads of the Church !

" Not the honorable Bon Marché itself," her companion answered her indignation, " but those rascally caissiers working off upon '*hors nous*' all their own store and all the store of their friends, of worthless Roman Pontiffs."

"Yes," said Mrs. Dove, dreamily, "I remember my Pontiffs, which disappeared from my purse, heaven only knows how, unless I paid them out in England for sixpences, and thus unconsciously made two cents on each pope. Also I remember the day we wandered into a remote country churchyard and sat in the shadow of a thousand-year-old-Norman church, listening to that melancholy sweet sighing of weeds and grass which we fancied the echo of plaints from the graves they covered. It was an over-crowded churchyard, now deserted by the newly dead. We sat in the cool shadow of the grim church and wondered if into its substance had entered any essence of the ten centuries of mourning it had coldly witnessed, where the dead have been buried over and over again in the same mould. Of all those graves only two were not weedy and neglected. Those two were well-rounded, as if they covered forms still shapely, and they were brilliant with flowers as fresh as if watered every dawn and evening, as we afterwards knew they were. These graves were far apart from each other, they were not of the same family. While we sat there watching the lengthening shadows creep slowly from the woman's grave to the man's, a bent and hobbling old creature, crippled with rheumatism, came first to one grave, then the other, plucking away fallen petals, straightening wind-bowed blossoms, and refreshing them with water from his garden can. We watched the tenderness with which he cared for both graves equally, and we wondered in whispers what to him could have been the two, evidently not related, — the man dead twenty-five years ago at thirty years of age, the woman twenty years ago at twenty-five.

"'*Parbleu!*' laughed Mademoiselle Jeanne when we told her of our wonderings. 'You 've seen old Dufour the gardener. Years ago, before I remember, he was the *fiancé* of Élise Petit. It was told that she did not wish to marry, and it is known that for one reason and another the marriage was continually put off. They had been playmates from childhood and betrothed soon after their first communion, which was made together. Why Élise seemed always averse to marriage, nobody knew. Suddenly the young curé of the village died and was buried in one of those flower-roofed graves that you saw to-day. From the hour the clods covered him Élise became melancholy mad. She spoke no more to anybody save in faint murmurs to her lost Édouard. Summer and winter she spent hours by his grave, planting it with flowers, tending them, and singing crazy lullabies as if to an infant in its cradle. Everybody wondered where she procured such rare and expensive flowers, and why with only her crazy care they flourished so beautifully; for even had she been trusted with money such hot-house flowers were nowhere in market. One evening, five years after the young man's death, she was found dead on his grave by Jacques Dufour, head gardener at the Château, the man who had always loved her, and who had watched over her during her brain-turned years. He has never married, and is n't it *une drôle de chose* that ever since he has taken care of both graves? We are wondering if he will leave his money for somebody else to keep his rival's grave blooming, or if three more graves will soon grow tangled and weedy before they sink away into the common mould.'

"Is n't that better to remember, *mon cher*, than my swollen pope's-jowls?" continued Mrs. Dove. "Is France *not* a dream of poetry without a Bon Marché, where love is as long as life? Don't tell *me*—"

"I won't!" said he.

France might have been ten thousand miles away for all they could see of it the gray misty morning that on St. Helier's pier they changed English gold into enough French money to last for four days. Yet they seemed already in France, a commonplace semi-sordid France, without hauntings or music, as they waited for the little steamer's bell to ring all aboard. For more French than English was spoken about them, several of the intending passengers wore the violently checked ulsters in which Frenchmen consider themselves at the very apex of the English fashion, there was continual jabber of francs and centimes, although none of pope's-heads. Three quarters of the passengers were French, or else Jerseymen who seemed so French one could not detect the difference; and those Frenchmen were largely of the bagman or *commis-voyageur* type from provincial cities. The few English were *avant coureurs* of the tourist season, with noses already in the air, giving their countenances the expression of contempt for everything un-English so familiar on the Continent.

A brisk little spin, peacock-blue banks of cloud, gray-green shores, then France *la belle.*

It were difficult to weave any imaginative mists about ugly Granville, and their landing in the very arms of the familar little douaniers with big moustaches and little use for soap, who never even peeped into their large kodak, though it might easily be imitation and brimful of the tea of which every travelling Englishwoman is suspected. Mrs. Dove even suggested that the type of douanier had grown smaller, rustier, duskier, dustier, and less inquisitive, than at the forty-two-or-so other times of their landing at France and in their arms.

"The Jersey boats come in too often to cause any excitement," he explained the slight inquisitiveness. "They know a smuggler by instinct."

The train was evidently kept in waiting for the arrival of their boat and the wise omnibus therefore did not "fash" itself because of the impatience of *Messieurs les voyageurs.* But the railway employés were markedly impatient, and shrieked, "*Dépêchez-vous, dépêchez-vous,*" from the station, till Mrs. Dove yearned to use choice French and answer back, "*Fermez vos bouches,*" which would not have been choice French after all. In the breathless excitement of bringing tickets to the incessant goading of "*Dépêchez-vous, messieurs, dépêchez-vous*" a large part of the company lost their heads and for a moment rushed wildly about in a *salle d'attente,* like mice in a cage, seeking and not finding the exit upon the railway platform.

"*Eh bien, messieurs!* have you come to France to amuse yourselves *comme ça?*" screamed the sarcastic ticket collector.

In the train bearing them on to Avranches, whence they would later depart for Mont Saint-Michel, they enjoyed the society of a Britisher, travelling with two Jerseymen. He had absorbed two English breakfasts that morning before the steamer left St. Helier's at eleven, knowing he should breakfast no more till he returned to British civilization; and he not only recounted with gusto the items of those breakfasts (both including bacon), but traced an imaginary menu for breakfasts for the future, when he should escape the barbarism of France. He would not condescend to flatter these Frenchmen by speaking their lingo, not he. The English language was good enough for any man; for any man who could not understand it, it was too good. So he talked of Mount Saint Michael, of Avranches to rhyme with cattle ranches. Saint-Malo was Saint Maylow, Dynan for Dinan, and so on. He would never stop in France more than a week at a time; ketch him stopping longer than he could help where you couldn't get beer on draught, nor a boiled pertater; but he had run cigars enough to last him through, and would his friends take a dozen or so? Whereupon he unloaded half a dozen packages from various places about his ponderous person.

"They know a smuggler by instinct," remarked Mrs. Dove.

It did not take the Doves long to agree, as they trundled through that corner of Normandy, that France was indeed *la belle*. Nowhere in all the world of their memories, it seemed to them, was ever anything so beautiful as the color of the landscape over which artists rave; and well they may. Nowhere else were the slopes and valleys, the little hills and meadows, of that exquisite sheeny blue-green (if coarse words may thus express it) that suggests peacock hues etherealized by an almost impalpable veil of silver-gray. Other landscape colors seem shockingly crude compared with the subtle gray-greens of France. America's green is cheaply glassy ; England's yellowish, as if grown for beef and butter ; Italy is a mighty chromo screaming to be copied ; even dear little Jersey suggests potato-green. The landscape in France allures, beguiles, intoxicates, — a very Circe, to make artists drunk with desire only to realize what mere swine they are when they attempt to paint it.

Against this prismatic background what marvellous orchards, every petal an illumined opal ; every orchard a glimpse of Eden. The solemnity of fortress-like churches, the huddled red roofs of quaint hamlets, the deep eaves and russet thatch of antique farm-houses and cottages, thrilled the Doves with realization of an old world picturesqueness such as is sadly trampled out beneath the energetic tread of the Anglo Saxon race to which they belong (although not of choice, since no choice was ever offered them where or of whom to be born. " Would have made no difference if it had," they comforted their dolefulness ; " we should probably have chosen milk rather than beauty ").

As the train unrolled this poetic panorama before their eyes, " Come, Love," said the foolish Dove ; "let us leave the train at the next station ; let us buy blouses, and quilted petticoats a mile round the hips ; let us buy caps and sabots ; let us forget our beloved libraries, theatres, and ice-creams, and dwell forevermore in French orchards under russet thatch."

"My yearnings are not infinite for sour cider, cabbage soup, *ventripotence*, and rheumatism," answered the wise Dove.

He had reason.

In their compartment three Breton peasant women flashed caps of snowiest muslin. They were quaint stiff caps with immensely broad bands, which looked as if designed to tie in bows under the chin. If such were the original design, centuries of contrary habit have thwarted it. Now those bands are looped up and fastened each side the cap in fashion to give the butterfly appearance which was not a novelty to the Doves, inasmuch as it is frequent in the street of Jersey, where Breton nurses are much esteemed, and many a Breton household established.

The three butterflies floated, nodded, beckoned, tossed, and danced, as if the heads they belonged to were sun-warmed flowers ; and the jabber was incessant of Jean and Jeanne, of Desiré and Desirée, of Jules and Juliette, of their rheumatisms, their *douleurs* of teeth and toes, of inside and out, upside and down, of body and members, till it would seem there could be no health whatever in the exquisite blue-gray-greenness to which they belonged.

"Low diet begets rheumatism ; damp thatch abets it," they agreed.

At Avranches they left their hand luggage *à la consigne* and climbed the aerial path up the hill which circumvents the winding and long carriage-road to town. Before they should wander at wayward will through the silent streets, gazing in at

shop-windows like *blancs becs*, discussing notices
of houses to let (none furnished), and hunting up
storied spots, they must even eat ; for men must eat
though they work, and eat women must though
they weep, else would there be no hiring-furnished
in far foreign lands, with delicious dashes into
lands even more far and foreign.

"Byron called his wife 'gormandizing beast,' "
remarked the lady, meditatively.

"Byron? What has fat Byron to do with our
little dash into France? Ah, yes, I remember, it
was when she ate cutlets; they *are* good in
France."

"Shall it be *déjeuner* or dinner?" they communed as they paused outside a portal, far enough
away from it not to be seized by some officious
garçon and dragged in willy-nilly. It was a natural
question at half-past three in the afternoon, and
nothing eaten since breakfast in the Jersey Dove-
cote.

"Dinner!" answered enthusiastic chorus.

So they dined, at three francs and a half a head
(or rather mouth), and enjoyed, as only pleasure-
catchers, not mere pleasure-seekers, can, their
cutlet and salad, fried potatoes, sweet biscuits, and
Pont L'Evêque, with cider *compris*, and coffee
following.

But when they came out the lady growled
ominously.

"Did you notice," she grumbled, "that the
water in which yesterday's cabbage was boiled cost
us four francs a litre ; more than a bottle of the
best Bordeaux?"

"What do you mean?"

"Did n't you see? We were going to be so

very clever, and not to be done while dashing. Already we are 'done.' We have had only the regular two-franc-and-a-half *déjeuner*, charged three francs and a half because we asked to dine, and the half-pint apiece of cabbage-water made it into a dinner."

She took out a tiny book and upon the stone where once an English sovereign knelt to be cleansed from the curse of excommunication, she *memmed*, " *Nr cd dr F we dr cn cd ;* " which is to say, " Never command a dinner in France where a *déjeuner* can be commanded."

If Avranches, dull, grass-grown, empty Avranches, once a great intellectual centre where Lefranc had a renowned school in the eleventh century, had no other claim to respect, its glorious position and more glorious views would make it never-to-be-forgotten. One view from the terrace of the public garden is said to be the finest in France; which saying the Doves took the liberty to doubt, having intimately known Auvergne and seen all that lies between the Alps, the Pyrenees, and the Atlantic. But it was a magnificent view of wide, rolling distance seen from a height, a manner of view by many considered finer than up-looking to stupendous heights.

The Americans seated themselves upon garden seats before a fine prospect of blank wall to discuss whether such difference of admiring was not human littleness and conceit preferring everything below its own level, as contrasted with the humility of a more inspired and illumined imagination lifting up its eyes to the eternal hills and to the glory of the heavens, and rejoicing because of spirits that soar though bodies are chained.

The view is of a vast plain far below, beginning with a sheer descent from the rampart-terrace. On two sides are river valleys, shimmering, dappling, as the clouds float over them, and deeply dimpled with thickets of trees. Directly in the centre, far away beyond wheat land and meadows, is a glimpse of sparkling sea with the faint far hills of Brittany behind the distant bay, where rises what seems a magic castle, at any moment to be rapt into the glory of the sky or to vanish into the glory of the sea, even while mortal gaze strives to encompass its fairy picturesqueness.

It seems a pinnacle of cloud upon a cloud pinnacle ; in the sunshine its spires become melting frost tipped with fire ; when shadow or dimness falls upon it it becomes a reft and splintered cloud, and in reality is the fortress-monastery of countless pilgrimages and as many fights and forays, Mont Saint-Michel.

Here in Avranches-of-the-View, as the Americans called it, is a small archway erected in the botanic garden, on which a brass plate gives a hint of one of the slow, creeping tragedies with which nature, red of tooth and claw, amuses its infinite leisure. The inscription states that this is all that is left of a church of the eleventh century. Elsewhere one learns that the church itself and its village stood, not in Avranches, but upon distant sands, which in time became quicksands and sucked the church and village down.

Very near, still with the marvellous view before it, is the church step upon which Henry Second knelt before the Pope's legate in humiliation for the murder of Thomas-à-Becket. On a brass plate on an ancient broken column is inscribed the story that Henry Second, King of England and Duke of Normandy, received on his knees the Apostolic absolution on Sunday, 22d May, 1172. A little beyond is a small heap of stones, a stone coffin, and the figure of a dog, a wheelbarrow-load perhaps in all, and all that remains of the grand cathedral into which a king was not permitted to enter till he had done bitter penance, and which once reared its lofty walls to be seen from Mont Saint-Michel as a magic vision of pinnacles and spires of frost and gold among the clouds.

"Providing it was not thus seen by a guide-book maker," sniffed a Dove. "Just hear this," reading from a book: "'To the left are Mont Saint-Michel and the island of Tombelaine, *too distant to be imposing.*'"

"Had n't the man an opera glass?" laughed the other one.

In the gathering dusk the dashers arrived by train at Pontorson and into the very midst of the infernal clamor at the station known to all arrivals there. How many those howling madmen were, they never knew; they seemed an innumerable multitude, those foaming, shouting charioteers raging about two or three dazed foreigners inno-cently wishing to reach Mont Saint-Michel just round the circle of the bay. The Doves were deafened by them, and for a time found not a word to answer, although one of them spoke French as if it were his mother tongue, and they were irritated almost to the extent of refusing all and every offer of conveyance and of starting to make the journey on foot.

Ten francs was the lowest price at which any-body could drive anybody over the quicksands at this time of night when all the regular omnibuses had done running and the return journey must be made in the dark. "Ten francs, and all the saints in heaven knew it was none too much, and if madame says she will walk, by the horns of the devil she knows not the dangers of the *sables-mouvants*."

"They think we are greenhorns," they laughed in each other's sleeves. "They fancy we have been reading-up, and are full to the brim of mediæval romances of these engulfing quicksands, such as " La Fée des Grèves " and the like. They fool themselves that we don't know all about that fine new causeway, level and smooth across the quicksands."

"Let us leave it," he continued chantingly. " Let us leave it, a land in which no man dwells, a phantom country stirring the passion of our desire for a fiery chariot — "

" *Tais-toi*," remarked his companion.

The clamor continued ; it even increased when one charioteer was discovered to be whispering "nine francs " in Mr. Dove's ear. Nine, verily it was eight, seven, six. Still the strangers refused, knowing that a franc and a quarter was the day-time price.

"Then five francs for monsieur and madame, all the two."

The besieged were about to accept this amazing offer when a fresh charioteer appeared on the scene from another shouting group.

" Four francs for monsieur and madame, all the two," he shouted in the manner of a Dutch auction, and to the manifest wrath of the others, at which he wickedly laughed.

As monsieur and madame, somewhat out of breath, clambered into the rough covered-vehicle, their charioteer confided to them that he had caught another *Anglais* for five francs, and that was why he could underbid all the others. This be-cozened Anglais thus paid for himself alone one franc more than the Doves paid for " all the two," even though one of the howling charioteers had aired his English by informing them that they were "two mans ; two mans pays more as one mans."

How many scores of times descriptions have been written of the arrival at the Mount, the meeting with handsome Madame Poulard, the warning by the kitchen fire, then the ascent of those interminable stairs to the Spartan plain chambers in la Maison rouge far up the rock. Nothing else was different in the arrival of these dashers. There was the weirdly picturesque swinging of Japanese lanterns to meet them as two rival hotels contended for their patronage. But nobody goes elsewhere than to the original Poulard's, " Poulard *aîné*," if it can be helped, not only because Madame Poulard is a renowned beauty as well as a renowned omelet-thrower, but because all one's acquaintances have always descended there (descended *up* two hundred and ten stairs), and have warned one to " descend " nowhere else. It must be gall and wormwood to the widow of the other Poulard, " Poulard *jeune*," who keeps up the title, to realize every day of her life that though her omelets are equally good, their secret learned from the same original Madame Poulard of a generation ago, she receives only the overflow from her brother-in-law's hostelry. Yet all the same her emissaries come out upon the arrival of every omnibus at night with also Japanese lanterns swinging and swaying like tropical birds of strange plumage. Madame Poulard *jeune* thinks her omelets better than those of her sister-in-law, whose omelets are moist while hers are as dry as omelets *should be, n'est-ce pas ?*

Madame Poulard *aîné* met the Doves with a cooing tenderness, as if she had waited all her life long for just this happy moment. " Madame has cold to the feet, of it I am sure ; let her approach herself to the fire before she mounts to her chamber."

Wood is thrown upon the low embers of the deep kitchen fireplace, flames leap flickeringly up, and Mrs. Dove is warmed clear through by so home-like a greeting, without an arrière pensée of *déjeuner*, two and a half francs ; dinner, three francs ; room, three francs ; morning coffee and rolls, one franc.

Mrs. Dove tells Madame Poulard that she has brought with her many compliments from Madame Say, who, she will remember, remained with her two weeks last summer.

Of course madame remembers ; she is enchanted to have news of dear Madame Say ; she is enchanted to know that this dear Madame Say has not forgotten how much she was contented at the Mount the summer passed, — and this charming lady, carries she herself very well in London?

" Paris," corrected Mrs. Dove.

"Ah, *oui*, Paris : elle avait toujours l'air très parisien. One would say her truly parisienne, n'est-ce pas ? "

" Why not ? " wondered Mrs. Dove, " since she is Parisienne."

"Blarney," laughed Mr. Dove, as they mounted endless stairs, "she had no idea whatever of whom you were speaking. It was not here at all that Madame Say wished to be remembered, but at Dinan."

Mrs. Dove wondered if this cooing was not as much as the omelets in the fame of Poulard *aîné.* For during every déjeuner and dinner during their stay this same cooing came over her shoulder : " *Dear* madame, just one little morsel more. *Dear* madame, you eat nothing. *Dear* madame, this is the last *plat;* eat then of it a little more, *dear* madame."

They were lodged among the clouds, in chambers like convent cells ; far, immensely far below, the village lived, in narrow, tortuous ways. One scarcely thinks of a village and living people on that great rock in the sea, crowned by a fortress-monastery which in its turn is surmounted by a church bristling with pinnacles. Yet the village is very quaint, and its people are picturesque, with wind-blown faces and storm-cracked voices, as they chatter from dusky doorway to dusky doorway, up and down the sides of the steep rock. Mrs. Dove had many chances to talk with them, for like most women she had no sense whatever of topography and the lay of the land, and was much given to squaring circles, or trying to. The rock is thridded with alleys winding in and out among sculptured walls, and walls rough-hewn, and without any mark, so the lady thought, to distinguish one from the other. From Sunday morning to Sunday night after their Saturday night arrival, she wandered in a complete maze whenever she wandered alone, and was more often lost and more often obliged to ask her way on that rock only three thousand yards in circumference at the base, than ever she was lost any one day in all of wide America.

They "did" all the architectural, historical, and legendary things, à la dash, for on Tuesday they must be back to their books and work in the Dove-cote. They did the regulation rounds with a young guide, son of the regular cicerone, who referred with sly frequency to his notes, and discouraged extraneous questions. Cloisters, dungeons, chapter-rooms, refectories, chapels, guard-rooms, *salles des chevaliers,* crypts, *dortoirs,* they saw them all, no doubt, and were glad to see them even if only in such bewildering confusion.

For half a loaf is better than no bread, and it is a peculiarity with these Doves that the half they get is always larger than the half they are obliged to leave. Besides the usual sights, they found others un-noted by guide-books and tourists. In a scrap of a graveyard, with graves hanging to the side of the rock like nests of mason bees, they found the grave of a young English girl drowned here some years ago while touring with her parents. The sight saddened them as they pictured the smitten family, leaving their dead on this far and rough rock, in an ugly enclosure without beauty of tree or flower, with no blossom or branch ever laid by loving hands upon her grave, and only now and then a loitering stranger to stand there a moment and wonder why a heretic foreigner was admitted to consecrated ground. Consecrated ground, indeed, that thin slant of soil over a crev-ice in a rock. One shudders to realize the farce of consecration of that tilting scrap of earth with an all consuming maw just beneath it. One shudders in realizing what that maw must contain. Generations upon generations have fed it for almost a thousand years, generations of dust once vital, and still it is not filled. How many times it has swallowed the entire village, grandsire, sire, and son, — who can tell? The rock must hold some hundreds of people, fishers and their families, relic-vendors, guides, guards, penny-grocers, hotel and café keepers, and their domestic and business entourage. All must die, and evidently all must go up to that horrible burial-place on men's shoulders, hustled up the same steps in the rock their feet have carelessly climbed so many times. It is almost strange to see the villagers indifferent to the monster who will devour them as it devoured their forefathers. It is strange to see women nursing babes on the steps of darksome interiors without weeping and groaning that half way up the Mount the hungry monster lies in wait for the babe as well as all its kindred. It seems strange that villagers are born, live, and die within arm's length of the dreadful maw, and never dream of running away from it even into the sea. Surely it must be a tragedy with alleviations when a Mont Saint-Michel fisherman's body is never recovered from the deep.

The Mount is really much more interested in brides than in this great yawning grave. Brides come continually from miles upon miles away with gay wedding parties, much noise and laughter. Madame Poulard always keeps large wedding-cakes on hand, hymeneally frosted and decorated by the confectioner, who furnishes her by the wholesale. Richard the Good of Normandy and his bride Judith of Brittany had no such cake for their wedding feast, here on the Mount, nine hundred years ago. The inquisitive one of the Doves would have liked very much to know what they did have and where they had it, on this dividing rock upon which and for which so much Norman and Breton blood had been spilt. It must have been a coarse flesh feast, with greasy beards and paws, and perhaps Judith received a few blows just to teach her what to expect. Brides wore crimson when Judith was married to the monk-governed and monk-flattered but harsh Richard in the tenth century, white being the widow's color. Mrs. Dove pictured this Breton bride in her two long and loose-fitting tunics, her hair parted in the middle of her head and much concealed under the long veil all women must wear or be refused the Communion by the priests. Whether she was a happy bride or not seemed to Mrs. Dove to be of very little consequence, for her married days were short, and she never wore the widow's white. It was in honor of his marriage here that Richard the Good built the second church upon the rock. Judith was a bride long before a Norman duke would conquer wild England across the Channel; her daughter would be Queen Emma of England, yet the day of her bridal her stockingless condition would put her utterly to shame in the eyes of the white-muslined and orange-flowered brides of these later days on the Mount. Norman and Breton brides bring money to the village; they buy souvenirs of the occasion; the elders of the party sit about in different cafés, while the younger romp up and down, in and out of all the queer angles and surprising recesses and corners of this most inconceivable village. The Mount enters into bridal calculations for miles of both Normandy and Brittany, and the wedding breakfast or dinner, albeit only the usual one provided by Madame Poulard, with one of her Paris cakes added, is very often the most luxurious repast the bride ever saw, or will ever see. It seems too bad, too, for she is generally so shy or so flustered, or else so intent upon her new matronly dignity, that she rarely eats more than a bird's allowance, although her spouse "tucks in" with might and main, and everybody cries shame upon her. Probably for years to come, in the kitchen back of the shop, as she and her husband drink sour cider and eat rags of beef from the soup, they will talk of the omelet, the salmon, the chickens, the golden potatoes, the salads, and all the cakes and sweets of their wedding-day at the Mount, and the wife will almost shed tears that one may not be a bride and have a glorious hunger at the same time.

During eight months of the year, Poulard *aîné's* is always full, and the dishes clatter incessantly. Wherever upon that steeply towering Mount one may be, it is always felt that the centre of life, the focal point of everything real, of all things not of the dreamy past or the imaginative present, is *Poulard aîné's*, the *salle-à-manger* and its satellite *cuisine*. Everything must fit in with the sacred hours of *déjeuner* and dinner in the long, white-walled *salle-à-manger*. Every plan of the day is subject to those two triumphant ceremonies. In fact, Madame Poulard is a magnificent rival to the marvellous architecture and history of the Mount upon which monks and kings have striven for victory, and an archangel looked down for ages upon deeds of popes and princes. Many a colossally paunched Frenchman, swollen with his two bottles of wine a day and unlimited cider, comes to "The Omelet" to pass a Sunday, and never climbs higher, but sits all day long in a dusky café waiting for the next meal. The fame of Madame Poulard's providing has spread far and wide. Fat priests (they all were fat that day of the Doves, perhaps the lean ones had climbed up higher) come now, not as pilgrims came once with crusts in their sacks, but with ruddy gills and wandering eyes to "swell wisibly before one's very eyes," at Madame Poulard's table. Every day of her life Madame Poulard throws those enormous omelets; sometimes, she says, using sixty dozens of eggs a day. These omelets are the fame of the house, of the Mount, made so a generation ago, by Madame Poulard's mother-in-law. The auberge is named "Omelet," *à la renommée de l'Omelette;* at the machicolated entrance gate of the village "*La Fameuse Omelette,*" stares straight from the walls at all arrivals.

Years ago, when fewer people came to the Mount than now, the original Madame Poulard had very little to offer her guests in the way of food. Eggs, to be sure, were always to be had and could be kept on hand; an omelet could be tossed up in two minutes, even after her people were at table. Naturally also, in those days before the present easy and safe causeway was ever imagined, everybody who reached Mont Saint-Michel did it after some peril. There was always more or less danger among the ever-shifting quicksands which have swallowed, so tradition says, many a knight and his charger, more than one -eloping couple, more than scores of fat priests; so that most travellers made the crossing in a state of some excitement. The way was long, the wind often rough; with excitement and fatigue everybody arrived at the little inn in a state of ravenousness. What then could taste better than Madame Poulard's speedy omelets? What was a more direct contradiction to the old monk who in some dead century wrote "There is nothing on the Mount worth frying"? Every pilgrim and stranger who stayed and comforted himself with omelets spread their fame abroad till the result became the present Madame Poulard's sixty dozens of eggs a day. The Doves scarcely thought to touch the famous dish themselves, so amused were they in watching the expressions of the countenances about them as buxom Madame Poulard herself carried the *renommée* round the table. Greed, nothing more nor less than gluttonous greed, was upon some men's faces, as the large spoon rapidly reduced the golden fleece long before it came near them. One Frenchman in particular seemed almost to crouch, prepared to spring like a panther before the English lady, whose expression was only of curiosity, should remove the last spoonful to her own plate. Happily for everybody a relay came, then several, and the Frenchman's anxious greed changed to greedy satisfaction.

"You may be sure that man always speaks of Mont Sainte-Omelette," remarked the elder Dove.

Strange that after all this talk of the golden fleece so sought by Jasons (and Medeas) of two not to say three countries, the tragic truth remains to be told that it is not so very wonderful after all ! Wherever a good omelet is made it is just as good, for French cooks everywhere have the knack of them, in some magical art of beating eggs and some magical turn of the wrist that tosses them exactly at the magical moment. Thus they, as well as the golden fleece of L'Omelette, seem always in three layers so to say, or rather a roll of the dry fleece wrapped about a middle of liquid gold.

Visitors at L'Omelette have been known upon rare occasions to decline *la renommée !* Mrs. Dove was one, she having no taste for eggs in any form. It would be amusing always to watch Madame Poulard upon these rare occasions. When l'Américaine declined the *chef d'œuvre,* Madame Poulard did not withdraw the dish, even in view of all the watering mouths lower down the table. She still held it over the lady's shoulder, incredulous that it should be intentionally declined, quite sure she had misunderstood, or that the lady did not quite understand what the blessed thing was, thus profanely negatived. When finally she could doubt no longer, the dish with gentle solemnity was withdrawn, and Madame Poulard's brilliant smile faded, till the next sitter dipped deeply into the sacred dish, when it pensively — oh, so pensively ! — dawned again.

Madame Poulard serves other things, and everything *cuit à point.* Thus she dominates the Mount ; she *is* the Mount, one might say, for from every family she draws her servants, — staid women who sleep at home ; into every house that has a decent chamber to spare she introduces her guests ;

of every house to let she takes possession. Thus it comes to pass that of the hosts who reach the Mount every summer one half gives no thought to the fact that some of the most beautiful ecclesiastical and military architecture of the Middle Ages towers above it, but only that here is the most famous best dinner for the price in all France.

It is entirely an *al fresco* life, that of the Mount in summer. Poulard *aîné's* bedrooms are bedrooms and nothing more ; one would as soon sit in a prison cell. Everybody — that is, everybody who is not waiting in cafés for the next meal — is upon the terraces, or sitting upon low walls gazing upon the sea, or wandering through the wondrous architecture that towers to the skies. The rock is circumscribed, but one easily loses one's self in such labyrinthine passages and wanders continually far more than of intention. Then when night comes and Madame (and Monsieur) Poulard must go to rest in their own stuffy little chamber over the *café* across the road from L'Omelette, then the gay Japanese lanterns are brought out with which every one must be lighted to bed. No other way could candles be used where beds are almost out of doors. Up the soaring external stairs, up the village street to chambers in private houses, these lanterns sway and swing like footless birds of Paradise and of fable.

The day beginning somewhat chill, the Doves passed the little iron tables of the balcony to reach the glass house at the end. They thus passed also so many half-open doors, with glimpses of toilets *les plus intimes*, that they were quite abashed, even though they knew that the open doors (or long windows) revealed only French people who did not care a rap, and that those who did or would care were English behind doors tightly shut.

In the glass house, sheltered from the wind, they expanded in sunshine. Others before them had taken coffee on the large circular table, but only one person took his at the same time. He was a Frenchman, of better than the *commis-voyageur* type in appearance, and of spare habit, as *va sans dire*, else had he taken his coffee in the café on the earth below, and not here among the clouds. He broke his rolls into the bowl of coffee, and bent his head almost into it, as if asking a benediction upon it. Mr. Dove gazed reverently through the clear glass of the walls, out upon the radiant expanse, which, far, far below, encircled the rock in silver and blue. A sound of rushing waters, of winds and roaring tides, suddenly rose up from the heart of tranquil space and filled that house of crystal. A storm among gothic forests, a tempest over a boiling sea seemed to burst upon their calm sunniness in one tremendous instant.

" Who would suppose we could hear the sucking and swashing of the tide at this height? " solemnly remarked Mr. Dove. Whereupon crimson Mrs. Dove bit her lips, but the Frenchman did not raise his head.

Then came the discreet and elderly *mère de famille* who served their *café*, to tell them that *déjeuner* would be at *douze heures.*

" *Douze heures!* " complained the lady. " That's your fault for making me do all the talking."

" *Making* you ! I like that ! when do I have a chance for an edgeways word ? "

" You *must* have been making me do it all," insisted the lady, " or she never would have said *douze heures* for *midi*. I 've a mind to tell her that you are half a Frenchman."

" And take my coffee as the tide takes the shore ? "

She did not run after the *mère de famille*, who talked pigeon-French for the benefit of *ces Anglais*. She ceased to wonder at that pigeon-French in face of the *Anglais* at dinner that night, who declined Madame Poulard's soft entreaty with, " Massy, madame ; je suis rempli jusker le cou."

With Monday morning came a flight to Dol, where they visited the cathedral, had *déjeuner*, a delightful drive to the Mont-Dol for a dollar, and where they snap-shotted like mad, including the famous Menhir, a strange ragged shaft in a field, thirty-five feet above ground, with no earthly clue to the mystery how it got there and by whom it was hewn. They pitied the dumb, lonely thing, unable to tell its pre-historic story, unable to taunt the modern world with ignorance of all the things it knows ; doomed to rear itself aloft in the daily companionship of hinds and yokels, with now and then a cow meditatively scratching herself, and a pig grunting piggish superiority because it can grunt, at feet that have stood still while century after century has passed on before it, powerless to stand still one instant.

Then came Dinan, much favored by the English as was evident at *table d'hôte*, where among a score of people was not one native of the country.

Some had just arrived from Jersey, some were on their way there, and the former gave the latter advice.

"You 'll get a *breakfast* at the Star, an *English* breakfast."

"That *will* be a blessing."

"You must not forget to get a candy shoe " (*canne de chou*).

"Candy shoe ! whatever is that ? "

"It 's a cane made of the cabbage stalks, which grow several feet high on Jersey. They are very tough, and everybody gets a few to carry away."

"Hope we shall have our rooms swept occasionally. Have n't been swept here since we came."

"Dassay," said the Englishman late from Jersey. "But I always manage that by sluicing my room with my bawth. They have to wipe it up then."

"You never know an Englishman not to mention his ' bawth ' in course of time," remarked the Dove whom the other Dove often named " Anglomaniac." "Yet Britons have not always been so ostentatiously clean. Did n't nasty old Pepys jeer at his wife because after a winter in the dirt she washed herself in warm water, and declared her intention of thereafter keeping herself very clean ? 'I know how long that will last,' jeered the vile creature. Then there was that dainty bride who became Mistress Alice Thornton during the civil wars. She was of an honorable house and lived in luxury. The day after her marriage and while yet in her mother's house she became dangerously ill. When she recovered she wrote, 'I cannot conjecture the cause of the fit, unless

it was washing my feet at that time of the year.'
When the Swan of Lichfield first saw her sister's
fiancé, she described him as looking 'very
clean.' "

Dinan offers many furnished houses to let, but
none tempted the Americans.

"What could we do with immense *salles-à-
manger* and grand *salons?*" they agreed, with
their usual philosophic disesteem for all things
beyond their reach. "We would n't take a coach
and four as a gift except to give away again."

Dinard after Dinan is beautiful and its breezes
are pure. It, like Dinan, is much affected by the
English, particularly by Oxford men, who come
over in an English steamer to join English friends
to spend a vacation in English villas, waited upon
by English servants, under the impression that they
are living in France. It has much of elegant-villa
style, but is saved from the deadliness of such elegance by exquisite views of sea and shore, still too
wild for villadom's encroachments. Here more
English bathe in the summer even than French,
being driven away from their own English bathing
places by that same force of English numbers that
has filled three quarters of the globe with the English language and made the Doves' own country
England's " dear daughter " when Americans be-
have themselves to England's liking, " that dangerous mixture of races " when they do not.

At Saint-Malo, after Dinard, the dashers would
have seven good hours before the steaming of the
Honfleur for Jersey. One spot claimed their first
attention, at some distance from the town. They
scrambled over a rough stretch of ragged shore till
they reached the promontory which at high-tide is

the island of Grand Bé. There they climbed an acclivity, ragged, outcast, and forlorn, reminding them so vividly of stony New England pastures around some " Poor-House " that they sniffed instinctively for tansy and penny-royal. On and on they came to a most melancholy spot enclosed within a rusty railing and marked by a weather-stained granite cross. This is the spot chosen in his lifetime for a grave, by a genius of France. This treeless promontory, an island twice a day, is where Chateaubriand willed to be laid when the last embers of his long life died out, and left but ashes. He wished to sleep thus without inscription over his dust, with the eternal sea sounding his perpetual requiem. For he was a vain man, he considered his perpetual requiem fit employment for the sea, and he fondly fancied his dust would make the spot a Mecca for pilgrims, who would need no inscription to tell them of the fire extinguished beneath that cross. Alas for the hopes of genius that depend upon other generations than its own mortal one for personal tribute ! Chateaubriand's tomb draws no pilgrims save rare and pensive foreigners such as the Doves. No footpath is worn about the grave, no care seems bestowed upon it to keep it from the inevitable decay with which nature begins her ever-living mystery of birth and rebirth. Sometimes on Sundays, it is said, bevies of servants stroll over from Saint-Malo to chatter and romp about the grave which Chateaubriand hoped would gather deeper and deeper solemnity with added years, not one of the rompers knowing or caring for whom the cross was raised, but only that the place is a good one for the game of *cache-cache*.

Also it is said that sentimental tourists, not fond of exercise or limited of time, write many poetic descriptions of this isle — as seen from Saint-Malo.

Chateaubriand was born in Saint-Malo to the sound of the sea and the wind, and his young feet must often have danced over the spot where the old man of fourscore was laid to rest, apart as he had wished, from all mankind, alone with the sea and the wind. He lived through various revolutions, he died in the very midst of the one which drove Louis Philippe 'into exile; perhaps it is no wonder that he wished to remove even his ashes from the companionship of his shifty and tumultuous countrymen, and his cross from their picks and shovels.

"If I die away from France," he wrote, "let my remains rest in exile till fifty years after my death. A travelling corpse is horrible to me. A skeleton white and light is more easily moved. Mine will be less fatigued in such a last journey than when I dragged it here and there under the weight of my trials. Let my remains be spared a sacrilegious autopsy. Let me be spared a search in my frozen brain, and in my silent heart, for the mystery of my being."

What cares the rolling earth, the teeming world for the mystery of a being that ceased to be, half a century ago? Had Chateaubriand died in exile, it is even probable that nobody would take thought in 1898 to move "the light and white skeleton" to Grand Bé, which in Breton means tomb.

The hotel in which the Americans took *déjeuner* was Chateaubriand's birthplace. One of the viands was not named for the author of "Génie du Christianisme," "Atala," and "René," as many

suppose, being, not a Chateaubriand, but a Châ-
teaubriant steak.

As they walked a plank to the Honfleur they
walked directly into England, and France *la belle*
was behind them, — beautiful, beautiful France,
with its exquisite landscape, its wonderful architecture, its romantic stories, its stirring history, its
peerless salads, and its renowned omelets. Everything now was aggressively English, even the hanging buckets and scent of toasted kippers ; the
stewardess tossed and caught her *h*'s as a juggler
his cups and balls.

" Probably a descendant of 'Enery the Hateth's
steward," remarked one of the Doves, referring to
an expense-book of that monarch in which was a
charge for " sope-hashes " (or soap-ashes).

" How long have we been on our Little Dash
into France ? " asked a Dove, as peacock-blue
shores grew dim and the winds of the Channel
whistled about their ears.

" Not more than four weeks," said the other, reflectively. " Let me see ; we left Jersey on Saturday ; Sunday we were on the Mount ; Monday at
Dol and Dinan ; this is Tuesday with Dinard and
Saint-Malo, and there is Jersey, looming large.
Yes, it must be four weeks. Wonder if Martin
will know us, with all our continental airs? "

Know them? At least they knew her, as she
smiled a welcome home in the green doorway of
the Dove-cote. Indeed it was home, a genuine
home-coming to their own vine and fig-tree, with all
the delicious sense of smiling familiarity in every
chair and table that returned voyagers always find
in their own homes. There was Martin with a
tray even before they had removed their gloves,

the teapot steaming upon it and two cups ready, with sugar or without, as each liked it. A bright fire was in the sitting-room; one needs all the brightness one can get after four days in that dirty France, and the twilight must have been chill on the water. A cheery table was spread in the dining-room below, everything was at perfection-point, the chops snapping like mad lest that point vanish before they were taken up.

"Ha, ha!" blinked an old-maidish object in the gay lamplight of the dining-room, "ha, ha! the bride is home again from a foreign shore. We have missed you, dear; I have not once been warm since you went away to foreign parts (I, you know, am English), and the cot has been dark without you, for Martin kept the doors shut. You have not seen so cosey and comfortable a friend as I am, have you now, in all your Little Dash? You yearned for me yesterday afternoon (a year ago), at your hotel in Dinan. You remember you were caught in a violent shower and had to hurry back. Then snug and dry in slippers and your comfortable two-franc-a-day chamber at the Hôtel d'Angleterre, with the rain pouring down, you sent for a *pot de thé*. When it came did n't you re-member me? Well, I guess you did!" (Here Rebecca spoke conspicuously through her nose.) "I am not handsome, I know; I am brown of com-plexion and squat of figure; you can't expect much beauty in a bridal purchase for a sixpence; but then, you know, I 'm neither too large nor too small, as you hate my kind, and my interior is not cor-roded by astringent servitude to generations before yourself. Me, Brown Rebecca, you bought to serve you with freshness, therefore you remembered me with tenderness yesterday afternoon (a year ago) when that hideous metallic creature with dull face and corrugated sides leered at you full of yellow water. You thought of me as you sneered at the one spoonful of tea in all that water (tea, you know, costs four times as much in France as in Jersey), and then you performed a clever little smuggler-trick of adding a big shake to the water from your own little parcel of tea. Thus your five-o'clock was quite of its usual strength, but, dear, dear, did n't you drink it with your back turned upon that pewter tea-pot? Now say again how pleasant it is to return to your bridal presents, made to yourself, all blinking and winking a welcome to the bride."

" Ha, ha ! " chuckled another, a taller more showy object. " Brown Rebecca tells the truth ; we all sadly missed you during these months of your foreign residence. The cupboard is not at all gay when the door is shut, and one seems to hear sighing among those dusty muslin flowers under glass shades on the top shelf ; we terribly miss your pleasant faces and your discussions of the charms and interests of this little island (for I am English, you know ; you bought me for a shilling, although but for that imperceptible limp of my foot I should be worth eight). We have all hoped nothing unhandsome would befall our Bride ; now I greet her return with my arms full of oranges, and congratulations that she is no longer, what she was all the time of the Little Dash, a commonplace little old — "

" Ha, ha, ha ! " discreetly interrupted tinkling and silvery chorus, " Ha, ha, ha ! " from spoon-vase, salt-cellars, cider-pitcher, " Ha, ha, ha ! don't forget us and our welcome upon your return home from ' *ler Continong.*' "

"Ha, ha!" laughed the lamplight. "Ha, ha!" the broadly grinning sitting-room fire. "Ha, ha!" carpets and curtains and the Victorian prints of baronial hall. "Ha, ha!" laughed even the door-knobs. "Ha, ha, ha!" shouted the two easy-chairs with wide-open arms.

The sitting-room table waited until the last with its welcome and its homeness of books and pages of manuscript scattered about. "Ha, ha, ha!" it laughed. "I am exactly the same as that long-ago day on which you steamed away. Martin has not dared to touch me, but kept me covered with a sheet; *ce n'était pas du tout gai*, as they say in the foreign country from which you come. You see there are the same flowers blooming on the deep window-seats; the same photographs of Sark and Jersey on the mantel-piece, with piles of books. It's all very much the same after all these years of your absence, except this four days' accumulation of postal matter, and, oh, yes, here's a bundle of new American magazines from the circulating library. Pough! how they smell of tobacco!"

"*Mong Doo !*" sighed the foolish Dove. "Let us no further roam, but remain Doves so long as we do live."

"The Channel Islands are all water," said a Dove.

A moment after, —

" I wish we could go by land ! "

Unnecessary to explain that this was the foolish Dove.

"Our Dove-cote ought to be named the ' Sea-gulley,' " continued Mrs. Dove ; " then, perhaps, we should not mind this spiteful Channel so much."

"There were the Seaworthys, however," remarked the other, "who leased that rugged old manor-house for a long term of years, and named it ' Sea Bright.' Seaworthy is a university don with eight months' vacation a year. You know they had to give up Sea Bright, in spite of its name, because they could not endure the Channel passage. The people who have it now call it Gladstone Villa or something of the kind, and live in it all the year."

It was apropos of a visit to Guernsey. For weeks they had been planning this visit, but one of them, with a most natural dovely aversion to boiling salt water even when cold, had, from week to week, put it off. It was a curious fact but a positive one that the Channel between the Gorey side of Jersey and France was the most enchanting

of enchantresses, beguiling, luring, till one of the
Doves, at least, almost spread wings to flee away
into the mystery of its enticing ; while the Channel
to be crossed from the St. Helier's side to England seemed dour and forbidding, no matter how
brilliant its smile. Had Guernsey been between
Gorey and Port Bail they would long ago have
added its memory to their rich possessions. Unfortunately for them, it was on the way to England :
they must even come down to the commonplace
manner of embarking in one of the regular English packets, for all the world as if they were
returning to drorin-room shoots and Cavendish
Square.

Queer, vastly queer, that after so much proing
and conning they steamed away from St. Helier's
on one of the grayest, windiest mornings of the
entire season. Safely ensconced in the wind-pro-
tected seats " for Ladies only," one of them set
firm lips over iron resolution that upon the other's
fund of pity and amusement no drafts whatever
should be made. The plan is recommended to
whosoever cares to profit by it. Long experience
of tumbling waters has proved to one person at
least, the sea-value of a stiff upper lip.

" Should auld acquaintance be forgot ? "

The air came thin and shrill across the glum
water from Elizabeth Castle. If ever there was
a chill sound in the world, that solitary piping was
chilly. It split the air like a cold knife. Some
of the passengers shivered at the sound, some
faces turned blue. One man was reduced to
tears. He was leaning over the railing below and
wiping his eyes.

"A soldier whose time is out," explained a ship's officer. "It's probably his chum whose time may not be up for years, saying good-bye."

Two long hours to Guernsey; but even two hours came to an end in time, and they reached Mrs. Bragg's quite in time to go marketing for the mid-day meal. Mrs. Bragg gave Mrs. Dove a dainty little basket, and the two set forth for novel observations, fresh experiences, and mutton-chops.

Their lodgings were on the Esplanade, close upon the waterside. The house had been recommended to them as "strictly honest, perfectly civil, obliging and neat; and where the cooking is all one could ask." The situation, too, had been recommended as "near everything," and where one could always see "plenty going on." This had seemed quite high praise enough. What Dove could ask more? So they walked straight from the steamer into the pretty sitting-room facing the water and the lesser islands of Herm and Jethou, with Sark behind them, which sitting-room, with two neat bedrooms and attendance (cooking, care of rooms, etc.), was theirs for twenty-five shillings a week, more in summer, less in winter.

They never repented their choice, even though later they criticised it. Mrs. Dove was disposed to grumble every time they climbed up the island's sides among the houses on the top. Whoever had so highly recommended Mrs. Bragg had neglected to inform himself, or herself, of the kind of "goings-on" preferred by the Doves. The arrival and departure of steamers, the bustle of hotels, the constant passing of trams and carriages,

all the business of a lively port, — these were the
goings-on before Mrs. Bragg's. Nevertheless the
Americans found them too exasperatingly near,
and in near things their souls and eyes took little
pleasure ; wherein they differed from Charles
Lamb and most other cockneys. From the
windows of houses high above Mrs. Bragg's roof,
were divine visions of things not near, dreamy
sails upon a silent sea, fairy islands, a nebulous
foreign coast, and at night a mystery of moonlight
and shimmering waters to lift one absolutely out
of mundane lodgings, no matter at how much or
how little a week.

All the same, Mrs. Bragg's was cheery, cosey,
homelike. But when the final reckoning came
for milk, eggs, bread, laundry, and various other
things, there was, alas ! a discrepancy between
Mrs. Bragg's reckoning and Mrs. Dove's.

Discrepancies of account between lodger and
landlady are not rare.

" However, as this one is to your own advantage,
I suppose you will say nothing about it," observed
Mr. Dove.

" It's a whole cent," said she, with satisfaction.
" I shall tell her, just to show what a clever keeper
of accounts I am."

How quaint and strange is Guernsey after more
gentle Jersey, indeed after almost anywhere.
Their lodgings were on the Esplanade, the narrow
edge of the island down upon which most of the
island looks. Behind the row of hotels and lodging-houses where their own tent was pitched, the
island steeply towered. Every possible road
soared, every path straightly ascended. In time
these Doves learned another way of rising to

Guernsey's heights without steep paths and roads. It was by means of a most extraordinary succession of stone steps, hundreds of them, grimy and of ancient aspect, grappling the side of the island like scaling-ladders. No description can give an idea of these steps or stairs, which perhaps explains the fact that all descriptions of Guernsey mention them, if at all, only slightly.

The steps began obscurely among the foreign-looking houses of the lower town ; Mrs. Dove often hunted for them in vain. Then they rose obscurely into perpetual twilight, till with dumb, cold malice they took possession of the unwary stranger like some Pit-and-Pendulum nightmare ending in doom. Alone Mrs. Dove was entirely lost among them ; she never could understand, she does not to this day, how wingless beings freely found their way among them. The spectacle of her fellow-creatures, or what seemed like such, passing indifferently up and down these sphinx-like stones almost took her breath away. A whistling butcher-boy, basket on arm, a schoolboy with his books, almost seemed to her creatures of Walpurgis night. She yearned but never dared, to ask them their clue to the dusky labyrinth, or if some other extra sense these island folk possessed, unknown to the rest of the world, to see daylight in a nightmare maze.

" You surely know when you are going straight up the side of the island," said Mr. Dove, who never lost his way in his life.

" No, I do not," she mourned. " I stop a moment for breath, in an instant three several and different stretches of stone steps sneak away from before my face, each climbing as much as the others. How am I to know which is the *up* I seek when all are *up* ? "

From the central and direct steps, as Mrs. Dove found, are various branchings. To take one of these branchings was to be lost among high and blank stone walls of gardens and dwellings. Sometimes the bewildered American walked into private gardens, sometimes she paused upon thresholds of kitchens, sometimes walls imprisoned her, only a tiny space of sky high above and countless steps before her. Then she felt comparatively safe, for step by step she was sure to arrive *somewhere*, whereas with branchings on every side she might wander forever, arriving nowhere every time.

These marvellous steps are for the convenience of houses whose fronts are upon the climbing streets. The labyrinth follows the convenience of each house clutching the island's side, hence so many branchings. Mrs. Dove hated them, — unutterably, inexpressibly hated. She looked down them from the top as into an infernal pit ; from the bottom she looked up as towards some sorcerer's cave in a mountain side.

" It is never of any use to ask where I am," she repined. " What difference does it make to me whether I am beside Colonel Jones's pantry or Major Smith's bedroom ? Neither is it of any use to try to tell where I want to go ; for I never know myself. I usually ask the nearest way *o u t.* I am always directed to it down the very way I came. They are called ' Constitution Steps,' I suppose because they are enough to ruin the best constitution in the world."

Almost everywhere else in Guernsey than on

those constitution-ruining steps it was pleasant to ask one's way.

"Will you kindly tell us what building that is?"

"That is the Royal Court House," answers the small boy, "erected in 1799, at a cost of seven thousand pounds, but lately enlarged and improved. Inside are many portraits."

They ask the same question of a youth in a chemist's shop.

"That is the Grange Club," he answers courteously, "frequented by the best society in town ; strangers are temporarily admitted. The tower you see is Victoria tower, built in 1848 to commemorate the visit of her Majesty in 1846."

"Where will this road lead us?"

"To the Bailiff's Cross, sir," answers the working-woman addressed. "You will find a flat stone a mile or two beyond. There the Bailiff of Guernsey in the thirteenth century took the sacrament on his way to execution. The place where he was gibbeted is near by, anybody will tell you where."

"Animated guide-books!" declared the Americans. "It is good to feel that one is welcome in a place, even as a tourist. In some places the tourist cannot get a civil answer unless he pays for it."

They remembered an occasion in Paris, one in London, one in Ravenna, one in Worthing, England. In Paris one evening they stopped a few moments before the window of a mean *boutique* in a mean street to read certain written directions in their hands. While they read a man issued from the shop and demanded a sou for the use of his light. In London they once asked the way of a bootblack, who called after them, "Told you wrong! You did n't give me nothin'." In Ravenna cabmen followed them with persistent entreaty because they chose to walk from the station to their hotel, — the entreaties, as the distance to the hotel lessened, changing to curiosity as to how much their shoes cost them a year, and if there were no carriages — in *Russia!*

In Worthing one bitterly cold winter's day in 1892, Mrs. Dove, while waiting the omnibus to Broadwater, stepped within a sheltering recess. It chanced to be the recess of somebody's front door, as she found when the front door opened and a forbidding face, evidently mistress of the house, informed her, "This is not for the convenience of the public." The rudeness was so entirely gratuitous that the American became almost speechless. Murmuring something like "Only five minutes' protection from the cold wind," she fled to the nearest open door and begged for a moment's shelter.

The grocer replied with the most kindly courtesy, "Certainly, madame, as long as you wish," and brought her a chair.

"Can you tell me who lives inside the door from which I just came?" she asked.

"Oh, yes, the postmaster," answered the man.

The Americans knew all about the wicked bailiff, a Guernsey tradition of ages agone. A field is still called by the name of his intended victim, and the place of his own gibbet was the place of public execution for centuries. It is only necessary to realize the semi-regal importance of a Norman bailiff to understand what a convulsion of insular nature must have witnessed the hanging of one, and how readily the story immortalized itself.

The bailiff's house is still shown. It is a low granite building, once thatched, with a round doorway and round tower after the Channel-Island fashion. Guernsey seigneurs, like those of Jersey, were not magnificently lodged. This bailiff owned a field across which a neighbor had a right of way to the spring used by both families. The bailiff was annoyed by the neighbor's use of the right of way and tried to buy him off. The neighbor refused to be bought off and doubtless made himself excessively disagreeable. Quite exasperated by the continual faring to and fro in front of his house by his neighbor's servants and cattle, he determined to rid himself of his neighbor. During the harvest of 1264, the bailiff hid two of his silver cups in a wheat-rick and then spread a report of his having been robbed, at the same time expressing strong suspicions of his neighbor. At the trial, witnesses suborned by the powerful bailiff gave such strong evidence against the accused that the judge was just passing sentence of death upon him, when one of the bailiff's servants came rushing in crying, "They are found! they are found!" The bailiff was so overcome with rage and vexation that he unwittingly exclaimed, "Thou wretch! did I not tell thee not to touch that rick?" This opened the eyes of the Court, who condemned the bailiff to the death meant for his victim.

"Do you suppose his ghost haunts the spot?" asked a Dove.

"Of course," answered the other; "else we should not now be walking all this way merely to see the spot where Gaultier de la Salle repented of his crime six centuries and thirty-one years ago.

What are memories but ghosts? What are traditions but ghosts of ghosts?"

Guernsey in some respects seems more foreign, less English, than Jersey. One reason of its foreignness is its currency. Both Guernsey and Jersey have the right of copper coinage, and both have thus penny pieces (or two cents) unlike each other's and unlike England's. But whereas Jersey's currency is entirely British, Guernsey's is entirely French. Francs and French gold pieces are in universal circulation. On the one tramline the Doves offered an English shilling and received a franc in change. A premium is upon English money, and to keep one's own, to lose nothing in buying with it, the stranger must never forget just how much his English coin is worth in French silver. To add to the bemuddlement, the price of an article is sometimes given in English money, and then the stranger is sure to have just changed all his money into French. When he has only English money nobody ever thinks to give a price except in francs. The post-office, being English, of course sells stamps only for English coin. Nevertheless, one need not be provided with any other than French money, for the officials are always prepared to change French money into English. Mrs. Dove became aware of this when she bought her first dozen 2½d-stamps for her American letters. She had changed all her English money into French before remembering that she needed stamps, then bought the English stamps with French money, paying a higher premium than she had just been allowed, — a most initiating transaction.

"What do you expect me to give you for this?"

asked the market-woman of whom the Americans bought their first Guernsey butter and to whom they offered an English half-crown.

Not yet had Mrs. Dove learned the queerness of Guernsey money, so she soberly answered, —

" Butter."

She was meant to say how little premium she would accept in place of the regulation one, perfectly well known to the woman. In time the Doves learned to insist upon English change for English coin when they found they had no French to offer. There was generally then a great fuss and pretence of hunting or borrowing, but in the end the English money was forthcoming from somewhere. It is said that the fine Guernsey market-house was built by the profits of francs given in change for shillings.

However that may be, the market-house seemed verily a *petite France.* French, or its cousin several times removed, was the language among the market people, although more English was spoken than in the Jersey market. The market-women had each her name above her stall, and every name was French. There were Marettes, Brissons, Longuevilles, Massarts, etc. Yet another anomaly of these anomalous isles, not one of the Marettes, Brissons, Longuevilles, was " Madame ; " every one of them was " Mrs."

" This constant change of currency tempts to crime," Mrs. Dove solemnly remarked. " It tempts, and to-day I fell."

" How much booty did you get away with ? "

"It is not the ill-gotten booty," she lamented, " but the innocent and smiling youth upon whom I have fastened shameful suspicions ! While you were busy with your letters this morning, you know I repeated our tramway ride to St. Sampson. When I paid my fare, the pleasant faced youth, no doubt as honest as the day, charged me two-pence to the end of the ride. You know the car stops half-way out and waits for the returning one. Like the simpleton I am, I left the car I was on, and took the return car, thinking we had arrived at the end of the line. The wind was blowing fiercely and I was bitterly cold, or I should not have done so. When I paid my return fare, the conductor took but a penny from me, and I remarked that I had paid two pence going out. Observe the honesty of Guernsey folk : the con-ductor seemed much disturbed that I had been over-charged (which I had not), and if you will believe it, gave me a penny from his own store !"

"Then your two penny rides cost you two pennies."

"Yes, yes; but I paid to St. Sampson, and stopped half-way there. That poor slandered youth, falsely accused and made an object of sus-picion to his fellows ! What shall I do? To hunt him up and give him a penny would add insult to injury. What shall I do?"

"Write a note to the management and state the facts."

Very conscientiously the lady wrote the letter.

Months afterwards in Paris, she found it be-tween the pages of a Guernsey Guide.

To-day while wintry winds beat about a New England home and snow wreaths dim every vista from the windows a writing woman is conscious that a gloom as wintry settles over certain of her summer memories. She knows that this very hour, upon a romantic rock against which the gray Atlantic surges forever, her memory is still green. Evergreen is that memory, as the London "deadbeat," who slandered one innocent man out of eight Guernsey Doubles, which in value make one English penny.

"I am thankful Jersey has no tramways," she murmurs. "No knowing how many rides I might have stolen there, even with a familiar currency."

Her thoughts dwell upon beautiful Jersey and its toddling babes of railway trains, till her brow clears amid dreams of many an enchanting little journey, till it even does not overcloud again when her companion says, —

"Guernsey with those Constitution Steps can never have a railway until we railway to the moon." Which may be sooner than we expect.

Guernsey is an island of flowers, as Jersey is of fruits and vegetables. From the last of February, it is a sight of itself, the wealth of daffodils sent by every steamer to Covent Garden. The year is a procession of flowers, every month with its queen flower of all. They are raised under glass, and in the open air, the hydrangeas, rhododendrons, camellias, of a splendor far beyond their kind elsewhere. Every now and then, even so early as May, when doors swing open in blank stone walls, one catches glimpses of gardens, all ablaze with color, and waves of fragrance surge forth as from some celestial country. Upon the arrival of all the steamers, men and women go on board with flowers for sale. To one coming from chilly England, and touching Guernsey only on the way to Jersey, the sight of all these dewy blossoms is scarcely less than heavenly. One seems really to have touched a clime ten thousand miles away from gray and misty Cavendish Square. Jersey people are rather given to tip-tilting the nose at Guernsey flowers when on their way to London, — "As if we had not as good of our own;" but the fact that the flower-venders present themselves upon England-bound steamers, just as much as upon Jersey-bound, proves that somebody buys them, even if Jersey people do not.

That Guernsey excels in flowers does not argue any want of vegetables. The argument would be foolish in face of all these island housekeepers returning from market. There are few or no wagons taking orders, and few if any delivery wagons. The housekeepers buy in the Paris fashion, enough for to-day but nothing for to-morrow, and carry their purchases home themselves. The prevalent custom of "cabbage nets," or string bags, makes the housekeepers' marketing of lively interest to strangers. No attempt is made at concealment; so through the nets' meshes one discovers that the tall lady in mourning will have lamb and pease for dinner, with strawberries and a cream cheese, while the little lady in blue has a family unusually fond of salad with their steak, judging by the quantity she carries. It is not the season for conger soup (although the monstrous creatures can be bought dried), else many of the cabbage nets would carry great sections of them. Guernsey, as well as Jersey and the other islands, is enormously fond of the conger eel. In their season they lie in the markets in huge serpentine coils, weighing at times even thirty pounds. While at Dove Cottage the Americans heard much of this rare delicacy; and one day dainty Lady Flo' quite pitied them that they had always come to the islands just as the congers swam, wriggled, or burrowed out of reach.

Guernsey has never done anything to make itself famous, yet in point of size it exceeds the immortal island of Ithaca, a rocky and mountainous bit of the world twenty-five miles in circumference. Yet Ithaca was long the home of Ulysses, whose adventures on his return to it from the Trojan War form the subject of the Odyssey. Small and unfamed as it is, romantic Guernsey has drawn more than one American to live and die within its seagirt walls. In the chief burial-ground one reads of these dead. One was a " spinster " " born in South Carolina, America, in 1794, died in Guernsey aged 74." Another was from " Kinosha, America." Beneath the name of still another may be read the words, " A friend sinsciere layeth here," — a proof that the Guernsey stone-cutter was more shaky in his English than Guernseymen usually are. It reminded the Doves of an inscription they saw over a Frenchman in Bethlehem, Pennsylvania, — " Pryie pour sonarm."

" Probably the American relatives ordered the marble and inscription," concluded the Doves, " and have no idea that their friend sincere lies on English territory under spelling very much worse than the English-despised American."

HAUTEVILLE HOUSE.

IT was all up hill the day, the one show day of the week, that the Doves climbed up to the Hauteville House, where Victor Hugo lived in exile for eighteen years. Before he came to Guernsey and bought Hauteville House he had lived three years in Jersey, surrounded by an uproarious band of also exiled Frenchmen. These men, with their domestic and social habits *à la française*, so scandalized the good Jersey folk, unaccustomed to seeing wives and non-wives live almost under the same roofs, that Jersey was made none too comfortable for the exiles. When in their furiously radical paper these French journalists openly reviled and insulted the Queen of England because of her welcome to Louis Napoleon in 1855, the excuse was gladly taken to expel them from the island.

Edmond Biré, in his book on Hugo, says that the exiles received a warmer welcome in Guernsey than would otherwise have been extended to them for this very reason. Mrs. Dove was quite ready to believe this when she heard one of the gentle Bragg sisters throw doubts upon the genuineness of Tom Thumb's trousers preserved in a museum, for no other reason than that the museum was in Jersey, and not Guernsey; and when the market-women sniffed at the name of Jersey honey and

butter, of which Chateaubriand wrote, " Le vent de
l' Océan, qui semble démentir de sa rudesse, donne
à Jersey du miel exquis, de la crême d'une dou-
ceur extraordinaire, et du beurre d'un jaune foncé
qui sent la violette ; " when mild Mrs. Bragg asserted that Jersey is the Paradise of English
'Arries, who always go past Guernsey without
stopping ; and when told of a Bible chained to a
stone wayside seat on one of Jersey's small in-
clines, is sure that Jersey needs such warning as
Guernsey never did.

The house in which Hugo lived in Jersey was
mean and low indeed, compared with Hauteville
House. It was but a stone's throw from the
Dove Cot ; the Doves knew it as an unattractive
boarding-house. The view from the front was
sterile and flat ; the house itself one in which
one could not imagine a poet unless in the poetic
stage where his effusions go down upon grocers'
brown paper. Victor Hugo spoke of this Marine
Terrace as flat, square, and " tombshaped." However, it is, and was in the fifties, like most Jersey
houses, turned with its ugliest side to public observation. Upon the other side is a garden and
terrace sloping to the sea, — the terrace upon which
sad Madame Hugo passed so many hours "alone
with my darning and my dead." Poor woman !
not only was she the neglected wife of a faithless
husband, but she knew that her supplanter, who
accompanied Hugo in all his wanderings and who
would openly take a wife's place in his household
after her own death, kept open house not only
for Hugo's friends, but for the poor wife's as well.
Even there in Jersey the supplanter one day
raised her glass at dinner, where was Madame

Hugo's cousin Asseline, and insolently said, " A la
santé de votre cousine."

Victor Hugo is remembered as untidy in his
dress, always wearing a black coat and gray
trousers very much the worse for dirt, and a shocking bad hat, as was becoming to a republican
proscrit. Nobody remembers ever to have seen
Madame Hugo, who lived in close retirement with
her *bas et chaussettes.* Hugo had not yet written
his most celebrated romances, although twenty
years and more had elapsed since the literary
revolution led by " Hernani " and " Notre Dame de
Paris." He was poet and dramatist until he came
to Jersey. Here, where even the wind forgets its
bitterness and the wintry sky its gloom, in the
Jersey of which he wrote, —

" Jersey rit, terre libre au sein de sombres mers,
 Les genêts sont en fleur, l'agneau paît les près verts,
 L'écume jette aux rocs ses blanches mousselines ;
 Par moments apparaît au sommet des collines,
 Livrant ses crins épars au vent âpre et joyeux,
 Un cheval effaré, qui hennit dans les cieux, — "

here, in this Jersey of lambs and blooms, this
Jersey where Chateaubriand found the springtime
to keep its youth longer than anywhere else, Jersey
a *lit de fleurs*, here Hugo wrote his " Châtiments,"
full of blazing, blasting, blighting hate, full of a sort
of demoniac fury, which in spite of its artistic form
forces one to remember that both Victor Hugo's
brother and his daughter died in lunatic asylums.
" Les Châtiments " was printed in Jersey. Its admirers called it *délire sacré.* Mme. Hugo wrote to a
friend, in fear of the poverty that threatened them :
" For my part I plan every day how I may give my

family a dinner no poorer than that of yesterday ; "
and to another: " Les bas et les chaussettes rac-
commodés, je fais un travail : mon mari me raconte
toute sa vie le soir après le diner ; cela fournira des
espèces de mémoires ; j'ai une belle terrasse, à mes
pieds est la mer, je vais souvent me promener, je
pense à mes morts."

The volume which came of these recountings
was "Victor Hugo : Par un témoin de sa Vie,"
written ostensibly by Madame Hugo, but really by
himself.

When the poet became many times millionnaire
and a glory, or at least a boast, of France, Madame
Hugo planned no more how to keep his dinners
from tasting of poverty and exile ; she no longer
cared for his *bas et chaussettes*. Neither, we may
suppose, did the ex-actress of the Porte Saint
Martin who took her place at the head of Hugo's
household, while the legitimate wife slept under
the sod of a poor little country churchyard in
Normandy.

The ex-actress, a very poor actress although
beautiful, is sometimes spoken of as "Madame
Strasbourg," having been the model for the
statue by that name in the Place de la Concorde.

During the Hugo sojourn in Jersey, from 1852
to 1855, the table-tipping craze was at its height.
Hugo was much excited by it, and devoted much
time to the tables of Marine Terrace. Madame
Hugo, we may be sure, asked very little else of the
" spirits," than tidings of her idolized daughter
Léopoldine, drowned at Villequier in 1843, eight
months after marriage, at nineteen years of age.
Victor Hugo spent sleepless nights haunted by
mysterious visions. Every morning when the

family met there was much discourse upon these dreams and visions, pale apparitions and mystic murmurs. Some account was kept of the poet's extraordinary dialogues with unseen visitors ; the manuscript is still in existence. Among the other ghosts summoned to Marine Terrace were a score of headless ones, ghosts of celebrated victims of the guillotine. André Chénier came to finish a piece of verse for Hugo, and once a table representing Marat bowed profoundly when Hugo entered the room, and announced that in a previous state of existence Victor Hugo had been a revolutionist of 1793, and had cut off, or caused to be cut off, the head of Louis XVI. We may imagine how the author of " Dernier Jour d'un Condamné" became imaginatively intoxicated in this grewsome company.

In October, 1855, the Jersey exiles, wrought to a French frenzy by the glory of " M. Bonaparte," after the fall of Sebastopol, his exchange of visits with Victoria, and the success of the Exposition universelle de Paris, his apogee in fact, wrote the screeching open letter to the Queen which compelled them to leave the island within six days. Hugo struggled, protested, covered the walls of Jersey with fiery proclamations, but all to no effect; at the end of six days he and his sons steamed away on an English packet to Guernsey, where he lived eighteen years, till the fall of the empire.

Hauteville House is more imposing than Marine Terrace, yet not more so than its close neighbors on each side. Since Victor Hugo bought it French journalists have industriously spread the superstition that one of its chief attractions to him was that it was known to be haunted. Guernsey people are not, however, acquainted with the ghost, who from all accounts was a Parisian not a Channel Islander.

The house has no sort of poetic aspect, as the Doves climb the steep paved road set thick with comfortable dwellings in the style of a country town. It is a large brown house with a wee bit of ground before it, two oak trees, and a high iron railing. The numerous windows upon the front never fail to attract the attention of Frenchmen, because they are "guillotine" windows ; that is, open laterally *à l'anglaise*, and not longitudinally *à la française*. Perhaps French journalists see something revolutionary in the very windows of Hauteville House, as well as in Hugo's illstanding with the Guernsey aristocracy because he refused to doff his hat in the presence of the national anthem, " God save the Queen."

They touch an electric bell, a curious thing to do at the door of a haunted house. When a sufficient time has elapsed for a pair of hands to be roughly washed and dried, a towsled head is thrust from a basement window and inquires their business. They answer, in Yankee fashion and surprise, with another question : " Is this not the day in which the House is shown ? " With that the head disappeared, to appear at the door a moment later with a markedly unamiable look, as if at intruders. They ask timidly again if they are mistaken in the day, and are answered by a short " No." The woman's manner gave reason to suspect that whoever profited by the shilling admission, it was not she. She evidently resented being called from her basement to repeat a monotonous story. It was almost apparent, too, if not quite, that although this was the day in which the House was announced to be shown, and quite in the Guernsey season, visitors were really not expected, for floors were up, gas-fitters and plumbers at work.

"Do many visitors come?" Mrs. Dove feebly asks.

Over her shoulder the woman coldly tosses her answer: "We get a good few."

Whereupon Mrs. Dove feels herself considerably more few than good.

In Hauteville House, so well named, Victor Hugo's pen was very productive. Here he wrote three famous books, one of them the "Travailleurs de la Mer," of which the scenes are mostly in sight of the high and far-viewing windows of his work-room. His pen was not idle, yet time was somewhat heavy on his hands, shut away as he was from the social diversions of his beloved Paris and the adulations of his worshippers. Time hung heavy, so he set himself to work to lighten it by decorating this House of Exile according to his own taste. He always prided himself upon his architectural and decorative skill, and frequently remarked to his friends that, in making a poet of himself, he had spoiled a better decorative artist, — a bit of mock humility which could have imposed itself upon nobody. Of course he never hinted that his cabinet-maker's skill was an inheritance.

How much of Victor Hugo and his decorative work does this woman know who whisks the Doves through the house as if they were dirt and she a broom? They ask a few meek questions, but receive such short and unsatisfactory answers that they ask no more, and listen to her perfunctory descriptions *faute de mieux*.

The interior and its decorations are curious beyond the point of eccentricity. The decorator followed no known style, nor was even a law unto himself. So far as canons of art go, the whole is perfectly lawless, except in the law that Victor Hugo, the poet and romanticist, could and would do as he pleased with his own. His decorative taste, like his poetic and imaginative, concerned itself chiefly with mediæval gothic, mixed with curious adaptations from both the Chinese and Japanese, and the art of the lower empire. The result is always as fantastic and unnatural as the gargoyles of his romances imitating the manners and deeds of men. The vestibule of Hauteville House presents an object, a sort of altar supported on a pedestal representing scenes from " Notre Dame de Paris," sculptured and gilded. Two reception rooms opening from this vestibule have the ceilings formed of faience in plaques, the wall completely covered with pieces of porcelain, no doubt well worth seeing if the cicerone were not in such a haste to be rid of one. She does deign to say that the shelves upon which the porcelain is ranged, and the brackets under them, were all sculptured and chiselled by the poet, and that a set of Sèvres upon the wall was the gift of Charles X.

The large dining-room was added to the house by Victor Hugo. It has a predominating gothic effect, with tall elaborately carved sideboards resembling altars of cathedral chapels, its high-backed sculptured chairs and antique, covered with tapestry, — yet even thus a queerly confused effect, with Moorish tiles, Florentine plaques, and Etruscan potteries crowding each other everywhere. Victor Hugo was very fond of driving bargains with the Guernsey fish people for the carved chests and chairs that had come down to them since they knew not when. He did not leave these genuinely curious things in their original condition, but cut them up and made them over according to his bizarre taste; here a bit, and there a bit, worked into some Hugoesque creation floridly mediæval, one might say, and often surmounted with " V. H." as a sovereign cipher.

In this room are many Hugo portraits, more of the poet than of anybody else, but the most interesting one of Madame Hugo. Victor Hugo's suffer in interest from the fact that they are too numerous in the world. With Victor Hugo portraits in every shop window, one does not need to gaze reverently upon them in Hauteville House. In fact, it would be rather difficult to do so in the face of the fact unanimously asserted by these portraits, that Hugo in his youth was decidedly insignificant-looking. For those who have seen only the coarsely sensual head of his old age, called " leonine " by his worshippers, and that through the glamour of his renown, it may not be easy to picture him anything else than a picturesque giant with Homeric head and hair, and stature of any number of feet and inches imagination may choose to give him. Homeric giants of franc-apiece photographs never stand upon their legs, hence it is a severe disillusionment to find that before he became famous Victor Hugo was not only under-sized, but upon occasions even known to smirk. Not one of the portraits gives one's idea of a poet, or of a gentleman, but rather of a lively sort of cabinet-maker.

The Doves re-read Victor Hugo during their stay upon Guernsey and within an easy stroll of St. Sampson, the scene of Gilliatt's semi-savage youth. They read with so many a pish and pshaw, so many a "just hear this," that a generation ago would have writ them down in the literary fashion-book of that time as souls deaf to the music of genius. A generation ago they might have claimed to hear clearly that music from the Hugo horn, when in reality it might have been the echo of some other horn, the fashionable critic's perhaps. Now they saw a genius overlaid with bathos; a genius made absurd by turgid striving to seem infinitely larger than it was.

The dado of this room is composed of inscriptions. Needless to say their guide gave them no time to read them. In this dining-room was placed the "Ancestor's Chair" by which Victor Hugo invited the hauntings he so much desired, seeming not to be satisfied with the original ghost thrown in with the house. This "Ancestor's Chair" is of oak, heavily sculptured with Hugo arms to which Victor Hugo laid unwarranted claim. From arm to arm is an iron chain preventing the chair's occupancy by any living sitter (unless Victor Hugo chose to remove it and sit there himself as the ghost's representative), and also chiselled and painted. Some of the fifteenth-century chair was the handi-work of the poet; he chiselled the inscription which declares that ancestral ghosts are ever present with their descendants, and he gave it to be understood in Guernsey that his father, General Hugo, often came to sit there in his uniform, during family banquets. In such case it was surely not the house that was haunted, but its owner. For why should that highly respectable ghost, evidently a *bonne fourchette* since he came only when feasts were on hand, take the trouble to haunt a house he had never entered in life, upon an island in no way connected with his history? Our guide does not believe in his ghostship. She has never seen such a ghost, and what she has never seen she evidently does not believe in. She is evidently a Guernsey matron ; probably the gallant warrior would not consider her worth wasting his ghostly time upon, the Hugos having always been notoriously fond of a pretty face.

"I wonder if Victor Hugo's carpenter grandfather is ever invited to sit there," whispered one of the infidels.

"As the great republican never mentioned any ancestors that were not noble, probably not," whispered the other. "His pedigree was as bogus as his piety."

The grand salon would no doubt repay long study. A mere glimpse showed walls hung with rich tapestries, cabinets crowded with *objets d'art* and various relics under glass, said to be of conquerors and kings. One table belonged to Charles II. of England, who strewed these islands pretty thickly with tables, to say nothing about boots and other things.

The Guernsey matron's haste would have prevented any clear comprehension of this richness even at best. As it was, the Dove did not ask to linger, seeing bits of feminine needle-work upon chairs by the noble windows, and both books and chairs overturned upon the balconies as if somebody or somebodies had taken sudden flight. Victor Hugo's daughter-in-law Madame Lockroy and family occupy Hauteville House as a summer home, and some of them had fled before the unexpected and unaccustomed visitors.

But the poet's work-room, his "crystal cage" he described it, was the most interesting of all. It is a bare little place scarcely better than a prison-cell, and built upon the roof in the recesses of chimneys and mansard windows. Hugo called it his "lookout," and told that he built it with the revenue of his "Contemplations." It is almost entirely of glass; in the winter it must be intolerably cold, in summer intolerably hot. Here upon a bare wooden shelf, to be lowered or lifted at will, he re-wrote "Les Misérables," wrote "Les Travailleurs de la Mer" and "Quatre-vingt-treize."

The Guernsey matron deigns to remark that he always wrote standing; and the strangers remark anew how few his inches must have been to make that shelf of comfortable writing height. Nothing else whatever is in this narrow glass house except a dingy divan decidedly *fatigué* as the French say, a porcelain stove, a wooden mantel, and a mirror upon which are now faded flowers painted by his own hand. During eighteen years Victor Hugo wrote almost daily here. His customary working-dress was as peculiar and striking as the monk's frock in which Balzac worked day and night when the writing fury was upon him. Victor Hugo did not write in furies, but most methodically. He began his work at three o'clock in the morning, and ended his working-day at noon. Every winter morning his lamp in that lofty eyrie could be seen from afar, even afar out upon the water, a tiny star in the darkness, the star of genius high above every head asleep or awake upon that steep rock in the sea. When the day broke the poet was to be seen of all men, by whoever passed in the street below and chose to lift his eyes, writing with might and main in a fiery gown red enough to seem a spot of flame, quite as Hugo was willing it should seem, who never doubted himself flame in a dull world.

The view from this roof-study is immense, taking in all the roofs of the island upon that side, many-shaped roofs of dwellings, and glass roofs of vineries glittering in the sun, the vessels of the Port, the far stretch of St. Sampson where Gilliatt lived, and the ever encircling sea upon which he toiled and in which he committed as impossible a suicide, in forgetting the automatic despotism of the muscles, as exists upon any page of romance in the world.

Gilliatt's rock-chair is invisible from those windows, from everywhere. It disappeared when the sea closed over Gilliatt's head. No doubt Victor Hugo expected to immortalize Guernsey, as a poetic return for its hospitality to him when Jersey cast him out. No doubt he expected that shrines would be made wherever Gilliatt set his foot. The sad truth is that few visitors remember that Hugo here posed as a Napoleon upon St. Helena, nobody ever asks for Gilliatt-shrines or relics; when "Nellie" points out the haunted guard-house of Hugo's novel very few even of reading people remember that in it Sieur Clubin meant to hide with his ill-gotten fortune. The views from all the windows of Hauteville House, save those facing the commonplace street, are scenes of enchantment. The most sluggish imagination must always be aroused by it. One does not wonder at Victor Hugo's attempts to grasp the infinite and give it out again to the world Victor-Hugoized ; that here he wrote so much, sometimes even intolerably overmuch (as when he wrote eighty pages in description of the storm in "Toilers of the Sea") of winds, of waves, of clouds, of mysterious ocean sounds, and immeasurable horizons ; one does not wonder that he seemed to lose consciousness of human limitations. On these islands he strove to encompass the ocean, the ceaseless mystery of its heaving tides, the sinister graces of its billows, its incomprehensible murmur, its inimaginable groanings, its everlasting youth, its awful antiquity. The ocean seemed to have entered into his consciousness and made it sublime, but it was a mistake when he struggled to turn that mystery into mortal speech.

From this crystal cage Hugo could catch dreamy glimpses of France, the coast almost as vague, almost as unearthly as the winds, the waves, the clouds which there gave his writings less of a mundane artistic form than even his admirers admire. One of the Doves thought he really had no rightful business to write of waves and the wind, for he had no ear whatever for music.

From this glass study a narrow space leads to the poet's sleeping-room, an original garret of the English-built house. The long narrow entry is covered with shelves ; they in their turn are covered with a disorderly array of ragged books. The guide briefly states that they are mostly old maps and French local histories which were used in writing one of Hugo's romances; the Doves decide at once that it must have been "Quatre-vingt-treize." The poet apparently took none of them with him upon his return from exile, for their ranks seem unbroken.

At the end of this alley is the poet's sleeping-place; it is scarcely a chamber. Of all that artistic, and even sumptuous house, it is the meanest place. No servant was lodged so poorly. The bed is scarcely more than a man's width, and only a few inches from the floor. It has nothing in the way of bedding; the Guernsey matron answers a question by information that the occupant never used sheets, but wrapped himself about in a coverlet and thus lay down, with his head upon a round block of wood which he himself had painted in imitation of a Japanese pillow. The walls of this garret are hung with faded stuffs, no doubt precious, but without effect under the guidance of the Guernsey matron. She lifts one or two curtains, to show how under them were bestowed ship-shape various literary and domestic conveniences, drawers for manuscripts, notes, old letters, all the odds and ends for which the glass work-room was too small. Here also are bits of Guernsey chests found among the fisher folk of the island and metamorphosed into great doors with vaulted tops. Victor Hugo added to them some carving of his own, chevaliers on horseback point-ing lances, and the usual beautiful woman of fable and fairy, together with an utterly indescribable mélange of other things, like a poet's confused dream of far-away ages. These two mediæval doors, or two sets of doors, serve a very practical purpose; one hid the hanging clothes of the owner, the other his bath tub.

From this Spartan bed he rose at three every morning without disturbing the household, and went to his writing on the wooden shelf in the glass annex. There he wrote until six or seven without intermission. At six or seven his coffee, with raw eggs, was carried up to him, after which he applied himself to work again till the family *déjeuner* at noon. With the hour of *déjeuner* his writing was done for the day. After that he could carve and paint at his own good will or wander among the fisher folk seeking *bahuts* and ideas. He must have found more of the former than of the latter, for his Guernsey folk of the " Toilers of the Sea " are as little like Guernsey folk, of to-day or any other day, as a gargoyle of Notre Dame de Paris is like Victor Hugo himself, or the towers of Notre Dame like the divine H., which represents Hugo, as certain admirers affected !

NELLIE PALMER.

NELLIE was a character.

Mrs. Dove declared that Nellie was also a "sight." Such a costume of the biggest, horsiest checks that ever were sold; the Doves even guessed that these checks must have been expressly designed for Nellie's own self and no other. Then such a body!—rotund as a beer-barrel, or rather hogshead, a big moon-face under straightly stiff red hair clipped close to the head, all set upon a pair of such ridiculously short legs that one wondered how Nellie ever walked at all. In fact Nellie seldom did walk, almost never, but sat enthroned high above the gaping and staring hosts that profited by curious eloquence and never forgot it.

"You can climb down there and hexamine them ere ravines, ladies an' gentlemen, if you wanter," said Nellie, "but hi ainter goin' with yer. Hi don't do no climin'; hi would n't do none to save this ere whole carload from tippin' hoff the hiland!"

Nobody wished to see Nellie climb. On the contrary, everybody would have tried to prevent that enormous body and those absurd legs from making any such tragic attempt.

On various mornings Nellie drove up in front of Mrs. Bragg's, with as many people as had gathered for the day's excursion, the Doves being usually the last. The Doves took seats already engaged, and away Nellie drove, with a clatter and dash of four horses that well knew their business for the day, and just how the exit from St. Peter Port should be made. Nellie realizes the dignity of that position up aloft, and holds no conversation with passengers, except in monosyllables, till the place is reached at which the day's lesson begins. For not only does Nellie Palmer handle the ribbons of four horses with distinction, but all day long, while the car is *en voyage*, answers questions with energy, and describes, with as much zeal and enthusiasm as if for the first time, gardens, farm-houses, churches, the residences of local worthies, ravines, chasms, precipices, vineries, " Victer Ugo's 'arnted 'ouse " and the " Japese " beautifulness of a pseudo Japanese house, like a ten-cent paper fan amid the dignified red roofs of its neighborhood. How Nellie ever attained to the extraordinary language in which the excursion's description was done, no man can guess. It is not a Guernsey dialect, for nowhere else is it heard than on the high seat of that excursion car. No French, however, corrupted it, as in the case of the landlady of the Doves in St. Helier's. It was as debased English as could possibly be, yet Nellie proudly claimed to be of Guernsey, root and branch. " They calls us ' Guernseyhasses ' (Guernesiais). Hime a Guernsey hass, and my mother were hanother ! " Nellie's pride in telling that prosperous farms and thrifty gardens were owned by " Guernsey asses " born and bred, no Frenchman and no Englishman, was proof that no kinship with other nations was for a moment to be suspected, at least aloud. The Doves did silently suspect that Nellie's father was an English hostler, whatever the mother might be.

Nearly at the top of the hilly street Nellie rose with dignity and faced the company.

"This ere, ladies an' gentlemun, is He-Lizbeth Collige, founded by Queen He-Lizbeth in 1563. You see, ladies 'n' gentlemun, the modern harchitecture reminds you of Orris Walp-Hole's carstle at Strawbry-Ill. Them ere battlements ain't made o' gingerbread ef the guide-book do say so. He-Lizbeth Collige sends many students to Hoxford."

Then, as the country road flashed away into the interior of the island from the steep town streets, —

"Now, ladies an' gentlemun, is before you this beauterful road, wich at your right 'and is the church, an' beyind is the lightouse wich you do not see, has is the reason of the aziness of the hatmosphere."

"Call this haziness?" asked an excursionist. "I should call it a pretty good specimen of fog."

"No, sir!" answered Nellie, unblushing, save of hair. "'T ain't no fog, it's a 'aze; fogses is wet, this ere's dry as a wistle wich air ten miles from a pub."

Nevertheless, the ladies got out their waterproofs and were thankful they had them. One elderly young woman, palpably English of complexion, teeth, hair, accent, and manner, in putting on her cloak showed a juvenile sailor-hat inscribed, "S. S. Chicago." Why she wore it the Doves would have liked very much to know; but they never did know, and can only wonder to this day why on far Guernsey they saw this familiar name in such unfamiliar companionship.

17

Nellie was very determined that the excursionists should see the views and hobjics of hintrist,
whether they wished or not, evidently making it a
matter of personal ambition to preserve the fame
already secured as the most entertaining of all the
car-conductors, — even whether they could or not
penetrate the mist, which so much oftener envelops
Guernsey than Jersey or Alderney because of its
more advanced position into the open Atlantic.
Whenever the car stopped at a regulation spot,
and some kept their seats for the 'aze, Nellie expostulated : —

"Hime a-bringin' you this ere drive, ladies 'n'
gentlemun, to see the scenry, 'n' you must see it,
an' not be a-settin' alwiz in this ere car. Ef you
don't never lighten this ere car you are a-goin'
'ome to Hinglund a-knowin' nothin' of our beauterful hiland."

Everything was "hour." Hour bayses, hour
treeses, hour Haustralian blue gumses, hour bird's-
nestses, hour Hamerican halouses, even "hour
Japese 'ouses, wich the way they gits into 'em is
through the roof," and our grapes (curiously enough,
they were not grapeses) wich was raised by a gentlemun wich his name is Mr. Smith. There were
five tons of grapes sold by this one gentlemun,
wich 'is name is Mr. Smith, at hatepunce a pun.
"I had a lady an' gentleman wich sat an' het them
grapes till I sez to myself, sez hi, 'Nellie Palmer,
you needs more 'osses to pull 'em 'ome!'"

The Guernsey cows were "hours" too, and
Nellie boasted of the greater size and coarseness
of "hour hanimals" over those of Jersey and
Alderney, even though those very things prove
less purity of breed.

"We don't shake no hiron tails over *hour* milk," said Nellie.

The early crops of beans, potatoes, and pease (or peases) raised on the ground space of vast vineries for Covent Garden were all " hours."

Even was " hours " (" they carn't git one for no price hover to Jersey ") the mystic Lady, roused from her dreams by the music of Nellie's winding horn.

"This ere Hecho, ladies 'n' gentlemun, is a Guernsey lady as wich got stuck on a gent as did n't recippercrate, so she bunked hout an' 'id 'erself someware among them air rocks, and nobody ain't never seen 'er since."

Hecho's voice had decidedly a martial ring. No heart-break shivered through those clarion tones. Rather was it an Amazonian Echo, riding upon the wings of the wind in the sky above, on beds of mist north, south, east, and west, in ocean caves below, Amazonian Echo answering Nellie's horn with fierce battle-cries and shrill calls to beat futile lances against her ringing breastplate and shield of brass.

" The gent as did n't recippercrate is wise not to show himself," whispered the Doves.

Then Nellie blew again.

From out the silvery haze shutting from the enfolded island any glimpse of earth, of sea, of heaven, came the answer. It came to make every nerve thrill, every pulse throb (at least of the Doves), with the passion of its mystery, a passion of desire, of longing, and of unutterable anguish. It might be the inarticulate sorrow and pleading of passionful ages, ending perpetually with that long-drawn wail of despair.

Nellie showed most unlovely teeth.

" You see, ladies 'n' gentlemun, I 'as more than one stick to stir Miss Hecho hup."

A little farther on, Nellie calls attention to the "Anway Rocks," near which Gull's Rock is seen, through the parting haze, to be completely covered with the beautiful creatures, floating, drifting, darting, to remind one of electrified snowflakes ; or as a Dove remarked, of small-sized angels just let loose from their celestial school.

Anway Rocks, " Hanway " in the Guernsey dialect, are none other than the Hanois Rocks which figure in Victor Hugo's " Travailleurs de la Mer." Upon these treacherous rocks, in 1808, the brave warship Boreas was lost, as many other vessels had been within a very few hours after leaving St. Peter Port. It was upon these rocks that Hugo's Sieur Clubin schemed to wreck La Durande, and from which he intended to escape to the guard-house on Pleinmont Point. By means of just such an 'aze as envelops Guernsey to-day the Sieur Clubin missed his reckoning, and wrecked the Durande on the more dangerous because more distant Douvres, where the octopus, or devil-fish, finished his iniquitous career, and where Gilliatt afterwards finished the devil-fish.

" This ere 's Victer Ugoses 'arnted 'ouse," explained Nellie. " There ain't a been no 'arnts in it since hi remember. Them ere ghostses o' Victer Ugo, he muster run um hin isself."

Victor Hugo describes this house very distinctly, not in what Omar Khayyam Fitzgerald called his " gurgoyle " manner, yet he manages to infuse that description with the mysterious gloom necessary to the ghostly effect. Every detail Hugo mentioned is truly there, — the walled-up windows and doors, the nettle-grown threshold, just as he wrote. Yet to the Doves, the evidence of their own eyes that the haunted house was a common guard-house, absolutely unimpressive in every possible aspect, even to the most imagination-glamoured sight, and walled up for its preservation's sake, and built in 1780, thus a quarter of a century after merry Fort Cheer, made Hugo's description forever more flat, stale, and unprofitable.

"To think that this is the haunted house of which I read in my youth on the rocks by the old Clifton House," said the elder Dove. "Europe, longed for with a passion that consumed me, was then a divine mystery, in the heart of which blossomed the most perfect flowers of human genius, of earth's aspirations, — Europe, which would lift and illumine even me, could my heavy feet but touch its poetic shores. From those Clifton House rocks, Guernsey was as remote and unreal as lost Atlantis. I scarcely knew where upon the earth it was, or where to look for it on the map. In all my dreams of voyaging on fleecy argosies, upon blue celestial seas, I never dreamed of reaching Guernsey, that sunless terra incognita, that cluster of stern rocks in perpetual twilight, where men talked so unlike human beings elsewhere, and did things no human being would elsewhere do. Then that octopus! I really imagined it the real old theological devil in one of his numerous disguises, and I never could see any sense in Gilliatt's sitting on the rock till the tide covered him, after having slain the devil."

"Nobody else," consented the other. "He did n't do it for 'sense.' None of Victor Hugo's

people have any 'sense.' They are all such sentimental or romantic maniacs that the world has
already shut the most of them up in its literary
lunatic asylums.   Such fantastic unnaturalism,
joined to such a grandiose manner, could only
be the fashion of a day, long or short.   Already
the man who was carried to the Pantheon by
such a concourse of common people is half forgotten.   Even on the *Jour des morts*, the only
flowers on his tomb are those sent by his own
family.   Few read him now for pleasure, although
many as a duty to nineteenth century literature."

   " That air Gilliatt were a hass ! " Nellie was saying.
   "As for your gloomy impressions of beautiful
Guernsey,"   the   Dove   continued,   "no   doubt
your mistake is paid in kind.   Even to this day
Guernsey mothers threaten their naughty children
with, 'I 'll send you to Boston ! '   What sort of
imagining would those children have of you, sitting on the Clifton House rocks?   After succes-
sive bad harvests in the years 1816–1817, the
distress became so great on the island, that many
of the laboring classes were compelled to emigrate
to the United States in vessels expressly fitted up
for them.   They clung together as island people
always do when possible, and some of them gave
a beloved name to Guernsey County, Ohio.   They
were not the first to emigrate.   In an American
paper of about 1752 was advertised, 'To be
sold, Guernsey boys and girls, for a term of time,
on board the sloop Two Brothers.'   They evidently paid their passage by this sale of a term
of their time.   What *are* you laughing at ? "

   The question was not unnatural, considering
the magnitude of the other's smile.

" I was only thinking of Victor Hugo's description of the bird's-nesting boys who were terrified by the ghostly doings within this very guard-house ; two Guernsey boys, you remember, and a French *gamin.* All the terror was in the Guernsey boys, all the bravery in the *gamin.* The Guernsey boys had never dared go near the haunted house till now they had a *petit Français* with them. The Guernsey boys were forever running away in fright, to be brought back by *le petit Français.* Even after the three had dared the ghosts and run away because nothing more was to be seen, the *Français* ran the fastest, not because he was afraid (perish the thought!), but because he was French ! Then don't you remember when we re-read the 'Travailleurs de la Mer' the other day how we laughed at some Guernseyman's retort upon V. H.? When La Durande struck upon the rocks one of the six passengers fainted (the same who, in eighteen hundred and *twenty*-something, talked with an American bible-distributor of William H. Seward and Stephen A. Douglas). When La Durande struck, Victor Hugo wrote, 'Le touriste s'était évanoui ;' over against it some reader had pencilled, '*A Frenchman ! ! !* '"

" How different was Chateaubriand's story," remarked a Dove. " Returning from America in 1791, in a vessel manned half by Frenchmen, half by Americans, they were so beaten and buffeted and driven from their course that they got between Guernsey and Alderney, near, if not actually in that frightful 'Swinge.' All gave themselves up for lost, except one or two Americans. When the Frenchman at the wheel gave up and let the vessel drift, one of the Americans took the

wheel and brought the vessel round. The Frenchmen were all shouting a prayer to Notre Dame
de Bon Secours, some of the scared Protestants
joining with them, but not the American at the
wheel."

"Tortevale church," Nellie was saying, and the
Doves remembered that Tortevale was the very
village where Sieur Clubin had so virtuous a reputation. "Tortevale church, built in 1816, on the
place ware used to was be St. Mary de Tourte-
valle in 1055, before hus Guernsey hasses conquered Hinglund!"

The car laughs; Nellie laughs too at this spon-
taneous recognition of the fact of a departure from
the legitimate discourse, and continues proudly,
" Said to be the hugliest church in Europe."

So it must be, with its ungainly martello towers
and broken spire, the very ugliest. It was built at
the same dreary period of ecclesiastical art, or
not-art, that characterless St. Prig's was built on
Sark. It took the place of an ancient one built
in 1130, upon the site of the earlier one of 1055,
by Philip de Carteret in fulfilment of a vow made
while struggling with death in the sea. Yet there
are many, many times when this unbeautiful church
becomes of almost unearthly loveliness. Its towers
seem shaped from the rainbow and set as a sign
of God's promise against the sky; its spire is of
pearl, its walls of alabaster, its architecture like
the clouds of the radiant heavens. Thus it is to
the sailor far away upon the water, whose keen
gaze joyfully distinguishes Tortevale church before
even so much as a shadow of the island is seen.
Until 1862, when the Hanois light was placed on
the fatal rocks, the spire was used for a beacon,

thus a star of hope to many a storm-tossed Guernsey mariner making way homeward from far shores.

" Hobserve, ladies 'n' gentlemun, our fishermun's 'ouses. You see them ere garrits stuffed so tight wich the seaweed is a runnin' hout? That ere seaweed we calls *vraic.* Hit's the fishermun's cookin' wood, he don't hav no hother fires. The vraic in the garrit keeps the cold hout hall winter, then it gits burnt wich the hashes makes our pertaterses grow. Hour baker's ovenses is all 'eated with vraic."

On all the Channel Islands the vraic is an important harvest. The gatherings are twice a year, during certain days (after the highest tides) appointed by each island's legislature. During the vraic harvests the shores are covered with carts and people, the town and village streets are scattered with straggling branches and twigs of the sea's harvest, the air is pungent with briny odors. The harvesting takes on a festive aspect, — a pleasant picnic quality; groups of families eat and drink together on the rocks, and a certain cake known as "vraic cake" is much in evidence. Hundreds of islanders have no other fuel, and what they do not burn as fuel they burn expressly for the ashes, which are sold by the bushel, usually about 9*d.* only, for fertilizing purposes. To think of the time and toil expended in securing a bushel of ashes ! The Channel Island farm-carts usually make a spring toilet for the vraic harvest, being freshly painted blue, the color considered lucky, — a superstition left from ancient Catholic days, when it was the Virgin's favorite color. A white horse is greatly prized with these blue carts; for how could the Goddess Luck fail to favor the Madonna's livery?

" Hobserve, ladies 'n' gentlemun, this ere ruined chapel of St. Hapoline as wich his license to build were granted by Richard Second in 1394. You can henter, ladies 'n' gentlemun, in a gitten the key as wich keeps the hold woman hoppizite. She don't speak no Hinglish, so I tells you the whole of the 'istry. Hunnerds 'n' hunnerds o' years that ere chapel was delappetatid 'n' used for a stable. The 'osses died so fast they gives it hup ; the hold saint wich howns the chapel did n't want no 'osses, so he 'arnted 'em to death. Beastly shame ! "

The Doves got the key and examined the strange old frescos — ghostly things as if seen at the end of a long vista of dark centuries — at their leisure, during the unnecessarily long halt for luncheon. "These always long halts of excursion cars are designed to persuade the excursionist that the drive he pays for is twenty-five miles, instead of only twelve, — a day's drive, rather than one to be naturally done in three hours," remarked a Dove.

"We could just as well have walked," agreed the Doves, "only, in that case we should never have known Nellie."

Never known Nellie ! The Dove-like reason tottered on its throne at the bare suggestion !

"We missed Creux Madi in the fog," said a Dove, reading a guide-book. "A great pity. My Ward, Lock, and Bowden says, 'The Creux Madi is of magnificent proportions. No traveller should miss seeing it. There is a tradition devoutly believed by some of the islanders that a subterranean passage runs from the cave to the centre of the island.'"

"Pity indeed!" said the other, also reading. "My Black's guide-book says, 'Creux Madi is an uninteresting cavity at the base of a cliff 200 feet long, 50 feet wide, and 60 high, formed by the decomposition of a softer vein of rock, which has entered the granite at right angles.'"

"In a multitude of counsellors is wisdom," they agreed. "But when you have only two counsellors who disagree, how know which has the wisdom? Moral, never carry more than one guide-book."

They made the discovery that Guernsey folk are more literal than Jersey; that is, if one single fact proves a law, as many travellers seem to think, — even as the Frenchman did, over a two hours' excursion to Folkestone, who wrote afterwards, "All English children have red hair." After their ferreting about the neighborhood while the rest were at lunch they returned to the hotel with just time, and no more, for a comforting cup of tea.

"A cup of tea," said Mr. Dove, carelessly, to a waiter as they took their seats at a little table in the tearoom, among other tea tables surrounded by some of their fellow excursionists, all with china teapots of the same size and pattern before them.

"Tea 6*d*.," read Mrs. Dove from the wall. "In this at least the two islands are of one accord, even if Jersey does elect its judges by the rate payer direct, and Guernsey by douzeniers representing the rate payers. Tea 6*d*. is common to all the Channel Islands. We get a good deal for our shilling."

Here the waiter appeared. He set one single cup of steaming tea between the two. "Sixpence, sir," he said,

"What do you mean by one cup when I ordered tea for two?"

"You said a cup, sir," meekly replied the man.

"Bring at once two teapots of tea, two cups and two saucers, two spoons, sugar, a milk jug, two small plates, and one of bread and butter."

"Yes sir," answered the man with cheerful alacrity.

"Lemme see if henny's missin'," said Nellie, after luncheon, mounting the box and counting the excursionists. "Ware's them air Jersey trippers?"

"Jersey trippers," indeed! It was for this, then, that Nellie all day long had refrained from any fling at the sister island, save once inadvertently to remark, "Hus Guernsey folkses is more haristocratic as what Jersey is."

Jersey trippers!

"Here we are," said the Doves, meekly.

During luncheon time the fog had lifted. Unfortunately the remainder of the drive was over the least picturesque part of the island, — picturesque, that is, in pinnacled cliffs, splintered rocks, and chasms, ravines, abysses, and caves beaten by the restless sea, the glimpses of magic gardens, radiant with subtropical flowers through ancient gateways of grave manor-houses, many the thatched cottages, quaint churches, and what stirred Nellie's eloquence most thoroughly, extensive vineries.

"Hobserve, ladies 'n' gentlemun, that ere vinery as wich air atop a cross. That air were once a church. Hus Guernsey folkses ain't a-wantin' so many churches as them fellers 'ad afore us was born; we don't tumble inter the hocean an' vow big things to git hourselfs hout! We gits hour savin' cheaper; 'n' puts vines instidder halters."

As the party dashed brilliantly into St. Peter's Port, the Doves again asked of each other, "Why is this big hostler given a feminine name; why is he not Pete or Bill?"

"Cos it's my name, sir, given to me by my sponsers in batism," Nellie was answering an excursionist.

THE ISLAND OF ALDERNEY, ITS PEOPLE, AND ITS COWS.

"ALDERNEY ! Wonder how long you will stay *there?*"

A suspicious unanimity was in these words. The Doves were not long in discovering that nobody thought they could remain long where, as everybody said, there was nothing to see, nothing to do, and nothing to eat. But they took into consideration that this was told them on Guernsey, and Guernsey has a sisterly way of undervaluing all the other Channel Islands. They were not to be discouraged from visiting Alderney; rather their determination was strengthened by information that nothing was there but cows and soldiers, and no man (or woman) ever ventured there without wishing he had not.

At times, from Guernsey, they realized that failing to reach that nebulous vision now faintly forming into a pale cloud-shape upon the farthest line of sea and sky, now melting utterly away, they should surely die. That the same result attended the tragedy of not seeing it, they did not consider important enough to draw attention. That bit of film on the horizon, to be hidden by a thimble's disc, drew them with the inevitable fascination of mystery and remoteness. When by the most powerful effort they could dimly descry it, their very souls uprose with entreaty to be let loose to their own wild wills. When with the very most powerful effort not the filmiest hint of a film could be discovered, they concluded to buy their tickets on the way home.

Twice a week from their pleasant windows they watched the Little Courier with laughter. For the Little Courier reminded them of a brisk schoolboy running home from school and the post-office with the day's mail. It raced across their windows with might and main, an hour or so after the large packets had arrived from England. Until the great packet arrived, the Little Courier would not budge an inch, and Alderney might cry in vain for its food and its friends, so long as the Lynx, the Antelope, the Gazelle were delayed in the Channel. Its steam was up and everything ready for departure the moment passengers (if any there were), mails, and packages could be transferred. Thus it often kicked up its little heels and capered across the windows of the Doves an hour or more before the still unloading majestic English steamer took up its stately way to Jersey. Alderney is very much out in the cold, and must continue there so long as two sea-voyages divide it from England. Its ambition is for a packet direct to England, but the day seems far that it will have one.

Alderney is the Cinderella of the Channel Islands, for whom no fairy godmother has yet appeared. The other islands think and speak of her as a little sister in the ashes ; very few Jersey people have ever visited her, and most Guernsey people only on a day's excursion.

But then, very few Jersey people even have

ever seen St. Peter Port, the capital of Guernsey, except from the steamer-landing, although
they cannot go to England without stopping at
the port of Guernsey from one hour to two. The
people of all the islands are extremely proud of
themselves as The Channel Islands, virtual republics under royal protection, but otherwise they
have very little interest in one another. Away
from home — in America, for instance — all Channel Islanders embrace each other as brothers ; just
as Chicago and Boston are Americans abroad, but
distinctly Chicago and Boston at home.

Alderney is three miles long by one and a half
wide, a lofty rock covered with grass and rough
weeds. It has not a native tree and but few
planted ones, and as the Doves saw it at the end
of a horrible three hours of boiling channel from
Guernsey it was anything but promising. The
steamer's departure from Guernsey had been telegraphed (almost the first use of the magic wires
that united long outcast Alderney to the rest of the
world), and the whole island of Alderney watched
them as they struggled past the lonely Casquets and
now tumbled among the breakers of the terrible
" Swinge."

This " swinge," by the way, accounts in some
part for Alderney's long isolation from the rest of
the world. Before the days of steam-packet
communication this foaming interval before the
harbor could be reached was dangerous to vessels,
except with expert pilots on board. It was not
only dangerous, but imagine the soul and body
anguish of tumbling and tossing, soaring and
sinking, for an hour or two in this elemental
churn ! Now the struggle of twenty minutes to

half an hour by steam over those sunken rocks and mad eddies and currents is bad enough in all conscience. Surely, nobody with a stomach ever got away from Alderney who ever reached it by sail !

Ten passengers were on board the little steamer; four only of them bound for Alderney. The others, Guernsey people, were going past Alderney to Cherbourg, thence on to Paris, — the usual way of reaching the continent from both Alderney and Guernsey. Jersey's way is nearer than this, her way to Paris shorter than those of all her sister isles, even though Alderney lies nearer the coast of France. Jersey people cross over to Granville or Saint-Malo, lower down the coast.

Among the passengers is an Alderney woman, perhaps a milliner and familiar with the " Swinge " from frequent crossings over to Guernsey shops and fashions. No sooner was Guernsey dim than she sat flatly down upon the floor, with eyes tightly closed and back against a mast. Nothing roused her ; she might have been dead for any sign she gave, even when the military man and his companions exclaimed at the fairy-like architecture of the terrible Casquets, those fatal rocks upon which many a ship has gone to pieces and many a soul to its doom. Not even did she open her eyes when the steward pointed out the rock Ortac, and the Americans told all they knew of it. It was once believed that Saint Maclou came to this bare rock at times. Many ancient mariners affirmed that they had seen him there reading a book. For this reason it was a custom among fishers and sailors to say a prayer or two and do a number of propitiatory genuflections whenever they sailed within danger nearness of Ortac. After a while it was discovered that Saint Maclou had never been on Ortac at all, but a devil, one of the minor devils of the great crew of devils, and had made himself appear for centuries as the Saint without detection, thus to receive the prayers of mortals. Victor Hugo tells this story in his "Travailleurs de la Mer." Apparently that devil took fright at sight of the new order of devil, puffing and snorting over the waves; for nobody hears of him now.

The milliner never opened her eyes to see whether saint or devil had possession of Ortac.

"Are you quite comfortable?" asked one of the Doves of the other, with suspicious anxiety. "Do you wish to go nearer the side of the boat?"

"A pretty question to ask!" she murmured. "I must die at my post unless that dignified military man takes his dreadful gaze from off my face."

The military man must have been a colonel at least. He was tall and gray, with a fierce moustache and eye, a firmly set mouth, and a complexion sallowed by tropic suns. In the very heart of the *swinge*, that horrible, horrible *swinge* which mixed sea and sky into such an elemental mess that one could not decide which to cling to, the military man stood fiercely erect, staring fiercely upon Mrs. Dove.

"What *is* the matter?" she thought. "Do I resemble his long lost love?"

With stern eyes still upon her, the military man made two fierce strides towards her.

"The other side, sir, the other side!" called the steward.

Then that smiling steward confided to Mrs. Dove's ghastly smile, —

"Gentlemen *do* make such a horation w'en they are hill."

"Why does he not sing to 'Our Lady of Suc-
cor,'" whispered the American. "It must have
been just about here that our own prayerless countryman took the helm in 1791, no doubt at the
bidding of Notre Dame, and in answer to that
shouted prayer in French.

The milliner never opened her eyes.

A Guernsey lady upon leaving St. Peter Port
had been heard assuring another that she was
never sea-sick in her life, never! She had crossed
the North Sea many times and voyaged to India
as well as to America, the very worst voyage of all,
with never a shudder or qualm. This lady was
one of the tender-hearted sort, in spite of her stout
stomach, one of the large-eyed, slim-waisted, weak-
voiced kind, with high, stainless foreheads, and no
chin to speak of, that were fashionable before
Rossetti painted, and Burne-Jones set Love among
ruins, or Du Maurier made Punch a drawing-room
of strong-chinned English beauty. She was one of
the ministering-angel-when-pain-and-anguish-wring-
the-brow kind, who smooth Pillows and wipe Brows
whenever they find a chance, — even though sometimes wiping and smoothing the wrong way.

Just as the steamer was about to start a party of
French women came on board with loud weeping.
Only one of them was to leave Guernsey; the
others had come to say good-bye to a girl of sixteen or seventeen returning to her own family in
France. She was a moon-faced peasant, probably
a farm-hand. She was returning in great trouble
and fear, not in the least lessened by the boisterous
lamentations about her, for she was returning not
alone. A tightly rolled bundle, stiff as a block of
wood, but from which goggled two watery eyes,

was passed from one to the other of the women, each receiving and passing it on with intensified howls.

The heart of the much-travelled lady was deeply touched by the spectacle of so much woe. She buried herself in the wailing group in the steerage and learned the whole story.

The women went ashore with a wail, the home-returning girl answered with another, her eyes swollen, her face distorted almost out of human semblance.

"The poor creature says she is always frightfully sea-sick," said the lady, coming into the first-class part of the boat with a bundle, which she tilted and joggled in a most amateur manner. "I am never, never ill, so I am going to take this poor ten-days-old baby down into the cabin with me. The wretched girl is terrified almost out of her senses at the prospect of meeting her father. He does not know about this baby."

Sea-sick !

Indeed the girl did not wait for the sea. The wheel had made scarce three revolutions, the wails on the pier were still audible, when her clamor changed from weeping to a variety of utterly indescribable noises, amid which that of weeping was least. Nobody had thought of giving up, when her perfectly unrestrained uproar filled all the space between bow and stern, and rose above the flag.

"How fortunate that poor baby is safe," observed Mrs. Dove. "She is such a lawless young animal I think she would throw it overboard."

"Best place for it," replied the other. Which Mrs. Dove could not deny.

All the way the girl *mon-dieued* in every possible animal tone, from wailing cat's to shrieking hyena's. Then the waves washed over the steerage, and the kindly steward lifted her forward among the first-class passengers. Evidently the change was for the worse, or at least she thought so, for —

"If I dared move, I would go downstairs," murmured Mrs. Dove ; "this is intolerable."

Some little time later, the steward came and stood between the sightless milliner and Mrs. Dove, three feet from the tumultuous young mother.

"A lady downstairs is frightfully ill," he said. "She begs anybody who can to relieve her of the baby she took into the cabin with her."

"Pas moi, pas moi, mon Dieu !" remarked the young mother, in the most human voice they had ever heard from her, then immediately recommenced her menagerie din.

With a somersault to strike the solemn stars, were any visible at high noon, the Little Courier bounds into Braye Harbour, and the milliner opens her eyes. "I keep them shut that my mouth won't spring open," she remarked to Mrs. Dove.

The lady with the tender heart comes up to the air, looking like death.

"It was that dreadful baby," she explains. "I think it has never been washed since it was born. If I had been on deck I should have thrown it overboard."

They go ashore, and then stand for a few moments stick-stock-still, merely to enjoy the heavenliness of firm earth beneath their feet, instead of alternately sea and sky. A score or so of people stand about the pier, the most of them brought there only by curiosity, although one woman, the Doves were sure, was she to whom they had written concerning lodgings, and who could be brought to name no other terms than "satisfactory." As "satisfactory" is an idea with two faces, as it might look to lodger or to landlady, they had not answered her last letter. Now as they saw her keen inspection of the Courier's passengers, they assumed an expression of joy, to meet a welcome among waiting friends, and passed her by. But first they watch the Little Courier unload, — Captain Whale, bound in the usual blue and gold, doing the major part. Almost everything seems for "The Canteen." Eggs, onions, potatoes, cases of bottles, "garden-sass," all go the same way. Even the mail bag is opened upon the pier, and the red-headed red-coated soldiers who take away the garrison letters leave but a shrunk bag behind. Alderney, like Gibraltar, is chiefly a garrison rock, every third person a soldier. The larger portion of the remainder are the descendants of English and Irish laborers, brought here for ill-fated English government works, abandoned in 1847 ; some are quarrymen and stone cutters from France, while a mere fraction are of ancient Alderney families, to this day speaking among themselves a queer jargon of mixed English and mediæval French. When they speak English, however fluently, their accent is strongly foreign.

St. Anne, the capital, has two hamlets for neighbors, both low by the water's edge, while St. Anne is enthroned on Alderney's summit. One of the hamlets has a poor French Catholic church, while St. Anne has a Protestant church, a gift from a former owner of the island, huge enough to house every islander. What in the world Alderney wanted with such misplaced grandeur and magnificence remains a puzzle, considering that the Salvationists have obtained a foothold there and other dissenters are not few. The only other large building, save forts, is a dynamite factory, sent to Alderney, doubtless, to get it out of the way.

They climbed a long hill to St. Anne's. It seemed an utterly deserted town, although a very modern one, and nothing ghostly or plague-stricken about it. Neither is it in the slightest degree picturesque, but resembling the newest suburb of an English manufacturing town, a suburb of working people, not of *nouveaux riches*. As the Doves pass through the one principal street, every door is closed, even of shops; every shop shade down. "Is everybody asleep?" they wonder.

At the rickety little shop inside a slovenly enclosure where the guide-book had bid inquire for lodgings, a dirty, deaf old woman told that her son was at dinner, and could not be disturbed. No business signs of any consequence attract the eye. The whole island of 2000 inhabitants is *en famille*, everybody knows the contents of every shop, hence no need of window displays or advertisements. Everybody, too, knows the contents of every clothes-press and chest, — likewise of every larder, for the butcher shops are open only on the days of the steamer's arrival, and everybody knows just what the steamer brought.

By a bright urchin's aid they manage to secure lodgings on " Blaggud Corner," in one of the few ancient houses of the best class, with the mullion windows peculiar to Alderney, and walls like a fortress. "Blackguard" is scarcely an attractive name for corner lodgings, although corners are fine coigns of vantage for viewing a town or island from a window. The blackguards, however, were not very black; they saw but two or three at a time, and they "guarded" only after working-hours. The junction of two roads where this old-time house stood always had one corner at least sheltered from the wind. It might be the corner of the dingy little general store, the corner of the dingy inn, or their own two corners, where idlers leaned and smoked and exchanged the stirring news of the rock. Twice a week the idlers can talk of larger news, of falling empires, and dying kings; but ordinarily, to whichever corner they cling as the wind comes from English meadows and hedgerows, or over the continent from Russian steppes, or up from African deserts, they discuss whether they like pork best or veal, or the benefit of an onion diet over one of cabbage. Perhaps the conversation is not much more inspiring among the upper circles, if one may judge from the quality of intellectual and spiritual pabulum furnished from the pulpit of the great church.

For Alderney has its "hupper suckle" of course. It consists of a few officers' families, plain everyday-looking people, the rector's family, a bachelor curate with an enormous lisp, and a few feminine odds and ends, with no particular object in life except to go to church, to play golf and tennis, always with the same partners, to dance occasionally, always with the same few partners, and now and then to picnic among the coarse weeds. To work among the poor, to re-create the slums, they have no chance, lacking poor and slums ; they cannot even cycle, lacking space. No library, no clubs, no theatres, no shops, no work, no real conversation, no change of faces, no news (except telegraphic) from the world oftener than twice a week, except a short season in summer, — if all things else fail to drive them to madness, the puerile drivel of their athletic curate ought to do it.

The Americans heard him for the first time the Sunday Mrs. Dove waxed indignant at sight of the surpliced choir. The boys looked quite angelic, and opened their mouths as widely as boys on a choric frieze. Out of those open mouths seemed to come angelic music, — sinless voices, newly come from the skies, chanting praises to an unforgotten Father.

"Humbug !" nudged Mrs. Dove. " Do you see all those girls in profane raiment hidden behind the organ? They are doing all this angelic choiring."

The drivel of the curate was such that the strangers did not wonder that the rector removed himself as far from it as decency and the chancel would allow. This curate has a salary of $700 from an endowment fund provided by the giver of the church. It is more than he could ever get in America, where flocks choose their own shepherds, even their own sheep dogs, and have neither forced upon them as in England. The Doves wondered what this big bachelor curate has to say of " Jersey hookers ; " for Jersey hookers let him slip every Jersey hook, and land in desolate Alderney still unhooked. Jersey girls are most unamiably named " hookers " by the spinsterhood of the other islands, for the reason that so few curates and officers ever leave Jersey unattached. It is not agreeable to Alderney girls, when a regiment or a parson is moved over from the principal island of the group, to see the young officers or the parson spending so much time on the point of land nearest to Jersey, scarcely moving his glass from the portion of the horizon where it lies. The spinsterhood guess why these interesting faces are turned away from them, even if they do not know ; hence the curling lips which speak of " Jersey hookers."

In windy, dull Alderney, the Americans found lodgings dearer than upon the gayer Channel Islands, even though house rents are extremely cheap. Forty dollars a year will hire a comfortable house, one hundred and fifty a great one almost suitable for an hotel. The reason of the dearness of lodgings is the scarcity of servants. Neither French nor English servants are willing to live on a rock two or three hours from everywhere, even in calm weather, and with that devilish Swinge between. Especially is a small rock dangerous to serving-maids, when a garrison is upon it, for though she be cold as ice and pure as snow, an English garrison always throws a taint of suspicion upon a girl's reputation. Neither will the island-born girls remain. From Alderney on clear days the glass roofs of Guernsey vineries, and her windows, blaze in the sun and lure Alderney girls away into the splendid mystery beyond the Swinge unto the larger isle which to them seems the world. Sark and Alderney furnish Guernsey largely with servants, Sark and Alderney go without. In the

Guernsey newspapers one may read piteous appeals from Alderney for cooks, nurses, and general servants.

On the other side of Alderney, only nine miles distant, looms a projection of France, a vision to tempt any untravelled imagination. Between the two how can any girl remain on narrow Alderney unless she be entirely without imagination? Then, entirely without that quickening spark, of what use is she as a serving maid? " Our Alderney girls prefer to join the Salvationists and bang tambourines," said Monsieur Duplain. So they somersault away over the Swinge, and Monsieur and Madame Duplain must give up taking lodgers and offer Blaggud-Corner House, nicely furnished, for rent at a pound a week, because they have no daughters of their own and can hire no other man's.

Their sitting-room on Blaggud Corner prettily furnished in old fashions and with ecclesiastical windows, had a library of four volumes. One of them was a French translation of " Little Women," one a gaudy French gift book, one " Stepping Heavenward," in English, the other Aldrich's "Story of a Bad Boy," in French. Some natural curiosity concerning the latter and its adaptation to the juvenile Gallic mind, led to the discovery that the chapter on Tom's sweethearts was expunged.

The bedrooms were like wax in neatness, with inside wooden shutters, as had all the house. One sunk to rest beneath a lofty canopy with solemn tester, and beneath soft homespun blankets, quite under the imaginative impression that one's knee breeches or hoop-petticoats decorate high-backed chairs and that one's hair still retains the daytime powder. George the Third is king, unless indeed hideous George the Second still holds the sceptre; and over the water a certain colony has increased too rapidly for its own good or indeed for anybody else's, and must be taught a sharp lesson or two.

Alderney does not invite to many walks, having so few to offer. It has not much in the way of scenery, for the sea seen too near is not scenery. Whatever is looked upon must be on the gazer's own level, or else below it. Ravines, chasms, cliffs and boulders, however rent by tempest, and by gnawing and tearing waves, are much less impressive to the imagination when looked down upon instead of with eyes upturned. So much is in mere bodily position and relation that man never feels his superiority so much, as the final and greatest work of nature, as when he looks down upon her creations. So on Alderney, where so much of the coast is entirely inaccessible except to indefatigable gulls, who chatter and skim water and air as if gulldom were the universe, nothing whatever cheats the senses and imagination with a vision of idealized things. On Sark, an island of the same size, one may find the light that never was on land or sea, the dream-forms of countries beyond the moon, but not here. The plateau is ugly, most of it coarse pasture land, and over it the wind blows continually till the rough furze, which elsewhere grows to tall bushes, here clings with its prickly fingers desperately to the ground and becomes a creeping vine. A struggle among Alderney furze is as much as a Dove's life is worth. Such walks as are described in the guide-books receive all the attention they merit. The paths run along the island's edge that the only interest the island possesses may be looked down upon. The paths are the width only of two human feet; parties must walk in single file or become either tangled in the clinging furze, or fall upon the rock below. The guide-books kindly warn the stranger of this last danger, and note the places where there is nothing but a thin layer of earth and stones below the turf. The Doves remarked the unanimously extreme caution with which strangers turned inland upon the furze at these indicated places, and left the path to more practised island feet. Also they smilingly remarked upon the dutifully trampled spots, islands of bareness in surrounding russet-green, where the guide-books had remarked upon something to be observed.

"Elizabeth's Earl of Essex bought the whole island for five thousand dollars," remarked a Dove; "what do you imagine he wanted it for?"

"Can't," answered the other, "unless it be true that he intended to carry his royal mistress off and hide her here till she consented to marry him."

Upon Alderney one has the sensation of being upon an enormous ship, where life and the outlook are quite as monotonous as they always are on a long voyage, and where one is almost equally apart from the world.

On Sunday afternoon the Doves attended a meeting of the Salvation Army. Before going with Zilpha, the little maid, they had remarked from their windows unusual animation round Blaggud Corner. All the population of Alderney seemed darting past Blaggud Corner, swift-footed, because of the cooling wind, and burdened with something hidden beneath a cloth. Earlier in the day the Doves had watched much the same island ceremony, although then the burdens were smaller and the feet less fleet. Among the noontide bearers was an elderly man to whom English, they knew, was a foreign language. His English was as fluent as their own, but every word un-Englishy pronounced. He was of the ancient Alderney race, now almost extinct, had never been in England in his life, although once in France, and had taken a wife from Sark whom he had met in Guernsey, and whose English was as fluent and accent as foreign as his own. Far away in the world somewhere they had a son, they knew not where ; perhaps he was in America, that strange far country where so many roving souls disappear in the western clouds. They had not heard from him for years, yet how cheerful they both were, how ready with pleasant tales and merry anecdotes ! Mrs. Dove pondered deeply and long that a mother could remain on a bit of rock in the surging sea, that she could hear the loud winds hasting from far countries to farther ones, that she could endure the distant shining of the stars, the cold sadness of the moon, that morning did not torture her, that evening did not appal, that she could relate laughing histories, that she did not beg her weeping way from port to port, from land to land, till she found her son, or till she reached the final Country of us all.

"But you see, madame, not every woman spells *son* SUN as you do," explained her companion.

Ten minutes later, when the hot and savory leg

of mutton graced their table *à deux*, they understood what their landlord had brought from the
baker's under that secretive cloth. "Our beans
are baked at the baker's every Saturday night the
same as the mutton, and we bring them away in
the morning," explained Zilpha.

"So do many in America," said Mrs. Dove.
"Many Americans, in a part called New England,
also eat beans on Saturday night."

The possibility of such a forestalling of Sunday's
breakfast had never occurred to the little Alderney
maid. She opened wide her eyes to exclaim, —

"How droll!"

Afterwards they heard her tell the strange story
to the landlady, whose comment was, —

"How droll!"

"Reminds me of an occurrence of my youth,"
discoursed the elder Dove. "Once upon a time
our New England minister preached to an audience
of baked-bean eaters upon the Sabbath-breaking of
having one's beans cooked at a bakery. The
sermon made a great uproar, as may be supposed.
All the week the congregation discussed it with
more or less heat; for New England's Sunday-
morning beans, you know, are not to be insulted
by any man, however sacred his office. When
the congregation gathered together the next Sunday morning, behold, the church steps were
thickly strewn with raw beans, as much as to say
to the Reverend Mr. Langworthy, 'Take your
beans like cattle.' Of course that made more
uproar; but the culprits were not discovered, not
even at the third bean-storm, which arose in the
congregation the following spring, by which time
the society had become generally known as the

'Holy Beaners.' The third commotion was when all the ground space about the Church of the Holy Beaners sprouted thick with beans, and continued to sprout for weeks, from those swept away from the church steps the autumn before."

After dinner to a little court apart from the narrow street, where the "Harmy" held a preliminary service. The "Harmy" consisted of a captain, a lieutenant, and perhaps a score of privates. The two officers were rustic English maids, who lived on their pay of ten shillings a week apiece, and tea'd every day with the privates, thus saving tea and fire. They were blooming dairymaids with tremendous singing voices, or what passed for such, and equal power in thumping tambourines, especially as contribution-boxes. This very Sunday was their last on Alderney, where they had been for a year. Their marching orders had come ; by the next steamer their successors would arrive and they depart, probably for Jersey ; they did not yet know their destination.

The services began with music by the band, "said to be the best Salvation band in the Channel Islands," patriotic little Zilpha declared, and prayer by the band-master, a round-eyed, flabby-mouthed, unintelligent looking youth, whose daily business was blacksmithing. Then came prayer by a decent working-man, in which was pathetic reference to the departure of " thy saints." " Saints," as applied to those chubby-cheeked girls, would have made the Doves smile had they not set their faces as adamant against any such levity. The pathetic reference was expected, for almost before it assumed any form at all the captain assiduously applied herself to her handkerchief.

But not for long did the dingy, crumpled thing dry her tearfulness, for her lieutenant gently insinuated it away to apply to her own. Then the captain's sorrow required it, then the lieutenant's again; so, to and fro, backwards and forwards, the unseemly rag travelled, till those meek Doves, peacefullest of their kind, yearned to charge the whole army and force clean handkerchiefs upon its officers. Not more than half a score of people were at the *al fresco* service, perhaps a score and five were at the service at headquarters. This was a room fitted with benches and a rough platform. The whitewashed walls were adorned with mottoes, and the congregation was largely of giggling young people. Certainly the most devout in manner were the even more youthful worshippers who arrived in what Zilpha called " prayambulators," and who kept their eyes devoutly shut till the braying of the band set them to shouting in shrillest army fashion.

" Prayambulators," communed the Doves; " how divinely named! What do you suppose they are on week-days! Can it be they are only the English ' pram ' which answers to our perambulator ? "

" Corporal Smith will make a few feeble remarks," announced Captain Susan, while Lieutenant Jane circulated the contribution tambourine. Corporal Smith's remarks may or may not have been " feeble ; " to this day the Doves decline to testify for either side. For, as Corporal Smith had no teeth and no palate, and his throat was husky with the granite dust of the quarry in which his weeks are spent, they were unable to distinguish a word he meant to say. Neither did he seem to care

whether he was understood of men or no, for he
began to prepare to reseat himself fully three
minutes before he and the bench came together,
and made the last of those feeble remarks quite in
the shape of a letter S.   Zilpha explained that
Corporal Smith had served as one of the light-
keepers on the dream-palace Casquets.   Nearly
all his life of twenty years he had lived with his
father on that rock which seemed so attractive as
a mere picture or as a dream, cradled by the sea,
watched by the heavens, sung to by ten thousand
winds.   " He had found it dull," Zilpha said, and
had come to brilliant Alderney to break stone and
flatter himself that he had reached a metropolis
of the world.   " He says he is tickled to death to
live on Alderney," said pretty Zilpha.   " I suppose it would seem quite small to him if he saw
London."

Before the present method of intrusting the
care of lighthouses to four men, each of whom
has a spell of holiday in turn, a family lived on
the lonely Casquets from 1821 to 1849.   Upon
one occasion the elder daughter paid a visit to
Alderney, but she soon grew weary of its bustle.
" The world," as she called it, " was too full of
trouble and noise," and in a few days she joyfully
returned home.   However, some years later she
was wooed from her rock to marry an Alderney
carpenter.

Two things upon windy Alderney were of great
interest.   One was the return of the cows, Alderney cows, every evening to the village ; the other
a drill of the island militia.   Those gaunt, fawn-
colored cows, with soft, wistful, intelligent eyes !
For the first time the strangers understood the

meaning of "ox-eyed Juno." Their interest in
them never ceased, even after they ceased reaching
out arms to touch the coast of France, so near that
houses were distinctly visible. Under the waters
of the Channel now lies the road which anciently
connected this rock with Normandy, and for which
to this day Alderney pays taxes for repairs.

The Guernsey and the Alderney breeds of cattle
are permitted to intermingle, being so much alike,
but the Jersey is entirely forbidden to both. The
Jersey breed is said to have deteriorated from its
condition of a century ago, probably for this very
reason. Men and women decrease in size and
beauty as well as in quality when too long insu-
lated and forced to blood intermarriages, and
naturally cattle are subject to the same law. The
Channel Island cows are always tethered, even at
pasture. They closely graze the grass within
reach of their rope, then lie down to wait to be
moved. It seems a cruel sight, that of these gentle
creatures tied to a stake, frequently also with head
harnessed down lest it reach up to apple-boughs.
It is said that in Jersey are fifty-eight cattle to
every one hundred acres. The breed in the
three islands is very similar, although decidedly
different ; in America we know no difference between them. Each cow yields from four to five
gallons of milk daily, and seven to ten pounds of
butter a week. The Jersey cow is the smallest of
the three breeds and the prettiest. None of them
is it possible to fatten for the shambles, and their
flesh makes very inferior beef, with yellow fat.

One of the guide-books consulted by the Americans stated that the prison of Alderney was seldom
used. "By the salutary influence of the Salvation

Army it has now seldom inmates." Considering that the island had found it advisable to erect a substantial prison of late years, and considering what they had seen of the "Harmy" on Alderney, this seemed a slightly insecure statement. When they visited the court-house and were shown about by the jailer, they asked if the prison was empty.

"No," was the answer. "I have three soldiers, nice fellows. They are in for breaking and entering one night when they were on a spree. I tell them what fools they are. You see they are tired of sojjering and are playing a game to be discharged from the service. It would ruin them, of course, in England; they could never keep a situation if they got one, and they don't really mean to be criminals. They are just headstrong, reckless boys, the eldest only one-and-twenty. They mean to get kicked out of the army, and then go to America under false names. They 're nice fellows; they are shut in together, and spend their time playing cards."

It seemed to the Doves that everything rascally and adventurous had gone to America, or was going.

"Were not our Pilgrim Fathers adventurers? Had they no spice of recklessness in them where should we have been?" communed those pilgrim Doves. "We inherit the pilgrim part of them, if no other."

But those cows, those cream-giving cows!

"Cream, solid, cream-colored cream!" they chuckled before the first supper. "Cream from brimming pitchers into brimming goblets!"

The next morning nobody chuckled. Nobody wanted milk for breakfast, or indeed anything else.

" You drank ze milk wizzout ze water," explained
their landlady.

They never did it again.

Every evening they watched those slow, dignified creatures, every one of them somebody's pet
and answering to its name with beautiful docility,
as they marched past their windows from the
island fountain, where every evening and morning
of the year they gather to drink (which water,
except for cisterns, is the island's only supply).
Every man's herd is by itself, but as all the herds
came at almost the same time, it seemed like one
long, stately procession, passing on to some flower-
decked altar of the pagan gods.   No cow straggled
or capered (perish such an unworthy thought !) ;
none flourished to one side or the other of the
alley-like street.   All was serious, even solemn;
no shouts disturbed them or the Doves.   They
marched two by two, sometimes four abreast, and
always with gentle countenances slightly inclined
towards one another.   Sometimes a herdsman was
with them, at other times they kept the even tenor
of their way without him.   The Americans sometimes
saw a herd halted before a shop while their attendant
bought his salt-herring or codfish for supper.   It
was halted by a word, as at a word it started again.
It was some time before they discovered that this
rhythmic twilight march, in which each pensive
marcher kept such perfect step and time, was managed by means of large loops of rope flung over
each cow's horns, thus uniting the whole herd.

These Channel Island cattle are very jealously
guarded.   No other cattle are permitted to land
upon the island, except to be butchered for food.
They never see another kind than their own, un-

less one be sold for a huge price and taken away over the sea. It almost seems as if these delicate creatures must be homesick when forced to associate with coarser beings of such different colors and forms from themselves. None of them upon their island home ever know their own calves, which are always brought up by hand upon *diluted* milk. If ze water was not put to ze milk of their supper they would refuse their breakfasts as the Doves did.

When Queen Victoria visited Alderney and drove the people out of their wits with proud joy in 1854, a grand procession was arranged in her honor of these gentle bovine creatures, decked with green leaves, flowers being beyond the island's reach.

One day the strangers became aware of some unusual excitement round Blaggud Corner. " Three o'clock," shouted one running boy to another. " No, two !" was the answer. " Pa told me himself."

" None at all," said a blaggud, leaning against the most decorative design on the island, a show window full of onions and oranges, divided into triangles by tins of tomatoes. " Is too," replied another, " we must be there sharp."

" A review of the militia," exclaimed a little serving maid, excitedly, almost throwing the dinner upon the table. " Mrs. Duplain says I may go." She danced about her duties with as pleased and excited expectation as if it were to be the trooping of the Queen's colors at the Horse Guards.

Two hours later the whole island was astir. It seemed scarcely possible that so many men and children belonged upon the rock. All tended one way, and thither tended the Americans.

There, upon a windy field called *Le But*, they saw sixty men, the island's army of defence. They were of all heights and sizes, and unanimous only in wind-beaten complexions and absence of teeth, or presence in hideous ruins. There must have been an officer to every half-dozen men ; indeed an invading army would meet an army of defence composed almost entirely of officers. Some of these officers did nothing but stand about in groups as if holding important councils of war. An extremely long-legged young officer in white gloves and much military braid, trailed a clattering sword incessantly. No darky with a watermelon was ever better satisfied with himself than he, with his sword and braids. His martial stride was almost too martial for the island ; one half expected to see him topple over the brink and scare the peaceful fishes to death by all that martial show. He did not concern himself with the rest of the army in the least ; his white gloves were more to him than any possible invader, the clatter of his sword was a visible ecstacy as he lurched and lunged from one army division to the other, in a way to strike admiration and terror to island maidens and our two Salvation lasses from rustic England.

The army itself could not forget Blaggud Corner. It tried to shelter itself from the wind. It played sly tricks and pranks under the very eyes of the officers. At rest the men pinched each other and grimaced at nursemaids from the garrison. It is safe to say that there were not a score of sound teeth in that army, and no dentist on the island. So far from hiding the hideous lack, every

one of those bold warriors seemed anxious to display it in grins from ear to ear. In the roll-call
each man answered to a number, but the officer in
charge sometimes had occasion *ex officio* to bawl,
" Now, John Heame, can't you answer to yer number? Ain't a-goin' to stan' no foolin'!" Or,
" Number Two, remember what you 'r doin'
of !"

The strutty young officer did nothing but strut,
even though a youth of tender age, having called
to a warrior bold, " Pa, I 'm goin' home now," ran
between his legs.' He did nothing but strut and
listen to maids whispering, " La ! Mr. Barbetson,
ain't he nice ! " even when another officer makes
a wide swish of his sword about him and shouts to
crowding boys, " Here, you fellers, clear out ! "

Another time, after " Eyes right ! " the other
officer shouted, " Bill Bray, what are you a-squintin'
at ? " and forgot that Bill Bray was cross-eyed till
the entire army shouted with laughter, and even
then never saw the gun that was prodding helpless
Bill Bray in the rear. This review was a village
sensation ; every boy on Alderney watched it with
eager eyes. Before many years he too could carry
a gun now and then, and wear a uniform on *Le But*
to dazzle nursemaids and frighten the never-coming
invader. So the boys gathered close upon that
warlike host in which were their fathers, uncles, and
big brothers, and in spite of shooings and booings
from both officers and men, nipped them irrever-
ently wherever was a chance, not scorning to
take unfair advantage in the rear, not fearing to
dash straight through the wobbling ranks with hoot
and yell, sometimes escaping gun jabs and sometimes not, sometimes made prisoners of war and

held by the slack of the trousers, till released with laughter and a thorough shaking.

All this time the swaggering young officer, whose legs would certainly elsewhere have led to their arrest as drunk and incapable, continued his clattering and ecstatic gyrations. He was conscious of stranger eyes upon him ; the more conscious he grew, the more his legs gyrated.

When all was over half or more of the island's defenders mounted a little child upon one shoulder, a gun upon the other, and Alderney grew lively with bold warriors marching home to supper behind their cows and each with a child upon his shoulder.

Probably even thus they would meet the Invader.

THE LADDER.

" Disgusting fog !" sighed the lady.

Her companion looked up in surprise.

" The sun shines."

" Really ! what business has it to shine in December?   It's pea-soup time."

" Ah ! I see : you are craving fogs as an excuse to leave London.   I do not know why we should not hire-furnished without one."

" Neither do I," she cordially acquiesced.   " I was only waiting for you to say so.   I hunger and thirst for that Wine-Cellar."

Among answers to their advertisements the lady had carefully preserved one which thrilled her to the very foundations of her being.   It was a lady's letter, a lady's stationery, penmanship, and manner of expression.   It gave the impression of a stately dame in black velvet and lace, wearing a long-tabbed widow's cap, and with a higher nose and color than an American of her position would have.   This lady, " Madame Noire," they called her, had noticed their advertisement in the Church Times (of course she was High Church) and " with sufficient recommendations was willing to let the advertisers have her house at B. for the sake of having it aired. There were seven rooms, gas, piano, and the Wine-Cellar."

When she read this letter the advertiser nearly broke into a cheer.

"Just think of it ! To own a Wine-Cellar during a whole winter ! What luxury ! What splendor ! What an atmosphere of 'hig-leef,' as our French friends say. What a flourish and finish to our letters home only casually to mention, 'He would certainly add a postscript had he not just run down to the Wine-Cellar' ! How the Smiths, Joneses, Browns, would all have bilious attacks, imagining the butler, the footman, the chief cook, and the bottle-washer, the men-servants and maid-servants, the everything that properly consorts with an English wine-cellar ! Of course there should be marble-floored stables, and no end of flowing manes and tails to accompany the Wine-Cellar. If there is not, we have no occasion to mention so small a discrepancy to the Robinsons."

"What will you put into it?"

"Into the Wine-Cellar?"

The lady reflected a moment. Then she named the fluid consumed between them in sufficient quantities to wake the horror of all their English friends.

Both laughed. For this fluid made a perpetual rift in the lute of their relations with their English friends who openly considered their perfect diges-tion and health an insolent flout in the face of of nature when they consumed vinegar *à l'améri-caine* by the quart, instead of mustard *à l'an-glaise* by the ton.

The Wine-Cellar settled the question. No mat-ter what inducements elsewhere were offered, be

it a softer winter climate (for little England's relation to the Gulf Stream gives it more climates than
you can shake a stick at, sometimes a pair of them
in one town) than briskly bracing Broadstairs, be
it "plate" included in the furnishing (with the
Wine-Cellar there was none), be it even an "extensive library," as one offer held, — no matter for
anything and everything, so long as there was but
one Wine-Cellar, one glorious, one magnificent,
one sublime, one unutterable Wine-Cellar !

It seemed consistently Wine-Cellarish that the
black-velveted and high-nosed owner exacted
references, though neither in the case of Villa nor
in that of Cot, had they been demanded.

"You see," remarked the financial manager of
the firm to the literary, — "you see it is not of our
solvency, inasmuch as we pay for the whole term
in advance ; it is of our moral and social status.
Madam Noire does not intend to insult her Wine-
Cellar with plebeian society."

"What will the Wine-Cellar say to the vinegar?
Is n't vinegar, associating familiarly with raw onions
and baked beans, a bit plebeian as compared with
Veuve Cliquot and Clos Vougeot?"

This was something of a blow.

But, after a pause, "I will cork the jug tightly
and label it *Sweet Malaga.*"

They arrived at the Wine-Cellar after dark, winding through the usual narrow and down-slipping
streets of an ancient fishing village. From high
walls and gabled gateway their carriage roused
sleeping echoes murmuring not of ancient glories,
of times and manners past, but, at least to the
lady's ears, sweetly singing, "Wine-Cellar ! Wine-
Cellar ! " She pictured at the foot of the descent

a high-nosed dwelling with black-velvet portals opening widely upon a spacious entrance hall, a glimpse beyond of a stately drawing-room and handsome dining-room, made even more dignified by their consciousness that beneath them the Wine-Cellar extended its noble vaults. "All," she chuckled, "royally condescending to be aired by vagabond Americans for thirty dollars a quarter!"

The carriage drew up in the darkness of a corner gaslamp many rods away.

"See!" cried the lady. Then with less haste and more dignity, she pointed to the level of the pavement where burned a low thin line of illumination, the only bit of light in the whole façade.

"Behold our Wine-Cellar!"

"Do English dowagers illuminate Wine-Cellars at ten shillings a week?" asked the other, with some inflexion of doubting.

Dreaming of that Wine-Cellar the lady had brought her best silver and napery. She had visions during all the railway journey of the flashing decanters she should find over the Wine-Cellar, the crystal goblets of finest cutting, the fairylike china to match, and to make their breakfasts and luncheons poetry, their tea-tray a dream, their dinners Music, Sculpture, Painting, and the Drama.

An intelligent, well-bred young woman, evidently more a confidential friend than even a confidential servant of the owner (as happens only in England), had come up from London for necessary domestic arrangements, and met them at the door.

Suddenly the lady's reason tottered on its throne. Even the throne itself uprose and reeled.

The Grand Portal was not of black velvet. It was scarcely wider than she was, scarcely higher than the partner of her hirings. There was no vista of drawing and dining room ; the Wine-Cellar did not make itself felt, the worn oilcloth of the narrow entry *did*, — likewise the steep and narrow stairs, cheek by jowl with the narrow front-door.

"The stairs are always covered with oilcloth in English seaside places," whistled the lady. "The sand you know."

Evidently his courage did not need whistling to keep it up, whatever might be suspected of hers.

"The 'sincere' English taste keeps its marble for its Wine-Cellar. Seems very comfortable here," said the wise one.

The foolish one wisely held her peace. Wisely, because later the indescribable, unparalleled queerness of the house largely compensated for its shortcoming of the mundane elegance so unreasonably pictured. Never in all their wanderings had any such odd creation met their sight. It sometimes seemed a dwelling in wonderland, where on windy midnights they heard the mock turtle's lament that he was not real, where the Cheshire cat's grin wavered to and fro in the sunny mornings, and where viewless Hatters took tea with viewless Dormice and March hares in the dining-room, whenever they left it.

When the Americans undertook to find a name for the house, as they always did name their hired-furnisheds, they found themselves embarrassed by the many peculiarities, any one of them characteristic enough to give a name.

"Why not call it The Wine-Cellar?"

The other partner's brow clouded.

"It is not a Pub."

"Of course not. It would n't pay. The Tartar Frigate, the Jolly Tar, the Man of Kent, not to mention the Dolphin are quite too near, the very youngest of them established in 1776."

They never quite decided upon a name, though "The Ladder" seemed most appropriate and was most in use. They wrote to their London friends of their "Crystal Palace;" the Smiths, Browns, Joneses, and Robinsons heard of their "Swell Front;" to each other, when time did not too much fugit, they named it, "The House-in-which-one-may-not-throw-Stones."

It had a swell front, one most decidedly swollen. But for that swell, swelling out toward the swells of the German Ocean, its width would have been scarcely more than twenty feet. The dining-room, drawing-room, and one of the bedrooms were largely composed of that elaborate swell. The house consisted chiefly (of course after the Wine-Cellar) of three flights of ladders (called stairs) climbing straightly up a white cliff of Albion, one of the very cliffs that Cæsar and St. Augustine may have made remarks upon before these ladders hid it. Thus while the rotund front of three rooms was chiefly of glass, in the form of bow-windows projecting even beyond the brick swell, the back was blank and rigid, being of solid rock. Every room of the six was on a different floor, except the three bedrooms. They spread themselves on the top level, three ladders from the kitchen, very like an umbrella on its stick or a mushroom on its stalk. Naturally, the Ladder-esque style of domestic architecture has some inconveniences. The sneeze and the handkerchief may not always chance upon the same level ; the needle may be with the thimble, but the buttonless garment three ladders away. Would the dinner-getter stay her soul with philosophic comfort between bastings of the joint, she must climb a cliff of Albion two ladders or three from the base to Marcus Aurelius, or else cry upward that her philosopher be cast down. One needs to adopt the Ladderesque style of housekeeping to realize how extremely wayward are the habits of many small adjuncts of civilization besides handkerchiefs and thimbles, to realize too how possible, even though so highly improbable, to live, love, suffer, and die on a space of earth not larger than a family burial-lot, without an inch of space beyond that covered by ladders up the face of a cliff. The Ladder had no outside space wherein to hang a handkerchief or to dry a stocking. From the door there was but one step to the pavement ; through that one door, for lack of any other, the inhabitants must receive their letters, visitors, and supplies, through it they must project their ashes.

The crystal part of the dwelling was about one third of the three front rooms. The enormous windows formed almost the entire façade and looked three ways upon the German Ocean, booming beneath. Directly in front, the crystal faced France, and framed at times a looming hint of Calais Heights. Close beneath, were fishing boats and a quaint little oyster shop, where the fisherman owner was rarely seen, and whoever entered to buy (in the winter) left his order and money on a shelf. Behind and above, were quaint, sunless streets, flintstone arches, and ancient walls, as well as modern streets ; to the left, the sea ; to the right, a succession of empty lodging-houses and fantastic summer villas gone to sleep.

The Ladder was its owner's summer home, that owner whose nose came down a few notches, and whose velvet and lace changed to merino and braid, when the Americans recognized how incompatible the Ladder's space with trailing raiment and any unusual altitude of feature. They believed in her honorable sincerity now, having before credited her only with the artificial simplicity of the aristocrat, when she wrote them that she had bought the house some years before as a vacation refuge for her nurses and children.

" It is n't quite an everyday nose, you see, even yet, and there 's plenty of velvet and lace in the winter wardrobes ; notice she writes nurses."

" How many would the house hold ? " asked the other, with mental calculation of the nurse-and-child capacity of three beds and a folding chair.

The house itself, by reason of the vagaries of the cliff at its back, as well as every room in it, was shaped like the very craziest patch of the craziest quilt ever evolved from crazy minds. This eccentricity was magnified and multiplied by mirrors ingeniously fitted into every angle, recess, corner, where a mirror could possibly be inserted, as well as broadly between doors and over the marble chimney-piece. They were mirrors long and mirrors slender, mirrors short and mirrors broad, all evidently designed to magnify space and dimensions. Two buffets in the dining-room below had mirror doors and backs, ditto one *étagère* in the drawing-room above. The result was less a magnitude of dimensions than a magnitude of glitter, of shine and shimmer, of high lights and cross lights, resulting frequently in such high and cross perplexity of vision that these Hirers gave way to dark suspicions. At times they mutually gazed aslant with an obliqueness consorting oftener with paganism and pigtails, than with American straight-forwardness, half expecting the fatal words, " How cross-eyed you are ! " and ready with that always effective retort, " You 're another ! "

The tiny drawing-room midway up Albion's cliff, and largely out of doors, being so largely of glass, was furnished with a Brussels carpet evidently reduced from the London house and larger rooms of its owner, and upholstered with green rep now considerably faded. It had Nottingham lace curtains and antimacassars without number. Muslin flowers (ah, the untold millions of them in England) and tuppenny ha'penny ornaments beyond count gave impression of æsthetic decoration entrusted entirely to nurses and children. The general effect was of the strangest. Somehow, in spite of its one side of everlasting rock, its other side of solemn sea, the room held yet the spiritual essence of a British matron, but one *en déshabillé* and given over to summer-vacation ways. The strangers fancied they could see her wearing a sailor hat in place of the wide-tabbed cap, and with a Trilby blouse and short petticoats tumbling in from the sands, to sprawl all over this green rep with a Keynote or a Yellow novel, regardless of the conventions that elsewhere keep her nose and stockings up, and her literary taste under guidance of the " Church Times " and " The Queen."

Deep down in the bowels of the earth was the kitchen, whence that low line of light had greeted the Americans upon their arrival; likewise there was the Wine-Cellar; likewise the space under the pavement called by all indigenes "coal-scubberd." In no such dungeon in America would "help" of any possible condition consent to be confined. No smutty scullion, however greasy, would stoop so low. It was nothing else than a grewsome cellar cemented top, bottom, and sides, and hung all about with fire-tried cooking utensils. Close under the ceiling two panes of glass, placed lengthwise and beside each other, not one above the other, touched the level of the street. They were always splashed thick with mud, and to wash them was foolish, for the next passing foot splashed them anew. Washed once a day, they remained in condition to afford a comprehensive view of the native foot, often a considerable object to view. The whole island might have been feet and nothing more, for all those panes revealed. During only about six hours of a sunny winter's day did twilight creep in, like a thing scared or ashamed. After three o'clock until nine the next morning, only by gaslight could a face be seen. There was no possible exit from this cavern save by a ladder, and no other possible entrance into it, unless for the trayful of dishes, which more than once during the American period somersaulted into the dungeon without so much as touching a ladder, albeit Nellie, the tray-bearer, knew familiarly from base to summit that House-in-which-one-may-not-throw-Stones.

The House-in-which-one-may-not-throw-Stones was delightfully clean, for it was an English housekeeper's own. Because it was the first of their hiring that really was somebody's own, and not furnished expressly to be let, these Hirers (at least one of them) was conscious of a delicious sense of peeping-and-prying, and the indulgence of that instinct of human nature which has created the Interviewer and the Personal Column, as well as made the quilting bee and the sewing society of our fore-parents, — the same instinct that makes Plutarch and Pliny of perennial interest, that has preserved dirty, mean Pepys from oblivion, that makes Boswell, the Duc de Saint-Simon, Horace Walpole, and Madame de Sévigné famous, and that swells the world's vast and ever-rising flood of biographies, autobiographies, correspondences, memoirs, and reminiscences. Many a time this peeper-and-pryer had inspected domestic interiors of England, but always under guidance. She had revealed the secrets of pandowdy, strawberry shortcake, and codfish balls in more than one indigenous kitchen, but ever with watchful eyes upon her. Never before had the bridle been taken from her neck, and she turned loose, without let or hindrance, among cupboards and clothes-presses not her own, not even of her own country; and it was with the delicious taste of forbidden fruit in her mouth that her face inserted itself between beds and mattresses, that she "hefted" pillows, peered into closets, and turned every kitchen utensil upside down with regret that it would not be turned inside out, and that it had no hind-side to be made a front one.

Blankets were fleecy and abundant; the counterpanes snowy, the beds martyred geese. Evidently Madam Noire was of the old school never modernized to hair mattresses ; although the feather beds were not of early eighteenth but late nineteenth century geese, and the ticking almost new. The chamber furnishing was extremely plain, but comfortable in every particular, as the English habit always is. In the dining-room-of-many-corners, the fireplace in the farthest one, the two decanters flashed as brilliantly as they would have flashed with ten companions ; wine-glasses were neat, and a full dozen minus three ; the china of the usual white-and-gold variety, and ample in quantity for a pair of Hirers with now and then a guest.

"Imagine," said the lady, " there is not a bread or cake tin in the whole Ladder. Not a steamer, a double-boiler, an ice-cream freezer, a custard cup, an egg whisk, a pie plate, a gem pan, a potato-masher, a flour-sifter, a pancake-turner, a coffee or spice mill, a can-opener, a fruit-strainer, an apple-corer in the whole House-in-which-one-may-not-throw-Stones."

The other one of them looked aghast.

" Go out at once and buy," he gasped, as if starvation already gripped them.

" No. I will manage as the English house-keeper manages in her summer home, and buy bread and all sweets from the confectioner and baker. But what under the sun can I do with the English housekeeper's implements for sub-stantial cooking? Do see this whole nest of baby bath-tubs ; they are for English puddings for which the eggs are evidently beaten with this pitchfork. Those basting hooks would bear a heifer ; here 's a fish-kettle for a mother whale, and a smaller for her daughter ; one could rock-me-to-sleep-mother in this chopping-tray ; this roasting pan is divided

into two hemispheres large enough to carry the
Zodiac twins. I fancy one is for the roast beef,
the other for the Yorkshire pudding ; one for fowl,
the other for sausages ; or perhaps Madam Noire
has a choice of joints for every dinner. These
colossal objects explain the gravy boats and meat
platters, in any one of which both of us might go
ashore from a wreck. We can use the gravy boat
platter for our roasts. I will buy a roasting pan
commensurate, and we need not invest in a cork-
screw, there 's one for every ladder."

That there was no lack of trays needs not to be
said. The god Tray is ever chief among the
household idols of England. Who ever read an
English novel into which the Tray did not enter,
visibly or invisibly? It may be the Tray of
breakfast, of luncheon, of tea, or of supper ;
but there Tray is, succulent, stimulating, grateful,
comforting, refreshing, solidly imposing, undeniably
British. Who ever forgets that supper tray in
Cranford, at sight of which the good mistress
exclaims, as if in pleased surprise, "Why, Betty,
what have you brought us ? " having herself been
cooking for that tray all day.

The English palace gathers unto itself trays of
silver and trays of gold. The English country
house is rich in heirloom trays ; the æsthetic
London house outlays upon much inlaying of its
trays ; Villadom adorns its trays with fine linen
and much stitchery ; the Cottager has her painted
idol ; the tramp steals every Tray upon which he
can lay his hands.

" Why do we make no account of the Tray in
America ? " one asked.

" Democracy's rights," explained the other of

them. "The Triumph of the Modern Spirit and the Rights of Man. In our country we can go to the tray, but the tray rarely comes to us, lacking legs. The English Tray and the English coal-scuttle are Molochs that yearly devour their thousands. Think of the endless procession of servile legs that toil, and have toiled for centuries, up and down stairs with them, under bodies bent broken and despairing, a servile class and nothing more. Think of it, thoughtless worshipper of your Five-o'clock, and try to imagine a 'help' in America 'accepting a position,' as they call it, where is a ladder between kitchen and dining-room, two ladders between the teakettle and the afternoon Tray!'"

For a brief space of time one of the Hirers looked almost as uncomfortable as she felt. Then her brow cleared.

"As you are no less a Five-o'clocker than I am, you may add your two legs to our tea-tray after this. But there are no ladders between our tea-kettle and tray, for there the kettle sings at the drawing-room grate on the trivet I bought the next morning after the evening of our arrival."

In consequence of this little domestic interlude, at five o'clock that very afternoon two tea-cups and saucers came up from the dining-room in a man's bare right hand, the tea-pot in the man's bare left, the tray under his arm. As the other of them climbed up from the kitchen with the cut bread and butter, she inquired : —

"Where are the spoons?"

"Daresay I dropped them somewhere," was the nonchalant answer. "You ought to keep the tea-things always up here."

" And wash them, where ? "

The rest was silence.

Nellie, their Maid of the Morning, came singing to the Ladder with every winter's dawn. She was a fisherman's daughter from a dusky interior three doors away, and served them deftly and honestly, albeit with various perfectly visible suspicions. Every morning the lady heard Nellie's blithe voice below, whereupon she rose for one little instant from her feathery couch and lifted the window a wee crack. The doorkey (there was but one, for cliffs of Albion do not permit of back doors), was thrust through the crack attached to a long string. When a pull came upon the string it was evident that Nellie had possessed herself of the key. The string was drawn up, and the feathery couch received its own again till Nellie's pleasant voice announced the hot water and breakfast.

Nellie was only sixteen, but already a clever cook. She was shyly but firmly convinced that she could cook " American things," if only once told how. The Hirers were wildly desirous of buckwheat-cakes, and Nellie, with amazement depicted upon her frank countenance, told them where buckwheat could be found, the only place in all Broadstairs. So the buckwheat was ordered, and with it a sealed can, or tin, of golden syrup, " two pounds for sixpence," the lady announced ; " eggs will come also, not at fifteen pence a dozen, but twelve for fifteen pence, oranges twenty the shilling, potatoes sixpence the gallon, apples fourpence the pound."

" Apples by the pound ! ar'n't you ashamed of yourself to order less than a bushel ? Tell me, at fourpence the pound for goldings, how much will a barrel of baldwins cost? "

The lady's face was troubled. It always was, when she was particularly reminded of apples by the pound. Until her arrival in England, many years ago, she had never seen apples sold by the pound, the most reasonable and just way to buy and sell them. She chanced to be passing a green grocer's, — never shall she forget the corner in a sordid neighborhood, a corner of Great Coram and Marchmont Street, — when she espied pleasant apples at something-or-other the pound. Experimentally she asked for a pound of those apples. When the boy gave her three, she exclaimed, " Is that all that goes to a pound? Then — "

She was about to add, " I must have five or six pounds," when the green grocer himself, hearing her exclamation, stepped up.

" 'Three ain't enough for a fourpenny pound, ain't it? Yer 'd better 'ave yer hown garding 'n grow happles fer yerself, er yer 'd better heat hunyuns 'n' leave happles till yer c'n hafford to pay for 'em ! "

The American was out of the shop by this time ; but for hours, " happles 'n' hunyuns, happles 'n' hunyuns," rattled in her ears, and not for months afterwards did she venture into a greengrocer's shop. When she did venture, she did not ask for apples, but for butter.

" Hain't yer gut no heyes? This is a greengrocer's," snarled the owner.

" In my country we buy our butter of the greengrocer," she ventured to explain.

The man looked her over from head to foot, then remarked superciliously : —

" It 's a rum 'un, then."

Years afterwards, this American heard an Englishwoman returned from six weeks at the World's
Fair lecture upon "Impressions of America."
She was a short, red-faced, dowdily-dressed
woman, the very type and pattern of John Bull's
wife, as American caricature represents her, who
showed by her every word, that, while in America,
she considered herself in a *Pays conquis*. It was
actually pitiable that this woman was as unconscious as a dead woman of the effect she really
had upon the taciturn Americans, supposed to be
speechless from admiration. The lecturer even
told of the excitement into which her English person and her " London frock " threw an entire village. The Americans in her audience did not
doubt it !

" The lower classes in America are unspeakably
insolent," said the lecturer. " I once went to a
Chicago express office to ask after a strayed box.
No sooner had I stated my business, than the
clerk bawled to another, ' If here is n't another
woman asking about a trunk !' 'Give me none
of your insolence,' I said to the man, ' I am an
English gentlewoman, and unaccustomed to impertinence.' "

" *Happles 'n' hunyuns ! happles 'n' hunyuns !* "
memory echoed in the audience, and an American
longed to match the vulgar woman's experience
of " American lower classes in an express office,"
during the rush and turmoil of a World's Fair,
with her own experience of that very day in a
Golden Grain tea-shop in Great Russell Street.
Finding her tea too strong, she had asked for a little
hot water. The girl who brought it, as she turned

away, remarked audibly to another. "She's goin' to get two cups outer one."

When the buckwheat arrived at the House-in-which-one-may-not-throw-Stones, its bulk was amazing.

"I don't believe it is ground," exclaimed a Hirer.

"Never heard of henny that was," said the man who brought it, and who knew it only as cattle fodder. The lady now understood the amazed expression of Nellie's face during the buckwheat-cake conference, and why she always sniffed at but never tasted the Johnny-cake.

And that relates to the Wine-Cellar. For to visit the Wine-Cellar, was invited the friend who brought with her the prepared package of American gold dust from which the Johnny-cakes were evolved, as well as the "baked Indian," upon which Nellie kept a wary and watchful eye, but of which she could not be persuaded to taste, not knowing if it were of a friendly tribe.

The lady was determined to live up to the Wine-Cellar, of which she had talked so much before leaving London, although to live up to it, with only willing but very youthful Nellie, was not so easy to do. She purchased the caps and aprons of a stylish parlor-maid, and Nellie was persuaded to wear them, with many blushes and giggling protestations of unfitness for so much elegance. Nellie was thenceforth observed to glance frequently into the multitudinous mirrors. Whenever a sudden giggle was followed by a dead, awful silence, it was known that a mirror had cast Nellie's reflection back at her in a guise of an over-powering swell. Yet she never could be enticed or deceived into wearing her finery out of doors. Even crossing over to the little oyster-shop for twenty-five oysters for two shillings, with no prospect of meeting a soul, she snatched off her cap and apron, and, in the twinkling of an eye, was transformed into a fishermaid again with tousled hair and bounding motion, till her return. Apparently, she thus avoided the comments of her acquaintances upon a towering ambition to become, without preliminary education, that *crême de la crême* of servants, a parlor-maid. She would make a perfect one, tidy, quiet, respectful, cheerful and capable ; the spirit of the lady repined greatly that clever Nellie was but a passing circumstance, and not a fixture of their hirings. Gladly would she have invited America to send for her, and be blessed in the acquisition, but for the knowledge that, with a net-ful of daughters, Nellie's parents had not enough of them to spare one out of their reach.

The Americans thus had not only a Wine-Cellar to welcome their guests, but a staff of servants. There was Mrs. 'Arris at the head of the laundry department, who carried and fetched the family washing in a wheelbarrow, to and from the front door, Mrs. 'Arris concerning whose existence was no possible doubt, she being rosy and rotund at past sixty-five, an age when she coquettishly confessed one ought to begin to "hexpect the little hitems and hincidents of hage." Besides this chief of the laundry department, was Nellie the parlor-maid, Ellen the cook, and Nell the butler.

Alas, it was in the latter capacity that the staff came to grief.

"Another bottle of claret, Nell," said the hostess one dinner-time when the guests were two.

"The yellow seal, top row, southeast corner of the Wine-Cellar," added the host, with a wicked smile.

"None there, sir. I brought them both up before dinner," said the unsuspicious butler. Fortunately the other bottle was yet unopened upon the buffet and multiplied by a background mirror into three or four; so nobody had occasion to weep, although much to laugh.

When Mrs. St. John's Wood, author of "Court Circles" and "Queenly Graces," came from St. John's Wood to the Ladder for a few days' visit, she seemed very much more English-you-know, that is, very much more unlike Americans, than she had ever seemed to the Hirers in her own home.

Mrs. Sinjonood, as she pronounced herself, had spent some time in America, and was given to much criticism of Americans, which was not unfair, as no people criticise other peoples more than Americans do. In fact, the absolutely unjust and conspicuously provincial criticisms by Americans of everything they see and hear away from their own country made these Hirers at times almost ashamed of their nationality. To hear nasal voices at their highest pitch proclaiming the cosmopolitanism of the "Amurricun Citizen" and the provinciality of "these Hinglish," in the very capital of England and almost of the world, was enough to make one speak disrespectfully of every stripe in the Starry Banner. In their own country these Hirers heard fifty offensive remarks concerning the English to one they heard in England of Americans. Hundreds of Americans return to their hot biscuits and ice-water every year, with nothing brought home from their travels but anecdotes and descriptions of European barbarism. When one considers the troops of ill-dressed excursionists gaping through Europe without change of linen, personally conducted at so much a head ; back-country Americans with their hideously corrupt English, in which every *a* cants over upon its back instead of standing upright like the *a*'s of Chaucer, Shakespeare, Milton, Tennyson, George Washington, and Daniel Webster, when one considers this annual " American Invasion " into the beaten highways of the tourist's England without a single glimpse of the real England, the beautiful homes and domestic, intellectual, spiritual life of a people whose character has made their speech and their blood to dominate the world, one is almost disposed to beat one's breast and tear one's hair three several and distinct times, — as a Mayflower descendant, a daughter of the Colonial Wars, and a D. A. R.

" It is positively amazing that English people who have never seen Americans in their own country think as well of us as they do," these Americans repeatedly agreed.

Mrs. Sinjonood of St. John's Wood was not of the old school ; she hated feather beds and lay abed, to prove it, till nearly luncheon-time. She took meantime an exact inventory of her chamber furnishing, and enlivened the breakfast-table by recounting the spots on the toilet-table and the cracks of the washstand. Everything on the dining-table, excepting of course the food, passed through the crucible of her criticism. The hitherto unsuspected duplicity of the china, the deceitfulness of the glass ware, the thinness of the carpets, the weak spots in the curtains, — she knew them all, and told of every one. It was only a hired-furnished that she thus mercilessly vivisected; it was not the Hirers' own, and she continually reminded them of her realization of the fact by saying, " Merely one of the seaside houses that English people furnish cheaply for the summer;" but for all that one of the Hirers grew very uncomfortable under the perpetual inspection and criticism of the hiring they enjoyed so much, and she knew that under the same circumstances, and a Sinjonood hiring, she would be less profuse of sarcastic comment. She believed Americans generally of the Sinjonood position would have the same reserves. She felt her nose rise not at the tip but at the bridge, and her color increase à l'anglaise. With black velvet and a tabbed widow's cap she would have resented Mrs. Sinjonood; without them she kept silence upon her conviction that it was not quite well-bred to make a hostess half ashamed of so poor a hired-furnished, and of realizing that poverty so incompletely as to invite a guest to share its misery even for three days.

"Do not generalize all Englishwomen from one," expostulated the wise one. "Not to generalize from the American who eats 'tomayto soss' on his apple pie, and does Yurrup in thirty days, is what you are continually impressing upon English people. Mrs. Sinjonood lacked tact, as the English largely do; but what did that pretty American girl lack last summer who bit an end from a Turkish sweet, and then returned it to the general quantity?"

"Mrs. Sinjonood lives among courts and queens,

at least in her daily work, and her father was a Q. C. The pretty American girl's father was a shoemaker who patented an invention, although, like all perceptive and receptive American girls, she had the dress and appearance of a princess. There's where the mistake comes, and all the friction of misconceptions; for no English person would ever think of expecting or excusing the manner of a shoemaker's daughter in her, but all exact the manners of the princess she manages to look. It is sometimes not all rose for the transatlantic plebeian in Europe that *his*, particularly *her*, appearance is so much better than that of the same breed in England. Neither is it *tout de roses* for the rest of us."

"Your table is very American," said Mrs. Sinjonood; "you use a sugar basin and a spoon vase. We English prefer to offer sugar, a few lumps at a time, in a wine-glass or glass saucer. It is cleaner thus than the same lumps repeated day after day in a basin."

"Ours is a clean country," feebly suggested a Hirer. "We do not use a nail-brush to our sugar, even though it be a month old, as London cooks have been known to do. You English do not use as many spoons as we, hence no spoon vases, now I am bound to say rather old fashioned even in America. You have fewer ' spoon-vittles.' All winter long you eat the same fork-vegetables, so to speak, onions, cabbage, turnips, sprouts, parsnips, all on the same plate. Our corn, squash, tomatoes, succotash, green peas, our peaches, cranberry-sauce, apple-sauce, etc. are saucer-served and spoon-eaten, hence our spoon vases."

The lady almost blushed one day in offering a

dish of Brussels sprouts to Mrs. Sinjonood, after three days of corn, tomatoes, green peas, and green beans. She imagined it so inhospitable to thrust eternal sprouts into mouths eternally winter-fed with them, remembering that English homes at the end of the winter always seemed to her per-meated to their inmost recesses, draperies, nap-eries, upholstery, even to the laces of the boudoir, the leather of the library, with the double distilled essence of roast mutton and Brussels sprouts.

"Now *this* is nice," remarked Mrs. Sinjonood with suggestive emphasis to the dish of sprouts. But to the dish of sugar corn. "It is sweetened porridge. Don't you hate porridge?"

The House-in-which-one-may-not-throw-Stones turned its swell front to the sun nearly all the day long. From morning till mid-afternoon, the little drawing-room was flooded with golden light, even until the writing-tables and reading-chairs must be moved into the least dazzling corners. All those bright winter days were filled with work and play, with books from a good circulating library, with long letters and long walks, with visits, even with a ball and dancing programmes mysterious in mention of *bd, gh, gd, ff, bt,* to be translated, "blue dress," "golden hair," "good dancer," "flat-foot," "big teeth." There was also one occult *I,* declared by one of them to indicate "Idiot," but by the other of them translated "Incognita."

"Our dear English friends highly resent the imputation of prominent teeth, and attribute the slander entirely to Gallic malice," laughed one of them, the morning after that delightful ball to which they were letter-of-introductioned from

Cavendish Square ; " but the fact remains that there are enormous dental displays among them, a peculiarity we in America have somewhat inherited. Whoever saw a Frenchman with conspicuous teeth ? "

" They have not sufficient osseous structure," explained the other ; " and I believe that is why they still keep up their absurd farce of duelling. They have not grown ashamed of flourishing swords, as the big-boned Englishman long ago grew ashamed of fighting with his fists. But why the English deny their valiant teeth I never can understand, particularly after a ball, or a walk down Regent Street. It was an Englishman, one Robert Coddrington, who, so early as the Commonwealth, warned his countrywomen against ' that simper of the lips with which many gentlewomen try to hide the greatness of their teeth.' "

In the month of January sunshine, however dazzling, is not to be depended upon for constancy. In time the Ladder was wrapped in cloudiness. Then the winds beat and roared upon the House - in - which - one - may - not - throw-Stones, the wild sea before the house lashed itself to thunderous fury ; no more the mock turtle's lament was heard in the elemental uproar that almost deafened them. Out upon that raging deep they knew poor souls must be struggling for their lives, perhaps to lose them even so near home ; for out there, but a little space of calm water away, although now distant by leagues upon leagues of shrieking foam, were the fatal Goodwin Sands, where many a brave ship and brave life have left their bones. Twice during the storm they saw the lifeboat manned and launched into the very heart of the tempest. Where it went, save into a great darkness, they could not see, nor did they see its return, with the half-drowned sailors of a collier at the bottom of the English Channel.

The Ladder did not rock one quarter-inch in all that turmoil as Pemsy Villa had rocked so many. The House-in-which-one-may-not-throw-Stones was much nearer the sea than Pemsy Villa, so near in fact that the salt spray almost dashed its crystal front; but it was too firmly backed by a cliff of Albion to shudder, even when the earth itself trembled beneath the booming breakers. Nevertheless the drawing-room was in a high state of excitement. Sheets of manuscript hopped and skipped all over the huge Brussels roses and green rep; leaves of books took their own time and pleasure, or rather the wind's, in the matter of turning over; the crystal side of the room seemed half a mind to come in altogether and spread itself on the hearthrug before the cheery fire. Again the paste-pot came into service, again every crack and crevice was thoroughly calked, and the Ladder put in ship-shape order.

Then Nellie came to assure herself that her timid city pair had not gone stark mad with terror, she brought up the tea-tray; and inside the crystal swell, beside a ruddy grate, peace spread its fair pinions over the cosy five o'clock.

But the Wine-Cellar!

Brother and Sister Americans, countrymen and women, fellow-citizens! Have we not in all our homes some grim dark place into which no man or woman enters, and of which the children are afraid? Is it not darkly haunted by gnome-like things, big-bellied and squat, wide-mouthed and iron-throated, hollow-faced and clanking, like chain-bound galley slaves? Are not unclean objects often there, shapes which certainly are not of honor, even if not exactly of dishonor?

From a gloomy mystery of this sort under the lowest ladder of all, a Hirer one day withdrew a laughing face.

"Call this a Wine-Cellar?" he remarked; "we have no end of them at home. In the American language, they are pot-closets."

CLOVER VILLA.

" NOT a gentleman," said he.

" Mr. Pumpkin Hood was not a gentleman."

"He did not pretend to be, which makes all the difference in the world. This man does. He does not know, however, that a gentleman would not ask concerning us of our banker, we having paid the whole term in advance. What can a banker tell save that our account is regular? We may be escaped convicts for all the ' London and County ' knows. This man's only idea of eligibility is a correct bank account."

The lady was quite of the same opinion concerning the good breeding of the offerer of Clover Villa. His letters were in every way correct; but how could she forget the day on which she had made a journey into Sussex only to look at Clover Villa? Mr. Boxworthy had written her how to reach the villa. She must take a certain train from Victoria Station, arrive at Hailsham in time for the omnibus for Hurstmonceaux, which would leave the Hailsham station ten minutes after the train's arrival. She had followed the directions implicitly, though to do so made a breathless departure necessary, before the house in Cavendish Square was awake. A hurried breakfast in the railway buffet, then an early morning ride and an early forenoon arrival at Hailsham, all as directed. But then, —

"'Ersmunsoo bus?" said men about the station; "it does n't call for this train; calls for the train an hour later."

"Why did Mr. Boxworthy rend me from my bed at such an inconscionable hour, to strand me here in a most uninteresting town waiting the omnibus?" she murmured disconsolately. There was ample time for a lunch at a neighboring hotel, a saunter about the town, then the omnibus gathered wiser passengers than she, who had known enough to take the later train from London, and all set forth over the four miles to Hurstmonceaux.

"Omnibus," it was called; it was really one of the long, heavy, black and clumsy covered wagons with a seat upon each side, as in other omnibuses, but the centre filled with commissions from Hailsham, and for Hurstmonceaux, — groceries, wooden ware, iron ware, flour and feed, furniture, luggage, whatever the little hamlet needed whither they were bound. There was scarcely room for the feet of the passengers who clung to the narrow seats as to a ledge upon a wall. The seats were thus narrow to enlarge the carrying capacity of the centre, filled now with both luggage and merchandise, the latter both added to and subtracted from by commissions at various shops and houses. The American noticed that everybody spoke of the thing as "carrier" not as "omnibus."

Mr. and Mrs. Boxworthy met her in Clover Villa, having driven from their own house in B—— in their pony cart. They had hired Clover Villa for their own summer use, they said, and furnished it for that purpose, but had concluded to let it to desirable tenants; they expected four pounds a month, but could probably let it at those terms not more than six weeks' of the summer; if the lady would take it for four months, as she said in her letters, she might have it at the rate of 15*s*. a week.

The man never spoke to her without repeating her name. Over and over and over again, till she wearied of it, and would almost have welcomed the touch more of servility in the English shopman's incessant " Madam," even the cabman's and porter's " Lady." The wife was less effusive, and made a better impression, as wives often do in England as well as elsewhere, even though she alluded more than once to the "exceeding luxury" with which her own house was furnished. The stranger gave a guinea to make the bargain fast, and the man gave her a receipt for it, a perfectly proper and business-like proceeding. Never in any other hiring had she paid such a guinea or been offered such a receipt. The consequence was that she utterly forgot to take the receipt upon her return to London, but left it in Clover Villa, to receive it by post the very next day. " Strictly business-like," she thought, " but not in the least like our other hirings, where payment in advance has never been exacted, but always our own choice.

" To-morrow I will send a check," she said, after binding the bargain with the guinea; "now I must get the omnibus for that four-o'clock train from Hailsham."

" What day is this ?" said the man reflectively. " You see, Mrs. So-and-So, there is no return omnibus to Hailsham on any day except Saturday. But you can hire a carriage at the Woolpack, Mrs. So-and-So."

" No doubt he is honest," thought Mrs. So-and-So, as she bowled along the pleasant road to

Hailsham at an expense greater than her fare from London ; " but he is not a gentleman. He knew very well there was no return omnibus to-day ; he knew there would be one to-morrow ; he did not tell me, because he wished the affair concluded as soon as possible for his own convenience."

These people did not fail to keep up the character in which they first presented themselves. All summer long, until late October, the Americans realized how useless to try to steal the piano or to levant with the drawing-room carpet. They knew that the kitchen poker would be missed within an hour ; they would run into the very arms of the Boxworthys round some corner if they fled with a kitchen knife. When they left Clover Villa and gave up the keys, lo, the Boxworthys were fleeing Clover Villa-ward on the wings of the wind, as no owner had ever rushed upon the scene of their dishonesty before in all their hirings. It turned out afterwards that they were professionals in the way of furnished houses, and the " luxurious home " at B—— was theirs for a home only in winter, being let during the summer, while the family lived in Clover Villa if it were unlet, or if it were let, took refuge in a four-roomed laborer's cottage at Battle. As one knows, there is a difference in manners, even the manner of letting a hired-furnished for the summer.

" What under the sun are you intending to peddle ? "

No wonder he asked. No wonder he endeavored to possess himself of the parcel. No wonder the lady tried to escape both question and the endeavor.

" It's only a little economy," she said, as airily

as if it did not weigh as much as a railway train or a cathedral.

"Little! You carry it as if a 'little economy' was something to stagger under. Let me — " and he made another endeavor, again upon space.

"Unh-a-n-d me, V-i-l-l-a-i-n! I assure you it's only an economy; I'll prove it when we reach Hailsham."

She dared not promise before that arrival lest he pitch her pedler's bag out of the train window.

"I have made the boxes as light as possible; but there are three of them, besides the boxes of books going down by goods-train, and they are heavy in spite of me. We shall have a pretty penny to pay for extra luggage; the South Coast is notoriously the most niggardly and least obliging railway in all England. We never pay extra on the Great Western, no matter what we have with us," she remarked, as trippingly as if but a dainty hand-bag hung from her arm.

To their surprise the porter who took charge of their luggage wheeled it directly to the train. There was no weighing, no receipt for extra luggage, everything seemed lovely and the South Coast enlarging its heart.

When, established in their carriage, the American gave the porter a shilling instead of the usual fourpence, the latter wore a disgusted face.

"Ho, no, sir. Hit must be 'arf a crown at least. You see I didn't take hit to the horffice. If I 'ad you'd 'a' been charged twenty shillin' for hextra."

"Why did you not take it to the office as was your business? It would be more honest to pay twenty shillings there than sixpence here — "

The train was about starting; the porter re-

ceived his 'arf crown. The Americans felt like thiev-
ish confederates ; the lady even worse, she felt, in
fact, completely done, thoroughly "sold," as she
hoisted her disreputable pedler's sack from the
floor where the porter had bestowed it, perhaps
under the impression that they were small iron-
mongers thus removing their stock-in-trade. She
would have disputed nobody who asked the price
of her shovels and tongs.

"My two little oil-stoves," she meekly confessed.
"I would not put them in the trunks because of
their weight."

He laughed. It would have been a bitter laugh
were any bitterness in him.

"We've cheated the South Coast out of seventeen shillings and sixpence," said he, "and carry
our house furnishings ourselves. Clever confidence
operators, are n't we ? "

Clover Villa was extremely inviting as they dismounted, one from his bicycle, the other from the
carrier-wagon, at its gate. It was enclosed with a
little garden and buried in shrubbery. The garden
and villa were higher than the village street, and
reached by two or three brick steps. The large
bow window faced the street, but was separated by
so leafy and bushy a growth of green that it was in
almost as great seclusion as with a park before it.
The front door was on the other side of the house,
and opened upon the tiny garden and brick walk.
Within, the "drawing-room" was one side of the
front door, the dining-room the other ; beyond the
latter, the kitchen with brick floor, whitewashed
stone walls, cook-stove, sink, and kitchen-table,
and open rows of shelves. Above, were two good

square rooms, above them two airy and comfortable attic chambers, decently furnished for servants,
or for anybody in times of pressure upon accommodations, as when, for instance, during that
exquisite summer a party of Harvard classmates
of Mr. Clover's stopped on their way from the
land of pumpkin pies to the land of the cypress
and myrtle.

"It is plain to see," said Mrs. Clover, "that
Mrs. Boxworthy is a model housekeeper. She has
delighted in furnishing and preparing the Villa,
much as I delighted in building a home in Dove
Cottage. A house could not be more complete in
the very small essentials that almost nobody thinks
of till the need for them presents itself. Not only
here is an abundance of bed-linen, not of superfine
quality and not of its *première jeunesse*, though as
white as driven snow, but also kitchen towels, flat-
iron-holders, chamois-skin for the 'plate,' an iron-
ing-board, even floor-cloths, glass and dish towels,
stove-brushes, carpet-brush, sink-brush, floor-brush,
every possible convenience for immaculate cleanli-
ness. In no other hiring have we ever found such
attention to detail. Even when we hire for only six
weeks, we must furnish these or go without. I, you
see, do neither. I manage that my staff of servants shall bring them all from its own home, when
our hiring is for less than months. Everything is
as clean as clean can be ; the good English housekeeper I find a perfect paragon of neatness everywhere. You see, Mr. and Mrs. Boxworthy enjoy
this matter of building many littles into a whole ;
it is their way of thrift, and their view of life and
human destiny is minute, not comprehensive.
Notice those chamber fenders, for instance. You

may knock your toes against them for a lifetime,
and the toes never complain; for the fenders are
the very lightest of black-painted pine, our landlord's own handiwork. He upholstered the drawing-room furniture himself; his wife made the chintz
coverings; he made the toilet-tables of packing-
boxes; she covered them with book-muslin over
pink cambric. The washstands were more than
second-handed and decrepit, he strengthened and
painted them; he matched the missing legs of the
dining-room chairs, and replaced that foot to the
dining-room-table. Only that large wardrobe
in the front chamber with its mirror, and the
furnishing of the drawing-room, do not plainly
show his clever handiwork; yet even in the drawing-room the mantel clock is his work, the dial face
marked with his own and his wife's name in place
of the usual numerals. Yet the result is extremely
good, the general effect one of refinement; the
drawing-room has none of the faded glare of the
Wine-Cellar, and there's not a muslin flower in
the house. The drawing-room piano is no better
than the Wine-Cellar's, but looks very much better;
there are solid iron fenders in dining-room and
drawing-room, fire-irons, a goatskin rug, and a
pretty and fresh carpet with lace curtains. We are
living on a much grander scale than in dear Jersey,
but — "

"Yes," said he, with the ready comprehension
of subtle differences that is not usually the masculine habit. "Yes — But — " Then he added
consolingly, "Fortunately there are no entrance
hall and no statues to live up to. You can live up
to flat-iron-holders, I suppose."

Whereby the masculine intelligence once more

proved its total inefficiency to grasp the logic of experience and of facts. From what premise reasoned he that the partner of his hirings would not immediately transform every holder into a pen-wiper? From what fact of their mutual experience did he conclude that she would not iron her ribbons and press her manuscripts, as she always had done, with the flat-iron grasped in a wad of paper? What made him suppose she would waste precious time in remembering that somewhere behind the kitchen stove was a corpulent holder, when she had a kitchen towel, if not in her hand, at least closely near it? What gave him the right to suppose she could live up to the intricate and perplexing conveniences of good housekeeping, when he knew that housekeeping was to her only a means of enjoyment of this glorious world in which we are for such a too-little season, not an end in itself, as the iron-holder woman so often makes it?

"Nay, my beloved," she remarked impressively. "Never so long as a daisy blooms on the ground can I rise to the altitude of kitchen-holders."

Indeed she fell so far below the iron-holder level that summer that when in crisp October they left Clover Villa, and took untold richness of pleasant memories with them to London, iron-holders were the only things the lady was obliged to replace. What Mrs. Boxworthy remarked to the inky ones left behind, she could only imagine.

Not that there were no disruptive disasters among those fair-faced furnishings. Apparently the table-ware had fallen from the higher estate of the "luxurious home." In falling into Clover Villa the vegetable dishes and covers had not always fallen together. During four or five months rattling and sliding dish-covers need not drive a housekeeper into the state of gibbering idiocy they would surely drive her to after a longer period. The more immediate Clover result in the paws of the Villa's "staff" was a somersaulting that left every dish coverless at the end of the first month. The bits were carefully preserved in proof of the misfititude which made their doom. That proof, the owners, to do them justice, did not demand, but preserved a discreet silence on the subject. Skill and finesse had worked miracles with those vegetable dishes themselves. Why queer-shaped little bits should separate themselves from the very substance of those dishes they could not at first even guess. They did not even guess that those bits ever had done so till their staff was heard loudly lamenting. Between tears and sobs, day after day, she showed little odd-shaped holes in various dishes, and in the hot water the bit that had matched and stopped each hole.

"Never mind," said the housekeeper, who was not model but only cheerful. "Never mind! The potatoes are bigger than the holes, and can't slip through. I can put a small white dish inside this blue and majestic one when we have peas."

The dining-room was not sunny, as the drawing-room was, all day. Yet here again had human thrift and ingenuity wrought a marvel. For some time Mrs. Clover did not solve the mystery of that streak of sunshine which every morning greeted her coming down to breakfast, a path of tender radiance inviting her feet to the kitchen-door, straightly across the north light of the only window. She did not ask why bright sunshine filled her spirit in an instant as her steps fell into that softly shining way, a way of chastened gold across the dull brown of the dining-room oilcloth.

"Sunshine," smiled her Superior. "Just your way of finding it anywhere. That sunshiny path to me seems only a strip of new carpet of the same pattern of all the rest, but of a yellower color. A bit of bright patchwork, you see."

It is a genuine English hamlet, untouched by change and remote from improvements, although not ancient as the word means in England. Its name dates from the Conquest and the marriage of one of the lords of Monceau, in Normandy, with the Saxon heiress of a family settled upon the place where are now only the picturesque ruins of a castle. The original hamlet gathered near this castle and about an ancient church (ruthlessly modernized) and a mighty tithe barn of the fourteenth century; the comparatively modern village consists of dwellings thrust among ancient farmhouses a mile from the church for which it is named. These farm-houses give its old-world charm to the village, a charm evidently not appreciated by the corrugated-iron-dissenting-chapel folk whose artistic taste is best served by illuminated scripture-texts. One may imagine the interior of that house opposite the village store upon which the illuminated-text taste has twisted and tortured a vine to spell "Praise the Lord," in green letters three feet long. Though Sussex itself is notoriously flat, the land is beautifully undulating, in this region rising sometimes to fairly respectable little eminences. From every one of these little eminences are exquisite views of many silent villages as white and vaporous as midsummer snow. From out these snowy drifts always rises a great Alpine flower, or rather a mystic blossom dropped through white clouds from singing processions of angels. Sometimes all day long for days these angelic flowers bloomed upon the golden distance, till one almost thought he saw the heavenly gardens in which they grew. Sometimes again the snowdrifts disappear in the vistaless dullness of the day, and the clearest eye could discover nothing more where the flower of Heaven had bloomed than a mere spectral stalk, leafless and wan, a very ghost of a flower fallen from the clouds so long ago that nothing of its origin remained. Then again, even in days less dull, the sight searched even for the stalk in vain ; the green slants, the vague distance, the pale horizon, would be as void of them as if they had never bloomed, or as if they had been caught up again to heaven. This mystery of bloom and fading, this continual enchantment of radiance and nothingness, haunted the Clovers. They could not forget, wherever they were, that the miracle was still at work. All summer long they sought the laughing little slopes and stood there seeking this strangeness of bloom and blight.

Thus were they the transcendent simpletons human beings must always be with more imagination than reason. Many and many a mile they walked and wheeled that summer merely to find exactly what they knew they should find, no heavenly flower at all, only an ugly, groaning windmill.

Sussex, being flat and without streams, grinds all

its corn with these mills. It is wonderful that they have not gone more into English poetry, for no shadowy ship upon the sea's horizon has more poetic effect than they; no angel of Paradise ever swept fairer wings through the gray of the dusky hours.

The Clovers reminded each other in wonder that only as noisy chatterers are these white visions usually mentioned. Even Stevenson, who carried the glamour of his artistic temperament almost everywhere, failed to recognize their haunting effect in a landscape. He saw them, but only as everybody sees them, near at hand, busy, garrulous mechanics at work, never spiritualized by the Elysian atmospheres of distance. "There are indeed," he wrote, "few merrier spectacles than that of many windmills bickering together in a fresh breeze over a woody country; their halting alacrity of movement, their pleasant business, making bread all day with uncouth gesticulations, their air gigantically human, as of a creature half alive, put a spirit into the tamest landscape. When a Scotch child sees them first, he falls immediately in love, and from that time forward windmills keep turning in his dreams." This is the canny Scot, to the life — " making bread all day," thriftily, even though with uncouth gesticulations to enliven a landscape.

Our American Indians showed more imagination in their terror of the "great white birds;" but even with the Indians it was less terror of their mystery of swirling wings and incomprehensible speech answering to the mystery of the many-voiced winds, than of their monster teeth biting the corn of the Dutch colonists of New

Netherlands. The red men never saw them as ghosts of white winds doomed to sad penance on earth in the service of these mites of men.

A Knight of the Rueful Countenance is our chief literary association with windmills. And that knight we cover with undying ridicule, and fix his name to every windy scheme and whimsical adventure, to valor without reason and honor without sense, because he saw giants where we see only — windmills.

Hotspur, with Shakespeare behind him in Henry IV., lacked the inspired vision of Don Quixote, and heard in their complaining only the airy gibber that most men hear. For he would rather eat garlic and cheese and live in a windmill, than with a complaining wife.

"You see," said a Clover, "windmills belong to low countries without water courses; and flatland people never have the imagination of hill-top folk. That's the reason they are so very little in English poetry and romantic prose. De Tabley's poem is almost the only one; do you remember it?"

Remember it, indeed! At least this much, —

"Emblem of Life, whose roots are torn asunder,
   An isolated soul that hates its kind,
Who loves the region of the rolling thunder
   And finds seclusion in the misty wind.

"Type of a love that wrecks itself to pieces
   Against the barriers of relentless Fate,
And tears its lovely pinions on the breezes
   Of just too early, or just too late.

"Emblem of man, who after all his moaning,
   And strain of dire immeasurable strife,
Has yet this consolation all atoning —
   Life, as a windmill, grinds the bread of Life."

Tradition and some histories tell that these wind spirits (let us avoid the word "mills") were brought home to Europe by Crusaders from the Holy Land. As the tradition has a suggestion of romance about it, a bit of poetry in its countenance, it of course has many contradicters. Some of these say, and their words are not foolish, they being learned archæologists, that mills were in Western Europe before the Crusaders, although not in France and England before the twelfth century. In 1216, Matthew Paris mentions the overthrow of many of them by a great storm; but before that mighty wrestle of the bond and the free they were in Normandy about 1180. At the battle of Lewes, May, 1264, during the flight of the troops of Henry III. before the victorious barons, Richard King of the Romans, the king's younger brother, took refuge in a windmill, barring the door, and for a long while defending himself from the fury of his pursuers. He was finally obliged to come out amid derisive cries. "Come out, you bad miller, you lazy mill master." A ballad of this event is among Percy's "Reliques." Chaucer mentions a windmill in the "House of Fame," and Dante in the "Inferno."

"Let them rave," said the least wise of the Clovers. "Let them archæologically rave of their windmills before the Crusades. I don't believe a word of it! For me the Cross-bearers saw them first, beckoning on the pale plains of Palestine. They saw them just as we see them, far away and ethereal, beings of an elemental world entirely unlike this to which they are bound. The returned Crusaders, with their travellers' yarns, never forgot their solemn beauty on mystic horizons;

and troubadours sang to harp and viol of their angelic floating in the hot winds of that fabulous clime. Then came some coarse Crusader, crusading, you may be sure, for booty, not duty, who told what practical works these mysterious visions could do : not till then did Englishmen capture for their own service these sad children of the white winds."

No railway whistle disturbed the peace of the village, no distant rumble of trains. The only excitements were the arrival at three o'clock of the postman on his tricycle, who served half a dozen hamlets, and the carrier-wagon bringing passengers and London papers from the same train.

The village post-office is an antique farm-house in a Shakespearian garden, the postmistress, a dusky widow with such a knack at harmless but piquant gossip as made her one of Mrs. Clover's most valued cronies. The village streets — there were two of them, both highways serving many scattered little hamlets — were as silent all through the long summer days as if all the world slept. At times the voices of children were heard at play, the lowing of distant cattle, the restless neighing of horses (who have no right to the privileges of "dumb" animals), and the sound of the village anvil answering the hammer.

Occasionally farm-wagons drove by, sometimes a light carriage, oftener the pedler's wagons, upon which remote villages so much depend ; but for much of the time the bees and the birds had all to themselves.

Several gentlemen's houses are within a mile or two, and the rectory is somewhat famous in religi-

ous biography, having been the home of Archdeacon Hare, known to pious American readers
chiefly for his relationship to the lady who caused
the book, "Memorials of a Quiet Life," and whose
home was here, but who seems to have left almost
no impression upon the memory of the village.
Otherwise than these more imposing homes, the
village is entirely rustic, its few villas quite of the
Clover order, its humbler but ten thousand times
more charming (to look at) dwellings of the rural
English village kind, with thatched or tiled roofs,
stone or half timbered walls, all half buried in living green. There was one gloomy general store,
from which came equally sugar, sewing silk, and
shoes, millinery, matches, and marmalade. Upon
the garden of this general store Clover Villa
depended, until Mrs. Clover learned the way to
other gardens. In the garden back of the black-
and-red-roofed post-office she found the earliest
apples, and straightway ate them up. The tree
in the cobbler's garden became flecked with gold,
and was rapidly consumed by the Villa, followed
in time by the tree a mile or two away, over-
topping a straw roof with eaves scarcely six feet
from the ground, under which lived, in antique
twilight, the wife of a gardener at the Great House
close by. Under these trees how many of the
gossiping chats in which Mrs. Clover delighted,
when gossipers unconsciously opened to her a
fascinating field of peculiar habits, and of characters shaped by an environment so different
from her own into an ever fresh romance. She
was supposed to be a Londoner ; that she might
be an American never entered heads to whom
America is as far as China ; and many a sly laugh

no doubt was laughed at the Londoners who do not know when the hop-season opens, and mistake oast houses for turrets of châteaux.

From the baker's garden came lettuce and peas, until the Clovers and the baker ate them all; whereupon Mrs. Clover began her intimacy with the primly-pretty and sweet-voiced wife of the village saddler, from whose garden came the vegetable-marrow which the purchaser once miscalled summer squash, to the intense amusement of the saddler's wife. There were no *h*'s astray in her dainty speech, and no suspicion of such wandering among the aspirates of the postmistress (who was not a Sussex but a Norfolk woman). But when the tidy young wife of the cobbler and her tidy children called at Clover Villa, or Mrs. Clover gossiped with her under the apple tree, or beside the poles of green beans, Sussex aspirates went fairly mad with delirious joy at finding so many soft places into which to nestle. The postmistress, Mrs. Clover soon learned, was step-mother to the saddler, and the feud was bitter between post-office and saddlery, between letters and leather. Each confided the story of wrong to the supposed Londoner, who received each as never suspected before, yet who thus was reminded anew that human nature is the same in a tranquil Sussex hamlet as in an American country village where wrongs that really are not wrongs at all are brooded over and kept warm for a lifetime, and families one in name and blood live side by side, never so much as seeing each other. The son of the village postmistress was half-brother to the saddler, and neither had wronged the other so far as the postmistress and

the saddler's wife told, yet they lived within
hourly sound of each other's voices, their trees
dropped fruit upon each other's ground, they
attended the same dissenting chapel, yet a wall
colder than stone, harder than adamant, forever
divides them. Sometimes the saddler's pretty
daughter brought plums and berries to the Villa,
as soft voiced as her mother, the same soft pink
complexion and the same bronze-gold ringlets
hanging quaintly beside her face, even as our
mothers wore ringlets, as they still wear them in
their youthful portraits. The saddler's wife has
been ringleted all her life, as doubtless her
mother was ringleted from her cradle to her
grave ; and the saddler's wife has never thought
to do else than twist her child's beautiful hair in
stiff curl-papers every night since her hair became
long enough to twist. The pretty child will grow
up with her ringlets, and will learn her trade of
the village dressmaker without changing them.
Then will come the village swain to swear his
adoration of ringlets ; when the bride sets up
housekeeping within her pretty mother's sight,
what is to prevent quaint, papered ringlets from
going on for generations ?

The saddler's wife is as cheerful as she is
pretty, as trim and neat as she is chatty. Her
daughter, her little toy and paper shop, and her
housekeeping, filled her heart and time to the
exclusion of yearnings, even such as haunted the
cobbler's wife. She did not torment the future
with questions ; but she liked to remember the
past, and her American gossip rejoiced to hear
her.

" Was it a love-match ? " " No, I should not call

it one from what I read in books of love-matches,"
she said. " Girls in the country do not make
such marriages, it seems to me. People cannot
love till they know each other; and how can they
know each other till they are married? I suppose
I married my husband because he has no palate."

Mrs. Clover had recognized this lack in the
saddler's speech. Yet she showed her surprise
that the lack should have won so desirable a wife.

" I came to school near here in that ivy-covered
house on Windmill Green. My husband was also
a pupil there ; but I never should have known it
had I not heard the other pupils mocking his im-
pediment. I took occasion to scold them, and to
make friends with him, but never to any great
extent. Then I went home and never thought of
him for years. I was twenty-five years old, and
working at my trade, when one day I chanced to
be driving with some friends, and we stopped at
an inn. Who should come up but my husband !
I should never have recognized him; he knew me
the instant he sat eyes upon me [those ringlets].
We talked of schooldays ; he came to see me; in
a year we were married, and there — my cabbage
greens are boiling all over the stove — don't go,
I'll be back in a minute ! "

The saddler's wife must be superior to her
position ; she was certainly superior to most of her
kind in New England rustic villages. Not only
was her language and pronunciation more correct,
but her acquaintance more active with the traditions and stories of the neighborhood. She could
always recognize, from Mrs. Clover's description,
any far away mansion, farm, or cottage come upon
in the long expeditions of the two Clovers, and

was ready with some bit of history or legend that made the object doubly interesting.

"That fine old mansion," she said of a certain delightful Jacobean picture, "is at a place called Carter's Corners.· If you go to the churchyard of Hurstmonceaux church and stand in a certain place among graves marked 'Potts,' you can just see it, miles away in the distance. It once belonged to the Potts family; when the head of the family died, he desired to be buried in a part of the church-yard from which the mansion could be seen."

The Americans had often stood on the very spot. Mrs. Clover wished she could ask Mrs. Saddler of certain of her own acquaintances, formed among Sussex Archæological Journals, to whom she gave many thoughts whenever she stood in that hill churchyard with its famous view, and, alas, its modernized aspect. She wished she could ask about Elyn Franklyn and William Longley, Thomas Bulke and John Honwyn, — all of whom were now the mould of Hurstmonceaux churchyard. But she knew how the pretty woman's eyes would stare at the very thought of knowing those Tudor English-men, whose wills only have kept their names on earth. William Longley, on the 28th of March, 1543, a husbandman of Hyrstmownsex, be-queathed his sowle into the hands of Almighty God the Father, to our Lady St. Mary, and to all the glorious company of hevyn, and his body to be buried within the churchyard of Hyrstmownsex. "Item, I will to be done for my sowle and all christian sowles thirteen masses, one barill of beere & a bushell of whete to be bake in brede & one fat shepe to be bake in pyes to refreshe the povyrte of the parishe." John Honwyn was also buried in "churcherthe," and willed that every priest at his burial, "to have for dirge and mass 8*d*." John willed 4*d*. to each of his god-children, "Best redde petycote, whyte fustyan doublett, blew cote with buttons, to James Swift, also old redde petycote & pair of whyte hose." In 1540, Richard Franklyn willed to Elyn, his daughter, "2 kyne, 2 tolmontyngis, 1 pot, 1 panne, 1 quern, 1 folcing table, 1 chere, 1 akere of whete, 1 of otis, 1 fedar bede, 1 bolster, 1 paire shetes, 1 blanket, 1 catel, 1 hog of 1 halfe-yere olde, all weanis, plewis, tyllis & yokis" (wagons, ploughs, harrows and yokes).

They are all of churchyard mould now, Elyn with the rest, dug over and over again with the spades, and for the dead of three centuries and a half. So, however Mrs. Clover longed to know how Elyn managed with but one pair of sheets and one blanket, one pot, one pan, and one chair, with evidently all her husbandman father's farm to carry on, it was of no use to ask, not even to ask what clod beneath one's feet was once these warm beating hearts.

"But you ought to know what a tolmontyngis was," Mrs. Clover complained to Mrs. Saddler.

Mrs. Saddler shook her head.

She might have retorted, "Why I more than you, since Tudor Englishman were as much your ancestors as mine."

Another time they spoke of Hurstmonceaux Castle, which, to Mrs. Clover's disappointment, had never been defended against assault by a woman, but only weakly haunted by one.

"She must be a great fool of a ghost," said the saddler's wife. "She tried to be very poetic and tragic, so gave out that she was starved to death by a cruel governess. The truth was she starved herself, trying to get a slim waist. Ghosts are usually humbugs, don't you think so?"

Mrs. Clover did think so, although she would give the world to see one that was not, and sought flesh-creepiness as she ought to seek wisdom. She asked them if the castle had ever known another ghost, a woman dressed always in white, and riding a milk-white palfrey with a milk-white doe running forever by her side. Mrs. Saddler had never heard of any such ghost, speaking only Greek to its English children, and living in semi-squalid grandeur in the castle, when not displaying its picturesqueness abroad. Evidently this lady, a very much affected one, and preposterously silly, haunts elsewhere. She was a wife of one of the Hares who owned the castle for a generation or two, and whose descendant was Archdeacon Hare. One day, in the course of a milky-palfrey and milky-doe display, dogs set upon the latter and killed it, upon which the Hare ran away from the hounds and refused ever to inhabit the castle again. In " Memorials of a Quiet Life," by that indefatigable book-manufacturer, Augustus J. C. Hare, the story of this airy *poseuse*, whose maiden name ought to have been March, is told with all the solemnity proper in writing of an ancestral Hare. He does not mention that the fantastic creature's widower speedily remarried, taking a bride who never rode a white palfrey through English lanes with a white doe running beside her white self, and who never conversed in Greek with her English children. This second marriage produced children as well as the first, and they put up a tablet to their mother's memory beside their father's in Hurstmonceaux church. Mr. Augustus Julius Cuthbert Hare gives a most elaborate and detailed description of the mural decorations and inscriptions of this church in his " Sussex," but leaving out entirely mention of the tablet to this second wife.

Mrs. Clover regretted that the palfrey lady did not haunt the lanes about the castle. It would have been worth a double admission fee to see her.

Of all the American's acquaintances, the cobbler's fair wife was the only one who mourned an ever-escaping ideal. The postmistress was content with her work, and above all with her son, whose dazzling proficiency in foreign languages had arrived at writing without fault, *Le marchand a les souliers du tailleur ;* the gardener's wife asked only of fate that it send less rain to mould her tomatoes. When the cobbler's wife lamented, " Ah ! " thought Mrs. Clover, " if but we Americans could mourn in such a ring-dove voice even grief would be a blessing to us as a nation."

The cobbler's wife was twenty-four with five children and a pensive face. She never left home without the five ; the children never left their house except as pinks of neatness. They were pinks from under a shower, and everything they wore was damp, wrung from the basin five minutes before they were dressed.

" Hit 's a great care," murmured the gentle voice, — " a great care to have so many. You never know wat may 'appen the minute your heyes are hoff. 'T is n't as hif we was wat I hexpected wen I married. I 'ad hideas then, as girls mostly 'as ; I thought hi married a shoemaker, but, to tell the truth," — her blue eyes here grew moist, — " to tell the truth he don't make a pair of shoes a year. Nobody can make 'em better ; he longs and prays to make 'em ; we dream at night that he 's made a pair for the rector's daughter or Lady Chatterton, and that everybody admires 'em. I tell 'im in the morning how beautiful they looked, how proud their arch from the 'eel was ; and he tells me how loving he drew every thread. Then he says, ' 'T was but a fleeting dream, Hethel, but sometimes dreams come true ; hile finish every bit of cobbling in the shop, then hawait my Shoes.' He goes to work very silent till the very last patch, then he puts 'em hall hout of sight in a row, and looks first at me then down the road. You could see he was hexpecting something. Sure enough, there was the rector's carriage driving hup ; I never saw Hedward look so strange. 'Hit 's a horder for shoes at last, Hethel !' he wispers. We both blush for joy wen Miss Hellis henters with no sign of a parcel. Then says she, ' There 's hate pairs of boots hand shoes to mend. Hi 've left hum in the carriage.' My 'art haked for poor Hedward."

Probably also his for you, poor wistful spirit, neither of you realizing that yours is but a common fate, to pursue an ever elusive Ideal, with only cobbling by the way.

" Very touching," said Mrs. Clover, " but I am obliged to say that the sewing she did for me was entirely on the cobbling plane, not the ideal."

The Idealist, the charwoman mother of S. S., and the washerwoman Elphick formed a circle of the village society. Although Mrs. Clover received and visited the first two, she never attempted to enter the circle, and thus never saw Mrs. Elphick, who washed for the Villa. It was enough to see her daughter, an insolent young hussy of fourteen, with character and manners evidently acquired in her father's stable, rather than at her mother's honest washtub. There was a prance in her gait; her neck was oftenest curveting; she seemed to repress a neigh when she brought or took away the clothes. No bend was in her back from washtub service; her dress was always as good as that of the saddler's petted daughter, who must have been a degree above her, amid the subtle distinctions of an English village. The Clovers looked with some interest upon this ill-bred young vixen, for she bore one of the most ancient and most dignified of Sussex names. Her far-away forbears were gentlemen living upon their own land, saying to this man, ' Come,' to that man, ' Go,' and obeyed with deference. They had the manners of the Sussex gentry, rough enough compared with those of modern gentry no doubt, but infinitely superior to those of their nineteenth-century descendant, who would jeer at their spelling and their pronunciation, and who has examples of far better behavior than her own every day before her eyes, if only in poor "S. S.," the Villa's staff of servants.

"Is it the high blood in her that makes her curvet and prance and neigh insolence with every breath?" the Clovers asked each other of this English girl. " Is it a restless, proud instinct of race, pricked and goaded by consciousness of the maternal washtub and the paternal carrier-wagon? Or is it the washtub and wagon instinct that knows no better? "

Only echo answered, " Knows no better."

"SILLY SUSSEX" was lank and long, like the days in which everything goes right and nothing goes wrong. She was shambling and loose-jointed, and although less than seventeen had no teeth to look at although many to speak of. It was rare to see her without at least one pasty cheek violently swollen, usually two, and at every blunder brought home to her those poor relics received the blame. Her eyes were pale and *à fleur-de-tête* (or "tater," a Clover remarked). The watery blue orbs never wavered in their dead solemnity of outlook beyond this fleeting world. They were the awful eyes of a soul "wropt in mistry," reflecting nothing finite, absorbing nothing earthly, like an inch-deep pool. She was of Sussex since Saxon days, and her speech bewrayed it. Her *ois* were all *eyes* and her *th* was often *d*, — dis, dat, for this and that. How many times her ploughman and milkmaid ancestors have inter-married none may know ; but from her wretched physique, her poor thin blood, and skeleton ever cracking at its joints, one may imagine those inter-marriages to have been many. The traditional Sussex Silliness in her was doubled, looped, knotted, twisted ; no two distinct lines of ancestry could ever have had such tangled wits as hers. In the olden days Sussex men were whipped as vagrants if found too far away from home, even though within Sussex borders. In 1615, Robert Kinge was thus whipped for being out of his native parish. A few years earlier, Robert would not have escaped so easily, but been hanged as a gypsy, choicest fruit of the gallows-tree at that time. The Clovers felt intense sympathy and fellowship with young Robert Kinge, never grown older to the world's knowledge than at the fifteen years of his immortal whipping. They would have called back to him through almost three centuries, had it been possible, that they too felt that same hunger for the horizon for which he was whipped; they too knew the enchantments of distance : yet they had never had half the whippings they deserved, while he had had at least one too many.

"Silly Sussex" was always " S. S." before her face, and never asked why she was not Martha as at home. As the Clovers so often spake an unintelligible lingo in her presence she probably supposed all Marthas were " *S. S.*" in the far land whence they came.

" S. S." came only for the morning's work. She early displayed such consummate genius in the way of mistakes that Madam Clover was obliged ·to keep an eye, even two eyes, upon her most of the time. Also to unlearn certain of her habits of speech. Several times it chanced that S. S. disappeared in the very midst of the morning's work, and came no more that day. There stood the little market basket, and its prepared list, just where it had been placed awaiting her errand to the garden from which Clover Villa was supplied. The dining-room was not dusted ; the parlor mats were loosely lying about the front door ; no water

was in the pails. The third time this happened,
one Clover complained to the other.

" You say you did not send her for anything ? "
asked that other.

" Of course not. The other two times I asked
her what she meant by quitting in the midst of the
work, and she replied by being even more ' wropt
in mistry ' than usual."

" What was she doing last ? "

A sudden light dawned upon a Clover, " She
was helping me turn the mattresses. When they
were turned I said, ' Now you may go,' I did not
add, ' to your work.' "

" She evidently stood not upon the order of her
going, but went at once."

" Has the rector's daughter lost her eyesight ? "
her mistress one day asked S. S. Silly Sussex
looked mysteriously away from finite things and
with sibylline vagueness answered : —

" She has lost her husband."

" Subtle Sussex," called a voice from outside the
door, " don't you see, she means she lost in him
the light of her eyes."

S. S. was extremely slow of motion.

" Come, fly round," said her mistress. S. S.
stared beyond time into the depths of eternity as
she answered, unhasting like the eternal stars :

" Dunno how."

" *You* need n't laugh," said he, when the Missis
repeated this to him. " When Billings, the baker,
told you he was late because he had ' overlaid,'
and that now he must ' move,' you gravely asked,
' Move where ? ' as if all his goods and chattels
were in the little hand-cart in which he brings
round the bread. He then seemed as bewildered

as you were, although you both claim to speak English. Had you told S. S. 'Come move,' she would still have stared poor Eternity out of countenance, but she would have understood you."

S. S. told that her father's grave was at N., an adjoining parish, whither the vagrant Clovers often walked with never a fear of the whipping-post, before which they always stopped to gaze and grimly meditate, on the way. It was easy to fancy ghosts there in the dim of the evening, when the ghostly wind, a thousand centuries old, and with a thousand centuries of bitter memories, sighed through the rough field. Easy to recognize the wretched spectres of Anne, "whipped for a waygoer," of Alice, "whipped for a runegate," and Jane, "whipped for a rogue," of the Johns, Williams, Roberts, whipped for many things besides a wicked curiosity to know how men lived and trees grew in the "furrin parts" of an adjoining parish.

"We must look for your father's grave, sometime," said the Clovers. "Has he a gravestone?"

"He had a wooden leg," replied the "Mistry-Wropt."

One afternoon the Missis came in to tea with three invited guests. She brought with her a paper-bag of sweet cakes from the oven-like shop of baker Billings (from whose ancient Sussex family Billingsgate was named) and three tiny packets of tea, the small currency with which she was wont to roam Sussex by-ways alone when her companion was too deep in his books to lead her in wider and more decorous ways. This small currency brought her many a curious history, that would have stopped often at stocks and whipping-post in other days. They brought her so many a moment's nearness to the life that held so much of poetry for her, that more than once she came home to beg her tyrant to let her go, away, away from roofs and walls, that she might become an "Egyptian," and know starlight better than lamp-light, and stand in the stocks, and be whipped at the whipping-post, with never a bit of starch in her petticoats again so long as she lived, or a ribbon to her name.

"Silly Sussex" chanced to be in the house doing some extra cleaning. She was enough as-tonished to drop her "house flannel" as the Missis escorted her guests to the kitchen, and gave them cool water in which to lave, and invited them to shake themselves free of dust in the garden-path. Two of them were time and travel, but not beer, stained ; yet Silly Sussex almost blubbered that she served a "Wild Woman" who could bring home tramp parents and their child to tea.

"'Op-pickers !" she ejaculated, with energy that quite amazed her mistress.

Hop-pickers of course, the whole countryside had swarmed with them for weeks. Every day two, four, six of them knocked at the front-door begging hot water for their afternoon tea. Every day the Americans saw groups of them by the roadside, sleeping off the fatigue of a long tramp, sometimes the wife making iron-holders or knitting dish-cloths, while the husband slept. They were a decent sort, a sort that chose a tramp of many days into fair Sussex, rather than the horrible companionship and orgies of East Londoners crowding into nearer Kent. These were usually decently dressed; they carried their *batterie de cuisine* on their backs; they answered respectfully when addressed. The only ones among them who ever begged were stout single men, who made but a bare pretence of willingness to "cleave some wood" in return for a bit of luncheon.

Therefore her mistress's idea of "'op-pickers" was not that of Silly Sussex, a hop-picker herself in the season, but always in one garden, never tramping miles for a job. There are social grades even among "'op-pickers."

When the somewhat abashed company was ready, the hostess called to S. S. to make the tea. The lank, blank maid received the order in silence, as was her habit. Then neither tea-pot or S. S. came, until the Missis, having made her choice of iron-holders and dish-cloths, grew impatient and called again, "Martha, have n't you made the tea?"

The Mistry Wropt appeared in the doorway with pale eyes to say, —

"Dunno how to make tea. My mother always buys hers."

"For mercy's sake, what *do* you do when you put tea in a tea-pot and pour boiling water over it?"

The Mistry Wropt withdrew her gaze from Eternity, to rest her eyes upon perhaps the thirtieth century, as she answered almost cheerfully: —

"*Wet* the tea."

"Do you suppose," said he, "that she would stoop to any unasked explanation before common 'op-pickers?"

Poor Silly Sussex, she had left a situation as farm drudge, with wages of eighteen pence a week, to serve in Clover Villa (at four shillings) — what wonder she found things queer, and the queerest of all a mistress who tea'd with tramps and expected *her* to make tea.

"Idiot!" spurted a Clover.

"Do you suppose she considers you anything better," said he, "when she remembers the stove?"

"Don't tell *me*," said the other with warmth. "Don't tell *me* that she remembers anything! How should I know the difference between two sorts of blacking! She had n't gumption enough to laugh when I undertook to teach her to black the cooking-stove."

"With boot-blacking!" added the other. "But never mind, she did n't have a fit even though she gasped when you told her always to wash the dish-cloths after washing the dishes. She knows you are a maniac; you know she is Silly Sussex: so it 's heads I win, tails you lose, with both of you."

One day starting upon an absence of many hours in pursuit of Windmills, her Mistress enjoined upon S. S. to leave the usual covered pitcher outside the kitchen door for the evening's milk, and to be sure not to close the dining-room window at the top, for, over it, the baker always dropped the evening's breakfast-rolls.

S. S. made every promise, with blank eyes lying loosely upon a certain lace fichu that she was suspected of dimly admiring, and that her mistress refrained from giving her, only because it was so absurdly unsuitable to her person and condition. (When the summer ended and the Villa closed, the rags of the fichu were cast into the ash-bin. The next Sunday S. S. wore them to church.)

After dinner that night in an inn eight miles

away, the Clovers came home. All the brick pavement of the little garden was streaked, spotted, splashed, puddled with milk. Mr. Clover straightway named it, "The Milky Way."

Mrs. Clover ran to the kitchen door. The pitcher lay upon its broken side with every appearance of having burst from a surfeit of bread and milk.

Then the lady lamented both loud and deep that S. S. had tightly closed the dining-room window, as it had not been closed for weeks, the baker had stuffed the rolls into the pitcher, the milkmaid had turned the milk in upon the rolls.

"Unmitigated Fools!" she remarked so many times, so emphatically, and in such various ways, that the other grew somewhat tired of hearing it.

"It's 'Silly Sussex,' of course, all round," he explained; "Borde's 'foles of Gottam,' were only two miles from that bread and milk, upon which the dogs have regaled themselves. Probably our maid's grandparents were 'foles of Gottam.' At any rate, we are no worse served than was poor Counsellor Burrell."

They had just been reading Counsellor Burrell's diary, and found it one of the most entertaining and picturesque of all the seventeenth and eighteenth century diaries unearthed by the Sussex Archæological Society. Counsellor Burrell illustrated his diary in a sort of missal fashion, with pen and ink upon the margins. Pipes, tankards, snuff-boxes, runaway-servants, kitchen and garden implements, old crones, night-caps, make those margins almost a history of themselves.

"Never such creatures in the world before! Oh, for the decent, docile, well-trained servants, of the good old times!"

It is the nineteenth century who thus moans over the utter decay of domestic service. It is a way the centuries have of grumbling that earlier ones have taken the cream of all things. But Madame Nineteenth Century has not the last word, or rather moan. Up pops the seventeenth century, in the guise of this Sussex gentleman, in knee-breeches, bagwig, and buckled shoes, to rap his snuff-box, and tell us that all was not color of the rose before he became a phantom. A grave, good man was Counsellor Burrell of Ockerden House, in far Sussex, a careful master and kind, sometimes even recording regret that, having taken the sacrament and resolved to live a better course of life, he had yet been " too irritable with my servants." He gave much in charity; he exercised a paternal care over his many men-servants and maid-servants ; he lived in the good old times, and kept note-books (with illustrations by his own pen) for us to read. Yet October 17, 1692, this good master is obliged to write :

" I pay'd Hollybone for setting the old pales by the orchard, 10*d.* per rod, which was a little too much, for he worked three days, but gently, 4*s.*"

Naughty Hollybone, to work but gently for your 4*s.* although two centuries nearer the age of innocence than we are !

The next March, the Counsellor continues : " Pay'd Frances - Smith her wages and discharged her, she being a notorious thief." Fie, Frances Smith, whose master paid you 50*s.* a year, and an extra 18*d.* at Christmas, if but you were honest ! Alas ! Frances was not the only Sussex servant whose fingers were light when William and Mary reigned over England in " good old times."

April 26, 1698, " Thomas Goldsmith came as footman, at 30s. a year and a livery coat and waistcoat once in two years, when he was to have a new one ; but being detected in theft, I turned him away. After a ramble in London, being almost starved, he came again as footman at £4, one livery coat and breeches, in two years ; if he went away at the end of the first year, he was to leave his livery coat behind him."

Goldsmith the footman was evidently quite worthy to have been born two centuries later, and to enter the service of our dames who grumble so lustily over the decay of servants. For on the 14th of September, he again departed, and again, " on the 24th of October, he repented and returned half-starved." This time, the uncertain footman is supposed to have returned with a wife, having rambled away a bachelor, for two pipes, instead of one, now adorn the margin. The good Counsellor " gave him hopes, if he proved a good husband, to consider him further ; but he several times rambled about all night, was frequently drunk with brandy, and spent all the money I got for him in half a year's time, besides his wages."

What became of Thomas the Rambler, we do not know ; henceforth he drops out of the story. But his good master must have suffered long with him, for did he not discharge him at 30s. and, after a drunken " ramble," hire him again for £4, as if in desperation at finding no better man?

Grave Counsellor Burrell in his stately home had no better luck with his coachman. Thomas Goldsmith the footman was always symbolized upon the margin of notes concerning him by a smoking pipe. " John Coachman " is always symbolized by a tankard. The Counsellor, in October, 1698, six months after a Goldsmith "ramble," and repentance, writes of John-with-a-tankard, "Pay'd in full of his half-year's wages, to be spent in ale, £2–6–6." At the same time, he "pay'd 6*s*. for John's breeches," in full assurance that the 6*s*. would also be spent in ale. The next time the tankard appears, John has "kept for ale" the half-crown his master gave him to pay for a "goos."

For some time, the tankard does not again appear; but, alas! John breaks out again. In July, 1705, the good old English gentleman whose "times" were so much better than ours, "Pay'd Gosmark for making cyder 1*d*. day whilst John by agreement was to be drunk on the carrier's money: and I pay'd the glasyer for mending John's casement, broken at night by him when he was drunk and could not waken the footman to let him in." This footman was no other than Goldsmith the Rambler. With the two the Counsellor was so much better off than masters are nowadays! Goldsmith was evidently a superior man, for he got drunk on brandy; poor vulgar John, upon ale or cider.

On the 17th of March, 1706, the master of Ockenden Hall writes: "Pd John Coachman, that he may be drunk all Easter week." Five months later, he pays 14*s*., for a "periwigg for John: and I gave him notice that I would no longer allow him for livery, since 't was to be all spent in drunkenness." Was it not more than Madame Nineteenth Century would do to allow John Coachman in December, something "to buy heartsease during the Christmas holidays"? Heartsease, too, that imperilled both casements and heads! Scant wonder that when in March John fell drunk from his box, his master made him pay for his mending out of his own wages.

But were the Counsellor's troubles confined to his coachman and footman? He had as many servants as the centurion of old, and this one came and this one went, as those other men ; but, alas ! not always at their master's will. Indeed, the continual change of names and faces at Ockenden House in those good old days was quite equal to such changes in these fallen times.

March 25, 1698, there was trouble with Bec Jup. Did the master order her forth, or did she flaunt and fling at him, " Please, sir, suit yourself with another "? The note-books do not tell us, they only say, March 24, 1698, " I pay'd Rebecca Jup her wages, £2-9-0. A bad servant." Then he adds in relenting, "To Bec at parting, 1s." How plainly these simple notes, made only for his own eye, and expected to perish before his death, reveal the kind heart under the grave face and manner ! When, in January, 1699, he dis-charged a nurse, he does not put in words her delinquency, but indicated it in his usual manner by a drinking vessel upon the margin. Perhaps it was only a suspicion, and repented of, for the cup is covered with lines, as if in second-thought attempts to cross it out.

Did Sarah Creasy take Bec Jup's place in Ockenden House? If so, the Counsellor gained naught by the change, for the next April he wrote : —

" I this day discharged Sarah Creasy from my service, having been faulty in taking vessels of strong beer out of the brewing and hiding the same."

Who was to blame, and who profited, that the "blew" for the "bucking" cost 1*s*. where formerly the master paid three-ha'pence for it? The "bucking" was the family washing, and derived from the Saxon *buc*, our bucket. It occurred only two or three times a year, and the Counsellor found himself better served to buy his soap and "blew" as wanted, and not at wholesale, as he preferred. Careful master and housekeeper that he was, Counsellor Burrell was evidently as powerless to stop leaks as if he had not lived in the "good old times." Can we not almost hear his sigh adown the long vista of years as he writes: "7th April bought a chees weighing 18 lbs. for 2¾ the lb. It was all eaten in the kitchen by the 18th."

In those good old days one's troubles sometimes extended to other people's servants; and the Counsellor hid in Latin the note, " Mr. Robrough's maid-servant came and took a cauliflower out of my garden without asking leave or saying anything about the matter."

Thus free in another garden, how much more so this maid-servant amid her own master's possessions?

After all, were those days so much better than our own? Or Bec Jup than Silly Sussex?

Only once was S. S. known to belie her title. That once she vaunted herself, when she came to the Villa one Monday morning.

"Sister 'n' me went to Ninfield yisterdy. It just poured-out and we had to move."

Which in the language of her mistress would be:

"The rain poured down, and we had to run."

AN ACQUAINTANCE OF MRS. CLOVER.

IT is what Carlyle called a " leafy Sussex lane."
It was a favorite lane with young Arthur Stanley
when yonder rectory was his temporary home,
and fame far before him. But a short bird's
flight away is the cottage in which John Sterling
lodged during the very brief time that he served
the Church ; through these hedgerows Frederick
Denison Maurice often passed, seeing only the
world within him.

It is a lane of English poetry and idyls ; withdrawn from a quiet highway, and winding through
cornfields, past a stately mansion with Jacobean
windows blocked up and Victorian children about
the door, till it dwindles to a mere track across the
ancient deer park to the ruined castle.

Because of its seclusion, it was chosen by one
easily mistaken for a lady gathering flowers, perhaps even for the châtelaine of yonder towers
gathering simples for the still-room, — one with a
dignified attitude, figure even stately, the dress
(twenty yards away) entirely ladylike.

But why that blue vapor rising timidly but an
inch or two above the grass ? Has a lady of the
olden times here set up her delicate laboratory
to distil sweet fragrances and perfumed oils and

essences, within touch of the vast and silent one of nature herself?

"I am not a good fire-maker," said a gentle voice, a voice that might have given command to many men and maidens.

The speaker wore a hat becoming her age and face. A queen of fashion could not have better chosen. It was a close, lace-trimmed, black hat, precisely such as dowager duchesses wear in their gardens, under its drooping brim, snowy hair, a refined but weather-beaten face, sound but neglected teeth. A faded cloak once elegant, the remnants of a cotton frock, and ragged boot-soles under more ragged white-cotton stockings had no suggestion whatever of the neatness which makes poverty respectable. Instead of neatness and respectability was an air those decencies rarely have, — *le grand air*.

In the midst of the timid smoke was a biscuit-tin, set among smouldering twigs gathered by the wayside. "Would you kindly smell of it, madam," she mildly said, "and tell me how it seems to one who fares daintily? I have scraped away all the maggots." Had she said "lady," the shibboleth of menials, Mrs. Clover would never have seen the inside of that biscuit-tin with contents gently seething, ornamented with a bit of parsley, and sending up no odor so far as she could tell.

"Thank you," re-covering the tin. "Now it will taste better. A butcher's kind wife gave it to me."

Her glances about her were as timid as her timid fire. "I asked a lady outside the lane if any trouble could come upon me here, and she thought not. I should like a cup of tea," she said "cup," but meant her rusty cocoa-tin, "better than this flesh food, and people will rarely refuse us hot water, though they refuse us everything else."

That "us" was the first actual clue to her condition.

"I did not sleep well last night. A cup of tea cheers without inebriating, after such a night;" adding naïvely, "Do you not find it so?"

Only in answer to questioning, felt under the circumstances to be grossly vulgar and impertinent, she told that, although last night's lodgings had been satisfactory, the sound of whistling outside had several times disturbed her slumbers.

"Who whistle are honest," said the visitor.

"Of just such we are, unfortunately, afraid," she answered simply. "The single woman seemed delicate, so I gave her my corner, away from the door; the married couple took the fagot-heap; so I had Hobson's choice inside the empty coal-bin, although I did not know it till I found bits in my mouth; but, as Shakespeare says, 'where ignorance is bliss 't is folly to be wise.'"

"Where are your fellow-lodgers? Why did you not keep with them?"

"Why should I? I knew not who and what they were. Doubtless they were decent enough; but one must be very careful in making acquaintance when one takes to the road. The single woman was rather clever; she told me not to be afraid of dirty water, for all comes clean when it is boiled. But she had biscuits and sugar, and the married couple had tea. I had nothing; so I left them all together."

The tanned and dirty hands were soft and still shapely. " Picking oakum is their severest labor," she said. " I avoid the Shelters as much as possible on that account ; also because in the most of them the officers speak as if you were dirt under their feet. The last one I entered, at Hastings, is a very ill-bred affair ; so is that at Hailsham. I have turned sixty, but I can still walk all night rather than bear with rudeness. I am getting on to the Hailsham Shelter now, but if the sky clears I shall make an effort to pass it ; they keep you in until eleven, the best time of the day. Hopping begins next week ; I shall probably have a pound at the end of it, enough to pay my winter's rent. I cannot earn now the wages of twenty-five. At twenty-five, I paid wages ; at fifty, I was servant in a clergyman's family, but I could not get on with his wife ; her accent was atrociously vulgar ; in Warwick we use good English ; so I took out a five-shilling license to sell the bit of lace I crochet ; and now I have neither license nor lace.

" Husband? He died of riotous living. Children? Both dead, and I have no abiding city, no home made with hands."

Was she going to cant? Did she take the Clover for a Bible reader, as van-people usually do?

"Sad, isn't it?" she laughed gleefully, seeing the Clover's perplexed face.

"You don't look your age, dear," when told it. "But it's sheets." Here she drew herself up as do tragedy queens. She flourished a rusty case-knife and a battered cocoa-tin, not violently, but in the grand manner. "Sheets," she crooned, — "sheets, white, clean sheets: under them a bed, over them soft, white blankets! In them one may turn as far as one's arms can reach. Oh, the blessedness of sheets, sweet-smelling sheets, sheets! Can such things be without our special wonder? the Bible says."

The Lady Tramp then deliberately turned her back on the Clover. She had asked for nothing, and the other felt dismissed with a whole Longer Catechism yet unanswered.

When Mrs. Clover returned, half an hour later, madam had tied her biscuit-tin and contents in a grimy cloth to sling upon her arm. She accepted a small parcel with a stately bow. "You are not a Christian," she daringly said; "Christians don't give away parcels of tea. You are better, — you are a lady!"

As she placed the parcel in her ragged satchel she saw an inquisitive gaze rest upon a few yellow rags neatly folded.

"My clean handkerchiefs," she explained.

PHŒBUS.

His Golden Chariot daily wheels with the sun. Often it wheels without that luminary, for those lanes and highways are frequently arched with clouds. That he dismounts from that Chariot at every bit of rising ground, and slowly pushes it before him, made them call him nothing else than Phœbus. He is bowed and bent, few and sad his teeth, his mastiff under jaw fiercely projects ; from Monday to Sunday his gaunt cheek is unshorn ; he is weather-beaten, wayworn, unlovely. Rarely he wears a coat ; and all the long wet English summer he brought the Clovers tidings from the uttermost parts of the earth in gray shirt-sleeves and dingy postman's cap. Many a time and oft he pushed the Golden Chariot before him even on level ground, while Mrs. Clover walked beside him and they communed of things seen and unseen, of earth's wonders and heaven's mysteries. Never in his long life has Phœbus crossed the borders of his native county. Naturally he is sure that no other space of earth equals it. He is very proud of those green wealds, of the almost riverless and quite hill-less but undulating part of Sussex in which they walked, and his heart was won by admiration of it.

"Come into the rector's grounds with me," he said ; "there's a fine prospect Eastbourne way,"

he said " Heastburn ; " "it reminds me of some of
the poetry I have read." There were other
" prospects," wider and more varied than " Heast-
burn-way," even with its tithe barn of thatch, three
centuries old, its more ancient church, and picturesque farm and manor houses against a background of silver sea ; but it did not take long to
discover that it was a cherished " prospect " with
Phœbus, who never mentioned "views." Why
it was favorite he never said.   One may thus imagine that the distant glimpse of sea was just that
suggestion of boundlessness, that mystery of the
infinite, which appeals most powerfully to the devoutly romantic imagination.   Back of every mystery to such lies heaven.   Phœbus daily wheels
his chariot seventeen miles between the rising and
the setting sun.   At three villages, several detached hamlets, many farm-houses and manors, he
delivers letters.   His own home, a lowly cottage
adorned with a red letter-box and sign of " Post-
Office," is in a tiny hamlet eight miles from the
usual meeting-place of Mrs. Clover and Phœbus.
It is a high-perched hamlet of thatched or lichen-
grown roofs and a windmill.   All those summer
days when the clouds hung not too low, the
Clovers saw that windmill from all their walks.   It
looked a phantom, a white, mysterious vision,
with filmy arms outstretched in wide benediction.
It is but a rude windmill such as thousands of
others in waterless Sussex, grinding the village
grain with harsh complaining, as wheat has been
ground here nearly a thousand years.   But between it and them an Enchantress spread her
magic veil to make its white silence seem unearthly ; and it is no wonder that Phœbus wheeled

towards it at every sunset with more solemnity than he wheeled away at dawn. Seven of these solemn windmills were visible from their village. All that summer they mystically allured the Americans; by the end of the summer the insensate and insatiate foolishness of longing had robbed the region of every mystery — save Phœbus.

He told of his little garden, his cow, his chariots to tinker (he had a mania for buying wrecks, and putting them together, till it was reported he had half a score of whole ones), and the feet of his hamlet to cobble. Where, with all this, could more than the labor of living find place?

Phœbus one day suddenly asked, "Do you ever read?" and Mrs. Clover's breath was almost taken away. When she asked in return, "Do you?" his satisfaction was manifest.

"A bit of an hour of the evening, when I can steal one," he said. "When I can't read, I think." "Of what?" the lady longed to ask, but dared not.

"Sweet is solitude," murmured the fierce mastiff-jaw, but whether spontaneously or in quotation she does not know. Asked where he got books, he answered, "Wherever I can. There's a circulating library in H., but it runs too much to novels," here Phœbus looked as if his head might be of the roundest, and his name a whole Scripture-verse. "Novels are a sin; they nauseate the spirit; praise God, I have never read one in my life. I read discourses and poetry."

"Have you never read Pilgrim's Progress?"

"Once for every year of my life," he answered. Evidently he did not suspect that immortal romance of anything in common with novels.

"I read Young's 'Night Thoughts,'" he continued, with grotesque smile. "I recommend them to you. They throw a wholesome awe over the spirit." Phœbus took it for granted that "'olsum hawes" would be grateful to the lady's spirit, and she did not say to the contrary.

He continued, "Then I read a grand poet named Tupper. Did you ever hear of Tupper? He wrote 'Proverbial Philosophy,' full of noble, hinspiring thoughts. Such a man is God's 'ighest work. Shall I lend you my Tupper?"

Mrs. Clover gazed far away over all she could see of the great universe that had once held a Tupper. Why should she say, even under her breath, "Poor Phœbus! from whom is hidden that his Poet of Poets is a babbler of the commonplace, mouthing sonorous platitudes!" Should she not sooner say, " Happy Phœbus! for, from their worshippers, idols ever hide their feet of clay. Happy he to whom something, even a Tupper, floats above the gross atmosphere of earth!" Why indeed should mere knowledge, earthly and earthy knowledge, bruise this devout, this poetic spirit, with sneerings? Why tell him that only to the poor in spirit is treasure offered by Martin Farquhar? Behold, have not the Poor in Spirit a promise, from which possibly we·are shut out? What right have we, and such as we, to shoot out the lip at another to whom even " Proverbial Philosophy" brings hinspiration, haspiration, and 'igh hideas ?

Upon mountain peaks, in heaven-pointing cathedrals, we, and such as we, continually seek in vain that which comes continually to Phœbus in a narrow room of a lowly cot, from a Poet who is no poet. Who are we, therefore, to say that M. F. Tupper, Esq., has not done even Heaven's service in many a silent, hidden place, while we, in seats of the scornful, have done nothing at all?

"Sometimes I read Cowper," he continued (and did not say "Cooper"), "I have tried to read Carlyle's 'French Revolution,' but the language is too hobtuse. I always return with pleasure to the Poet Tupper and my Ten Virgins."

Ten Virgins! Alas for the wisdom of the wise! Mrs. Clover knew nothing whatever of that lovely band, save that by far the most famous and interesting of them all was "foolish." Phœbus knew all about them; their inmost thoughts, the object of their being, even, one must believe, their names. Every Day of Rest he lives in their fair company with shaven cheeks, clean raiment, and unpostman-capped head, meet for such companionship.

To think that to mere Clovers they can never be anything but a "discourse"! He promised to leave that favorite "discourse" for Mrs. Clover some day at the Post-Office, in the door of which now stood the postmistress in a blue check apron, scowling at their slowness.

He did not leave it, nor yet Tupper. Evidently his Sundays would be too disconsolate without them.

Phœbus knew the lady to be an American, but not her name. He even asked her if she should ever go to war again with "South America," and if in the Mayflower or Speedwell her "folks" went over. One day he tapped his pedals more vigorously than usual to overtake her.

"Something to show you," he said; "can you tell me what language this is?"

"It is Italian," she said, but did not add that the postcard was addressed to herself.

"Why *don't* those people learn our language?" he asked almost impatiently. "It is much more simple and natural than theirs; and we must all understand each other in heaven. But perhaps they are Cath'lics."

Evidently in that case they would never need to know our celestial tongue.

"I used to like my cobbler's trade," Phœbus often said; "as I worked I thought of the time when our feet will be holy and our countenances shine. I'm a Methodist." He meant no pun. He did not remember that such "holey" feet were the cause of his earthly trade. What being a Methodist had to do with the rest of his sentence, is not plain unless he meant to indicate in which denominational quarter of the New Jerusalem he should be found.

Still another day the basket velocipede overtook her. He fingered a parcel with disdain, not to say disgust. "I forgot to leave this as I came through the village," he said; "will you leave it at the Post-Office in passing?"

It was a novel from the circulating library at H. Mrs. Clover did not believe he forgot it.

WINDY HOW.

THEY met at Euston Station when June was young. The hour was that in which churchyards yawn and graves give up their dead. She was in proper travelling costume; he was not. There was even an air of disguise in the unseasonable overcoat hiding his classic lines.

" Have you the other clothes ? " he whispered.

"Hush ! here they are in these shawl-straps. Here are the luggage receipt and the tickets ; I did not wish you to be seen getting them."

" I hope we can have a carriage to ourselves," he said ; " I can change in a jiffy."

" No chance of it," replied the lady. " Everybody seems going north to-night."

Not everybody, but six somebodies who, after all, were probably nobodies except to themselves, were in their carriage. During three or four hours the eight sat bolt upright, lacking opportunity to do otherwise. Boltly upright they slept also, if one might judge from the gaspings and growlings of the darkness. Every time the train stopped, the Americans hoped somebody would get out ; that everybody should leave the carriage was too wild a hope to be encouraged. All that time the mysterious gentleman in the overcoat wrapped the drapery of his disguise about him and sat up to as pleasant dreams as were possible to a man fleeing from London in the costume a man might wear driven from his club for cheating at cards.

Then day broke upon the sleepy company. It broke also upon a significant expanse of white, upon which the lady fixed a warning eye. The overcoat was hastily drawn over it; if the others saw, they made no sign. Then, one by one, the six descended, until at Oxenholme, within a few miles of Windermere, where they also were to leave the train, they saw their last carriage-companion depart. The lady then discreetly gazed from the window upon the awakening beauties of the famous Lake Country, as the little local train into which they had changed ran up beside Lake Windermere. She did not need to ask the cause of the mysterious rustle and evident haste behind her, for she knew that the Man in the Overcoat was changing his clothes.

"There!" he said, as he came into view in proper travelling costume with full evening dress over his arm, "it takes an American, does n't it, for adapting himself to circumstances? I wonder if an Englishman would think he could see a Lyceum 'first-night' out, and trust to changing his clothes on a train."

From Windermere they drove four or five miles, up hill and down, on the Coniston Road, through hamlets and villages that seemed not to have stepped out from a picture because still in one. It was all poetic ground over which they drove; Wordsworth has made almost every rood of it, if not immortal, at least immortal for our generations. Here upon this shining road he met the old dismissed soldier going home. Here, he roamed and loitered when a boy at Hawkshead grammar school, the roamings and loiterings used to such profitable account in the wearisome " Prelude." Others, too, have used Wordsworth's playtime here to profit. The amount of Wordsworthiana spun out of Wordsworth trivialities must have made much money for the compilers, money that the parsimonious poet would doubtless much begrudge them, were begrudging possible where he has gone. This, however, has nothing to do with the pleasantness of the road to Hawkshead, whither the Americans were driving. Exactly here is " the brook murmuring in the vale," exactly here the " long ascent " written of in the " Prelude." Too many Wordsworthians have busied themselves about the spot for any traveller to mistake it. All the same, there are a thousand more ideally picturesque spots and aspects of the road between Windermere and Hawkshead, than those Wordsworth chose to mention ; and the Americans considered that however Wordsworth might make over nature into Wordsworthian poetry, he certainly did not choose his material from nature's richest store. This brook murmuring in the vale does not " murmur," at least not from June to October of a dry year ; one would not know a brook was there had Wordsworth's admirers not written about it.

" Wordsworth did not need to choose the best that Nature offered," said curling lips ; " he quite fancied he could gild her primroses by the river's brim, and make poetic the asses of tinkers."

Perhaps it is as well to explain that one of the pair had a supreme aversion to Wordsworth the man, seeing him as a type of a now almost extinct monster, the anaconda on the domestic hearth, to whose deglutition of his womenkind, and battening upon their comfort, the New Woman absolutely refuses to contribute.

Half a mile before this Coniston Road reached Hawkshead, they dismounted at the hired-furnished in which the next four months were to be passed. That H. F. was in a lane, a true English lane, tangled with ferns and vines. It was a gothic lane, vaulted with springing boughs, the grassy ground beneath an ever-shifting fretwork. From either end, looking into the lane, it seemed as if cut through a forest, even though three dwellings and a Quaker meeting-house met the eye with strange surprise. One of these dwellings was Windy How, another Windy How Cot. The former was an important affair, two stories high, well furnished, with flower-garden and orchard, and a lawny little hill of its own, all let for £2 10s. or £3 a week. During that summer it had a succession of tenants, families hiring it for a month or so at a time, according to length of vacations. They were oftener Quaker families than not, of the north of England. The little meeting-house was the centre of a community of Friends, who often communicated with distant acquaintances that Windy How was to let.

Beside Windy How, Windy How Cot seemed but a baby-house. It was originally a laborer's cot, built a hundred years and more ago, when laborers did not demand as much light and air as now. It was exquisitely picturesque, gleaming like a pearl through masses of vines and vivid splashes of floral color. It was built flat against the How, or hill, hence had but one door, a low and narrow one at that. The door opened directly into the chief, indeed the only, lower room, which was at different times kitchen, dining-room, or study. A commodious scullery, where the oil-stoves were kept, relieved this room of the roughest work, although the modern range, set deep into the antique fireplace, was almost its chief feature, except when a handsome screen of golden storks and foliage upon a black ground was drawn before that range. Above, under a slanting, but not too low roof were two comfortable chambers with windows of pocket-handkerchief size, set with infinitesimal panes. The two houses were let by an ex-school teacher who had invested her money in them, and had furnished them in most excellent taste, as well as with every necessary convenience. The Cot she had furnished with an eye to women-artists, who every summer haunt this fair region. A party of four at least could comfortably share its accommodations, that is, in a dry season, when the day is chiefly spent out of doors ; and for such parties, fresh from London studios and art galleries, she had bought pretty china, a handsome art-square for the sitting-room, and had set blooming flower-boxes outside the windows. To be sure Windy How Cot was as dark as a pocket when the front door was shut ; but then it almost never was shut until the autumn rains came, which was another story. During all that long bright dry summer, so unusual in that rainy Lake Country, the Cot was as dark as a pocket to be sure, but a pocket with a good many slits in it. Through one great rent which answered for a front door, the sunshine broadly came for three long months, illuminating every corner, gilding and glorifying even the objectionable necessity of clearing the study table and tumbling French romanticists and German classics cheek by jowl upon the already piled window recess, at every mealtime.

"Imagine it," said the lady, "lace curtains, triple-plated spoons and forks, nice knives, an abundance of pots and pans, even towels, sheets, and pillow-cases included, for two guineas a month! I can't see where Miss Newlyn makes her profit, unless she got the Cot for nothing."

"Very likely it was thrown in with Windy How House," suggested her mate. Whereupon the first speaker clouded a bit, not exactly pleased with the thought of such delight as theirs with a merely "thrown-in."

Stately Mrs. B. from the third house in the lane greeted them with dignity, fresh butter, cream, new-laid eggs, and lily-white bread and a glorious handful of flowers from her own garden. Mrs. B. would help them through the summer with many a kindly service, with the very snowiest linen they ever saw in their lives, with many a sage suggestion and bit of wise advice. She was the caretaker of the House and Cot and evidently included the occupants in her careful and pleasant supervision, when she liked them. In contrary case, she turned upon those unliked ones the very coldest of countenances, and was as enigmatical as a sphinx concerning the best butter and the price of fresh raspberries. Once even the Cotters, upon whom she looked kindly from the first, perhaps in gentle commiseration for occupants of a mere "thrown-in," nearly forfeited her good opinion. It was when Mrs. Cotter borrowed bread for dinner. Mrs. B. was one of those perfectly regulated housekeepers to whom a house without bread was as foolish as a church without a Bible, or a Christian without a creed. Her own house was as dark as those North country farm-houses oftenest are, with low walls and small deep-set windows; yet sheet-lightning or a conflagration could not bring to light a spot, or stain, or dust-mote in it. She never seemed at work, moving with apparently slow stateliness about her affairs; yet she accomplished wonders. She was like a queen in exile, having been a serving-maid. Doubtless she excused the Cotters upon reflection, as she could never have excused the people of the House, cot-keeping being not exactly housekeeping, even with the nicest of beds and bedding, the most artistic of art-squares and screens. She must even have a different set of rules for nomads who hired-furnished for four long months at a time.

"Plenty of people are richer," they heard of her saying; "but not many are nicer than this summer's Cotters, even if Mrs. Cotter does dig potatoes."

Which leads to say, that there was a bit of garden to the Cot with a thicket of gooseberry bushes and a space planted with potatoes. While the gooseberry season lasted, Mrs. B.'s perfect gooseberry pies and puddings were no rarity on the Cotters' table, and many an after-luncheon and after-dinner hour the Cotters spent in the ripened thicket upon the golden slope of Windy How, whose whispering summit looked down into their humble chimney. There, too, almost every day when the sun sank in the west, and the Cotters were not abroad upon their frequent, often protracted, always poetic pilgrimages, for a little moment might have been seen a strangely gyrating figure against the golden sky. For an instant or two it bent profoundly low, as if in earnest entreaty of the mysteriously fecund earth, then sprang erect with even a suggestion of Pan-like dancing in the folds and curves of fichu and tea-gown. To the unimaginative eye this was merely Mrs. Cotter digging four potatoes for dinner.

" Digging," indeed !

Was it " digging " to summon forth with enchanter's wand (double pronged and wooden-handled) those golden spheres, fragrant of the loamy crucible in which the richness of innumerable bygone summers are daily distilled? " Digging potatoes " indeed, that gladsome, graceful, health-ful, happy, that ladylike and most æsthetic magic, which makes golden moons to dawn, and little stars to gleam, upon the pungent darkness? " Digging potatoes ! " Out upon you, base realist, and find your chief interest in the fact that the Cotters did not buy a potato that summer, though bushels of them, with everything else in the line of " garden sass " was daily brought to their door ; likewise flesh and fowl, eke fish from the lakes and from the sea ; likewise milk and cream twice a day from a neighboring farm, freshly churned butter, berries, and eggs over which the hens had not yet ceased cut-cut-cut-ker-dar-cutting.

Mrs. Cotter was well aware that she seemed to be digging potatoes on that picturesque garden slope, up so many mossy steps from the lane, and level with the Cot's eaves. She well knew that curious eyes watched her at times from the hamlet doctor's house (or rather the doctor's rich wife's) just outside the lane in the road. She knew that through lace curtains eyes sometimes gazed at her to set up many proud peacocks in tails, and that various bucolic minds wondered how a potato-digger could so well imitate a lady's appearance. That they were known to be Americans, probably accounted for much that was peculiar in this vagrant pair, but even that could not account for the potato-digging by the woman (or lady) just back on foot from a week's excursion, while the man (or gentleman) hid himself inside the Cot. The eyes little supposed that whenever that man (or gentleman) expostulated with the lady (or woman), as she sallied forth with pitchfork and • basket, like a maid in a pastoral, her reply invariably was, like a Miss Ferrier heroine, " Kill me, oh, kill me ; but do not ask me to abstain from mining my daily gold ! "

Mr. Cotter preferred his luncheon to his other meals ; for Mrs. Cotter, breakfast was the favorite repast ; as to dinner, especially after a long tramp, they both were agreed that it was a very poor meal to do without. Hence, the three meals must be properly provided for, beginning with the exquisite booterboons, without which breakfast was but an empty show, at least to the lady. The booterboons came from Hawkshead, and a tiny dark shoplet kept by two little white-haired old maidlets. Rather should it be said that one of the sisters kept the shoplet, the other baked the booterboons. The sisters were not regular bakers or professionals, being simply ancient maidens with a knack at making three or four usually home-made things, and adding these three or four to the scanty stock of pepper-

mints, toffy, candles, snuff, and tea, which was all
their other stock in trade. Every afternoon at
four, booterboons, whigs, and tea-cakes came from
the little brick oven back of the shoplet, — that
shoplet so obscurely placed amid other dark-browed
houses, so microscopically windowed, so sullenly
indifferent to the public eye, that Mrs. Cotter spent
many an hour that summer in exasperated search for
it, knowing exactly where it was the day before, exactly where it would be to-morrow, exactly where
it should be now, yet looking for it exactly where
it never was since time began. And each time
she returned airily to Windy How as innocently
smiling as if not desperately afraid her tyrant
would find her out and inquire, with aggravating
sweetness, "Been trying to square the circle
again?"

Once or twice a week from the shoplet's oven-
let came also the famous Hawkshead cakes which
every North countryman remembers with longing
wherever he may be, as the New Englander remembers his mother's flapjacks. The daily summer
excursion-breaks, driving between Windermere or
Ambleside and Coniston, always stop at Hawkshead
for the celebrated cakes ; and all that summer, tourists and travellers walked about or drove with the
renowned disks in their hands or under their arms.
It was a necessary part of every excursion to
make, or renew, acquaintance with this delectable
dainty ; with the Cotters it was enough once to
make, they never sought to renew.

Hawkshead cake is two layers of the very richest pastry, rich enough to fur the tongue, turn the
whites of the eyes yellow, and the complexion
green upon sight. Between these layers of bilious-

ness is a layer of lively headache. The Cotters never learned of what that layer is composed. They saw it black ; they tasted it sickeningly sweet ; they knew that many Zante currants went to the mixture; they never knew more, not even why it was called Cake when it was palpably of the genus Pie.

But those booterboons !

What mortal pen can describe their snowdrift whiteness, their delicacy, their crisp tenderness, the exquisite suavity with which they lie upon the tongue, the subtle smoothness as of vanishing cream with which they melt from it?

Every morning when the sun came topsy-turvying into the Cot with the opening door, and capered like a schoolboy all over the place, booterboons of the evening before went into the oil-stove oven on the scullery table. They went in cold, pale, semi-lifeless, flat, and of tea-saucer size. In a few minutes they came out again buoyant, joyous, golden-tender, with radiant souls eager to meet their fate, which was to be eaten with supreme satisfaction and fresh butter by the two Cotters.

" Lily-white muffins," Mr. Cotter undertook to call them, but was instantly crushed.

Once upon a time Hartley Coleridge promised to give a lecture on Wordsworth in some church or chapel of this region. Nobody was quite certain that he would do it, if left to his own devices, so two villagers went over to Nab Cottage to bring him to his appointment. The place was full, for the villagers had learned that Wordsworth was much talked about; and they knew so little about him themselves, although perfectly familiar with his awkward appearance and solemnly didactic manner. Hartley stood before his audience, opened his mouth and cried shrilly.

"Lily-white muffins! Lily-white muffins!"

Only this and nothing more could he be induced to say.

"Of course it was in our present village," agreed the two, "and he meant *our* booterboons."

"'Booterboons'!" said Mrs. Cotter. "Let them ever remain in our memories by that blessed name. As butter-buns they could never be half so sweet."

For luncheon came frequently another kind of cake favorite with Mr. Cotter, and for these something must be brought in a lump from Hawkshead. For a long time the Cotters thought this something was "balm," and wondered if its peculiar smell had ever suggested an ancient and decayed Gilead. It was sold from an enormous lump always standing, daily changed, upon the counter of the Hawkshead general store. The young clerk did not understand Mrs. Cotter the day she asked for yeast, he knew it only as "barm;" and although he did not know the word came from the Anglo-Saxon *beorm*, was doubtless well aware that it answered to the leaven of his Sunday-school lessons.

"Whigs" are a species of plainer booterboons, specked with caraway seeds of which rustic England and plebeian London is so inordinately fond, of which England was unanimously fond when the ladies of castles and manors consulted receipt-books in the gloomy Black Letter, which to the nineteenth century makes an innocent damson tart seem a dreadfully occult dose. Nowadays caraway seeds make not a patrician sensation upon the tongue. How can they, having, with weak tea, built so many dissenting chapels, breeched so many unlucky savages, and become recognized as distinctly of the world of Miss Squeers and the Uriah Heaps. Monsieur Mirobolant never imagined anything so Squeery and Heapy in his culinary wooing of the author of " *Mes Larmes.*" The Cotters could not explain why this Squeery taste did not go over in the Mayflower, that cargo of dissent; they could only rejoice that it did not.

" Whigs " are invariably named " Wigs " by London and South country tourists, who always seem beset with dread lest the letter *h* trip them unawares. This dread makes Mayfair pronounce the English language not one whit (or *wit*) better than Whitechapel. The former avoids the *h* as a pestilence, because the latter brings it so much in evidence. As the latter learns at board-schools to pronounce the final *ng*'s, the former takes to *goin'* and *comin'*, to *eatin'*, and *drinkin'*, lest it be considered of the same race.

" Suppose the Carpenter's Son had spoken English," remarked the younger Cotter, " how would he have used his *h*'s and his *ng*'s ? "

" Ask me another," replied the elder Cotter.

" Windy How seems four miles from everywhere," one of the pair remarked. " It is four miles from here to Windermere ; four miles through the fields to Ambleside ; four miles down hill to Coniston, although thirty-two miles back. Then from Ambleside, Grasmere is four miles, although we know short-cuts that reduce the whole distance from Windy How to Grasmere to but little more than six miles."

All summer long the two patronized these short cuts, and sauntered many a delicious mile through billowy pastures and farm lanes, over deep dank ditches spanned by tottering planks, up sunny knolls and down their sunny sides, through expanses of waving grain, through fields of cabbage, purple as pansies, stepping from stone to stone of bubbling brooks, passing even through the house-yards of silent farms far away from the almost equally quiet highway through which rustic carts crept and giddy bicycles dashed as if half afraid to make a noise. All summer they walked till fair Grasmere, gay Ambleside, brisk Windermere, and Bowness, became as familiar to them as even little Hawkshead, the metropolis of Windy How. Often they went farther to Keswick, and memories of Southey, to the Falls of Lodore and gloomy Buttermere, where lived famous Mary of the Inn, to Ullswater and all that lies between, delighting to consider themselves " literary tramps."

The Literary Tramp is no new thing. Thousands of years ago a blind one sang of the beauty of Helen and the valor of Achilles. Nearer our own days, palmers with scrip and scallop-shell told tales for bread as they tramped on towards the Holy Land or home from it. Troubadours sang as they strolled from castle to castle and became the Fathers of Literature. Then literature ceased to go on foot. When it could not ride as Chaucer did, it stayed at home. Bad roads, sparse habitations, above all the growth of cities, did away with literary vagabondage. Literature almost forgot nature in time, and the tramp took to garrets rather than to highways, and wrote idyls in bed to keep warm. Only within the last hundred years has literature again found feet, and the pleasant spectacle of its makers tramping alone, or in couples, again become prominent.

Almost the first of literary tramps, if indeed they come within the description at all, were Shelley and Mary Godwin. They have left little trace of their adventures; yet that they could walk, or thought they could, is evident in their plan to go on foot from Paris to Lausanne. We catch a fleeting glimpse of them trudging with Jane Clairmont through the dust, and grumbling bitterly at the evil fare and housing of vagabondage, the two women riding by turns on their own donkey, till a sprained ankle promoted Shelley himself to ride, and they had to buy a chariot. The poorest of tramps they must have been, for not love of nature but scarcity of gold put them on their feet. What the natives of the country thought of them, no man may say, for the girls trudged in black-silk gowns, and were of the hated nation. Doubtless they trudged along in the kid slippers and silk stockings and the corded and iron-busked stays that were of that day. No wonder the poet got a sprain.

A stouter, if less romantic pair of pedestrians were James and Harriet Martineau, who, in 1822, made a tour on foot together in Scotland, walking five hundred miles in a month. Miss Martineau was always a capital walker, while she had health; and Wordsworth accused her of walking the legs off of half the gentlemen of Ambleside. For all that, she was the most unimaginative of women. She had a manly stride, and never nymph or pixy, elf or dryad lured her to follow streams or to dream beneath rustling foliage.

Robert Browning and Sarianna were another brother and sister who covered miles upon miles together. The peculiarity of their journeys lies in the fact that they did not begin them till both were middle-aged. They formed their companionship after Mrs. Browning's death, with whose feeble steps neither of them had ever kept pace. Browning speaks of seventeen-mile walks with Sarianna, and records nine miles accomplished in less than two hours, which certanly required more than the usual manly stride from his companion.

The Wordsworths, brother and sister, were splendid examples of literary tramping. Mrs. Wordsworth told Harriet Martineau that William and Dorothy sometimes walked forty miles a day. Tours on foot were a large part of their experience together. The first thing they did after their reunion in 1794 was to start off upon a little stroll of which Dorothy wrote : " I walked with my brother from Kendal to Grasmere, eighteen miles, and afterwards to Keswick, fifteen miles, through the most delightful country that ever was seen." In November, 1797, they started upon a pedestrian tour, with Coleridge, along the sea-coast. A little later in the same month, the three set out at half-past four of a dark and cloudy afternoon, walking eight miles for a start, while the two poets laid the plan of a ballad, with the sale of which they hoped to pay the expenses of the excursion. The methods of the two did not run easily together, and "The Ancient Mariner" was soon given over entirely to Coleridge.

Dorothy did not walk in a black-silk gown. Doubts are reasonable if even she had one. Her usual walking costume was a little jacket and brown dress. Coleridge we may imagine in the same raiment in which he afterwards travelled with the two in Scotland, the soiled nankeen trousers, the blue coat with brass buttons, in which he mounted a Unitarian pulpit and preached a candidate sermon. Wordsworth, doubtless, also wore his usual suit of dingy brown, with a flapping broad-brimmed straw hat to protect his weak eyes. They were not three graces, this distinguished trio of tramps; Wordsworth was not a handsome man, not even an impressive man. In spite of the fact that the brother and sister walked, according to De Quincey's calculation, between one hundred and seventy and one hundred and eighty thousand miles, his legs were the worse part of him, and the total effect of his narrow person was even more uncomely in movement than in repose. His walk was a roll and a lunge, with eyes fixed on the ground, — mumbly on his legs, the neighbors described him. Once Dorothy, walking farther behind him than usual, and thus getting a better view, was heard to exclaim discontentedly several times, " Can that be William ? " Dorothy herself was short and slight, with such a gypsy tan as is rarely seen upon an English face. Her eyes were not soft, nor were they fierce or bold ; but they were wild and startling, and hurried in their motion like those of some wild wood-creation. This same glancing quickness, according to De Quincey, characterized all her motions, although, like her brother, she stooped awkwardly in walking. Humming and booing about, the peasants saw the poet and his sister, of whom he wrote : —

" She gave me ears, she gave me eyes."

"Miss Dorothy kept close behind him," a neighbor said, "and she picked up the bits as he let 'em fall, and took 'em down, and put 'em together on paper for him. And you may be very well sure as how she didn't understand nor make sense out of 'em, and I doubt that he didn't know much more about 'em either himself; but, however, there's a good many folks as do, I dare say."

Wordsworth sometimes had another foot-mate. Once he found Christopher North directing some road-building near Ellcray Wilson's own cottage. Christopher was in slippers, but, joining Wordsworth, walked miles with him till, not only the slippers were worn entirely away, but socks as well.

Wordsworth wrote of his own zest for walking : "My lamented friend Southey would have been a Benedictine monk in a convent with an inexhaustible library. Books were his passion, wandering was mine. Had I been born in a class deprived of liberal education, it is not unlikely that, strong in body, I should have taken to a way of life such as that in which my Wanderer passed the greater part of his days." At seventy-one, Wordsworth wrote of being four hours on foot, even though he confessed, at fifty-nine, that he was unable to take so much out of his body by walking as formerly. Yet, at sixty-one, he ran twenty miles a day beside the carriage in which his daughter Dora drove. Poor Dorothy gave in sooner. The twilight of her reason settled upon her and confined her to her own home for more than twenty years, till her death in 1855.

Another brother and sister were good foot-mates, although no great lovers of nature. They prattled of pleasant walks, but never of ardent mountain climbs and plunges into wild abysses. Mary Lamb wrote, after a visit to Brighton in 1817, to Dorothy Wordsworth (she being fifty-five and Dorothy nine or ten years younger). "Charles and I played truant, and wandered among the hills, which we magnified into little mountains and almost as good as Westmoreland scenery. Certainly we made discoveries of many pleasant walks which few of the Brighton visitors ever dreamed of; for, like as is the case in London, after the first two or three miles we were sure to find ourselves in a perfect solitude. I hope we shall meet before the walking faculties of either of us fail. You say you can walk fifteen miles with ease; that is exactly my stint, and more fatigues me."

Smooth roads and easy footfalls were evidently the ideal of pleasant walks to the Lambs, to whom the Brighton downs were as good as Westmoreland mountains. It almost seems that they walked chiefly to rid themselves of nervous irritability. There is nothing to indicate love of nature in Mary Lamb's writing, and Charles openly declared himself a stranger to the shapes and textures of the commonest trees, herbs, flowers. "Not from the circumstance of my being town-born, for I should have brought the same unobservant spirit into the world with me had I seen it first on Devon's leafy shores." Nor did he care for the sea. "I cannot stand all day," he wrote, "on the naked beach, watching the capricious hues of the sea shifting like the hues of a dying mullet. When I gaze on the sea, I want to be on it, over it, across it. It binds me with chains as with iron. The salt sea foam seems to nourish a spleen. I am not half so good-natured by the sea as by the milder waters of my native river." He cared no more for mountains. Rather would he be shirtless and bootless in London, than amid such summits and mists as Ossian sang. The scenery of the Salutation Inn was more to his taste. He did not hunger for the horizon. The mystery and enchantment of distance never lured him over moor and mountain, brake and fell. He liked near things, neighborly smiling open-hearted objects, books, tankards, pipes, cards, snuff-boxes, smiles, chatter. Still he liked to walk. Doubtless, like Leigh Hunt, he felt a respect for his leg every time he lifted it up. He could not sit and think, he said (which suggests nervous irritability), so when he was not reading he was walking. Afterwards, as the Superannuated Man, he looks back half wistfully upon the ancient bondage which made holidays so fair and precious, and laments that now is no need to walk thirty miles a day to make the most of those transient delights. Then what a cockney's-out-upon-a-holiday is the retrospect in "Old China" of pleasant walks, lunch-baskets, ale, table-cloths, landladies. Their walks leave them only such memories as may be acquired within sound of Bow Bells.

The best foot-mates, far and away, of our century were William and Mary Howitt. They began to walk on their wedding-day, two prim young Quakers honeymooning among hedgerows, like the rustic *ouvriers* of France, and they continued to walk vigorously together during the space of almost two generations of men. A year later, they walked five hundred miles among the Scotch mountains,

carrying light luggage on their backs, and resting
at rough inns or rougher cots. They climbed
Ben Lomond, wading streams, crawling over bogs,
and finally grappling hand and foot with a terrible
cone, from the peak of which they gazed upon a
prospect to fill the eye of the gods. It was a
wild tramp taken in 1824, and was surely a return
of primeval instincts under the quaint serenity of
the Quaker guise.

Walking was not fashionable then. Respectability went in gigs, and he who walked, particularly
she, was, in popular esteem, a vagrant. To see a
fair English girl springing across torrents on stepping stones, or carried on a brawny Highlander's
back, scrambling through bracken like some wood-
land creature, and sliding down sheer defiles, was
enough to make the peasants fancy the two stark
mad. They heard among the mountains of another crazy pair who had lately passed that way.
These were Christopher North, the leaping, wrest-
ling, cock-fighting Professor of Moral Philosophy
at Edinburgh, and his young wife, he carrying
about a quarter of a hundred weight of provisions
on his back, she about fourteen pounds.

The Howitts loved nature, but not as poets and
artists do, those pagans of our world. They loved
it in the sober, old-fashioned way of the intelligent
and cultivated multitude, with no illumination as to
moods, intense or occult, transfiguring the landscape. Trees were trees to them, not sentient
rapture and agonies, mountains were mountains,
rivers were rivers, just as they were to Gains-
borough and Lawrence. The actual nature and
its wholesome physical influence upon themselves,
in mind and body, were enough for the active,

objective pair whose own natures had no mysteries, no subtleties to be mirrored in a landscape.

During all their long married life, these devoted
companions never missed an opportunity for a
protracted excursion, and in their daily rambles
they walked miles enough to go round the world.
In the fifty-first year of their marriage, they might
reasonably be considered old people, Mrs. Howitt
seventy-four, her husband eighty. At such ages
the most faithful and sympathetic, as well as the
most active companionship, has usually become a
fireside one, and memory, not legs, the enduring
bond. Yet here is this mighty couple, stronger,
more enduring than any running youth and maid
of classic story, starting forth one August morning
to climb an Alp of the Tyrol. To be sure they
do not now carry their personal belongings and provisions, but hire a man for the work. Seventy-four
and Eighty started from the village of Taufers up
a steep and ever-mounting road, too steep for
vehicles. They walked five hours, till they were
getting weary. It began to rain ; but these dauntless youths walked on and on in narrow paths,
through grassy fields full of flowers. At dusk
they came to the châlet of a tenant farmer. The
wife was baking cakes for supper, the husband and
his men eating them. The apparition of the out-
landish couple, so high above the earth, a height
where old age is almost absolutely unknown,
created as much astonishment as a comet would
have done. But they were made welcome, and
cordially entertained to supper. Where did they
sleep ? In the barn, to be sure, on fresh, sweet
hay, the bed most affected by youthful vagabonds.
Seventy-four and Eighty slept two nights on the

hay, climbing twice to the mountain-top between times, with strong longing to reach distant glaciers, but finding daylight too short. On the second morning when Seventy-four woke, Eighty had already left his hay for a morning stroll. He returned to breakfast, jauntily sporting his hat trimmed with flowers in Tyrolean fashion.

The open-air feeling of space, atmosphere, largeness, freshness, and beauty pervades the Autobiography. The excursion planned for dear old father's eighty-fifth birthday was abandoned only because of the rain. They climbed Monte Cavo together, and they wandered, like youths in an idyl, over the Campagna, gathering flowers. In the eighty-seventh year that William saw, when Mary had seen fourscore-and-one, she wrote : " Father and I have just come in from a pleasant walk right into the country, amongst picturesque houses and such ancient orchards and park-like fields scattered over with grand old Spanish chestnuts."

Mr. Howitt died in 1879, aged eighty-nine years. No more the faithful foot-mates of sixty wedded years trudge side by side. But not yet does the widowed one sit down quietly at home, and know the pomps and glories of this radiant world no more. She writes that she takes quiet little strolls, and gathers the flowers her husband loved. She lives to see eighty-nine years, then gently falls asleep, at exactly the age her husband ceased to walk.

One fine summer evening of 1824, the inhabitants of a primitive northern village saw two travellers, apparently man and wife, come into the village, dressed like tinkers or gypsies. The man was tall, broad-shouldered, and of stalwart build, his fair hair floated, redundant, over neck and shoulders, his red whiskers were of portentous size. He bore himself with the air of a strong man rejoicing in his strength. On his back was a capacious knapsack, and his slouched hat, garnished with fishing-hooks and tackle, showed he was as much addicted to fishing as to making spoons. The appearance of his companion contrasted strikingly with that of her spouse. She was of slim and fragile form, and more like a lady in her walk and bearing than any tinker's wife that had ever been seen in those parts. The natives were somewhat surprised to see this great fellow making for the best inn, the Gordon Arms, where the singular pair actually took up their quarters for several days. They were in the habit of sallying forth, each armed with a fishing-rod, — a circumstance the novelty of which, as regards the tinker's wife, excited no small curiosity ; and many conjectures were hazarded as to the real character of the mysterious couple. So wrote one who saw burly Christopher North and his wife on the vagabondage which Mary Howitt described as, " A species of bee and butterfly flight, sipping pungent juice and alighting upon bloom ;" for whenever they found a particularly romantic spot, or an attractive cottage, there they stopped for days, while the husband fished, the wife rested, and both explored the region round about.

One morning in Glenorchy, Wilson started out early to fish in Loch Toila. Its nearest point was thirteen miles from his lodging. On reaching it, and unscrewing the butt-end of his fishing-rod to get the top, he found he had forgotten it.

Nothing daunted, he walked back, breakfasted, made his rod complete, and walked again to Loch Toila. All the long summer day he fished round the loch, and after sunset, started for home with a full basket. Feeling somewhat fatigued, and passing a familiar farm-house, he stopped to ask for food. It was near midnight, and he routed the family from bed. The mistress brought him a full bottle of whiskey, and a can of milk. He poured half the whiskey into half the milk, and drank it off at a draught. While his hostess was still staring in amazement, he poured the remaining milk and whiskey together, and finished the mixture. He then proceeded homeward, having performed a journey of not less than seventy miles.

Between the 5th of July and the 26th of August, this couple walked three hundred and fifty miles in the Highlands, fishing, eating, and staring. Professor Wilson wrote, "Unlike bee and butterfly, he carried death and devastion everywhere." One almost shudders to read how much of harmless happy life went out forever to make a giant's holiday. He killed one hundred and seventy dozen of trout,— one day, nineteen dozen and a half, another, seven dozen. From Loch Awe, in three days, he took seventy-six pounds of fish, all with the fly. He shot two roebucks, and he wrote, " I nearly caught a red deer by the tail ; I was within half a mile of it, at farthest."

On their return, the pair, particularly the lady, were the lions of Edinburgh. So far from presenting the weatherbeaten appearance expected, Mrs. Wilson was declared to be bonnier than ever. It is a little curious that this lady, who walked on one day of this tramp twenty-five miles, should have died prematurely some years afterwards, because of insufficient bodily exercise.

Various good walkers have died, and left no literary trace of their ramblings. Mr. and Mrs. S. C. Hall were of these who covered untold miles together and made no note of them. Others do not come within the scope of this paper, for the reason that they walked not in pairs, but alone. Mary Russell Mitford declared herself perfectly uncomfortable without a daily walk of ten miles, and congratulated herself that a friend, come to dwell nine miles away from her, was within calling and walking distance There is a funny description of this spinster taking long solitary walks at night with a lantern. This would seem to argue no love of nature as incentive to tramping. The dainty Pre-Raphaelitism of the natural descriptions in her books, however, shows that she loved it in her own prim small way.

The Brontë sisters appear to have been almost always walking, one or the other of them coming into every picture of that dreary Yorkshire parsonage, as fresh from the breezy moors. But they walked little in pairs, and carried their passionate hearts and fettered longings out under the gray skies in solitude.

Of our own day, George Eliot and Mr. Lewes, miserable invalids though they were, made no mean showing as foot-people. George Eliot's letters and diaries show that scarcely a day was without its walk. One day the pair, in company with Mr. Herbert Spencer, are five hours on foot. But no gypsy tramps and romantic adventures were in that united history. Their walks too were never counted by miles, but by the time spent on

them out of doors. Those slow walks were as
eminently respectable as the pursuit of queer
insects and strange fish and fleeing health could
possibly be, as decorous as George Eliot's own
highly moral and self-conscious letters. There
were no wanderings. Never was there a saunter,
delicious relic of fair, ancient beggary when *sans-
terres* lived more gayly than lords of broad
domains. They took constitutionals, and for the
stomach's sake, not the imagination's. George
Eliot's was the shut-in view of one born in a
flat country, — mere peeps at hedgerows, orchards,
meadows, gardens, commons. She sees color
strongly, but not tender or subtle color, always the
bright yellow of the broom, the vivid green of the
grass, the red and gray of rocks, the gold of sandy
beaches, the smart hues of flowers. The wide sky,
to be sure, comes continually into her glimpses and
her letters; but never the beckoning horizon, never
the beguiling distance, only and always the well
behaved blue directly over her head. She hated
the wind, and incessantly complained of it; but
breezes were sweet and sunshine necessary to her.
She rarely, if ever, sees the radiance and grandeur
of earth from a height, or in limitless expanses.
Neither was she in love with the sea, in her mild
admiration of it standing midway between Charles
Lamb's nourished spleen and poor Dorothy
Wordsworth's rapture, who wept at her first sight
of it.

As we count these walkers over, we find not one
romantic visionary among them. None of them
hear lullabies in the air or haunting voices in the
wind. They never lose themselves in the shadow
of a cloud upon a distant mountain, or brood with

a sunbeam over the heart of a voluptuous rose. No mystic thrills and pangs are in their love of nature. Such amorous dalliance they leave to weak legs and narrow chests, to summer hammocks and heated libraries.

"It seems to me you have taken a great fancy for starting out alone," observed Mr. Cotter, when the summer had grown mature. "This is the third time you have told me to ' catch up ' with you, and then you must have run every step of the way, for I did not overtake you till close upon Ambleside."

The lady smiled. It was an inward smile as well as a vague one, and escaped the other's observation. She said nothing, but continued to start first and alone upon those of the tramps that were to extend beyond Ambleside or Grasmere, and she continued to reach the trysting place under green trees before him. Mr. Cotter labored with the puzzle in vain that Mrs. Cotter walked so very much faster without him than she ever did with. The lady recognized his bewilderment, but made no sign.

Not even to say " scalloping."

In their long tramps over the romantic Lake District, to-day seeking memories of Felicia Hemans near her Bowness cottage, to-morrow of Ruskin half a score of miles away at Coniston, one day in the footprints of Dorothy Wordsworth at the Wishing Gate, where many a sob must have burdened wishes for selfish Coleridge, another day at lonely Blyntarn farm, where once young Agnes Green watched three days, for her parents, dead in the snow, and touched a nation's heart with her sorrow and her bravery, another up steep

Elleray path to the picturesque home of the leonine poet who became professor of philosophy and writer of Noctes, up and down, hither and yon, seeking by tarn and ghyll, by lake and wood, by crag, gap, and pass, the most obscure and the most famous spots upon which poetic illumination has fallen, Mr. Cotter strode and his companion scalloped. Always they started out side by side, step by step. They did not talk much together; none do who think much the same thoughts at the same moment, and to whom is no necessity for ecstatic whinnies in the face of august nature. Thus for an hour or two they strode in joyous sympathy, though mute. After ten stout miles or so the lady's devotion to nature began to grow apace. From time to time she called her companion's attention to flecks and flashes upon far hill-tops, to the gloom of distant vales, to the silvery winding of remote highways, the singing secret of near springs, the mystic murmur of wayside pines.

With heroic patience the longer-legged Cotter stayed his strides and gazed just where he was bid, to see just what he was told to see. With each taking to his stride again, however, he found himself in a measure alone. Sometimes three feet, sometimes six, sometimes a good many yards behind, the lady was meditatively engaged in what she called a Pursuit of the Ideal, but for which he had another name. This "pursuit of the ideal" was to all appearances and purposes a vague crossing from one side of the road to the other, with no visible purpose in such wavering, and with very visible increase in the number of steps to a straight-forward mile.

"Step up! Step up, my Lady!" he some-times called to her. "You are beginning to scallop."

"No such thing," she would answer, "only you know the other side of the road from that on which I walk always seems smoother."

"Never for the first two or three hours," he laughed. "The first ten miles is never em-broidered."

And this is why one hapless, never-to-be-forgot-ten day she started alone for Grasmere, arranging to meet her companion, too busy to start so soon, at the tidy Moss Grove Hotel, where they always tea'd and lunched, then to proceed with him up the long slope to Parson Sympson's abode.

"Now be sure not to tire yourself by too fast walking," he enjoined, as she departed. "Don't take the lower of the cabbage-field paths; take the middle gates. Don't climb any fences; don't wet your feet; don't miss the pasture-turning; don't climb any fences; don't lose your way; don't climb any fences; *don't* try to square any circles; don't — "

"I won't," said she.

The long morning was all before her, the sun still rejoicing in the east. She could saunter as slowly as she chose, with as many poetic rests as she pleased beneath rhythmic branches. The dew lay very heavy on the tall grass, and for a time she sped on with huge English boots like men-of-war, defiant of the wet and with skirts held to their tops, which was very high indeed. She did not even drop them when she met the farmer, who

bade her a cheery " Good morning," in his cabbage field, and told her the day would be pleasant,
as he knew by his cows ; and she had not occasion to
drop them again, until that awful moment the memory of which makes her flesh creep to this day.

Beyond the cabbage field a meadow, then a rest
upon a billowy mound with white clouds, blue sky,
singing insects, and a radiant world for company.

Whither do vagrant thoughts wander from under
the trees of a day in mid-summer? Are they
thoughts at all, those dreamy wanderers, gathering
sun-tinted wool from yon floating clouds drifting
away to the shining Beyond no mortal eye has
seen, as they pluck radiant wool from the wings
of summer winds, singing as they fleet, as they
pick it rainbow-hued from the waving horizon
line of distant trees, as they woo it from grass
and humble flower, from expanses of dimpling
grain, as they win it from shining bits of water,
from far hamlets, seen in a vision? Are they
thoughts at all, bringing wool of enchantment with
which to weave the magic carpet, that never
touches earth, yet never rises too far above it?

Then another saunter of a mile or two towards
a dark depth of green water, beyond which were
certain iron bars, slender but strong. A full quarter of a mile before this deep ditch, the saunterer
began to smile. It was really but a delicate suggestion of a smile at first, widening, by very slow
but sure degrees, into what a vulgar mind might
even describe as a grin.

"Would n't I catch it," she thought, "if he
only knew."

With one foot on the lower bar, she balanced
herself with care. The time had been that she

was less cautious, and the result not flattering to her self-respect to remember. She would not have had her tyrant know how she went over that fence the third and the fifth times of trying for the world. Or anybody else, indeed!

This time the bars did not give unreasonably beneath her weight, and with some perhaps more majestic than bird-like flutterings, she was over, decently and in season to fall into a man's open arms.

"Perfidious woman!" he exclaimed. "*This* is the short-cut you kept to yourself to steal marches upon me, is it? How dared you climb such a climb without somebody on hand to gather up your fragments in baskets?"

The culprit could not speak for some time.

Then she murmured tremulously: —

" How in the world did you find out?"

" Merely by wandering this way myself one day. The moment I set eyes upon that tell-tale waver of the bars it was revealed to me in a flash, ' Here's where somebody always climbs in the same place who is short-cutting upon my usual short-cut from the Hawkshead road.' It was none of the farmers I knew, for there is no path; so to-day when you started out I started too, and passed behind you while you wool-gathered in the sun."

WORDSWORTH'S "PARSON SYMPSON."

As for Sympson, who was he that these Americans thus jeopardized for him the urbanity of their relationship? Who was this dusty parson for whose sake two simple Cotters grew thus serpent-wise and wily, for whose sake one climbed frail iron bars, for whose sake one lurked beneath a hedge, for whose sake both walked on beyond Grasmere up the aspiring road he climbed so many thousand times?

Nobody knows anything about him in the district, that is, among the everyday folk. The ever busy catchers-up of every unconsidered trifle concerning Wordsworth, even they know very little indeed. Having ransacked records and memories even to the extent of finding out that the dalespeople found Mrs. Wordsworth a hard woman to deal with, and that Wordsworth was fond of legs of mutton, and that Dorothy had more wits than all of them, these gleaners and winnowers are baffled in any and every desire to know more of Parson Sympson, Wordsworth's "Patriarch of the Vale," than Wordsworth himself has told. Even the intelligent care-taker of the Hawkshead library, pleasant Mrs. Black, who chatted with them of Kit North's mad rides over the countryside, playing midnight huntsman with the

farmer's cows, who could tell them of poor Hartley Coleridge with teeth on edge, that his father
ate sour grapes, of radiant Dorothy Wordsworth
gibbering and nodding in a garden chair, the miserable victim of her brother's anacondaism, — even
Mrs. Black could tell nothing.

Strange to say also, Parson Sympson's cottage seems unknown to the drivers of excursion-
coaches and to the indefatigable photographer
whose mill finds grist in the most minute of
picturable Wordsworthiana. Only a passing mention of it is in one of the many Wordsworthiana
booklets, — such a booklet as is not likely to come
under the observation of the unliterary tourist.

The Cotters knew the house by sight some time
before the day on which they knocked at its door.
The smoke from its chimney they had watched
from afar, with tip-tilted noses that now the tea-pot
steamed upon a hob and did not nestle in hot
ashes, as when that chimney smoked for Parson
Sympson's evening meal. They knew familiarly
the tiny deep windows, the walls of lime-washed
stone, and the farmyard before the door, long
before the figure of a pretty young woman out-
lined itself against the darkness and pleasantly
invited them in.

Up the long ascent to this Cot came one day,
a century and a half ago, a motley train of pack-
horses with jingling bells and pillioned riders,
followed by more ignoble beasts, backed more
shapelessly than desert dromedaries. It was exactly such a train as Macaulay describes when,
throughout the country north of York and west
of Exeter, all goods were carried by long trains
of these pack-horses, the sturdy breed of which

is now extinct. Travellers of humble condition often made long journeys mounted on a pack-saddle between two baskets, moving at snail's pace, and often with great suffering from the cold; such as this train did not suffer in that month of June.

At the lowly door of this stone cottage the company finished a pilgrimage as picturesque to our times as any royal pageant, a merry journey, rich in pastime, cheered by music, pranks, and laughter-stirring jests, mischievously designed to mystify gaping yokels, and ending at this once bleak and bare cottage which would house for half an hundred years the head of that gypsy band "till from manhood's noon" (at forty-one), he became the Patriarch of the Vale, standing alone within this cot, "left void and mute as if swept by a plague."

Wytheburn Chapel, where he, "Parson Sympson," was shepherd of a flock of mountain shepherds for more than half an hundred years, has more honor. The Keswick and Ambleside coaches stop before it every day, just long enough and no longer for a snapshot view of the interior. They stop, not because of Wordsworth, not because of the Wanderer, the Vicar, the Solitary; neither do they stop because of that Priest by Function, once so irregular and wild, by books unsteadied and by pastoral care unchecked, — for none of these, but because "It is the smallest church in England!"

That it is directly opposite the "Nag's Head," has perhaps nothing to do with the case.

The "Nag's Head" replaces the famous "Cherry Tree," now retired under a thick veil of ivy to the tranquillity of farming life, after a somewhat lively career. A buxom landlady who pronounces the coach-load a " bad lot," because it seems not athirst, replaces him of whom Matthew Arnold wrote : —

" Our jovial host, as forth we fare,
Shouts greeting from his easy-chair."

The little " Cherry Tree " was famed for good cheer long before Wordsworth's Wagoner yielded to the enticing of a fiddle's dinning, and met his ruin at the village Merry Night.

A quarter of a century before Wordsworth came to Grasmere, a " Laker " wrote of the " Cherry Tree": " They gave us a breakfast fit for laboring men : mutton, ham, eggs, buttermilk-whey, tea, bread and butter, and asked if we chose cheese, all for sevenpence apiece." Scarce wonder that this Laker added, " Do not imagine, good reader, that we gluttonized."

Continued this writer: " Two grandmothers were in the kitchen ; one of the old women was between eighty and ninety. She was a chatty old lady ; and as both my companion and I wished to give free scope to every one we spoke to, she had the clack of her sex and the privilege of years to say what she pleased. She performed both parts of questions and answers, and told us she had been a pretty shepherdess in her time, and that she had been too often upon Skiddaw in her youth to be ill in her old age. I mention this," adds our tourist, " to make known how healthy and cheery they live under the ' Cherry Tree.' I think a chatty old woman, when she is not too much upon the diffusive, is a most cheerful companion, and ought to command a respectful hearing."

This chatty old woman of the "Cherry Tree," born before the eighteenth century, was one of Parson Sympson's flock. She knew that rustic figure, striding up from Grasmere Vale, carrying even yet something of its old-time air of the grander world beneath its later habit, as well as she knew the sound of the two little bells in yon humble belfry. Many a time, without doubt, she had eaten trout of his catching, and exchanged her own geese and ducks of the earth for his sky and water. She knew the amount of tithes she had paid him, and the sound of his home-made harp and viol. She was twenty years or more older than he, and remembered, without doubt, that first occasion, a score of years before, that the poor little mountain chapel had first a curate of its own — was served no longer by a beggarly and uncouth "Reader." She could well remember the jokes and gibes at the new parson's Northumbrian accent, amid the rugged accents of the Cumberland and Westmoreland Dalesmen. She possibly remembered something of the sermons with which this ex-courtier become parson (whom Charles Lamb afterwards declared the most delightful figure of "The Excursion") greeted his new charge. Parson Sympson was considerably alive. and in the vigor of something like three-score years that summer's day of 1773, when our Rambler chatted in the "Cherry Tree." Even while that Rambler did not gluttonize, the parson may have passed up or down the road.

Why did not our Rambler espy him then, with weather-beaten complexion and bobbing queue, and turn some of that diffusiveness upon a future phantom in English literature? Parson Sympson was of a class grown smaller in the nineteenth than in the eighteenth century. As a shepherd of souls he could scarcely be counted a direct guide to heavenly pastures, wherever he might end at last. He was a type of shepherd far older than the Christian pastor, piping amid his flock, rather than to them, with pagan tunes and music of wassail upon pan-pipes of coarse sound. Wordsworth's Priest was simply a good-hearted, kindly sort of humble hamlet squire, better born, better educated than his flock, but, like them, giving no thought to other than mundane things. He wore the livery of heaven, not to serve the devil in, but his own tastes, pleasure, and needs. That he devoted time vowed to his Master's service to fishing and shooting, rather than to cards and racing, was more a chance of taste and circumstances than of conscience. He was very much a boaster of the better days that were more roistering, and he reviled his Grasmere days as a downfall from them.

Why did that early Laker not have prophetic sense enough to ask about the motley train which, about 1759, — when those rough and forbidding mountain-roads offered no access for wain, heavy or light, — wriggled itself slowly into the Vale?

Who knows that the diffusive dame was not one of the parish matrons who met that train at the cottage door? Even she, it may have been, who plucked the ruddy children from their well-poised baskets, drowsily rocked by the motion of a trusty ass. Perchance she gazed with curiosity, not unmixed with rustic awe, upon the comely Matron riding close behind, a woman of soft speech, and with a lady's mien, all so unusual to mountain-bred eyes. And that whiskered Tabby, was its mew Pasht-like and occult, as befitted the mystic familiar of a vagrant and prophesying train? How demeaned itself a cat contemporary with Sir Charles Grandison?

How far more interesting this Laker, had he encouraged non-octogenarian diffusiveness to be too diffusive, and served us a spicy dish such as austere virtue condemns when new, and savors with delight when time hath seasoned it well.

De Quincey supposes Wordsworth's story of Parson Sympson's entrance into the Vale to be literal.

In "The Excursion," Wordsworth says that the good pair often described their fantastic, yet grave, migration with undiminished glee in hoary age. When disgusted Curate Sympson, weary of bootless promises from titled friends, and having revelled long and frolicked industriously while waiting preferment, accepted angrily at last this beggarly curacy in what was then an uttermost part of the earth, Wordsworth was not yet born, a fact the inaccurate Opium Eater failed to observe.

The "Chapelry remote" was in Cumberland. No parsonage went with it; and our Priest by Function was obliged to house his family seven good miles over the marshes into Westmoreland, whence he had a tough climb to the chapel by a road " winding in mazes serpentine, shadeless, and shelterless, by driving showers frequented, and beset with howling winds."

He must always be in good season, too, buffet and trip as those Northern blasts might, for it was the priest's business to gather his flock by ringing the bell with his own hands.

Wytheburn Chapel was then a dependency of Crosthwaite, and was equidistant between the parsonage and the mother church. The stipend was £31 a year.

Naturally, the parsons must have another trade, even though so late as Arthur Young's "Tour," beef was but 2*d.* a pound, mutton 2½*d.*, cheese 2*d.*, bread ¾*d.*, milk 1*d.* a quart, laborer's house rent 20*s.* a year. Even thus, few could live on their stipends and fees, but like "Wonderful Walker," of Seathwaite, must work at a dozen trades or more.

"Wonderful Walker" was hedger, ditcher, tailor, clogger, sheep-salver, and shearer, weaver, brewer, harvester, schoolmaster, village lawyer, clerk, etc. ; and he married a domestic servant, as many did in those days, when not put off with a fly-blown reputation, as Bishop Tusher was.

He worked at his loom in his schoolroom, and at day's labor for his parishioners. He died at the good age these active Dalesmen often attained, almost an hundred, having brought up and educated many children, to whom he left £2000.

Sympson's predecessor at Wytheburn, whom the old lady of the "Cherry Tree" probably well-remembered, had a salary of £2, 10*s.* 0*d.*, a hempen sark (or shirt), a pair of clogs, a whittlegate, and a goosegate. Whittlegate was the right of laying a whittle or knife at a parishioner's board two or three weeks every year, according to the householder's means. The whittler was obliged to furnish his own knife, few houses having more than one or two. Sometimes this knife belonged to the church, and was lent by the wardens. He

marched from house to house with his whittle,
seeking fresh pasturage ; and, as master of the herd,
he had the elbow-chair at the table head, which
was often made of a hollow ash tree. A parson
was thought a proud fellow who demanded a fork
in those days ; he was reproved for it, and told
that fingers were made before forks.

The goosegate was the right to pasture geese
upon the common. One wonders how his children fared at home while the shepherd browsed
thus, with his flock, " on taters and bacon on a bare
fir board."

Even with priestly perquisites from brides,
babies, and bodies, not many sevenpenny dinners
could they afford, however the " Cherry Tree "
tempted with savory scents of mutton and ham.

" Priest, come to your poddish " (porridge),
" Priest, come to your taties," " Priest, come to
your poddish," one of them told in old age had
been his call three times a day for half a century.

Naturally there was very little of the typical
clergyman about these six-day farmers and artisans.
Fustian jackets, corduroy or leather breeches,
stockings of the coarsest gray yarn, and wooden
clogs, stuffed with straw or dried bracken, was their
frequent garb. Sometimes the sark, instead of
unbleached hemp, was of coarse blue check, and
over corduroy breeches, without braces, was worn
a weaver's apron. For weddings and christenings
the only change was to a black coat, the convenient surplice hiding all the rest. One of this
bucolic clergy was an excellent judge of sheep,
and drove superior bargains home. With due
respect to his Sunday clothes, he took pains to
retire and turn them wrong-side out whenever he

wished to examine flocks. When his examinations were over, his costume was turned again to its reverend side. This same parson was so keen at a bargain that it was well understood by the sharpest that, dealing with him, Greek was meeting Greek.

" Well, I find this," said one to him, " self niver sleeps but wi' ya ee oppen."

" Eh, Johnny," was the answer, " thou has nobbut learnt hofe thy lesson. Self niver goes to bed."

Still another (the Reverend Mattison) whose ordinary income was £12, and never more than £24, died the year Wordsworth was born. He was so industrious and penurious that he left behind him more money than the whole of his salary for fifty-six years at compound interest. He and his wife carded and spun wool ; he taught a school for £5 a year.

His wife acted as midwife, at a shilling each lying-in. She also was the cook of christening dinners, and pocketed every possible perquisite. This wife had done her part in swelling her spouse's fortune ; but at his death she and his children spent every penny he had amassed, and she was obliged to seek shelter in a charitable institution for widows of clergymen.

This woman's father at her marriage boasted that he had married his daughters to the two best men in Patterdale, — the priest and the bagpiper.

Still more remarkable was one who died about the time our " Priest by Function " came to Wytheburn Chapel. He was curate during forty-seven years of the neighboring chapel of Threlkeld. He lived like a Diogenes, upon eight pounds, sixteen shillings a year. His dress was beggarly ; he lived alone, and slept upon straw with two blankets. In aspect a sloven, his wit was ready, his satire keen and undaunted, his learning extensive ; he was an agreeable companion, and, although fond of the deepest retirement, in company became the chief promoter of mirth. He left no fortune behind him, but an excellent library and several manuscripts of great merit on conic sections, spherical trigonometry, and other mathematical pieces, says Clarke's " Survey."

Most of his poetical pieces he destroyed before his death. Once the sub-dean, whose business it was to visit the inferior clergy in his district once a year, to see that they acted becoming their function (and could demand to see any corner of their houses), found great fault with this curate's house, dress, furniture, and probably food, as the priest was his own cook. " Dean," answered the dirty curate, " you have not seen the most valuable part of my furniture. There is contentment peeping out of every corner of my cot, and you cannot see her, I suppose — you are not acquainted with her. Upon the walls of your lordly mansion and in your bedchamber is wrote ' Dean ' and ' Chapter,' after that ' Bishop.' No thought of these here, nor of equipage ; contentment keeps them off." Then he repeated to him the sixth Satire of the second book of Horace : " *Hoc erat in votis : modus agri non ita magnus.*"

" A little farm, and a pleasant clear spring, a garden and a grove were the utmost of my wish. The gods have in their bounty exceeded my hopes ; I am contented."

Sometimes these clerical hewers of wood and

drawers of water, toilers of field and farm, were obliged to brew and sell ale, and make alehouse and parsonage one. Perhaps this explains a certain old woman's complaint that her daughter's husband, or suitor, kept bad company, — "the parson and such." Another old lady, defending a too jovial minister, declared : —

"Well, I 'll not say but he may have slanted now and then at a christening or a wedding, but for buryin' a corp he is undeniable."

Neither is it surprising that particular evil smells were said to be as bad as chapels in sheep-salving time ! The chapels often were no better furnished than their ministers. At Wythop, the communion service consisted of a pewter cheese-plate and pewter pot; the baptismal font, an earthen basin. Here the minister's stipend was tenpence a Sunday, the exact wage of a day laborer. Both minister and ploughman received their wage with victuals, the former in form of whittlegate. The poughman's day was from six to six ; but his week had six days, the parson's only one.

Why should these rough Dalesmen waste time and work to write sermons ? — especially as the Lake District peasantry have always been a practical, never a very religious people, and always averse to long sermons.

"What shall I say next ? " asked one of these mountain preachers in the midst of a somewhat lengthy discourse.

"Amen," said an audible voice from among the congregation.

In 1767, the poet Gray one Sunday passed the " Cherry Tree " and the little chapel of Wytheburn, out of which the congregation was

just issuing. He says no more than this of the
chapel in which thirty people would have been a
throng; but we know from Clarke's "Survey,"
a dozen years later that "the chapel was a very
poor low building and not consecrated; their
burying-place is Crosthwaite." So late as 1792,
when Parson Sympson had been thirty-five years
its minister, Walker's "Tour" described the chapel
as "wretched, in a scattered group of poor houses,
everything about it cold and comfortless."

Had the poet Gray stopped to peep in, he
would have seen very much such an interior as
Kit North described even sixty years later at
Wastdale — about a dozen benches, the reading-
desk scarcely to be distinguished, humble the
pulpit, and lowly the altar, and earthen floor, and
bare stone walls, weather-stained, with penetrating
damps and driving tempests.

On that October day of 1767, in all probability,
it was our Priest who read the usual prayers in
the chapel, and for his gracious majesty King
George, third of the name, as he had ten years
earlier prayed for the second of these German
dullards. A picturesque issuing that (to us), a
company of mountain shepherds who spun the
fleeces of their own sheep, and knew themselves
fine in Sunday best of undyed homespun, the
white and black fleeces mixed. How dandy the
full-skirted coats ornamented with huge brass
buttons, and the waistcoats opened in front, if
perchance the home-woven sark boasted a snowy
frill. Breeches were buttoned tightly across the
haunches, so as to keep up without braces, not yet
invented. Many are the bows of ribbon and
bright buttons on these Sunday breeches; some

of the richer Dalesmen's breeches, of buckskin, intended to endure long after the owner grew too large for them or shrank too small.

Buxom belles and matrons are in homespun linsey-woolsey gowns, well above the ankle. Brightly buckled shoes were of coquetry as well as of service, and many a foot in those days sought the fender without need of the fire. Our Priest by Function is not long after the others, for he doffs his surplice behind a curtain. He is in clerical black, knee-breeches and yarn stockings, all probably somewhat weather-rusted from their thirteen miles' struggle every Sunday through frequent sunshine and tempest, and he wears a cocked hat somewhat worse in form and color than the day it finished its caravan journey, a dozen or more years ago.

Wytheburn Chapel is no longer wretched or grim, but snowily neat. It has spruce belfry and pleasant-voiced bell, a bell-ringer, vicar, and a memorial window, but not of our Priest.

The chancel, of recent addition, is considerably higher than the original building, which gave it a singular appearance. It is still : —

> " Wytheburn's modest house of prayer,
> As lowly as the lowliest dwelling,"

and into it every season pour tens of thousands of Lakers, with never a thought of Parson Sympson, whose name shall endure when not one stone of these walls lies upon another.

They were guided through the dusk of walls scarcely higher than one's head, beneath heavy black oaken beams, and beside windows of only doll-house size. The floor was of the same blue slabs of mountain-stone of Wordsworth's time. The slabs are worn now into ruts and furrows. In the great fireplace comparatively modern conveniences are set; but they knew from the flickering light and flame just where Mistress Sympson cooked the timely treat of fish or fowl, " by nature yielded to her spouse's practised hook or gun." They knew where all winter long in the peat smoke of the great chimney hung, with flitches of bacon, the burly hams and quarters of beef and mutton, making the well-stocked chimney considered by eighteenth-century Dalesmen the most elegant furniture that could adorn a house. " Well-stocked " those chimneys surely were ; for an eighteenth-century tourist mentions one in which he saw eight whole carcasses hanging at once. Beside the chimney, how easy to imagine still the high-backed settle, where the master sat by the light of tallow-dips, and sorted his hooks, and set his poles.

Here we seem to see the " hospitable board," just by the " charitable door." This dim room was the general living and sitting room of Priest Simpson's family, the self-same room trimmed and brightened by the matron's care. It was also the clergyman's only study, amid pots and pans, and the bustle of daily needs, of butter and cheese making, spinning, weaving, dyeing, washing, pickling, quilting, preserving, herb-distilling, fat-rendering, candle-dipping, fowl-plucking. " He might be considered lucky, if he had a dozen dog-eared volumes among his pots and pans," wrote Macaulay of such as Parson Sympson.

To cover these very slabs, Mistress Sympson

wove a fair carpet of homespun wool, dyed with gay hues; not for daily use, but kept for festal days, when three unknown poets came to tea, or Dorothy Wordsworth came with her work, while William and the Priest joined Southey and Coleridge, to fish in Wytheburn water till supper-time. Mistress Sympson hung snow-white curtains to these mites, of windows; and, for mats, at thresholds, she braided tough moss and mountain-plants. She was a pattern wife, devoted to her home, which she apparently rarely left, and to all appearances without tastes that craved a wider earth and higher sky. She was contented, for so also is a snail in its way; but what she really was in potentiality, who ever knew? Till the sun kissed it the goldenest field was but clods. Without attrition of other minds, in books, newspapers, or conversation, without even a weekly sermon, that only stimulus of so many bucolic minds, why should a mind, however full of latent fire, give out one single spark?

Dorothy Wordsworth speaks of Mistress Sympson in old age as, " mild and gentle, yet cheerful and much of the gentlewoman." This seems to imply that she was only " much," not "altogether," the gentlewoman. Probably she was really more the eighteenth-century mountain-shepherd's help-meet, than the equal of the showy courtier her brother's pen represents the husband.

Probably also that showiness was chiefly in the old man's bombastic talk.

Mistress Sympson's kitchen-parlor is now the farm-house kitchen, and Wytheburn's Vicar has a parsonage within stone's throw of the church. The present occupant shows her parlor, rich in framed photographs and antimacassars, proud of her modern Brussels carpet, its white ground strewn with immense roses.

The Wordsworths and the Sympsons were very "neighborly," albeit three miles were between them, and the Sympsons already aged when the young people came to the Vale. Dorothy writes in one of her letters that the old man of eighty was as active as a man of fifty. Her Grasmere Journal contains various mentions of the household.

On a June day of 1800, when the Priest by Function was eighty-five, we read: "William and I walked up to the Sympsons'. William and old Mr. Sympson went to fish in Wytheburn water."

A little later in the same year: "On Sunday, we made a great fire and drank tea in Bainriggs [wood], with the Sympsons."

Coleridge and his wife were of this party. It was not a hymning and psalming one, we may be sure, though on a Sunday and with three parsons, present and *ci-devant*.

One was Coleridge, the ex-Unitarian, who had preached a candidature sermon in nankeen trousers, blue coat, and brass buttons; another, Priest Sympson's ordained son; and Priest Sympson himself, who still retained a flashing eye, a burning palm, a stirring foot, a head which beat at nights upon its pillow with a thousand schemes.

On September 3, 1800, our Priest by Function climbs Helvellyn with William and John Wordsworth, the elder of the two brothers a third his age. On a May day of 1802, Dorothy and William met Coleridge at Wytheburn, and found the Patriarch fishing there. Again Dorothy considers it lucky that Miss Sympson comes into Dove Cottage and takes William from his struggle with the " Leach Gatherer."

Dorothy, on her way home from her long walks with her brother, sometimes stops at the Sympsons' to borrow a shawl. The Journal abounds with mentions of walks to Keswick and Wytheburn. Scarcely one was without a call at the parsonage, a word with its inmates, even when no note is made of such. " Mr. Sympson came . . . and brought us a beautiful drawing which he had done." This could scarcely be the fiddling, scheming, climbing Patriarch, but probably the poetical son, a clergyman who had preceded Wordsworth by ten years or more at the Hawkshead Grammar School, where both spent eight or ten years, and whom Wordsworth (many years later) considered entitled to that place among Westmoreland poets which has never been accorded him. His principal poem, now perished, " The Vision of Alfred," Wordsworth thought " in versification harmonious and animated, and containing passages of splendid description."

" He was a man of ardent feelings," wrote Wordsworth, "and his faculties of mind, particularly of memory, were extraordinary." With him one day Wordsworth talked of Pope, and found fault with his versification. The other defended Pope with warmth, almost with irritation, till Wordsworth said, " In compass and variety of sound, your own versification surpasses his."

" Never," continued Wordsworth, " shall I forget the change in his countenance and tone of voice ; the storm was laid in a moment ; he no longer disputed my judgment, and I passed immediately in his mind, no doubt, for as great a critic as ever lived."

Another son of the family, not one pannier-poised into the Vale, but native of it, inherited his father's early disposition towards revelling and frolicking.

Something, too, of the Matron's gentleness may have fated him to failure. He was sent forth from that primitive Vale to try the paths of fortune in the open world, — Birmingham perhaps, or Manchester, even perhaps only small Penrith. Whichever it was, proved too much for him. The son of a long revelling and industriously frolicking father failed entirely, " before the suit of pleasure."

After what dusty fallings and angry disappointments at home, we know not, but may imagine, he returned to the Vale humbly to till his father's glebe. Wordsworth, after 1820, suppressed the lines of " The Excursion " relating to this son and to the youngest daughter, who : —

> " In duty stayed
> To lighten her declining mother's care ;
> But ere the bloom had passed away, which health
> Preserved to adorn a cheek no longer young,
> Her heart, in course of nature finding place
> For new affections, to the holy state
> Of wedlock they conducted her, but still
> The bride, adhering to those filial cares,
> Dwelt with her Mate beneath her Father's roof."

This daughter died five years before her mother. Her ever-active father outlived her six years and more, outlived her child and the glebe-tilling wanderer, his son.

The Sympson graves are no longer " unsociably

sequestered," as Wordsworth described them in his "Churchyard among the Mountains."

Death's harvests have been rich since those words were written.

Very near the graves are those of all the Wordsworths, and of Hartley Coleridge, whom the Sympsons knew only as a blithe and buoyant child, never "untimely old — irreverendly gray."

Jane, the youngest of the Sympsons, died first, aged thirty-seven, in 1801. Mary, the mother, twelve years our Priest's junior, died in 1806, at eighty-one. In June, 1807, after his glebe-tilling son's death, and the far absence of his only two children, the old man went one afternoon across the road to note the growth of his garden. Perhaps at that very moment lower down in the Vale the family of the poet wondered how he would pass those remnant days, that stanch old man bearing the wintry grace and comeliness of unenfeebled age. "What titles will he keep — will he remain musician, gardener, builder, mechanist, a planter and a rearer from the seed?"

Even while they asked each other if it were possible, with his household swept away as by a plague, and hillocks grown green in Grasmere Churchyard, he could still remain the man of hope, with forward-looking mind, he had always been, — even then death fell upon him.

The long life came to its end amid June scents and sounds in his garden. Perhaps his aged eyes saw in those swift-flitting shadows of clouds, shadows of things celestial. Perhaps to him came visions of his manhood's noon, and the cloud shadows seemed visions of the fantastic caravan which half a century before stopped at almost this very spot. There, perhaps, he saw the gentle wife riding her pony with the grace of immortal youth. He saw her bending forward to gaze upon the cot where the old age of earth stole upon her. Perhaps he saw bounding children dancing upon those gray hills of earth and time. Who knows even that he saw not the well-remembered Tabby (how often had they spoken of her long after every atom of her had come up again from earth in grass and flower !) float dreamily across Helm Crag, just as all grew dim to him — even the blue June sky.

> " Like a shadow thrown
> Softly and lightly from a passing cloud,
> Death fell upon him."

The Sympson garden still remains almost precisely as it was that day. A new gate replaces the old ; but the weather-stained oaken posts may very well be the same that the old man touched in passing through them for the last time. These things remain, and his phantom presence. Not one single memory of him would exist on earth but for an unknown and unpromising youth, lower down in the Vale. Parson Sympson himself had no love for the pen, that little instrument which preserves lives and histories. While Minister of Wytheburn he kept no records even of the church, and no scrap of his writing remains in the world. Yet because of that obscurely writing youth he became one to whose receding footsteps upon the sands of life and time an occasional pilgrim listens with rapt interest, and for whose soul breathes, perhaps, even an unconscious prayer.

MONA.

ONE glorious morning they left Windy How Cot to stately Mrs. B., and went wandering o'er land and sea for a space of four days. Mr. Cotter, as usual, had certain hesitations and even got so far as to say, "Cheap trippers! Week-enders!"

He wished he had not, for then his companion remembered all the "I told you so's" kept in reserve since their bank holiday on Sark.

She remembered.

So now does he!

They walked four radiant miles, all blessedly down-hill through a winding road that continually took them almost off their feet with delight. They saw Ruskin's home, the one to which Mrs. Lynn Linton went as a bride; they saw Wordsworth's mountains near and far, and placid Coniston water. Also they met a little mountain maid who said she had got the dinner ready, and now was going to call father and mother. She looked so very small that Mrs. Cotter asked in surprise :

" How did you cook the meat?"

" Only pertaters for dinner," answered the little maid.

At Coniston they took a train for Barrow, — " Barrer," the Manxmen name it, — and a short time after were trundled down to the water's edge.

Mona or Manxman? You may have your choice between the masculine and feminine form for the little steamers plying between England and the Isle of Man, although the steamer is always " she," whatever her name. They ply on alternate days, and the Cotters happened upon the Manxman's day.

Whether you buy your ticket for Mona, for Man, or for Manxland, you will get there all the same. And whichever it be, in your imagination you will not wonder that Mr. Gladstone fell in love with it at first sight. He, we may be sure, never thinks of the island as other than Mona, dainty name holding within its music the very essence of the island's poetic beauty, as it was when Gladstone fell in love. The islanders themselves never name it else than "The Island." To them " The Island " is the universe, the rest of the world but fringe upon Mona's raiment.

The Manxman was not crowded with passengers, for now was the ebb of the season. The most of them seemed Manx people, those in the steerage almost entirely so. The Americans, with first-class tickets, voyaged part of the way in this open and airy steerage, more interested in the conversation of humble islanders than in the silence of those whose passage cost fifty cents more.

One old woman, neatly dressed but with poverty's neatness, gazed tearfully upon England's receding shores. A younger woman tried to comfort her by saying, " It will not be for long ; as you say, nothing is long when you are nearly eighty."

Strange to say this was less comforting than it was expected to be. The old woman in tidy mourning still strained her eyes for fading England, and a dry sob broke from her throat. " If only I could be buried in dear England."

" She has just buried my father," explained the daughter to Mrs. Cotter. " All her children are dead but me, and I married a Manxman. I am taking her home to live with me. I think she will not bear it long ; to go out of England, as she considers it, quite breaks her heart."

Two people opposite were eating and drinking as if they had never eaten and drunk before. They were an elderly couple of Manx people ; and the Cotters took for granted that they had made the voyage often enough to know how best *faire passer le temps*, and also ward off possible misery. Three bottles of beer, uncalculated bread and cheese made the pair merry with quiet and decent merriment. The Manxman forged steadily on, though the sky began to roll queerly from one side of the steamer to the other, and the waves seemed trying to catch it. The kodak was nevertheless brought slyly forth and quietly prepared for a snap-shot at the jolly eaters.

It was never done.

In the twinkling of an eye a battered umbrella opened before the banqueters and from behind it came sounds of mourning.

" Come," said Mr. Cotter, hastily, " come up stairs ; they are snapshotting us in the steerage from above."

" What impertinence ! " remarked the kodak-bearer.

For fully an hour from the deck of the Manx-man the Americans strained their eyes trying to discover Mona in yonder bank of cloud. With soft, silent grace, as still and cool Diana floats from out her filmy drapery of a summer's night, Mona gradually revealed herself. She seemed a very Diana in her majesty of tall and silent beauty. Her pensive head rose among the brooding clouds of heaven, her calm feet were kissed by the murmuring sea as she welcomed with a wild halloo —

" Don't crush ! Beware of Pickpockets ! "

Alas ! Had they come from Barrow in England, daring the dangers of a four hours' voyage, to be thus greeted, as no different from the factory gangs which every summer descend Third-class-from-Saturday-to-Monday upon Mona? Was it nothing to their credit that they had brought to Mona's feet their very goldenest sheaves of imagination, that she must thus yell at them in letters three feet long ?

No, it was not Mona, fairy isle in mystic waters, — not Mona, cool goddess with warm modern soul, — but those of our own Gladstonian race who built that enormous semi-circle of flashy lodging-houses, those tawdry Palaces of Delight and Temples of Music and Dancing, to make the Isle of Man a paradise for the 'Arrys and 'Arriets of Lancashire.

Fortunately 'Arry and his 'Arriet do not care for dells and caverns or for night-wanderings beyond gaslight. For thus the interior of the island is in a measure preserved from their horse-play and horse pleasures, and only the outer edge fur-belowed with music-halls, gaudy shops, and flashy caravansaries. These people who smoke and loll on an hundred doorsteps in intervals of tossing and tumbling each other, never even heard of Mona. To them she is only " Ilerman," and a capital place from which to cast their year's accumulation of dirt into the sea. Douglas, the capital, on the edge first touched from England, is a perfect Pandemonium when midnight empties its Temples and Palaces into the streets. One needs to remember that these bellowing creatures are not devils, but (the majority of them) hard-working human beings let loose from bondage. Hall Caine writes with great consideration of these annual invaders of Man. These invaders bring money to the island and make Man rich, so no Manxman audibly complains, even seeing beautiful Mona trampled under foot, dishevelled, and insulted. For great is Mammon even to romance writers.

" If it is pleasant to you to see how people enjoy themselves," he says of these howling throngs, " and if you have a taste for enjoying yourself after the same fashion (! ! !), you cannot do better than to pitch your tent in Douglas." Which is to say, if you like your chaff of the coarsest quality, and monkey-tricks to abash monkeys, you need not flee Douglas the capital longer than for a few hours' car-excursion, from which you may return with your head on your young woman's shoulder, or with your best girl in your lap, and yelling to wake the dead.

There were fortunately no 'Arries and best girls in the particular Douglas boarding-house that took the Cotters in ; evidently their tickets-of-leave had expired, and only a few undistinguished mortals were left. These were in holiday dress, and probably petty shop-people with longer leave and more expensive tickets than the factory folk. But the house was so precisely like the others of the vast crescent that they almost needed to tie a ribbon upon the door-knob to distinguish it from two miles of the same showily set tables, all with snowy cloths, shining cheap glass, and brutal flowers of muslin and paper, ostentatiously displayed through gaping windows. They managed to distinguish it by the three brilliantly red heads and three pairs of glaring pince-nez of their three landladies and by a fat father, who lounged at the gate. These three young women, the Landlady, are from Barrow, and come over every year for the season. The whole mean starving business is done by themselves, their fat father, lean mother, and shifty brother. Mamma cooks; papa washes dishes, blacks boots, run errands, and points continually to the picture of a brig in which (he says) he long sailed master; the sisters manage chambers and tables; and the son touts for guests at the arrival of every boat. He caught the Clovers from the Manxman, but did not tell that the breakfast bacon would be yesterday's boiled ham limply fried over, that the coffee would be in a dead faint, and that the whole rough-and-tumble management was such as might be expected of campers who flee to England and dressmaking before the earliest frosts. As this fleeing was a constant practice among the lodging-house keepers, and hundreds of huge draughty houses yawned empty all winter, a regulation is now established that no house shall be left empty between "seasons." This accounted for the maundering ghost that they saw through the kitchen windows, the tottering grandmother of the ruby-headed Three, who would be left to inhabit the house between seasons. Would she be happier then? for surely the poor old remnant must be aught but comfortable now,

28

driven from pillar to post in the bustle of the season, with not even a chimney corner, that refuge of superannuation, to call her own. In the winter she could sit by a fireside, even if she had, as was probable she would have, the range of but one room. She could watch the firelight; she could have her cup of tea; and if she wanted ghosts for company, why there were doubtless many of them in her memory who could make the day cheery with echoes of the far away years. Yes, she must be happier when she inhabited the deserted jerry-built house alone. One could imagine her tottering from silent room to silent room, and smiling to imagine herself the mistress of so much splendor, above all to be alone. *We* shudder at the haunting of our ancestors; we groan for the aches and stains they leave with us : but worse sometimes the shudders at the haunting of our descendants, beings we cannot shake off, in whom we too often see our early selves, not at our best.

The Isle of Man is celebrated for its Three Legs, its tailless cats, its Hall Caine, and a few minor things, such as druidical remains and Peel Castle, immortalized by history and Walter Scott. Hall Caine writes romances in Mona, about Mona, wherein he shows himself to have more method in romanticism than Walter Scott, who romanced about the island without ever having set foot in it. The island thanks Scott for his romancing by naming various restaurants and hotels " Fenella," and by giving the realistic tourist a definite map of Fenella's flight from the castle, as well as one's choice in Fenella rocks and other Fenella souvenirs. Hall Caine has not yet given his names to any island monument, as doubtless will be given a few generations hence. None of the Manx people regard his work as other than a joke, for do they not know he tells things that never happened, to work upon the credulity of the rest of the world?

The Caines of Man are almost as numerous as the Christians. Caine was originally MacQuaine, and, as one sees, of Irish origin. Manxland is principally of Irish and Scotch origin and mixture, a fact which Manxmen deny or deplore in spite of the similarity of their Gaelic and of their un-English names, — Cronk-ny Irey-Lhaa, Knock-sharry, Ballaugh, Ballaglass, and Dhoon. The Three Legs, The Arms of Man (the joke is too old to be wicked), are said one to spurn Scotland, one to kick at Ireland, the third to kneel to England.

So determined are Manxmen, even when Mac-Quaines, not to be Irish, that they insist upon pronouncing their Port Erin in their own island fashion. They have a right to do so, no doubt; but when Americans hear 'Arry ask his way to " Port Herrin," and hear natives describe to him where " Port Iron " is, no wonder their ideas are confused concerning the Port Erin on the map.

Hall Caine has worked the Christians of Man into as many guises as a French *chef* works a potato. We have the Christians good, the Christians bad, the Christians of every degree between these two extremes. One wonders how the real Christians like this romantic liberty with their family name. Perhaps they all claim the good Christians as of their own branch, while the bad are of those other Christians, you know.

Everybody knows now the inevitable Hall-cainesque cruel father and two rival brothers, of which the good one gets the worse luck ; but not everybody knows that Hall Caine brings into every one of his romances bits of Manx local history and tradition that would make the island famous even were it less charming than it is. In " The Deemster" is a tradition, or bit of fact, changed into Hallcainesque concerning the Calf of Man. This unimpressive projection, an island at certain tides, was once the refuge of a philosopher (or possibly only a madman) in Bacon's time, who hid himself there to experiment with a diet of herbs, if perchance with such a régime evil passions might be killed, and the mind grow clairvoyant in a philosophic atmosphere.

In Manxland the Americans grew sure that the author of " The Deemster " does not love the Manx cat, else why never immortalize that peculiar creature ? The Manx pussy has surely mystery enough about her to make her worthy of romantic treatment ; for who knows her origin, who knows her fate, who knows the purpose of her creation, who has ever fathomed the mystery of her taillessness, varying according to circumstances ? Many a visitor has paid a fancy price for Pussy, and carried it carefully away, expecting families like it. What mystery in the almost invariable disappointment ! Usually the Manx papa or mamma Felis, no matter how stumpy their own caudal pretentions, adopt the fashion of tails for their foreign-born offspring. The real Manx cat is quite common upon the island. Mated with an ordinary cat, the Manx species has kittens with tails betwixt-and-between, that is, longer than the Manx stump, but shorter than the ordinary appendage. With a predominance of the ordinary breed in the mating, the tail in time forgets its Manx proportion. A physiological problem may be in the fact that, even when Monsieur and Madame Felis are Manx born and tailless, their children are sometimes entirely unlike them. The Manxmen are hard at a bargain, greedy and grasping; but far from any one be it to say that ordinary kittens are ever *detailed* for sale to tourists. It would not be easy to pass off an artificially tailless cat for the real article upon a lover of animals; for there are many other traits of difference between them. The Manx cat is clumsy in form and ungraceful in motion compared with the ordinary feline. It waddles, has high and awkward hind-quarters, with coarse head and curiously sinister face. Its peculiar motion and form has given rise to an unfounded superstition that it is a cross between the ordinary cat and the jack-rabbit. But the Manx cat is not solitary in its taillessness. The Burmese cat is the same; and there are tailless cats in China.

There are two funny little narrow-gauge railways on the island, trundling and tooting with a speed that would leave our electric cars out of sight — in advance. The Cotters named them Thunder and Lightning, and took Thunder across the island to Peel, fleeing the horrors of Douglas. In one of Thunder's mites of carriages, they sat cheek by jowl with sad-faced Manx people whose remarkably long upper lips would have betrayed their origin had the Emerald Isle been three thousand miles away, instead of a score or so. When the strangers spoke a foreign language to each other, all these rustic faces, the long upper lips and gloomy eyes, turned suspiciously upon them.

To speak French does not redound to one's

credit in an island which bends a knee to England, and where even the loudest of 'Arries is more esteemed than a member of the Académie française. Years ago the Manx laws of debt and credit, as well as many other matters, were very different from English laws, and no person on Man could be pursued for debts incurred elsewhere. The various revolutions of France sent many queer customers into exile, some of whom were exiles only of choice. After exhausting their credit in England, many of these (as well as many English absconders) fled hither from their creditors. They were a reckless, roistering, spendthrift gentry, and their fantastic deeds and manners not only astonished the natives, but passed into grotesque tradition, and a mighty distrust of all foreign speech. A popular rhyme represents a crowd of this gentry upon the shore, greeting an incoming vessel with the chorus : —

" Welcome ! Welcome, brother debtor,
    To this safe and jolly isle
    Where no jailor, jail, or fetter
    Dims the sweetness of our smile."

Of herself, Mona is beautiful. The climate, made languorous by the Gulf Stream, and found too relaxing by many visitors (although Mr. Caine declares it bracing), is conducive to marvellous floral and arboreal growth. Fuchsias grow like trees, and houses are often entirely enfolded in their scarlet embrace. Many of the farm-houses are thatched and many of snowily-washed stone. The interior of these sylvan pictures is less attractive. The same climate that makes vine-arms and tree-trunks strong has other effect upon those of Manx housewives, and tidiness is not a Manx virtue. The children are tow-headed, bare-footed, and ragged, and more frequently stand on their heads than feet, — that attitude being found more productive of tourist-pennies. In fact, the summer occupation of these youngsters is following strangers about, some with gymnastic performances, others with a monotonous chant continued for miles, till both the stranger's patience gives out and his pennies. Nothing makes one yearn toward King Herod so much as to stand upon one of these dizzying cliffs, and to find æsthetic raptures strangled at birth by a thicket of these paddy-looking beggar-brats, some of them sopping wet from standing on their heads in the water.

Most of the rustic cots from which these young cut-throats rushed, upon news of the strangers' coming, bore the poetical inscription : " Plain Tea, 4*d*. Knife-and-fork-Tea, 9*d*."

Indeed, Tea was omnipresent. Strangers were evidently supposed to be gasping for it at each instant. The Lancastrian's money burns in his pocket when he leaves the factory for his annual vacation on Ilerman, and many a cup he accepts for the mere joy of paying for it. Very many of them spend thus in a fortnight's vacation the savings of a year, and do it year after year in exactly the same manner. Hall Caine tells of some who have come here every summer for forty years, always with the same money, to spend it exactly in the same manner, to remain exactly the same length of time, then return to the mills for exactly the same routine of eleven months and two weeks. They come for a " regular old blow-out," and they get what they come for.

The scenery of the island is solemn and rugged, and dulcetly smiling. In variety, it is like Jersey, almost a continent in miniature, with its wildest glens tupp'nce. From various points the Scotch and Irish coasts are sometimes visible, also the ethereal mountains of Cumberland, those poetic heights of "Wordsworthshire." From Peel, a tiny excursion-steamer puffs over to Ireland and back in a few hours ; while Scotland is so near that many a Manx dinner has gone down a Scotch throat. One of the Manx ballads represents a husband grumbling at his wife's slowness in serving the dinner, while the chimney-smoke attracts the greedy eyes of Scotsmen on the opposite shore. To retaliate for the loss of his dinners, the Manxman was not *advised* by the Manx law to kill his Scotsman, but if he did kill one he was to pay a fine of a sheep. Sheep were the cheapest of a Manxman's possessions !

One never forgets that poetic Mona, practical Man, literary Manxland, is an island. "Going to England," "Coming from England," is as much in the speech of the natives as it is the speech of England's farthest colonies. Like all the islands attached to the great central one called England (all except sad Ireland), it has Home Rule ; and like the Channel Islands, Jersey and Guernsey, would rather sink to the bottom of the sea than to give it up. Like all the other islands, its chief officer or governor is appointed by the Crown ; but, as in all the others, save Ireland, its legislative body is indigenous and of an antiquity as picturesque, even if sometimes as grotesque, as the undated gargoyles of crumbling shrines. Two islands, by the way, Man and Jersey, were the last to surrender to the royalists during the Parliamentary War, and both were long held by women. We are told that women may not vote, because they cannot fight ; we are not told why Lady Carteret, who held the Jersey Castle of Orgueil so long for the king, and the Countess of Derby, who held Man, were not stronger in command of men than if they had fought beside them. The Isle of Man, unrepresented in the English Parliament and enjoying Home Rule, has done its share in solving the Woman Question by giving them equal rights. Women exercise all franchises, including voting for the local parliament.

As they trundled across the island in a toy carriage, they were reminded again and again of the sadness of the Manx faces. They were reminded afterwards, too, that Mona is very small after all, even with its four towns, its rich history, its shrines, relics, and monuments of by-gone ages. For a melancholy Manxman, hearing that they had walked across the island in less than three hours, was moved to sad-voiced bragging. "What a walker *I* was when a boy ! I did n't think nothin' of ten miles, *nothin' !*"

Neither did the Cotters. But had ten miles been the diameter of their universe perhaps they might have given them more importance.

How the winds blow upon Mona, — soft, wistful winds, breathing that melancholy of Nature's soul which makes art's deepest poetry ! Those mystic winds, come from the distance into which no man has entered, seem never to cease their homesick sighing. They gather under the thatched eaves when a child is born, and murmur of the tears which life must not withhold from him. When the bride goes forth from her father's home, the same prophetic sighing goes with her to her new home, where her welcome is soft wailing. Every dead man who lies over night among mourning kindred leaves to the watchers eternal memory of long hours of invisible elemental grief, the plaints that will never be long still over his grave. This wailing wind becomes an integral part of a Manxman's memory, associated with all the sad and pleasant events of his life. When one remembers, too, that the Manxman is remarkably superstitious, as islanders usually are, no wonder his face is sad amid the mystery and sadness of all this unimaginable world.

"It would be hard to find in the world a more bright-eyed, cheerful-toned, humorous, and happy-looking race than the people of the little Manx nation," writes the author of the gloomy "Deemster" and the gloomy "Manxman," sad-faced Hall Caine, with gloomily-drooping head in all his portraits. "Cheerful, humorous, happy!" Whence then the scowling hates, the skulking spites, the long-cherished revenges, that make the little Isle of Man seem in our author's pages something almost forgotten of God?

That reminds one that in Manxland and the Channel Islands the laws against witches were in force later than anywhere else. Only so lately as the forties, a Manx jury tried a Manx woman for commerce with witches. They had just asked her a leading question, when suddenly a deadly fright seized them. A strange, uncanny object, night-hued and wild, sped round the room.

"The Witch! The Witch!" screamed trembling

audience and jury. Somebody caught the witch, and placed it in a suspiciously empty basket, when it immediately assumes the appearance of a terrified rabbit !

Peel Hill is a somewhat breathless little climb that paid for itself by a delightful view over the very top of the castle and of the sea beyond. Even Nathaniel Hawthorne, had he reached this hill-top during his one brief visit to Man, might have spoken the encouraging word, the unspokenness of which the guide-book meekly resents.

" Nathaniel Hawthorne, the gifted author [how strange to name Hawthorne thus, as if genius itself were only of the tribe of Gifted Hopkins] of ' The House of the Seven Gables' and several other famous novels, visited the Isle of Man when he was consul at Liverpool for the United States ; but he only gives a brief note of what he saw, and that note had reference to Kirk Braddon Church-yard, the rural appearance of which, and the surrounding belt of green trees, he greatly admired ; and as Hawthorne was one of those Americans who found very little to admire in the old country, his approval is rather noteworthy." Thus the Ward and Lock guide-book, which also says, " Peel Hill is steep and trying to the breath of climbers, which makes it desirable to stop at Fenella's restaurant, and then we feel, if we have any romance in our nature, that we are approaching very nearly indeed the spot, almost enchanted ground by the force of genius, which we read about [and were so unwilling to leave off reading about] when ' Peveril of the Peak' first came into our hands." This same guide tells that the gloomy towers on the very summit of Peel Hill

are known as Corrin's Folly, and were erected
about seventy years ago by a Nonconformist of a
very advanced type who especially disliked the
burial service of the Church of England, and therefore built these towers as a resting place in uncon-
secrated ground for himself, his wife, and their two
children. This is the bald truth, the kind of
guide-book truth than which the ordinary tourist
and tripper asks no more. So tourists and trippers
struggle up Peel Hill from the Fenella restaurant,
with cakes and cheese in paper bags, and bottles
under their arms, to lunch near Corrin's Folly.
They crack coarse jokes at the Noncomformist
who would not be buried with better folk than
himself, they prance and curvet, they scream and
chase each other, and think, "wot larks," on the
very spot where once a soul wrestled with the
Angel of its God. They scrawl their names on
the towers, and aim chicken-bones and crusts at
the ragged mounds. When neither tripper nor
tourist amuses himself there, sheep wander among
the crackling weeds and stretch themselves upon
the polluted graves.

For if a man builds a Folly, what else can he
expect than to be the butt of witless jokes without end? If he undertakes to strive with nature,
what else can befall than that nature takes her
slow time to undo all his foolish doing?

Corrin was a silent Manxman who now sleeps
in Kirk Braddon Churchyard, — the one admired by
Hawthorne, and where also sleeps Henry Hutch-
inson, Wordsworth's brother-in-law, under an
inscription by Wordsworth as commonplace and
prosaic as Wordsworth was himself. In the same
enclosure is also the dust of the Reverend Patrick

Thompson, vicar of the parish in 1680, who left three dollars to the church, so tied up that only its revenue of eighteen pence a year is available; where also is the grave of Reverend John Kelly, L.L.D., J.P., who compiled a polyglot dictionary in the Manx, Gaelic, and Erse languages. Whilst conveying the manuscript of this laborious work to England, he was wrecked, but with great fortitude supported himself in the sea and held the manuscript at arm's length above the water for the space of five hours.

In early life the silent Manxman Corrin lost his idolized young wife, who was soon followed by their two young children. The deaths came so suddenly upon him that he had no time to prepare a place for the precious dust other than the usual tomb in Kirk Braddon Churchyard. With the sweeping away of his entire family, the Manxman's broken spirit naturally dwelt much upon the resurrection; for whoever went down into the dust without longings unspeakable for that promised Day? He was unlearned in books, and the sorrows of the great weeping world wrought out no hope for him, who knew only the island and scarcely more even of that than his farm in which uprose Peel Hill. But he believed unreservedly in the final resurrection of the body, the actual earthly substance of wife and children to meet him one day in the same fresh young beauty in which the grave received them. Among his lonely imaginings came also the idea that places first touched by sunshine on that glorious Morning would be the ones from which the seal of death would be first removed. Every day of his anguished life he saw the sun lighting the top of

Peel Hill long before Kirk Braddon graves came out from the grayness of early morning, and he was convinced that upon that golden hill-top he would earlier be united to his family.

From that time the silent Manxman began his heroic folly. Stone by stone, he built these towers with his own hands, toiling up the steep, rough hillside day after day, bowed beneath heavy burdens, as much a martyr to his faith as any treader of hot ploughshares. Inch by inch, foot by foot, the clumsy towers grew, catching the very first gleams of light that uprose from the encircling sea. Month by month they grew, summer and winter, till the three stood there, gloomy almost as death itself when no sunshine was upon them, but transfigured in the morning light, and seen from below to be shining like a stone most precious, even like a jasper stone, clear as crystal.

Then came the time to remove the precious bodies to the towered hill-top. Corrin chose the night, that no prying eyes should watch his work of faith, which to them was " folly." With the assistance of only one man, his own hired farmhand, he removed the three coffins from the churchyard in the dead of night, and toiled up Peel Hill with them on his back, each stumbling step lighted by a flickering lantern. With his own hands the silent Manxman piled the earth above his dead, and gave them to time, till time should be no more and death fled away from the sunrise of the Great Morning.

Alas ! It was folly to contend with nature, to insist that wounds should always gape and bleed, that nature would not cover them up with fresh interests, fresh hopes, as she covers the torn earth with new grass and flowers.

In time Corrin married another wife, and became the father of other children. He lived to be an old man, with children and grandchildren about him. When he died, there was no thought of carrying him up to the towered hill-top where once his soul had agonized and his grief breathed a thousand prayers. What to those living sons and daughters was the long dead story of their father's vanished youth, however ecstatic, however bitter it had been in its time? So Corrin was carried to the very tomb whence he had stolen his treasures; and there his dust lies in longer darkness, but in decency, while on the golden hill-top (now sold out of the family), cheap trippers make bone and bottle targets of his towers, and jeer at his "Folly."

All this was told the Cotters by one of the scholarly and refined Manxmen of whom the island has its share, although in the hurly-burly of the season one sees no sign of them. The Cotters wondered what became of these archæological, antiquarian clergymen, and others of Douglas who love their beautiful island with devotion, during the weeks that the Lancashire factories belch their thousands upon Douglas and its neighborhood. Do they retire into their studies and draw the shades down, waiting the storm to be overpast? Or do they leave their island to its annual frenzies, and take their own vacations elsewhere, only to return when the steamers cease to come loaded and shouting from England, and the doors are closed of these flashy caravansaries? If so, it is not pleasant to think of them driven away when their island is so beautiful. However, the tripper does not go everywhere. Many an elegant dwelling, castle, mansion, villa, and substantial farm-house is far removed from their presence. In these handsome homes the refined life is in no ways affected by the summer's debauch.

SUNDRIES.

" I TOLD you so, " said the lady Hirer. " I told you the Smiths, Browns, and Robinsons would die of envy of our Wine-Cellar. Just hear this :

" 'We are dying with envy of your House-in-which-one-may-not-throw-Stones, and of all your other houses. Why, when such exploits as yours are possible, cannot we take our nervously pro-strated husbands, our over-worked wives, our poor but honest novel-writing, our robust ambitions but not robust fortunes to England for a year or two ? Please tell us if there are other houses, or if you took them all ; how does the general cost of living compare with ours at home ; what do you pay for bread and butter? Tea you say is cheap, how much for servant's wages, etc. ? '

" *Etc.* means too many things," continued the lady. " I might as well write a book and have done with it. The more simple and general questions I will answer, such as Mrs. Robinson's ' How much do you pay for the doing-up of a shirt ? ' and Mrs. Brown's ' Do you think the tips would reduce us to squalor ? ' — but the *etcs.* are beyond me."

DEAR MR. AND MRS. BROWN, JONES, AND ROBINSON, —
There are many other villas, cottages, and houses besides those in which we were so happy. As I told you, we had many answers to our advertisement,

from all over England. I have no doubt we should have just as pleasant memories of our hirings had we never seen Pevensey or Clover Villas, or our soaring Ladder. Of the Dove Cote, we make an exception ; not because of the Cot itself, but of the ever-to-be-cherished friends we found on that radiant isle. Except in the height of the season, furnished country cottages are easy to find at an even absurdly low rent, for the dampness of England is an enemy to unoccupied houses.

There was one at Rickmansworth, in the town itself, close by all shops, and the railway station, hired unfurnished by the year by a party of three friends. The three Englishwomen were artists and teachers with comfortable incomes. They desired a little place all their own, for the three summer months ; the other nine, they wished to let it, not for profit, not even for economy, but to keep the dampness from their dainty furnishings. Everything in the cottage was just what women of elegant tastes and not restricted means had "picked up," to beautify and make comfortable this workingman's cot of six rooms. During the last two or three winters parties of ladies have occupied it, from September to June, at a rent of six shillings, or $1.50 a week. One party of applicants, by the way, did not appreciate the privilege within their reach, when they asked, "How much plate goes with the furnishing ? "

Then in the Lake District, not a thousand miles from Windy How, an American teacher, with a class of six young American girls, had hired for £5 ($25) a year an ancient stone farm-house, near village post-office and library, shops and "booterboons." The house was roomy, but dark, and the teacher must furnish it herself, was doing so at last accounts.

Sometimes owners of cottages do not wait for applicants. During several years, we noticed every autumn a furnished cottage, at Walton-on-the-Naze, advertised in our "Chronicle" for six shillings a week. The Thames Country exudes dampness from every pore.

My advice to all you Smiths, Browns, and Robinsons is, to select the part of England in which you prefer to begin your hirings, then to advertise in a local paper (be sure not to give an American address, but have all letters forwarded). The great dailies do just as well, although more expensive, and will not forward letters.

The owner of Windy How House, Miss Newlyn, has a number of comfortably furnished houses to let in various parts of the Lake District. One of them is in the most picturesque village of all England, Troutbeck, a picture of red roofs and antique gables climbing a glorious hill. During the season, these houses let for three guineas a week, including everything. During the other nine months, they may be had for a song. The Lake Country is glorious during the summer; but its lovers declare that its period of divinest beauty is from October to June.

As for the general expense of living in England, compared with ours at home, *cela dépend*. Walter Besant has lately written that a chop and potato, cooked at home, need not cost more than 4*d*. I doubt if the chop and potato can be cooked in an American home for only eight cents. I am bound to say also, that I never saw it done in England; but naturally many things may be cooked there, unseen forever by Americans. Boston and London expenses do not vary widely, except during the annual American invasion of England. Then every boarding-housekeeper gets what he can without reference to any ordinary scale of prices. American invaders must expect to pay $20 a week in very modest houses, where the regular boarder pays exactly half the sum for precisely the same accommodations. At the very height of the rush, hotel prices are frequently demanded in boarding-houses of the central and popular Bloomsbury district; and the American may take or leave at that price, as he pleases, it is all one to the proprietor, who knows that no room goes empty at that season, no matter what its price. Not only are the summer prices inflated ; but "extras" are piled on, to amaze our countrymen accustomed to see everything comprised in the terms. Unless by special agreement, lights, except a bedroom candle, are an extra, and the American is disgusted to be charged a shilling a week for a lamp in his room, whether it be lighted or not. Coals again are a monstrous extra; Americans frequently pay for them at a rate of $25 a ton ! The only way to avoid this is to arrange for a fire at a stated sum per week. It may result to be a ghostly fire of kitchen cinders and ash-bin relics ; but it cannot cost $25 a ton. The best manner of "doing" London by those who have time at their disposal, and no money to throw away, is not to go into hotels, lodgings, or boarding-houses at all. Comfortable rooms without board may be obtained in every quarter, at all prices. Breakfast is usually taken in the house; but the other meals wherever the sight-seer may chance to be. In a metropolis of countless restaurants and lunch places, such as London is, no man need go hungry with a shilling in his pocket, and none need spend more money than he intended to spend before leaving home.

Housekeeping in London is no dearer than in American cities, perhaps a trifle less. Ordinary provisions, such as meat, fish, and winter vegetables, are about Boston prices ; the greater cost of fruits, summer vegetables, and rarer provisions is equalized by the cheaper rents and labor wage. Gas and coals are cheaper than in America, at least in New England; very many wealthy English women absolutely refuse to keep warm when coals rise to $5 a ton.

Country housekeeping is cheaper than in our own

country. Rents are excessively low compared with ours, and so are servants' wages. It is nowhere difficult to find an excellent general servant for $2.50 a week, often less. They are almost always to be found, even for a few months, for the long terms of faithful service of which we hear and read are not for ordinary employers, but for great families who raise generations of faithful servants on their own estates.

Milk, butter, eggs, summer vegetables, and garden fruits are no dearer than in our own country villages of New England. Strange to say, bread is a trifle cheaper; whether because of baker's wages, the comparative cheapness of fuel, and the less cost of the ovens, or all together, I do not pretend to say. Some things, such as tomatoes for instance, are always dear; some, green corn, for instance, one never sees at all.

As for tips, they need not threaten squalor. Settled quietly in one's own hired-furnished, the American scarcely remembers that the tip system exists. Nobody expects tips for ordinary every-day service, even though in towns the Christmas-box is a part of one's dealings with butcher, baker, and grocer. After fifteen years in Europe, I remember my surprise that Christmas morning in Pevensey Villa, when a youth in his Sunday best came to ask if there were "henny horders." I answered, innocently enough, " No, everything was ordered yesterday. I did not expect to see you to-day ! " The young man withdrew, looking extremely foolish. Unconsciously, I had given him the very best rebuke possible for calling for a Christmas-box (a tip), upon people served during only four or five weeks. In the country, where orders are not taken, but given directly by the purchaser, and purchases usually taken home by himself, no Christmas-box is given, unless one chooses to be generous. Tips, in fact, are chiefly used in travelling ; and the practice is gradually decreasing in England, as it is gradually increasing with us.

As for laundry bills, they are indefinite. In all English housekeeping, everything is usually sent away to be washed. Definite terms are made for such work, so much a month, be the parcel what it may. Where bills are separately made, one each week, the payment is not by the dozen, as with us, but by the piece. Thus, two handkerchiefs or two towels are generally a ha'penny, a shirt "done up" fourpence, — everything in less proportion than in America.

In all these country villages there is free postal delivery every day ; in nearly every one is some sort of a library, free or by subscription. In the hamlet which was the metropolis of Windy How was an excellent library and reading-room, with not only London and local newspapers, but some of the literary journals and many leading magazines, including the American. It happened me there to drop a leaf out from the London "Academy" every time I opened it. It seemed to me that the leaf was placed there for a purpose, so I very carefully replaced it each time. One day I expressed my pleasure at finding the "Academy," to a bright-faced lady whom I frequently met there, and who had kindly helped me find the books I wanted.

" I am glad to hear you say so," smiled the lady; "my sister and I give the ' Academy ; ' we were about to withhold it as never read. I put a leaf in every one to detect a reader, but seldom find it removed."

An agreeable feature of these little libraries is that they always contain books of local interest, books concerning the history of the region, biographies of celebrities connected in any way with it, volumes of poetry relating to it, and all novels and romances of which it is the scene. Thus, the Hawkshead library furnished everything necessary for acquaintance with Wordsworth, Southey, De Quincey, Coleridge, and poor Hartley, Christopher North, Mrs. Hemans, Harriet Martineau, the Arnolds, — all whose lives are inwrought with the lives of the people and the places. Where the village library proves insufficient, Mudie's is always at hand, his boxes of books travelling incessantly all over England, from Oxford Street into the remotest corner of the farthest province.

You see, dear Browns, Joneses, and Robinsons, I have answered your questions, even to some of the *etcs*.

Yours,

L. H.

THE END.

Foam of the Sea.

By GERTRUDE HALL,

Author of "Far from To-day," "Allegretto," "Verses," etc.

16mo. Cloth. Price, $1.00.

Miss Gertrude Hall's second volume of short stories, " Foam of the Sea and Other Tales," shows the same characteristics as the first, which will be instantly remembered under the title of " Far from To-day." They are vigorous, fanciful, in part quaint, always thought-stirring and thoughtful. She has followed old models somewhat in her style, and the setting of many of the tales is mediæval. The atmosphere of them is fascinating, so unusual and so pervading is it; and always refined are her stories, and graceful, even with an occasional touch of grotesquerie. And there is an underlying subtleness in them, a grasp of the problems of the heart and the head, in short, of life, which is remarkable ; and yet they, for the most part, are romantic to a high degree, and reveal an imagination far beyond the ordinary. " Foam of the Sea," like " Far from To-day," is a volume of rare tales, beautifully wrought out of the past for the delectation of the present.

Of the six tales in the volume, " Powers of Darkness " alone has a wholly nineteenth century flavor. It is a sermon told through two lives pathetically miserable. "The Late Returning" is dramatic and admirably turned, strong in its heart analysis. " Foam of the Sea " is almost archaic in its rugged simplicity, and " Garden Deadly " (the most imaginative of the six) is beautiful in its descriptions, weird in its setting, and curiously effective. " The Wanderers " is a touching tale of the early Christians, and " In Battlereagh House " there is the best character drawing.

Miss Hall is venturing along a unique line of story telling, and must win the praise of the discriminating. — *The Boston Times.*

There is something in the quality of the six stories by Gertrude Hall in the volume to which this title is given which will attract attention. They are stories which must — some of them — be read more than once to be appreciated. They are fascinating in their subtlety of suggestion, in their keen analysis of motive, and in their exquisite grace of diction. There is great dramatic power in " Powers of Darkness " and " In Battlereagh House." They are stories which should occupy more than the idle hour. They are studies. — *Boston Advertiser.*

She possesses a curious originality, and, what does not always accompany this rare faculty, skill in controlling it and compelling it to take artistic forms. — *Mail and Express.*

Sold by all Booksellers. Mailed, post-paid, on receipt of price, by the Publishers,

ROBERTS BROTHERS, BOSTON, MASS.

FAR FROM TO-DAY.

𝔄 𝔙𝔬𝔩𝔲𝔪𝔢 𝔬𝔣 𝔖𝔱𝔬𝔯𝔦𝔢𝔰.

BY GERTRUDE HALL,

16mo. Cloth. Price, $1.00.

THESE stories are marked with originality and power. The titles are as follows : viz., Tristiane, The Sons of Philemon, Serviroi, Sylvanus, Theodolind, Shepherds.

Miss Hall has put together here a set of gracefully written tales, — tales of long ago. They have an old-world mediæval feeling about them, soft with intervening distance, like the light upon some feudal castle wall, seen through the openings of the forest. A refined fancy and many an artistic touch has been spent upon the composition with good result. — *London Bookseller.*

"Although these six stories are dreams of the misty past, their morals have a most direct bearing on the present. An author who has the soul to conceive such stories is worthy to rank among the highest. One of our best literary critics, Mrs. Louise Chandler Moulton, says: " I think it is a work of real genius, Homeric in its simplicity, and beautiful exceedingly.'"

Mrs. Harriet Prescott Spofford, in the *Newburyport Herald:* —

"A volume giving evidence of surprising genius is a collection of six tales by Gertrude Hall, called 'Far from To-day.' I recall no stories at once so powerful and subtle as these. Their literary charm is complete, their range of learning is vast, and their human interest is intense. 'Tristiane,' the first one, is as brilliant and ingenious, to say the least, as the best chapter of Arthur Hardy's ' Passe Rose ; ' 'Sylvanus' tells a heart-breaking tale, full of wild delight in hills and winds and skies, full of .pathos and poetry ; in 'The Sons of Philemon' the Greek spirit is perfect, the story absolutely beautiful ; 'Theodolind,' again, repeats the Norse life to the echo, even to the very measure of the runes ; and 'The Shepherds' gives another reading to the meaning of 'The Statue and the Bust,' Portions of these stories are told with an almost archaic simplicity, while other portions mount on great wings of poetry, 'Far from To-day,' as the time of the stories is placed ; the hearts that beat in them are the hearts of to-day, and each one of these stories breathes the joy and the sorrow of life, and is rich with the beauty of the world."

From the *London Academy*, December 24th : —

"The six stories in the dainty volume entitled 'Far from To-day' are of imagination all compact. The American short tales, which have of late attained a wide and deserved popularity in this country, have not been lacking in this vitalizing quality; but the art of Mrs. Slosson and Miss Wilkins is that of imaginative realism, while that of Miss Gertrude Hall is that of imaginative romance ; theirs is the work of impassioned observation, hers of impassioned invention. There is in her book a fine, delicate fantasy that reminds one of Hawthorne in his sweetest moods ; and while Hawthorne had certain gifts which were all his own, the new writer exhibits a certain winning tenderness in which he was generally deficient. In the domain of pure romance it is long since we have had anything so rich in simple beauty as is the work which is to be found between the covers of 'Far from To-day.'"

Sold by all booksellers. Mailed, post-paid, on receipt of price, by the publishers,

ROBERTS BROTHERS, BOSTON.

𝔗𝔥𝔢 . . . .
𝔖𝔱𝔬𝔯𝔶 𝔬𝔣 𝔞𝔫 𝔄𝔣𝔯𝔦𝔠𝔞𝔫 𝔉𝔞𝔯𝔪.

A Novel.
By OLIVE SCHREINER, author of "Dream Life and Real Life," "Dreams," "Trooper Peter Halket," etc. 16mo. Cloth. 60 cents.

It is written with so constant an intensity of passionate feeling, with so much sincerity and depth of thought, with such a terrible realism in details, with so much sympathy and high imagination in its broader aspects, and finally with such a tense power, as of quivering muscles, that the reader, at once repelled and fascinated, cannot lay the book down until he has turned the last page. — *Boston Daily Advertiser.*

"The Story of an African Farm," by Ralph Iron (Olive Schreiner), is one of those books which are remarkable because they voice with power the passionate characteristics of the age in which they are written. It is in the first place a graphic picture of life in a South African colony; but even its novel phase of existence is of far less importance than its passionate earnestness, its intense emotion, its profound sympathy with the struggle of a mind naturally devout with the restless unfaith of the time. The reader is stirred so deeply that it is hard to say whether what he feels is pain or pleasure, only that he cannot shake off the hold of the book's fascination. It is one of the most emotional of recent novels, and not to read it is to miss a profound sensation. — *The Courier.*

There is power of a peculiar sort in this little volume of sketches of farm life among the Boers in South Africa. Each of the characters has a striking individuality, and the descriptions of the manner of life they lead have so much of the color of reality, that they must rest upon a basis of actual experience. The contrast of types is sharply accentuated, and the development of character is cleverly indicated. The book, in fact, is not so much a story as it is a study of character as affected by peculiar surroundings. Yet a strange fascination attaches to the fortunes of the headstrong young English girl, Lyndall, whose singular career and pathetic fate supply some of the most effective pages in the book. There is humor of a grim sort, too, in the picture of the hypocritical adventurer, Bonaparte Blenkins. — *Book Buyer.*

"The Story of an African Farm" is in many ways a remarkable book. Of downright power, yet written with poetic delicacy of touch, as absolutely original in method and treatment as its scenes are novel and its people new, it throws itself across the level of ordinary fiction like the shadow of a great rock in a weary land. In its structure the romance, as its author calls it, is as intricate as a spiders' web, and as full of surprises as if one of its objects was to lure the reader of light literature into the very heart of a psychological jungle ere he suspected whither his steps were tending. — *The Critic.*

Sold by all Booksellers. Mailed, postpaid, by the Publishers,

ROBERTS BROTHERS,
BOSTON, MASS.

LOUISE CHANDLER MOULTON'S WRITINGS.

SWALLOW FLIGHTS. A new edition of " Poems," with ten additional Poems. 16mo. $1.25.

The appearance of the new editions of Mrs. Moulton's volumes is something for the lover of poetry to be glad over; for Mrs Moulton is one of the few real woman poets of the present day. Her work has an exquisite quality, and there is no lover of poetry but should make speedy acquaintance with her verse. — *Review of Reviews*, London.

SOME WOMEN'S HEARTS. 16mo. (Paper, 50 cents.) $1.25.

These stories are written in charming style, and with a naturalness that shows the earnest woman, writing of what she has seen and felt, without affectation or strain. — *Post*, San Francisco.

RANDOM RAMBLES. 18mo. $1.25.

English thought is touched with a delicate and graphic hand. French liveliness and Italian weather, Rome, Florence, and Venice, the Passion Play and Munich, a French watering-place, Westminster Abbey, London literary life, the streets and shops of Paris, — these are the things about which Mrs. Moulton writes, and which she tells of in that delightful and sparkling manner that one cannot grow tired of. — *Thomas S. Collier.*

IN THE GARDEN OF DREAMS. Lyrics and Sonnets. 16mo. Illustrated. $1.50.

It is a book which none but a true poet could have written: and of which any poet might well be proud. — *John G. Whittier.*

OURSELVES AND OUR NEIGHBORS: Short Chats on Social Topics. 16mo. (Paper, 50 cents.) $1.00.

It is wholesome counsel for young and old on topics pertaining to love, engagements, marriage, married life, social relations, etc. — *Springfield Union.*

MISS EYRE FROM BOSTON, AND OTHERS. 16mo. $1.25; paper, 50 cents.

Her style is piquant, and her satire almost unconscious in its felicity — *The Beacon*

BED-TIME STORIES. With Illustrations by ADDIE LEDYARD Square 16mo. $1.25.

Her pretty book of " Bed-Time Stories," is spotless as an open calla ; and so rich in beautiful lessons attractively conveyed that every mother should present her children with it, as a text-book on children's manners towards parents, servants, and companions. — *Chicago Times.*

MORE BED-TIME STORIES. With Illustrations by ADDIE LEDYARD. Square 16mo. $1.25.

NEW BED-TIME STORIES. With Illustrations by ADDIE LEDYARD. Square 16mo. $1.25.

FIRELIGHT STORIES. With Illustrations. Square 16mo. $1 25.

STORIES TOLD AT TWILIGHT. With Illustrations by H. WINTHROP PEIRCE. 16mo. $1 25.

ROBERTS BROTHERS, PUBLISHERS,

BOSTON, MASS

Lazy Tours ∴ ∴

In Spain and Elsewhere.

By LOUISE CHANDLER MOULTON,

*Author of " In the Garden of Dreams," " Swallow Flights,"
"Random Rambles," etc.*

12mo. Cloth. Price, $1.50.

EXTRACTS FROM ENGLISH OPINIONS OF "LAZY TOURS."

Mrs. Chandler Moulton's chapters of travel on the European continent are *charmingly chatty.* There is a literary flavour about them which
reveals the accomplished woman of letters under all the guise of a lazy
tourist. *Acute and discriminating art criticisms, apt personal allusions,
and literary illustrations come in upon every page.* Geneva is the more
interesting to Mrs. Moulton because near there is the Maison Diodati,
where Byron and Shelley lived for a time, and where Mrs. Shelley wrote
" Frankenstein "; a visit to Florence naturally calls forth loving references
to the Brownings ; a sojourn on the Yorkshire moors suggests " Jane
Eyre " and Charlotte Brontë. These " Lazy Tours " are of value not
only as a record of travel in pursuit of pleasure and health, but also as
reflecting something of the writer's very charming personality. *It is
delightful to attend to the impressions of so cultured an observer.* — *From
the Daily Mail, London.*

The author gives us her impressions with much brightness and vivacity.
She seeks less to inform than to interest ; and in interesting she thoroughly
succeeds. These " Lazy Tours," in fact, are eminently the work of a
clever and cultivated woman. — *Daily Globe, London.*

Vivid and imaginative sketches of places and people render Mrs. Moulton's " Lazy Tours " a pleasant book into which to dip at random. The
book reveals mind, as well as mood ; for Mrs. Moulton has ideas and the
courage of them, and they leap to light in artistic criticism, and sometimes
in subtle appreciation of much more than the mere pageants of life. . . .
These Lazy Tours are recorded with a picturesque and cultured pen, and
a fresh audacity of social judgment. — *The Speaker, London.*

The author of " Lazy Tours " is a well-known American writer ; and
these essays are brightly written and entertaining accounts of tours in
Spain, Italy, and Germany. — *The Times, London.*

Many are the women-writers who crowd our shelves with unquickened
pages, but Mrs. Louise Chandler Moulton is not of these. Her " Lazy

Life of Her Majesty . . . .
QUEEN VICTORIA.

BY

MILLICENT GARRETT FAWCETT.

12mo. Cloth. Portrait. Price, $1.25.

In writing her "Life of Queen Victoria" the author has very wisely refrained from any attempt to narrate, even in outline, the history of the salient events of the Victorian era. She has concerned herself chiefly with what she calls the formative influences that have helped to develop the character of Queen Victoria, and have largely determined her position as a woman, and her career as a sovereign. Even in treating the political and personal events of Queen Victoria's later reign, Mrs. Fawcett has selected and dwelt upon those which serve to illustrate the character of the queen and her understanding of her responsibilities as a ruler. The tone of the biography is naturally laudatory, — it could not well be otherwise, — but in its portrayal of a sympathetic, considerate, and unpretentious nature it keeps well within the limits of that impartial spirit which should always animate a biographer. The book is exceedingly readable, because it presents the leading events in the queen's career in an orderly and definite way, and it is moreover very gracefully written. Selections from contemporary memoirs and from the queen's own correspondence and diary are judiciously used, and help to give animation to the narrative. The book has a fine frontispiece portrait from a recent photograph of the queen, and is provided with a chronological table and index. — *The Beacon.*

Roberts Brothers, Boston, publish in a volume of about two hundred and fifty pages Millicent Fawcett's useful and instructive life of Queen Victoria, in whom, the author conceives, modern constitutional government has found more support and development than in any other royal person. Aided by the queen's sagacity and devotion to duty, that phase of human polity has been created, in the author's opinion. And this theory is well developed in the chapters of the book which give the childhood and education of Victoria ; her accession to the throne ; the mingling of politics and love which followed ; the leaning in difficult affairs of state upon her young German husband, without alienating her loyal and faithful ministers ; the loss of that husband at the difficult time of the American Civil War, in which he showed himself a friend of the North ; the queen's retirement from society in consequence, and her quiet life ever since, while always ready for her duties as queen and Empress of India. The home life of the royal pair, and later, of the queen alone, at Balmoral and Osborne, and her more stately residences in London and at Windsor, takes up several chapters of exceptional interest. Chapter IX. is entitled "The Nursery," and its duties alone would have engrossed most women ; but the queen has been active for more than fifty years in large affairs of peace and war, and shown excellent judgment and conduct through them all. There are portraits of Her Majesty taken in 1835, and again by photograph in later years. — *Brooklyn Eagle.*

One of the special charms of the book is that it is more personal than political, — that it gives us the always to be desired insight into the home and the domestic life of one who lives so much in the glare and glamour of publicity. — *Advertiser.*

Sold by all Booksellers. Mailed, postpaid, by the Publishers,

ROBERTS BROTHERS, Boston.

THE RIGHT HONORABLE

WILLIAM E. GLADSTONE

𝔄 𝔖tudy from 𝔏ife

By HENRY W. LUCY.

12MO. CLOTH. PORTRAIT. PRICE, $1.25.

The obvious difficulty of writing within the limits of this volume a sketch of the career of Mr. Gladstone is the superabundance of material. The task is akin to that of a builder having had placed at his disposal materials for a palace, with instructions to erect a cottage residence, leaving out nothing essential to the larger plan. I have been content, keeping this condition in mind, rapidly to sketch, in chronological order, the main course of a phenomenally busy life, enriching the narrative wherever possible with autobiographical scraps to be found in the library of Mr. Gladstone's public speeches, supplementing it by personal notes made over a period of twenty years, during which I have had unusual opportunities of studying the subject. *Author's Preface.*

Mr. Lucy begins with the boyhood and early home-life of his subject, and in a series of twenty-six graphic chapters, some of the titles of which are "Member for Newark," "Chancellor of the Exchequer," "Premier," "Pamphleteer," "The Bradlaugh Blight," "Egypt," "The Kilmainham Treaty," "The Stop-Gap Government," "Home Rule," "In the House and Out," Mr. Lucy has drawn, we believe, the most accurate portrait of one of the greatest men of the century yet drawn, and has told most graphically, tersely, and at the same time comprehensively, the story of a great career not yet finished. We have nowhere seen a better description of Mr. Gladstone's methods, of his strength and weakness as a debater, than Mr. Lucy gives us. — *Boston Advertiser.*

Mr. Lucy entitles his new book on *Gladstone* "A Study from Life." It is more than this, for the book covers rapidly his whole life, from birth to the present time, describing with tolerable clearness the great events of which he has been a part. For an outline biography the reader will find this narrative satisfactory and readable. But the greatest interest attaches to those incidents in Gladstone's life of which the writer has been an eye-witness. He describes with great vivacity the parliamentary function known as "drawing old Gladstone out." — *Advance.*

Roberts Brothers, Boston, have just published an interesting book by Henry W. Lucy, entitled "Right Honorable W. E. Gladstone: A Study from Life." Though not necessarily so intended, this history of Gladstone is virtually the history of his country during the period of his ascendency at least, and the book is valuable from that standpoint, because it is evidently fairly conceived and executed. The sketch o Mr. Gladstone is that of an admirer, but that will not tell against it with the world a large, which is alone an admirer of the "Grand Old Man." Beginning with his boy hood, it pictures him with friendly but faithful hand to the end of his career as head of the English Government, in language which gives an additional charm to the book tracing his course from the day he became Member of Parliament till he was th acknowledged champion of Home Rule, and showing how, as his mind develope with experience, it cast off original errors growing larger day by day. — *Brookly Citizen.*

Sold by all Booksellers. Mailed, post-paid, on receipt of price, by th Publishers,

ROBERTS BROTHERS, BOSTON

Dream Life ᴬᴺᴰ Real Life.

𝔄 𝔏ittle 𝔄frican 𝔖tory.

By OLIVE SCHREINER,

AUTHOR OF "DREAMS" AND "THE STORY OF AN AFRICAN FARM."

16mo. Half cloth. 60 cents.

These are veritable poems in prose that Olive Schreiner has brought together. With her the theme is ever the martyrdom, the self-sacrifice and the aspirations of woman ; and no writer has expressed these qualities with deeper profundity of pathos or with keener insight into the motives that govern the elemental impulses of the human heart. To read the three little stories in this book is to touch close upon the mysteries of love and fate and to behold the workings of tragedies that are acted in the soul. *The Beacon.*

Three small gems are the only contents of this literary casket ; and yet they reflect so clearly the blending of reality and ideality, and are so perfectly polished with artistic handling, that the reader is quite content with the three. It is a book to be read and enjoyed. — *Public Opinion.*

There is a peculiar charm about all of these stories that quite escapes the cursory reader. It is as evasive as the fragrance of the violet, and equally difficult to analyze. The philosophy is so subtle, the poetry so delicate, that the fascination grows upon one and defies description. With style that is well nigh classic in its simplicity Miss Schreiner excites our emotions and gently stimulates our imagination. — *The Budget.*

All the sketches reveal originality of treatment, but the first one is a characteristically pathetic reproduction of child-life under exceptional circumstances, that will bring tears to many eyes. — *Saturday Evening Gazette.*

Sold by all booksellers. Mailed, post-paid, on receipt of the price by the Publishers.

ROBERTS BROTHERS, Boston.

In Foreign Kitchens.

WITH CHOICE RECIPES FROM ENGLAND, FRANCE, GERMANY, ITALY, AND THE NORTH.

By HELEN CAMPBELL,

Author of " The Easiest Way in Housekeeping and Cooking,"
" Prisoners of Poverty," " The What-To-Do Club," etc.

16MO. CLOTH. PRICE, 50 CENTS.

While foreign cookbooks are accessible to all readers of foreign languages, and American ones have borrowed from them for what we know as " French cookery," it is difficult often to judge the real value of a dish, or decide if experiment in new directions is worth while. The recipes in the following chapters, prepared originally for *The Epicure*, of Boston, were gathered slowly, as the author found them in use, and are most of them taken from family recipe-books, as valued abroad as at home. So many requests have come for them in some more convenient form than that offered in the magazine, that their present shape has been determined upon ; and it is hoped they may be a welcome addition to the housekeeper's private store of rules for varying the monotony of the ordinary menu.

Sold by all Booksellers. Mailed, postpaid, on receipt of the price by the Publishers,

ROBERTS BROTHERS, BOSTON.

POWER THROUGH REPOSE.

By ANNIE PAYSON CALL.

" *When the body is perfectly adjusted, perfectly supplied with force, perfectly free, and works with the greatest economy of expenditure, it is fitted to be a perfect instrument alike of impression, experience, and expression.*" — W. R. ALGER.

One Handsome 16mo Volume. Cloth. Price, $1.00.

" This book is needed. The nervous activity, the intellectual wear and tear, of this day and land requires a physical repose as has none other. Every intellectual worker finds so much stimulant in his associations and in the opportunities for labor that he takes on more and more responsibilities, till he has all the strain it is possible for him to carry when everything goes smoothly, and when complications arise he has no reserve for emergencies." — *Journal of Education.*

" A book which has a peculiar timeliness and value for a great number of people in this country is ' Power through Repose,' by Annie Payson Call. This volume, which is written in a very interesting and entertaining style, is a moderate and judicious effort to persuade Americans that they are living too hard and too fast, and to point out specifically the physical and intellectual results of incessant strain. To most people the book has a novel suggestiveness. It makes us feel that we are the victims of a disease of which we were largely ignorant, and that there are remedies within our reach of which we are equally ignorant. We know of no volume that has come from the press in a long time which, widely and wisely read, could accomplish so much immediate good as this little book. It is the doctrine of physical rest stated in untechnical language, with practical suggestions. It ought to be in the hands of at least eight out of every ten men and women now living and working on this continent." — *Christian Union.*

Sold by all booksellers. Mailed, post-paid, by the publishers.

ROBERTS BROTHERS, BOSTON.

A BOOK FOR MOTHERS.

Mother, Baby, and Nursery.

By DR. GENEVIEVE TUCKER.

Fully illustrated.   Small 4to.   Cloth.   Price, $1.50.

The object of the author in presenting this work is to furnish
a practical summary of the infant's hygiene and physical development.   The aim of the book is to be a guide to mothers, particularly young and inexperienced ones.   It purposes to teach and help
a mother to understand her babe, to feed it properly, to place it in
healthful surroundings, and to watch its growth and development
with intelligence, and thus relieve in a measure the undue anxiety
and nervous uncertainty of a new mother.   The book in not intended in any measure to take the place of a physician, but rather
to aid the physician in teaching the mother to care properly for her
babe when well, that she may better nurse it when sick.

CONTENTS.

Heredity.	Crying Babies.	Bowels and Kidneys.
Prenatal Period.	The Eyes.	Posture.
The Little Stranger.	Nursing.	Exercise.
Growth and Develop- ment.	The Wet-Nurse.	Habit.
	Weaning.	A Study of Babies.
Bathing.	Feeding after Weaning.	The Baby's Basket.
Dress.	Teething.	Nursery Pointers.
Sleep.	Hand-Feeding.	Nursery Don'ts.

Mailed, postpaid, on receipt of price, by the publishers,

ROBERTS BROTHERS,

3 Somerset Street, Boston, Mass.